MW01643858

Remy vs. Rome

Bonnie Callahan

This book is a work of fiction. All of the names, characters, events, organizations, locations, incidents, and artwork portrayed in this novel are either products of the author's imagination or are used fictitiously. Any resemblance to actual persons, living or dead, is entirely coincidental.

No part of this book may be reproduced in any form or by any electronic or mechanical means, including information storage and retrieval systems, without written permission from the author, except for the use of brief quotations in a book review.

REMY VS. ROME. Copyright © 2022 Bonnie Callahan

All rights reserved.

FIRST EDITION

Cover design by Gia Thompson

ISBN 979-8-9860846-9-5

To V.P, e un amore piú veloce della luce.

Chapter ONE

I, REMY CAMPBELL, SOLEMNLY SWEAR, I start to type. The blinking cursor taunts me from the laptop screen, and I stretch my neck, sore from being stooped below the top bunk. Across the room, a unicorn-shaped clock emits a series of whinnies, rubbing in the fact that I woke up in my niece's bedroom on New Year's Day, alone and no longer engaged.

I promised myself I would write my resolutions before falling asleep—new rules for a new Remy, a fresh start, less crying in the tub—but all it took was a couple of glasses of prosecco and an after-dinner bath to make me a liar. Now, my head is a disaster (my sister's three screaming kids don't help), and I'm in no condition to draft any sort of document that's meant to dictate the renaissance of my dating life.

I reach for my phone, digging through the pile of stuffed animals that seven-year-old Camila forces me to sleep with and lift it by the corner like it might bite. The illustrated orange blossoms on the case are not enough to fool me into trusting that whatever I see on the screen will be equally sweet. I'm already cringing when I tap to pull up my notifications and discover multiple missed calls from Cassie, along with an assortment of vividly worded texts from her and a few of our other friends. Last night they went out for a multicourse dinner in

Scottsdale and then downtown for the countdown. I'd said I'd go, but a party was not worth the risk of seeing Eric.

That traitorous bastard.

Taking a deep breath, I put the phone down and hit the backspace key on my laptop. I am a twenty-year-old woman, and I shouldn't start my resolutions like some third year at Hogwarts.

Fine, I am a twenty-five-year-old woman—almost twenty-six.

A whimper lodges in my throat. I am an almost-twenty-six-year-old woman whose fiancé left her just before the holidays and who's been forced to move in with her sister and brother-in-law and their brood of wildlings.

I'd venture that the new year could only be an improvement, but I don't want to tempt the universe into proving me wrong.

There's a thump against the bedroom door, followed by two more and the sound of hysterical giggles. I close my laptop, slamming my head into the top bunk as I sit up to slide the computer under the bed. A very unsexy moan escapes my mouth as I massage the permanent bruise on my forehead.

The door flies open, and the kids tumble into the room. They all have their dad's black hair, dark eyes, and tan, olive skin, like *The Village of the Damned* in negative—way cuter, but not necessarily less scary.

"Mom wants to know if you'd like pancakes," Cristian, the serious second-born, says. The baby, Carlito, tackles me. I smoosh my face into his hair as his grimy little hands press into the sides of my cheeks. Perhaps this has something to do with my recent bout of adult acne.

Camila strolls to the bed and sits down. "Are you sick?" she asks, cocking her head as she eyes me.

"Why do you ask?" I pry Carlito off my neck and set him down on my lap.

"This," she responds, gesturing toward everything from my neck up, "looks…bad."

Cristian nods in agreement, lips pursed in concern.

I sigh. If Camila thinks I look like crap, I'm sure I do. My highlights, which were due for a refresh at the beginning of December, have crossed the line from ombre to embarrassing. The lack of regular washing doesn't help. My face hasn't gotten any love beyond the occasional coat of tinted sunscreen, which my beauty brand boss and my pores are not pleased about.

On a positive note, all the crying has really made the green in my hazel eyes pop.

"Tell your mom I want all the fu…I want all the flipping pancakes."

Camila's lips turn down. "You were going to say 'fucking.'"

"You aren't allowed to use that word," I say, pulling her off the bed. "Now get out of here. Tell your mom I want chocolate chips, too."

"Not fair. I want chocolate chips if Tia Wemy gets them," Carlito whines as they walk away.

I'm searching for my bra when my phone buzzes.

6:57 am

Cassie: Happy New Year, Remus! I missed you last night. In an Uber. I lost my shoes. Definitely a good one.

Me: Why are you awake?

Cassie: Escaping!

Me: Do I want to know?

Cassie: She's the breakfast in bed type.

Me: Poor you.

Cassie: Details over wine later, but first, I need a big ass Berto's burrito in my belly and a nap.

I'm still staring at my screen when the next message comes in.

Cassie: Eric was looking for you.

My pulse quickens, and I'm mad at myself for how quickly I text back, how desperate I am to hear more. My hands shake as I type.

Me: He was?

I watch her text dots bounce, holding my breath.

Cassie: The asshole was with someone.

The room tilts, and my stomach threatens to sink into the carpet. I consider tossing my phone in the toilet, but then I remember how much I dislike scrolling through Instagram on the computer. Instead, I throw the phone onto the My Little Pony comforter I've been using and pull on some pants.

On my way out of the room, I pause by the door to adjust the map of Ancient Rome that's taped to the wall. It's mine, one of the few things I've bothered to hold on to over the last decade, and it's hung in every room I've slept in since the day I tore it out of a *National Geographic.*

Eric hated the map.

There is a heart on the west side of the Colosseum that I drew in black ballpoint—the site of my very first kiss the summer after eighth grade. The memory still makes my knees weak. The kid had on a shiny, silver jacket and leather sneakers and didn't speak a word of English. I had on red high tops and a modest J-Crew button-up and couldn't have found words if I'd tried. I was in love the moment I saw him. I remember the way the stone echoed the sunset-pink of the sky, the smell of warm grass, and the sweet brush of his hand on my cheek.

Stepping closer, I rest my forehead on the map, just above the Temple of Jupiter Optimus Maximus. I wonder what my Italian is doing now, what kind of man he is.

I bet he, at least, would never have dumped me via email while I slept in the next room on the organic mattress we bought together.

My eyes fill with tears, and I swipe at them as I head for the kitchen, where the sound of wailing kids and clanking plates portends a lovely, relaxing morning.

"Mimosas?" I ask no one in particular as I nudge Cristian with my hip and take over his seat at the kitchen island.

"What's a mimosa?" Camila asks.

"Special orange juice for mommies," my sister Lilian answers, shoving Carlito toward her husband, Javier. Javier wraps an arm around his youngest son and reaches down to ruffle Camila's hair.

"*Eres mi niñita mimosa*," Javier tells her.

Camila pushes him away and frowns. "*No me toques*."

I pick at the bacon and nod to my sister. "She gets that from our side of the family."

Lilian and Javier met in Salamanca while Lil was studying abroad in Spain. She imported her husband, and he imported his family's olive oil. Now, they own a boutique Spanish goods shop in Old Town and have three kids whose names all start with C. My sister is living the dream.

Meanwhile, when Eric called off our engagement, he employed the painfully derivative, "You'll be better off exploring your options." Which meant he was ready to explore his. My stomach turns. I look around for those mimosas.

"So, where's that mommy juice?"

Javier and Lil glance at each other. "Rem, you drank all of the bubbly last night," my sister says, avoiding my gaze.

"What's bubbly?" Camila asks.

"I only took one bottle," I protest. But then I remember seeing a mostly empty prosecco bottle on the bedside table, which isn't the one I left on the side of the tub. My chest heats. "Shit."

"Shit, shit, shit," Carlito echoes.

"Remy, please." Lil shoots me a look over her shoulder, a pancake balanced midair on the spatula.

"Sorry," I say, slumping into the chair.

She turns back to the stove. "Did you talk to Cassie? She called me last night to check in on you."

I groan. "Are the pancakes ready?"

Lil pinches the bridge of her nose and exhales. "It's been over a month since you and Eric split up. You can't hide in the house forever. Maybe seeing him would help."

My hands clench into fists, Cassie's text flashing in my mind. But still, my lip quivers. A face-to-face with Eric would be a horrible idea. As hurt and angry as I am, I still ache to snuggle into his chest and feel his arms around me. I don't trust myself not to beg him to take me back.

"Tia's going to lose it again," Cristian says, scooting his chair away from me. Javier grabs a plate of pancakes and shuffles the kids into the living room. I hear the TV pop on: *Peppa Pig* in Spanish.

Lil stands in front of me, hands on her hips. "Hey, you

know what? Maybe this isn't the worst thing that could happen. Eric is great, but is he great for you?"

"He's not great. He's an ass." My throat tightens. Admitting out loud that Eric sucks still hurts. He didn't always.

"He's also got a great ass."

"Don't remind me," I grumble, pressing my palms into my eyes to erase the image of Eric's magnificent rear end.

"But were you happy with Eric, or were you complacent?" Lil asks.

She pours a cup of coffee from the French press while I consider her question. I only accepted the job at PetaLuna Boutique Skincare after college so I could stay in town and help support Eric who was two years into his post-grad in public administration at the time. I chose marketing luxury face creams in Phoenix over grad school at Williams, which Lil has never let me forget. But I loved Eric—still love him, unfortunately, and worry I always will. "I was happy enough."

Lil raises her eyebrows. "I think this could be good for you, a chance to figure out what you want for yourself and from a partner. But that won't happen if you keep moping around here." She turns back to the stove, plops a short stack on a plate, and brings me the steaming pancakes. I reach for the butter and syrup and smear on an inappropriate amount of both.

She watches me chew for a minute. "Why don't you go with Cassie?"

"I don't think I'm Cassie's type," I say. "Do you remember Rebecca?"

"Not go out with her, you idiot. I mean, go with her *to Rome* when she leaves for her internship in March."

It is no secret that I've been jealous of Cassie ever since she got the job. Rome isn't only the location of my first, and arguably most romantic, kiss. The Eternal City is also the reason

I studied art history in college, the reason I watch Season 1 Episode 2 of *Stanley Tucci: Searching for Italy* every night before bed, and why my Instagram feed could double as a Roman guidebook.

I shove a piece of pancake in my mouth and shrug. Lil makes a good point, but I can't let my sister win that easily. "I'll think about it," I say. Lil mumbles some choice words and joins the more enjoyable members of her family in front of the TV.

Alone in the kitchen, I tuck my legs beneath me on the seat and use my fork to sketch the Arch of Constantine in a puddle of maple syrup. The thought of returning to Rome fills my tummy with wine-colored butterflies, and Cassie would be happy to let me join her. Still, I'm not naïve enough to believe I can *Eat, Pray, Love* my way to normalcy. A few weeks of vacation in Italy may sound great, but Eric and I were together for seven years, and there is no way I could consume enough pasta in that time to fill the gaping hole that kind of loss leaves behind.

But I suppose I could try.

I have to try. Eric is already moving on, seeing other people.

I let out a long breath.

New Year's Resolution: *check*. I'm going back to Rome.

Chapter TWO

I SHAKE CASSIE OUT of her half-a-Xanax-and-red-wine-induced cross-Atlantic nap as the plane touches down at Fiumicino Airport. We both smile, watching the umbrella pines zip past the window as we taxi to the gate. When the captain's staticky voice welcomes us to Rome, I press a hand to my chest. My heart hammers against my palm in excitement.

Or possibly panic.

I reach for Cassie's arm to steady myself, the seat belt sign fading out as the realization that I left my senior marketing position at PetaLuna and burned through most of my savings to bankroll an indulgent six weeks of food, wine, and self-discovery lands on the heels of our Boeing 777.

"Easy," Cassie says, prying my white knuckles off her wrist.

I wrap my arms around her neck instead and kiss her cheek. "Thanks for letting me invite myself to stay with you."

Cassie pushes her pink silk sleep mask further up into her dark curls and yawns. "Your sister made me. Lilian didn't want Camila to internalize any more of your emotional trauma."

"Poor Camila," I sigh.

Cassie leans in and rests her head on my shoulder. "Regardless, there's no one else I'd rather pub crawl into my new career with."

"Pub crawl," I repeat in a high voice that I hope sounds enthusiastic and not pained. I'd envisioned something more like small cafe tables with checkered table clothes in Piazza Navona for our first night out. "Is there not, like, an age limit?"

Cassie raises a hand between us, huffing her hair out of her eyes as she shifts in her seat so she can make sure I see the dirty look she gives me. "We are young *and* single." Her gaze drops to my bare ring finger. I wince. "And you promised we'd have fun."

"Why would you believe me?" I joke. Only, it's a fair question. I spent the last few months binge-watching Disney movies on the weekends and eating chicken nuggets for dinner.

I've given Cassie no reason to trust that I even remember what fun is, but I'm ready to be reminded.

"Don't make me regret this, Remy Campbell," Cassie says, swatting my hand away when I try to pinch her.

Phones ting in the cabin as passengers start to collect their things, and I dig mine out of my shoulder bag. When the phone comes to life, my breath catches on a sharp inhale. The first thing that pops up is a text from Eric. I bite my lip, turning the screen away from Cassie.

> Have a good time on your trip, RC...but maybe not too good (winking face). I can't wait to see you when you're home.

I shove the phone into my back pocket without responding. Flirty texting with my recently repentant ex-fiancé is at the top of the list of things that would make Cassie reconsider her decision to let me tag along.

Eric embraced his three months of bachelorhood, but he had a sudden change of heart when he heard about Rome. For better or worse, his backpedaling coincided with the purchase of my nonrefundable ticket and the two weeks' notice I gave at PetaLuna.

"It was a break, Rems," he insisted the night before my flight. "In the end, of course I was going to choose you." We decided that when I return to Phoenix, we will talk, re-evaluate. Eric is ready for the next step. But as Cassie and I walk away from the gate into the rolling hum of Italian and the scent of freshly ground espresso, I realize I have just taken my first real step away from him.

Outside of customs, we find a middle-aged driver sweating through a brown suit and holding up a piece of paper with C. MARTINEZ printed in bold letters above the logo of Cassie's company.

He duals as a tour guide as he drives us into the city, looking back at us as much as at the road as he talks. Cassie drops some prayers that contain more bad words than I assume are customary, and by some Roman automobilist magic, he delivers us unscathed to a peach-colored, six-story apartment building flanked by cafe tables and potted plants.

As we get out of the car, a woman shouts "Emilio!" from a window somewhere above us. On the other side of the street, a group of kids kicks a plastic bottle down the sidewalk past two old men standing together at the corner with their hands clasped behind their backs. When someone flies past us on a motorcycle, so close it tickles the hair on my arm, our driver turns around, pinching his fingers and shaking his hand in the air at the back of the bike.

I step onto the sidewalk and let my head fall back. The day

is beautiful, and the air smells like simmer sauce and diesel and citrus and cigarettes. I swallow it into my lungs and grin.

The lingering fear that I made a horrible mistake and will be single and unemployed for the rest of my life melts away in the soft sunshine, and the last few months of heartache give way to the fluttering in my belly.

I've spent hours tracing the roads of my Rome map since deciding to come with Cassie, and now that I'm standing here, I know I'm where I'm meant to be.

Eric enjoyed his freedom, and I am going to enjoy mine.

I scan the buzzer and hit the tarnished metal button next to an engraved number six. "*Benvenute ragazze,* third floor," a gruff voice answers, and the door clicks open. We drag our luggage up what feels like endless flights of slippery marble stairs until we meet a sturdy, balding man on our floor.

He introduces himself as Cosimo Rinaldi, the world's best landlord, and then gives us a lesson on how to use a three-inch bronze key to open the 200-year-old door to Cassie's apartment. He's making us practice when the only other door on the floor swings open, and a gray-haired woman in a flour-dusted apron appears. She starts talking very loudly, and I worry we've already managed to annoy our elderly neighbor.

"Mamma, *tranquilla,*" Cosimo says to her. Then to us, "She wants to know if you are hungry from your trip?"

Cassie and I shake our heads—even though I am—and smile. Cosimo's mother grunts before shuffling back into her house. When she reappears, she has a pie in either hand.

"*Grazie,*" I tell her as she shoves them toward us. She reaches up to pinch my cheek.

"*Che bella signorina,*" she says. My Italian isn't great, but I know enough to understand that this nonna thinks I'm pretty

—which makes me inordinately happy. If the old ladies of Rome like me, their grandsons can't be far behind.

I hope they're into weekday pub crawls.

The bar is dark and loud, and somehow, I've misplaced Cassie. I teeter to the counter and slide in beside a very pretty blond girl perched on the edge of a wooden stool. She's tall, tan, and healthy-looking; I assume, based on no other evidence, that she must be Australian. "Have you seen a cute little brunette running around?" I slur in her direction.

She leans down. "You'll have to be more specific," she shouts over the din of the music, waving a hand toward the dance floor. She has an accent and sounds a little like Steve Irwin. I congratulate myself in my head for my good guess.

"A cute little brunette wearing pink kitty ears?" I clarify.

"Can't say I have."

She is kind enough to talk to me while I scan the crowd with blurry eyes. She asks what I'm doing in Rome, and before I know it, I've word-vomited the entire story of Eric and how I forced Cassie to let me come with her to Italy.

"Now that I'm here," I tell her, "I'm just looking for someone who makes my legs crumble when they kiss me, or better yet, my long-lost Italian boyfriend from the Colosseum, so we can get married and live happily ever after."

"Wow…"

"Yeah," I breathe, pressing my fingers to my mouth. I'm still chasing that damn kiss.

Someone bumps into me, and my drink splashes onto the Australian's shoes.

"Watch it!" I shout, turning unsteadily to face the culprit. But when I see the man behind me, my mouth slams shut. He's wearing immodestly tight red pants and a light button-down shirt that is one button short of decent and fitted to show off his entire upper body.

His lips turn up at the corners, and I almost faint. He's the most perfect human man I've ever seen.

My first instinct is to ask him for a photo together, assuming he must be an actor or model and therefore used to the attention. The thought of Eric seeing the picture makes me giddy. My hand shoots into my purse.

Then I give myself a shake. Why am I thinking about Eric?

I'm supposed to be discovering myself or something. Maybe this well-groomed, impeccably dressed male could help with the process.

When I look up, his eyes are ranging over my body, lingering in all the places where propriety says they shouldn't. They stop on my lips, and I hope my lipstick hasn't smudged all over my chin.

Someone's arm slips into mine, and I glance sideways. Cassie is making doe eyes at me.

"Who's your friend?" she asks, and I'm staring at Red Pants again, but she shakes her head and points to the girl I've been camped beside. I shrug, but Cassie introduces herself, first to the girl, who it turns out is from New Zealand—*so close*—and then to the gloriously sexy man who caused me to spill my drink and who I haven't even spoken to yet. He takes her hand and murmurs, "Fabio, *piacere*," before kissing her cheeks. I swallow my snort.

Fabio, of course. Cassie looks at me and raises her eyebrows.

"Shot?" the Kiwi asks.

"Yes, please!" I answer very quickly and way too loudly. I glance at Fabio, and he lines up beside me at the bar instead of running away.

My bare right shoulder is pressed against the Italian's expensive-feeling shirt. I turn to him and smile. I don't even know if the guy speaks English. I'm not sure it matters. His eyes seem pretty good at communicating. My belly tightens as his gaze meets mine, and I regret that I didn't take the time to dig my razor head out of the drain when it popped off in the shower.

"So," I say, using my finger to chart the path of the Tiber River in the spill on the wooden bar. "Are you from Rome?"

"I am from a small town in the north," he answers in perfect English. "I am in Rome for work." A pang of disappointment fills my gut, but it passes. He's not my Italian—but he is *an* Italian—and a very good-looking one at that.

I push ahead. It's not like I expected to have that boy come knocking at my door. Or into my back, in this case. "What kind of work?" I ask.

"I am in special collections. I am here investigating a piece of antique jewelry that we believe inspired a certain project by Michelangelo. I follow the trail he left—the art, the notes, the history."

I smile. "Right, the famous Michelangelo Code," I manage with not even a hint of sarcasm in my voice. He doesn't elaborate on the particular job but does tell me he's part of an international effort to recover Renaissance works throughout Europe.

My pulse drums in my ears, Fabio's words waking up little parts of me that have lain dormant, been tucked away to make enough space in my heart for Eric and his future.

Fabio's eyes shine—with admiration or desire, I'm not sure. But he looks impressed as we debate the advantages of tempera versus oil and discuss the evolution of perspective in Proto-Renaissance portraiture.

"Tell me more about your undergraduate thesis," Fabio says,

and it is almost criminal how hot he makes those words sound.

Eventually, Cassie and Shay the Kiwi excuse themselves and head for a more private corner of the bar. I wave them away, enthralled by Fabio's stories of secret acquisitions between Italy's museums and collectors around the world.

Somehow, I've ended up with a glass of red wine and a bag of potato chips. I'm about to tell a story about how I once identified a forged triptych by Giotto on an antiques television series when Fabio looks at his watch, then at the door, and my heart drops.

"Expecting someone?" I ask, hoping I don't sound too disappointed. I guess I had assumed this gorgeous, fancy Italian had come with the purpose of picking up an indulgent American girl. (I volunteer as tribute!) Why else would he be in a bar that's play-ing Paula Abdul's greatest hits on repeat?

"Yes," he answers. He smiles when my face falls into a pout and takes my hand. "But if you are free tomorrow morning, I would love to see you again." I turn his hand over in my own—no wedding ring.

My skin tingles when I look back up, and our eyes catch. "I think that might be a possibility."

He pulls me closer and kisses my cheeks. "I will be on the back steps of Santa Maria Maggiore at eleven," he whispers against my skin. "See you then."

I want to grin, but instead, I play it cool and say nothing as Fabio walks away. He meets an attractive woman at the door and then turns and waves at me. She studies me for a second before they push back a curtain and disappear into the unlit space behind it.

Hot damn, I mouth as my hand fishes around inside my empty chip bag. Rome is not messing around.

Chapter THREE

I WAKE UP STILL BUZZING from my conversation with Fabio and only slightly hungover. It's nothing some Illy Bold Roast espresso and a chocolate croissant can't cure. After wiping the pastry flakes off my face, I jump in the shower, pry my razor head out of the drain cover, and get to work.

I pull a short, button-down dress out of my closet—a silky, sand-washed number I purchased before the trip as an ode to Audrey Hepburn in *Roman Holiday*, but sluttier. I slip on a pair of comfy rose-colored sandals, swipe on some lip gloss, and shove my phone, credit card, and a handful of euros in my brown leather shoulder bag, pinching my cheeks like it's 1950 before leaving the apartment.

Cosimo's mother is sitting on a chair in the hall, and she gives me a wink as I head down the stairs.

The walk to Santa Maria Maggiore is short, but not so short that I don't have time to second-guess every decision I've made that's led to this moment, my choices now laid bare in the light of Roman day.

My pulse teeters toward panic, and I force a full breath into my lungs. If nothing else, Fabio looks like fun. The kind of fun Eric doesn't want me to have too much of, which is a good thing.

The street opens to Via Cavour, and there is Fabio, leaning against the base of a reddish brown obelisk. He's dressed in very snug burnt orange pants with a matching jacket slung over his shoulder and hanging from a fingertip: a pose that Cassie and I have already cataloged in the list of "Italian Man Stances."

I wave at Fabio and wait for the Roman drivers to acknowledge my presence at the crosswalk, tucking in close behind a local and her kid when they step into the street.

"The trick is not to make eye contact," my Latin teacher had told me during my middle school trip, but that always just sounded like an excellent way to get run over without knowing who was about to hit you.

Being taken out by a Vespa is not how I'd like to start our date.

Fabio walks toward me, slipping his phone into his jacket pocket as I make my way through the piazza. His lips pull back in a dazzling grin, but the intimate fit of his pants provides another salutation. Gulp.

"*Buongiorno, Bellissima*," he says, dropping his head in a slight bow. When he looks up again, his eyes flit over my outfit, pause on my mouth, and then meet mine. He nods approvingly, and my body floods with heat. If this were a regency romance, I'd swoon.

Fabio offers me his hand and leads me around the corner to a shiny, yellow sports car parked behind a row of motorini. He opens the passenger's side door.

I hear my mother's voice in my head. "Do not even *think* about getting in a stranger's car in a foreign city!" Then my dad, "To hell with that. That's a Ferrari 488 Pista with carbon-fiber wheels. Tell him he's not getting any unless he lets you drive."

"Nice car," I say as I slip past him and onto the black Alcantara seat. Fabio leans over me and reaches for the right shoulder strap. He smells like mountain air and sharp soap, and I realize I might still be a little drunk when I have to keep myself from licking the perfect curl of his ear. I feel his hand below my belly button and try not to grunt as he clicks the buckles into place. I'm harnessed and locked in when he pulls away and shuts my door.

As Fabio settles into the driver's seat, I run my fingers over the "LAUNCH" button on the console.

"Careful," he says, and there's a note in his voice that sends a shiver over my skin.

"Where are we headed?" I should shoot Cassie a text and let her know, so if something horrible happens, at least my mom won't think I'm a complete moron. He reaches over and brushes a strand of hair from my face.

"It's a surprise, *signorina*." I bite my lip, and he seems to anticipate my good sense kicking in. Fabio gives a light laugh. "I would like to take you to the Vatican Museums and then for lunch along the Tiber, if that is okay for you, Miss Campbell."

Art and food? It's like he already knows all of my weaknesses. "That sounds wonderful," I answer, crossing my leg toward him.

Fabio starts the car, and the purr brushes right up my spine. "Exciting, no?" he asks. And I'd respond, but I'm worried it would come out as a moan. He slides out of the tight spot with minimal maneuvering, loops around Santa Maria Maggiore, and soon we're flying past a bunch of buildings I recognize from my art history books. As we drive, tourists and Italians alike turn their heads to look at the car. Living in the Eternal City doesn't make you immune to beauty, especially when it's in the form of a sparkly new Ferrari. Even the police in Piazza Venezia stare.

In less than eight minutes, we have cleared half the city, and Fabio pulls through the front gate of an enormous palazzo. "It's hard to find parking near the museum," he says as if that explains the man with coattails opening his door.

"Grazie, Stefano." Fabio hands the man the keys to the car as he steps out.

I try to undo my belt, but he must have the kid-lock on or something because I can't get out. While I wait for Fabio to come free me, I pull out my phone and take a selfie to send to my dad.

The courtyard is cobbled and golden and glorious. "Are you staying here?" I ask. A second man reads a newspaper in the corner, sitting at a small table with a full ashtray and a glass of beer.

"Yes, a friend of mine is renting the house."

I wonder if he means the leggy woman from last night, but I don't ask. "The whole thing?" I say instead.

Fabio looks at me, then up at the five stories of yellow walls, windows bordered in decorative white stone, bronze scrollwork on the glass. "Yes."

He takes my arm in his as we walk and stops at a bar on the corner, where he orders us both an espresso and sparkling water. When we come out onto Viale Vaticano and see an infinite line of tourists stretching along the ancient brick wall, I regret not using the bathroom when I had a chance.

I'm about to high tail it back to the bar before I have to start clenching my legs together to avoid peeing my pants, but Fabio waves at someone near the entrance, who raises his hand in return. Fabio ushers me across the street by the elbow—all the cars stop for him, of course—and he tips his head at the museum guard. The man, a green-eyed Hercules type with golden brown skin, guides us through the crowd and away from security, then unclips the retractable belt on a black stanchion and ushers us through. Some of the people in line are watching us, and I imagine we look like VIPs. I keep my sunglasses on until I'm in the bathroom to keep up appearances.

We spend at least two hours going through the rooms of the Pinacoteca. Fabio points out things my professors never did, and I catch almost all of it when I remind myself to listen and stop staring at his jawline. He stands close enough when we walk that our arms brush, and when he's speaking, he rests his hand on my shoulder or the small of my back. I'm squirming—I need more Fabio hand in more places.

We pull up in front of a good-sized DaVinci, and he laughs. The piece of art is a bit nightmarish—an unfinished painting of a suffering old man with a lion at his feet. "St. Jerome," I say, reading the plaque, which is met with a solid "Ha" from Fabio.

"I don't see the humor." I wait for him to elaborate on the painting's secret source of whimsy.

"That lion," he begins before shaking his head. "*Il maestro sapeva la veritá*," he says at last and pulls me to the next room. I need to brush up on my Italian so I can understand all the sexy art things Fabio has to tell me.

My stomach starts to produce an obscene cacophony of rumbles while we observe Veronese's *Vision of St. Helena*, who looks a lot like my mother when she's disappointed.

Fabio rests his fingers on my belly, and his lips graze my ear when he whispers, "One more stop, and then I will see to this." I'm pretty sure he means he'll feed me, but my face flushes anyway. He gives me his arm, and I hook mine through his elbow.

He sweeps me back toward the entrance. The super buff guard who let us in is still there, but now he's dressed in flattering street clothes—we all need our lunch break. Fabio leads me past the doors to the upper level and into the Museo Gregoriano Etrusco. There was a chapter on the Etruscans in one of my early art and architecture books, but I don't remember much, and the gaping emptiness in my stomach is distracting. My family always said there was nothing scarier in our house than a hangry Remy, and I'm not sure I'm ready to unleash the hunger demon on my date.

While Fabio is looking around one of the rooms, I sneak into a corner and dig through my purse for a half-eaten granola bar that I intend to illegally shove in my face, but there's no food. I grab my phone instead and see a text from Cassie, making sure I haven't been abducted.

I reply with a selfie of me grinning in front of the nearest bronze—*Mars of Todi* in contrapposto, gesticulating over my shoulder.

Me: Just chillin' with my homeboy, Marty.
Cassie: How do you say "you're a nerd" in Italian?
Me: Love you too.

I startle when I feel a hand on my back. "Photography is not encouraged in the Museo," Fabio says near my ear. My chest heats. I've been naughty.

Spinning around, a thrill runs through me at how close Fabio is standing. "I was just checking my makeup," I lie, then bite my lip. He huffs, and a rush of cool air brushes against my cheek. For a moment, it is not food at all I'm hungry for, but that doesn't stop my insides from whining loud enough for everyone in Room III to hear.

"*Andiamo*," he says, and I follow him back downstairs and to the exit. A vaguely familiar guard with wild, yellow eyes that follow me a bit too closely pulls back the security belt and sees us out.

Fabio's Ferrari is parked right outside the museum exit. Stefano, who'd taken the keys in the courtyard, tosses the Ferrari keys to Fabio without a word.

This time, Fabio doesn't open the door for me, and I hustle to get into the car and get myself buckled. He starts driving before I can figure out the straps. Maybe he really is pissed that I took photos in the museum. He obviously takes his art *very* seriously.

We are held up for about ten minutes beside Castel Sant' Angelo while a string of blue police cars goes blazing by.

"What do you think happened?" I ask, turning my head to follow them.

I'm still looking out the small rear window when I feel his warm hand on my knee. My thighs ache. Someone has gotten over my unlawful photo misstep in the Etruscan room.

"What piece did you like best at the museum?" Fabio's words say, but his eyes pin me in place, and my mind goes blank.

The traffic starts to move, and he tears his gaze away. We speed down along the river and onto a small, one-way street in Trastevere, lined with peachy pink and yellow buildings with green doors and lush balconies. He seems to have forgotten his question, which is good because the only piece I care about right now is his. I wonder if he is as intense in bed as he is behind the wheel of a sports car.

Though, I might be getting ahead of myself. We haven't even kissed yet.

Fabio is back to his gallant self and opens the door for me after finding a parking spot in an alley behind the taverna. A wooden cafe table is prepared outside, and a young waiter fumbles when pulling out a chair first for Fabio—who glares at him—and then for me. He comes back with a bottle of Gewurztraminer and a small, brown envelope that Fabio promptly grabs.

The wine is a little perfumy for my taste, but I don't really care once I have the glass to my lips. It pairs well enough with the basket of bread and breadsticks the waiter brings out, and I'm very grateful when Fabio excuses himself so I can placate my hunger in peace. In between bites, I take a picture of our very picturesque setup: the glasses glimmering with moisture in the warm air, the flowers in the middle of the table. I'm about to send it to Cassie when I notice the brown envelope on the ground beneath Fabio's chair. I stick it in my purse for safekeeping until we get back to the car, then pick up another breadstick.

"I ordered inside, so you won't have to wait," Fabio says with a smile as he sits back down. Annoying, but probably for the better. The bread is just waking the beast.

"Carbonara?" I ask between bites.

"Better." He winks. I don't believe him because nothing is better than carbonara, but at this point, I could eat an ox. He fills up my glass and rests an elbow on the table as he tells me about the wine. *I know, I have taste buds, too*, I want to tell him when the waiter appears at our table with two plates hovering in the air.

"*Coda alla vaccinara*?" He is looking anywhere but at our faces. Sometimes I forget how awkward teenagers are.

"*Per la signorina*," Fabio says, and the kid rests the plate in front of me. Fabio ordered me actual ox. I look at his plate, and all he has are a few slices of salami and hard cheese.

"Watching your figure?" I ask as I get to work on the oxtail.

He raises his eyebrows at me. "I like to be aware of what I put in my body."

I fork a huge piece of meat and chew while he watches me. There is a hint of a sneer on his lips, and I feel one forming on my own. He ordered me the damn dish; what did he expect me to do with it?

Eric and I had our issues, but he was a good guy for the most part. He never commented on what I ate, or how, or my body, other than the parts he loved—which were most of them.

I have no idea how to handle Fabio, and I'm confused as hell. It is like he can't decide if he wants to ravage me or run away, and I'm starting to feel the same.

I empty my wine glass, and he lifts the bottle to refill it. I let him. There is a steady drone of sirens in the background. No one brings it up. In fact, neither of us speaks for the rest of the meal. Part of me is in awe of how quickly things got weird. In my experience, food makes everything better. When we finish, Fabio disappears back inside for a while.

I stand when he gets back to the table.

"Thank you for the lovely day," I say. If nothing else, it's a good story.

He smiles like we just shared a wonderful and not-at-all uncomfortable lunch together. "*Grazie a te, signorina.* Shall I escort you home?"

I nod but notice his eyes on the front of my dress. The look is a little blatant, even for him. I glance down and see three drips of tomato sauce on the light silk. "You have something on your dress," he says, and he seems offended that I would dirty myself in his presence.

"You know what? I think I'd like to walk."

"It's very far. Let me drive you."

"No. I'm good." I swing my purse over my shoulder and turn toward the river. He grabs my arm.

"I really must demand that you—" I look at his hand pressing into my flesh and think of Bernini's *The Rape of Persephone* and the smug look on Hades' face that is way too close to the one Fabio is giving me right now.

I pull my arm away and shoot daggers at him with my eyes. "Demand?" I shout. A couple on the street stops and looks at us. Our waiter edges himself behind the door frame. "Touch me again," I breathe. "I dare you." I don't know what I will do if he does. Scream bloody murder, kick and scratch. But he just shrugs.

"Have it your way," he says, and I step back. "*Addio*, Miss Campbell."

Addio, *my racy Italian fantasy*, I think. Thank God I have a decent Eric waiting for me at home. I'll be grateful to Fabio one day for making me realize that.

When I cross the street and am a reasonable distance from the restaurant, I look back. Fabio didn't seem eager to follow, but he is also a creep and a controlling misogynist to boot. My mother would never forgive me if I ended up in a prime time special just because a hot foreigner flirted with me when I was drunk.

He's bent over, looking under the table, and I can sense the tension in his shoulders even from a block away. Beside him, the waiter's hands are waving all over the place. Fabio stands and slams a fist into the wood. My wine glass lurches off the table, shattering on the ground. Fabio starts to turn, and I hurry into a group of tourists cloistering among the trees along the Lungotevere.

During the forty-minute walk to the apartment, I design bridal bouquets in my head. Tomorrow, I will call Eric. I'm ready. If this is what is out there in the world, then being complacent with Eric Armstrong is what I want.

Chapter FOUR

THAT EVENING, CASSIE CALLS ME when she's done at work and tells me she's meeting Shay for drinks. She invites me to join, but I pass.

"How was your date?" she asks before I can hang up.

"Interesting."

"Will you see him again?"

I think of Fabio's "*addio*" and chuckle. "God, I hope not."

"Dammit, Rem, tell me what happened."

"We can talk when you get home." She concedes and tells me she will stay in touch in case I change my mind. I'm already in my pajamas. There's an open bottle of grechetto in the fridge and a platter of *pizza al taglio* on the counter. I'm not going anywhere.

When my glass of wine is empty, I contemplate sending Eric an email, telling him I'm his, asking him to set the date. Then I think of the pictures he was tagged in this winter. The huge smile on his face as a series of women dangled off his ripped arms.

I take a deep breath and try to compromise with myself, find some middle ground between love and hate. After all, I'll be back home in six weeks, and if today made me realize anything, it's that I still want to marry the guy someday. I settle on spite.

Squinting at my phone, I scroll through my photos and select all of the highlights from the past twenty-four hours. There I am with Cassie and Shay, there's my selfie in the Ferrari, the beautiful trattoria in Trastevere. I even include the photo I took with Mars in the Vatican—because culture, and because you can see Fabio's perfect face in the background.

I caption the post with the wonderfully cliche "When in Rome." See, Eric. I can have fun, too.

My phone dies as I wait for more likes to appear under my photos, and I fall asleep on the couch watching *You've Got Mail* dubbed in Italian. I wake up in the morning to the sound of Cassie trying to use the Moka.

"Need help?" I ask, rubbing the sleep from my eyes. She has a leftover slice of pizza in one hand and a lighter in the other.

"Yes, please," she manages through a full mouth.

I take the lighter from her and am trying to get the flame to spark before enough gas leaks out for the blast to take off my eyebrows when I hear her gasp. "Shay told me about this."

A warm gust brushes my face when the stove lights. After getting the Moka situated for Cassie, I join her in front of the TV. The Italian news flashes image after image of the Vatican tangled in police tape.

"What happened?" I ask, reaching for the controller to turn up the volume so we can continue to not understand what they are saying, but louder.

"There was a heist at the Vatican Museums." She looks at me, and her eyes are wider than I've ever seen them. "Oh my god," she squeals. "What if you were there when it happened?"

"Huh," I murmur, watching the police lights on the television cross-fade into an Associated Press image of an ancient amulet. Three pendants fall from the chorded gold chain, each ending in a small grouping of meticulously detailed lion heads. Too bad I was too busy drooling over a megalomaniac douche bag to have noticed anything. But I did catch the stream of sirens that were blaring all through our lunch. "Maybe I was."

"So cool," Cassie says as the Moka begins to bubble over. She rushes into the kitchen and turns off the stove. "By the way, cute post last night." She knows what I was going for, and I give a guilty grin as I reach for my phone to see if it worked. I feel a revolting twinge of hope at the prospect of making Eric jealous, of hurting him just a little. I tap the screen, but it stays black. I forgot to put my phone on the charger before I passed out.

Cassie swears when she notices the time and bolts for the door. Before she leaves, she looks at me and narrows her eyes. "You still haven't told me about your Italian lover man."

"I'll meet you for an *aperitivo* when you get off this evening. Prepare to be disappointed."

"Goody, I can't wait," she says over her shoulder as the door shuts behind her.

I pull out my laptop and scroll through my Instagram notifications. There is no like from Eric. There is no message. I throw on a sports bra, a tank, and a pair of shorts, intending to run away from whatever the hell yesterday was.

I tug on my red sneakers, and the lace breaks off in my hand. Of course.

Where to buy shoelaces in Rome?
How do you say shoelace in Italian?

I am conducting a rather ineffectual Google search when there is a knock at the door. I go to the cloudy peephole, but it's not Cosimo or his mom who keeps trying to feed us crostata. There are at least three men, two for sure in uniform.

Any hint of lingering jet lag evaporates. "Hello?" I say, feeling a little queasy.

One of the officers steps in front of the others. "Remy Campbell," he says, his deep voice drawing my name out in a subtle Italian accent. "Could you open the door?"

"Um."

"Now," he commands. I run through different scenarios in my head. It's unlikely that a bunch of Italian police officers are here to do something bad to me, but it also doesn't make sense that they are here at all. Unfortunately, I am short on options. I pop the top lock and swing the door inward.

"I am Detective Lorenzo Rossi of the Polizia di Stato," announces the one who has been growling through the door. He glances down at my hand, where the broken lace still dangles between my fingers, then at my shoes. He looks at me and blinks. He shakes his head. "We need you to come with us."

"Excuse me?" I ask in a breathy laugh. Detective Rossi can't be much older than I am. He's wearing scuffed sneakers, jeans, and a t-shirt that's so wrinkled, you can still see the creases despite how tightly the fabric is stretched across his chest. Rossi runs his hand through his thick, unkempt mass of espresso-brown hair while I give him the once over. When he pulls his fingers away, the strands are poking out in different directions. I have an inappropriate urge to reach up and touch it.

I have seen the movies—this is *not* what an Italian detective looks like. It is much, much better. Younger. Hotter.

Rossi sighs. His dark eyes look tired. "Ms. Campbell, I need you to come with me to the station. We have questions."

"What kind of questions?" I ask, crossing my arms.

"The kind we need to ask you somewhere private. And safe."

"Do I have a choice?"

He ignores me and checks the watch on his wrist, then drags his hands over the shadow of stubble on his face. "Ms. Campbell?" he tries again, gesturing to the staircase.

My hands are shaking when I turn back into the apartment. I toss my dead phone and lip balm into my purse and then follow the two uniformed officers down the stairs as my foot slides in and out of my shoe.

Rossi walks beside me, and when I look up at him, I see him biting his lip as he watches my feet. I want to vomit. Not only do I have no way to get in touch with anyone, but I can't even entertain the fantasy of running away if I need to. By the way his thighs flex under his jeans, I don't think he's the kind of cop who skips the gym for a morning *ciambella*. I wouldn't stand a chance with a bum shoe.

The officers go out the main door of the complex before we do. "Wait for the all-clear," Rossi whispers in my ear. The hairs on the back of my neck rise. The others give a signal, and Rossi grips me by the upper arm. I wince as his fingers press into the marks Fabio left. He notices, and his hold loosens, but he doesn't let go until I'm secured in the backseat of an unmarked Fiat Panda. He slams the door behind me and heads for the driver's seat.

Holy shit. "Am I under arrest?" I ask.

He shifts the car into first. "Not exactly."

I make a face at him in the rearview mirror, which he chooses to disregard. We drive in silence for no longer than five minutes, and in that time, he takes us in at least four full circles. If he is trying to make sure I have no idea where we are going, it's working.

He pulls up in front of a white building, and I feel my face pale. A large stone sign beside the central arch reads QUES-

TURA in a 1930s serif. The whole station looks like a place where Mussolini would have hung out. Above the entrance, three flags—EU, Italian, and Roman—lay limply against each other in the still air.

We pass through a series of guards and into a tiny room with an enormous wooden desk. To calm myself, I try to imagine how they got the oversized furniture through the door because if I think about how I've been dragged into some sort of Italian crime drama, I might pass out.

Files cover the desk's entire surface. Rossi points to a chair, and I sit down as he blunders about for a minute, shoving things into precarious piles. He takes a seat across from me and huffs out a slow, "*Allora*," then stands again. I feel slightly reassured, seeing him so flustered. If he is the bad guy, he is doing a terrible job.

"Coffee? Water?" he asks in a gentle voice, confirming my suspicion that he's not this episode's villain. A lock of dark hair falls over his forehead, and he pushes it back. For the first time, I realize there is something familiar about his face.

"Water, please," I answer. I'm staring at him, trying to figure out who he reminds me of. He clears his throat and bumps into his chair as he steps back from the table.

"Yes, water. *Va bene*," he mumbles, then looks around like he's not sure what to do with me. His eyes flit to his handcuffs, and I tense, my knuckles white where I grip the edge of my chair. When he looks back up at me, his face goes a little red before he fumbles his way out of the cramped space.

While I wait for Rossi to return, I run my hands over my knees to stop them from bouncing as I try to work out how the hell I ended up here. My fingers freeze when I notice a spot on my leg that I missed with the razor yesterday, and it makes me remember how Eric used to brush his fingers over those patches. How he called me Duck.

Maybe his bitch ass would message me if I posted a selfie from the police station. My stomach twists as I think about my phone sitting uncharged in my purse.

Rossi comes back with two paper cups, each the size of a shot glass: one filled with water for me, the other containing espresso for himself. The guy seems pretty jacked up already, and I'm not sure the extra caffeine is going to do him any favors. He scrubs his face, looks at me, and looks away. He makes a weird cough sound and tries again, leaning across the table and clasping his hands like he's doing an impression of a serious cop.

Thank God he's so cute. Otherwise, I might have wet myself by now.

"Ms. Campbell, the current best-case scenario is that you were witness to a serious crime. Worst case, you were complicit. Which means that my job now is to understand which one it is."

"The Vatican Museums?" I ask, putting all the pieces together. Rossi nods and chews his full lower lip.

Oh, no.

My date with Fabio. The gift that keeps on giving.

"Am I going to jail?"

"This is Italy. We have an apartment you'll stay in until we work through some of the details. But it is my duty to keep my eye on you, and I don't want you doing anything funny."

"Like what?"

"Trying to get away."

"Where the hell would I go?" The gravity of the situation hits me like a ton of ancient bricks. It doesn't feel good. I'm in police custody in a foreign country for what I imagine is a pretty serious crime. I curl into myself on the chair.

"What about Cassie?" I ask. "Is she okay? Does she know what's going on?"

"She's fine. We will move her into a rental near her office. She'll have a police detail."

"Is she in trouble?"

"No, it's to make sure she's safe."

My head sags so low it almost hits the table.

Rossi is talking, but I can barely make out what he's saying over the pulsing in my ears. "We aren't sure how much Bumgartner knows, but we don't want him or his associates looking for her to get to you."

My head shoots up. "Bumgartner?"

I see his mouth tighten like he's holding in a sigh. He pulls his phone out of his pocket and scrolls, then passes it to me. It's a screenshot of the picture I took in the Vatican, the one I posted last night on Instagram; above me is the *Mars of Todi*, but Rossi has zoomed in on a spot over my shoulder—a man in burnt-orange pants.

"You mean Fabio?" Is Fabio's last name Bumgartner? That makes this so much worse.

He looks at me like he's checking to see if I'm joking, and I'm flooded with fear. Because I'm not joking, and I have no idea what's going on. Detective Rossi takes a deep breath. "This man's name is Lewin Bumgartner. And what we want to know is how you know him and why you were with him yesterday morning."

I gape at him. He raises his eyebrows, waiting.

My best defense is the truth, and the truth is I knew nothing about fake Fabio or his plans. I tell Rossi about the first night in the bar and the woman Fabio disappeared with at the end of the night. (Rossi tells me her name is Maelle Toussaint, and she just got out of prison in France.) I explain how I met Fabio the next day on the steps of Santa Maria Maggiore. I tell him about the car and show him the picture I took in the front seat. (He tells me the Ferrari was stolen and dumped in a hangar at Ciampino Airport just this morning.) I describe the palazzo we parked at (which he tells me was rented and part of the setup).

"The whole thing?" I ask, interrupting my own story. I guess Fabio wasn't lying when he said his friend rented the house. "Whatever he stole must be worth a fortune."

The face Rossi makes is incredulous, almost offended. "It's a 2,500-year-old piece of jewelry from the Vatican Museums. What do you think it's worth?"

I feel like a jerk and keep talking. The only time Rossi's face changes is when I tell him about my farewell with Lewin née Fabio on the bank of the Tiber. His eyes flash, and a muscle strains in his jaw, but I can't tell if he's angry or trying not to laugh at me—which makes me glad I neglected to mention anything about why I'm in Rome in the first place.

"Your phone usage from this moment on will be monitored, and we will need you to hand over your device so we can download any pertinent data," he says when I finish.

My eyes are wet. How will I get in touch with Cassie? What will my parents think if they don't hear from me?

"My family will worry," I blubber.

Rossi's gaze softens, and he glances at the door, his eyebrows drawn tight when he turns back. "You may call them now," he says. "Be quick."

My lip is trembling as I pull out my phone and show him its useless black screen. He studies me, frowning. I wipe the tears from my cheeks with the back of my hand.

Rossi tilts his face to the ceiling and expels a huge rush of air, then pulls his phone from his pocket. He sets it between us and heads for the door. "I'll be back in five minutes."

"But you said phone use would be…." He is out of the room before I can finish.

I stare at Rossi's phone and consider my choices. If I call my mom, she will be so overcome with rage, the whole five minutes will just be her yelling at me. Lil would die laughing.

I dial my dad's number. "This is Joe," he answers.

"Daddy?"

"Howdy, Peanut, how's the pizza treating you?"

My throat is so tight I struggle to breathe. *Come save me*, I want to yell. But I pull myself together. I don't want him to worry. "The pizza is great. The wine is better."

He laughs.

"Hey, Dad, I got a tour of Rome in that 488 Pista you've been drooling over in *Motor Trend*."

"The hell you did."

"For reals."

"That's great, kiddo. You sound a little funny; everything else okay?"

"Dad?"

"Yeah?"

"I think I'm in trouble."

"It's about damn time. I was wondering when you were finally going to live a little."

"I'm serious, Dad. There was this guy and this thing at the Vatican…."

"Remy. You'll figure it out. You always do. If you need anything in the meantime, give me a call. And for once, just try to enjoy yourself. You're in Rome for Chrissakes."

I sniffle. "Love you."

"Love you too, kiddo." He hangs up first. I'm swiping at my eyes when the door opens again.

"Ready?" Rossi asks. I wipe my nose on my arm and hand him his phone. He pulls a pack of tissues from his pocket. I take one and try to give the package back.

He hesitates, looking at my puffy face. "No, you keep it."

I go to stuff it in my purse and remember the little brown envelope that I'd shoved inside after lunch. I pull my bag off my shoulder and crouch on the ground, dumping its contents all over the terrazzo floor.

"Ms. Campbell?"

"Ugh," I groan, realizing for the first time that Fabio had been using my last name, though I'd never given it to him.

"Is there a problem?"

What a stupid question. "Here." I jam the envelope into Rossi's hand.

"What is this?"

"I don't know. Fabio—whoever—dropped it at lunch."

"And you just *kept* it?"

"I forgot to give it back to him when he tried to yank my arm out of its socket."

He nods. "*Mi dispiace*," he says, slipping into Italian for the third time since we met. I didn't realize I was keeping track.

I incline my head to show him I accept, and we both look at the envelope in his hands. "Are you going to open it?" I ask.

He glances up and seems surprised, probably because I've gotten very close. He smells like warm bread and grass and books, things that feel safe. I lean forward as Detective Rossi unfolds the top of the envelope, popping the sides in. The opening is too small for his finger, so I push his hand out of the way and use mine to scoop out the teeny piece of paper inside. He holds it up to his face, his lips moving over the words.

"So?" I ask. Maybe it is a hint or some clue that will lead to my freedom.

He turns it over, and I step closer. In a very tiny script, someone has written three lines of characters that are not part of the English alphabet.

I shake my head. "What does that mean?"

"I have no idea. Gather your things. I'll drive you to the apartment."

Chapter FIVE

THE STUDIO APARTMENT IS CUTE in an IKEA display sort of way. And the space is not at all prison-y, for which I am grateful, but I still feel miserable when I sit on the bed and slip off my dysfunctional sneaker.

I had been a shy kid. I liked that my mom dressed me in khaki and neutrals. It was my classroom camo, allowing me to disappear into the general gloom of adolescence. But it drove my dad crazy. He didn't want his daughter to fade into the background. He tried to raise girls who fought for what they wanted and what was right, girls who trusted their voices and power.

That was not me. Especially not at fourteen.

The night before my school trip to Rome, my dad came home with a big box, gift-wrapped and tied with a bow. Inside, there was a pair of red Chuck Taylors. "So you've got something on the outside to remind you of the fire on the inside," he said as he hugged me.

I was wearing those shoes at the Colosseum when I closed my eyes and puckered up for my first kiss. They were the only things holding me up when our lips met and my knees went out from under me, and I've been wearing red shoes ever since.

Rarely have I felt that fire on the inside, but it's nice to believe that I'm not all khakis and creams. Even if, for years, I let myself blend in enough to be part of Eric's vision without detracting from it.

I want to be more than a bland, unremarkable accessory to someone else's future—or their crimes.

When my stomach protests loud enough for me to assume it must be lunchtime, there is a knock at the door. I jump up off the bed and straighten my shirt. I hope it's Detective Rossi. Maybe he is back already to tell me he deciphered the secrets in the envelope and has come to release me.

My shoulders slump in disappointment when I open the door. Standing in the hall is a salt-and-pepper-haired officer who introduces himself as Alberto and smells like he sleeps in a bottle of Acqua di Gio cologne. But Alberto has brought me three bags of groceries.

Italian state-provided room service isn't all that bad: bread, pasta, garlic, olive oil, salt, basil, tomatoes, mozzarella, Parmigiano, pancetta, prosciutto. The essentials. I'm disappointed that they didn't trust me with a bottle of wine, but as I dig around the bottom of the last bag, I come up with another surprise—a pair of red shoelaces. I try not to cry again.

Alberto tells me Rossi will come by at some point to brief me. Or at least that's what I gather with my limited Italian.

I eat two rolls and then curl up in the upholstered full bed, perhaps overly sophisticated for a glorified jail cell. I pass out hard.

Then someone is shaking me.

"Fucking hell!" I jump up. My head connects with the sharp bone of someone else's arm, and I swear again.

The light in the room is dusky. Rossi stands beside my bed with his shirt half untucked and his hands in his amazing hair.

"Sorry, Ms. Campbell. I was worried when you didn't answer the door, and then when you didn't wake up when I called your name, I thought...."

"I'm fine," I say, massaging the burgeoning goose egg on my head with one hand while covering my mouth with the other. It's been a while since I brushed.

Rossi exhales and shakes his hands out, causing the muscles in his upper arms to flex. My mind goes blank. It should be too early in the process for me to develop Stockholm syndrome, but I'm beginning to see how an attractive and concerned Italian detective might increase the future probability of an inappropriate crush.

"Is now a good time to talk?" he asks like I've got something else I might need to do this evening.

"Now's fine." I walk to the small table and am about to sit down when I notice a heaping dish of pasta on the counter. Carbonara. How did he know that it's my favorite? Perhaps this is some sort of advanced Italian interrogation method; they ply you with food until you speak.

Rossi follows my gaze. "It's for you," he says, bringing it to me at the table. He sets it down, then adds, "You don't have to eat. I just thought it might be easier—"

My laugh interrupts him. Yesterday he heard the whole story of me in the Vatican Museums losing my mind because I was hungry. He didn't want to have to deal with a hangry Remy. He wants information, not insults.

Rossi is pretty good at this whole detective thing. He brings me a fork and a paper towel, and I get to work. I don't even care that I'm basically drooling as I shovel it in my face. The carbonara is delicious, a perfect balance of egg, Pecorino Romano, and guanciale. At one point, I think I even moan but only realize because Rossi shifts his face away.

I clear the plate and am pretty sure Rossi looks a little impressed. "*Grazie*," I say as I wipe the sides of my mouth.

He gets up and rinses my dish, which seems almost more suspicious than the pasta. I'm trying to figure out why he looks so familiar, partly to distract from the way he somehow makes drying his hands look incredibly sensual, when he asks me if I have heard of the Zalśar. I shake my head.

"You studied art history, correct?"

I narrow my eyes. "Yes," I answer.

"Do you know much about the Etruscans?" Rossi asks. I shake my head again. He goes to his bag, pulls out a pen and a notepad, and sits next to me at the table, scooting his chair away when our elbows graze. Or maybe it's because of my breath.

"The Etruscan civilization flourished in Central Italy before the Romans." He draws the Italian Peninsula on the graph paper and starts marking boundaries and cities: Veii, Velzna, Tarchna. "The Romans owe much of their culture to the Etruscans. And according to some scholars, so do the Medicis and the Florentine Renaissance in general."

"Okay," I say, not at all sure what this impromptu history lesson has to do with my captivity.

He runs a hand over his stubbly chin and takes a deep breath like he is deciding where to take this next, how much he should say. "Lewin, or, you know, Fabio, belongs to a group of criminals that call themselves the Zalśar. The cooperative was founded during the First World War by twelve Italian families. Their intentions were noble: to protect what was left of Italy's Etruscan heritage from the ravishes of war. The word Zalśar means twelve in Etruscan, for the twelve great city-states of Etruria." Lorenzo counts out the cities he has drawn on the map, then adds two more.

"When Germany surrendered in 1945," he goes on, "the

original Zalśar were disbanded. But one of the members had different plans for the organization, and through time, the syndicate became the illicit enterprise it is today. There are twelve higher-ups that form a council, and they meet once a year to elect a leader from among themselves—a *Zilath*, they call them, from the Etruscan. This person governs the group's operations for the year."

"What kinds of operations?" I worry I sound like I'm playing dumb, but I must look genuinely uninformed because though Rossi considers me a moment, he doesn't hesitate to go on.

Rossi tells me how the Zalśar believe that the Renaissance artists of Tuscany hid messages in their notes and artwork, and this makes sense because Fabio pretty much told me the same thing at the bar. The group contends that the secrets belong to the Etruscans. Many of the civilization's records were lost or wiped out by the Romans. Some were later destroyed by Savonarola at the Bonfire of the Vanities—at least, according to the Zalśar. But the Medicis attempted to conserve what remained through their patronages in art and literature.

A massive effort is all that saves me from melting into my chair as Rossi speaks. First pasta, now a condensed but passionate history of the Etruscans and their influence on some of Italy's greatest artists?

Rossi clears his throat, and I drag my eyes away from his mouth.

The objective of the Zalśar, he says, is to track down the remnants of Etruscan records that have survived or been concealed in art throughout the past two thousand years and to reclaim them as their own.

Usually, they keep their affairs quiet and out of the public domain, which makes the high-profile theft of the amulet from the Vatican a little alarming. The group prefers dealing in circles that are not inclined to draw the attention of law enforcement.

Rossi goes on to explain that most of the remaining Zalśar aren't Italian citizens; their families left Italy after the fall of Mussolini and resettled in other parts of Europe. Fabio, for instance, is Swiss. The Zalśar use the claim on the Etruscans as a claim on prestige, something ancient and powerful that they can tie themselves to.

"But the Etruscans do not belong to them. The people of Etruria grow gardens and orchards on the same land their ancestors did. They walk the same streets and go to church in buildings built upon temples where the Etruscans worshipped. They don't dirty the legacy of the Etruscans with crimes and petty politics," Rossi finishes, and I almost applaud. It seems the Roman skill of oratoria has persisted through the millennia.

"What can you do?" I ask. "The amulet is already stolen."

"The Zalśar like to play games, even among themselves. The theft is just the beginning. Based on what we've seen from the group in the past, this is some kind of test or competition. We believe Fabio was working with others at the Vatican Museum, and now their superiors will make them struggle. From the intel we've gathered, it seems the amulet will be hidden somewhere, and Fabio will have to find it. Though he won't be the only one looking. I haven't figured out what the prize is yet or why the Zalśar are being so brazen. I don't think Fabio and whoever else is involved would risk so much for the amulet alone."

"What about the envelope?"

"I believe the envelope held his first clue. Which is why I—*we*, must make sure they don't find you. As far as Fabio is concerned, you are the only other person outside of the state police force that has seen it."

That makes my blood run cold, and I wrap my arms around myself. Rossi doesn't seem to suspect me of foul play, but he does seem to think I'm not out of the woods yet. His hand makes a fist on the table when my eyes threaten to spill over.

"Your family knows where you are and what is going on. But if you would like to talk with them, you can use my phone." He starts to slip his cell out of his pocket, but I shake my head.

"Not even your sister?" he asks.

"My sister?" I reply, wrinkling my nose. The man has been doing plenty of research on me, as well as the imposter-Etruscans. I cringe, imagining him reading my text threads with Eric.

Rossi looks appropriately embarrassed for having pried into the details of my life. He's right, though. I would love to talk to Lil. But, for a number of reasons, I would not like to have that conversation in front of him.

Rossi stands up. "Ms. Campbell, I want to assure you, you are safe in the apartment. I am here on watch most of the day, and when I am not, Alberto or another officer will be." Alberto, the officer who, after dropping off my groceries, paced outside my door for hours, smoking and shouting at his phone.

"I know," I say, walking him to the door. "And Detective, you can call me Remy."

He bites his lip—right on a red spot I noticed while he drew Etruria in his notebook—and looks at me. "Good night, Remy. I will be by tomorrow to check in."

I start to shut the door, but then I remember the groceries. "Hey, Rossi," I say as he walks into the hall. "Thanks for the shoelaces."

For the first time since we've met, Rossi smiles, and I have to lean against the door frame to keep from falling.

A knock wakes me, and the room is already flooded with sunlight. It is Alberto at my door again. This time he has come to deliver my bag, which is great news because the room is warm, and now my nervous stink from yesterday and my heat stink from the night threaten to overwhelm my nostrils. I need a shower and a change of clothes.

I also need the espresso he hands me, winking.

My attempt to ask Alberto if there is a plan, when Rossi will be back, is halting. Alberto's English is spotty, and my Italian is limited to four semesters in the classroom. Our conversation is mostly us looking confused and chuckling at our inability to communicate, but it feels good to laugh with someone.

Alberto stays outside my apartment for the next few hours. The door does little to filter the sound of his footsteps and sudden loud outbursts of what I assume are swear words over the noise of livestreaming sports games.

I spend most of the day rereading the Rome guidebook that was buried in my suitcase. I write a few of Alberto's favorite curses on the front page to look up later and then visit all the places I won't get to see in real life. I turn to the section on the Colosseum. "This is all your fault," I whisper at the page, then flip forward to the next chapter.

Hours later, I'm reading about the earliest iterations of the Circus Maximus when I smell something so delicious, I feel light-headed. It's safe to say that I am not one of those people who lose their appetite in stressful situations. If anything, I try to eat my way out of them.

Whatever that smell is, I need it.

Resting the book on the bed, I walk over to the door and crack it open without undoing the chain lock. Alberto left at some point, but somewhere in the complex is a police officer whose job is to keep me safe and likewise keep me from escaping. The chain can protect me from whoever they think is out to get me and also signal that I remain stuck inside.

The scent of warm garlic and basil and other yummy things I can't identify wafts into the apartment, rounding out the hints of savory goodness that had already crept in. My mouth waters, and I go to the kitchen.

I prepare myself *pasta al pomodoro* to the best of my abilities and eat with the aroma of someone else's dinner in my nose, making my meal no doubt taste better than it actually does. My chest aches as I rinse my plate, trying not to think too much about Cassie and what she's doing or the fact that I still haven't talked to Eric.

Is this my new life? Until Rossi can prove I'm not guilty, will I be forced to eat tear-soaked pasta all alone in this apartment? Without wine?

Snuggling into bed with the guidebook, I flip back to the Colosseum. I think of my red Chuck Taylors and the flame my father is convinced flickers somewhere inside of me. I'd been willing to risk it all—at that point, expulsion or a call back to my mom—for that first kiss.

I run my finger over the stone arches, tracing the curve of the walls. I wonder if I will ever feel as brave again as I did under that pink sunset sky when I saw a metallic-jacketed teenage Italian boy and knew in my bones what I wanted. I wonder if life will ever be as magical again as it was in that moment when someone unironically played Backstreet Boys' "I Want it That Way" over a speaker on the ancient stones, and I leaned in carelessly, breathlessly, toward a perfect pair of lips.

If my love life peaked the summer after eighth grade, I think I deserve a consolation prize. Right now, getting out of Italian house arrest would cut it.

Chapter SIX

I WAKE UP IN THE MIDDLE OF THE NIGHT and can't breathe. Something warm and heavy is pressing down on my chest, and my heart pounds so hard it hurts.

My entire body starts to shake. I never shut the door.

What if the bad guys found me? What if Fabio has come to exact his revenge. For what, exactly, I'm not sure. Denying his offer of a ride home? Taking the photo in the museum that landed me here?

Probably for stealing his envelope.

A slight whoosh of air rushes against my chin, and something sharp digs into my collarbone like I am being stabbed by an oyster fork. The sensation alternates from one side of my body to the other, and then the silence of the room gives way to a quiet, rattling hum.

Rising onto my elbows, I come face-to-face with the fattest cat I've ever seen. She is round and white and unfazed by my interruption, drooling as she continues to press her claws into my flesh.

I giggle a little wildly as I pet her, the trembling in my limbs calming as the adrenaline works its way out of my system. Once the cat is satisfied with the level of damage her claws have inflicted on my pajamas, she curls up on me and passes out.

When she's sleeping deeply enough that I won't disturb her, I slide her off my chest and get up to close the apartment door.

Perhaps it is because I want to keep her safe, or maybe I'm just happy to have my own captive—the company of someone other than myself, or some*thing*, in this case. Either way, I'm not ready to let her go yet.

Back in bed, I wrap myself around the cat and bury my face in her warm scruff. It smells like fresh bread.

The cat's incessant meowing drags me from sleep the next morning. I scan the fridge, coming up short of anything feline-appropriate, even for an Italian cat. When I pick her up to kiss her face and apologize for my lack of cat food, I notice a blue metal tag hidden under her thick fur and rolls. It's obvious someone loves this cat. I should make an honest effort to give her back.

The tag is shaped like a fish and says **Mnemosine 4B**.

I recite the name in my head a couple of times and then out loud, wondering if I'm pronouncing it right, imagining what kind of person gives their cat a name like Mnemosine. I can't judge, though; I once named a goldfish Heliogabalus.

I change out of my PJs for the first time in just under twenty-four hours and put on a shirred linen midi dress that will probably never see the light of Roman day—not outside of this building, at least—and a pair of berry-colored ballet flats.

Grabbing my Rome book off the bed, I scan the conversation guide in the back, but there is nothing in there that says, "Excuse me, your cat wandered into my apartment in the middle of the night and nearly gave me a heart attack. Would you like her back?" Likely, it won't matter. The situation seems pretty self-explanatory.

With Mnemosine tucked under my arm, I wander into the hall. I call out to see if my guard is there, waiting to find out if

I will get in trouble, but no one appears. I check the back of my door and see 3A in three-inch brass characters. I follow a set of stone stairs up to the next floor.

Maybe whoever lives in 4B will let the cat visit me. I could be her daytime babysitter, give her attention while her family is away. I wonder what Rossi and Alberto would think if they found me with a cat in the apartment.

Better a clandestine pet than an ancient amulet, I suppose.

When I find the door, I take a deep breath, hoping that the whole building doesn't know me as the girl locked in 3A for her alleged lawlessness, that my picture hasn't been splashed all over the Italian newspapers. I'd like to see my new therapy animal again, and if her owner slams the door in my delinquent face, I don't think I will handle it well.

I cling to the cat and knock three times. A door shuts somewhere in the apartment, and I hear a muffled, "*Aspetta.*" I wonder what time it is and start to panic. Maybe it's too early in the morning to go knocking on neighbors' doors, especially neighbors with whom you intend to ingratiate yourself. I consider running away, but I can hear someone approaching. And besides, Mnemosine needs her breakfast. I tell myself to be strong for the cat.

The door swings open, and I gasp—loudly, embarrassingly. The man before me has just stepped out of the shower. Water runs down the dusting of hair on his chest and along the deep ridges of his abdomen. I follow the rivulets lower, over the chiseled muscles, before forcing my eyes back up to his face.

"Rossi?" I breathe. I pull Mnemosine over my chest like I'm the one standing there wet and exposed. Holy shit, Detective.

He is naked, except for a thin towel slung low on his hips, and he is so upsettingly hot. I tell myself to close my damn mouth.

"You have my cat," he says. He looks at her, then at me, pushing his hair back from his face. I shiver. "Why were you out of the apartment?" he asks, his voice accusatory.

I adjust Mnemosine so I can put my hand on my hip. "I wasn't. She came to me."

He looks at the cat again. "How'd she get in?"

"I had the door cracked open," I admit.

"Why?"

"There was…a smell." He cocks his head at me. "A good one," I clarify, my mouth twisting.

Rossi's free hand is ranging over the stubble on his chin. Then he says, very seriously, "I—we need to keep you safe."

I press my lips together to squash my smile. "Okay."

At this point, we are at a standstill. Mnemosine is starting to squirm in my arms, and I'm sure Rossi doesn't want her taking off again. If he reaches for her, though, he might risk exposing me to more than just his amazing chest and the fact that we've been sleeping in the same building, a thought that makes my pulse quicken.

"Want me to feed her?" I offer. I drop my eyes to his towel to imply that I know he's in a bind and could use my help, but this is a mistake because as my eyes trace down his body, I go hot everywhere. He fidgets a bit under my gaze, which makes it worse.

Rossi steps back from the door and points. "Her food is in the kitchen, under the sink." I don't dare look at him again as I step past for fear of tripping over my own feet, but I hear him shut the door behind me and pad down the hall. "I'll be right there," he calls before closing himself in what I assume is his bedroom.

I empty a can of food into a ceramic dish decorated with lemons and leaves, like the big majolica serving platter my grandmother has from Sicily. Mnemosine has got it pretty good.

While the cat eats, I take in the details of the kitchen. The space looks neat but used. A copy of Artusi's famous cookbook *La Scienza in cucina e l'arte di mangiar bene* is open on the counter, and a single plate and small collection of cooking utensils dry on the rack beside the sink. The stove is covered in cast iron pans of varying sizes, and beside the fridge are two bottles of red wine—Nero d'Avola and Etna Rosso—and a bottle of white I've never heard of. I would drink any one of them.

Beside me on the counter is a stack of mail. The top letter is addressed to Valeria Piccini. I'm pushing the envelope out of the way with my finger to see what's beneath when Rossi appears. I might blush harder than I did in the hallway, not least of all because even though he is no longer naked, he now has on a pair of very suggestive sweatpants and a tight white shirt. I bite my lip so hard I almost draw blood.

"Thank you for bringing her up." He looks away from me and to the spot on the floor that the cat has littered with tuna flakes.

"Mnemosine?" I ask. The shorter the question, the less opportunity I have to fall into a trance staring at his face. He catches my meaning—what the hell kind of name is that?

"I was reading *The Theogony* when I found her," he says by way of explanation.

I shake my head.

"Mnemosine," he repeats. "The goddess of memory." He looks at me like he's waiting for me to have some sort of ah-ha moment. I don't, of course. Instead, I wonder why he went with that particular option, as I am pretty sure there are several deities with names far more manageable than Mnemosine.

But since he just caught me snooping through his mail, I don't want to be nosy, so I don't ask.

I bend down to scratch the cat behind the ears. "I like her."

Rossi leans against the counter behind me. "I was going to come talk to you this morning." I glance back at him, his outfit. *Dressed like that?* "Have you had coffee? Can I make you an espresso?" he asks.

I tell him I don't have any coffee downstairs—hint, hint—and that an espresso sounds great. We are both quiet as Rossi prepares the pot and the cups, except for when he offers me sugar. When it's ready, I follow him to his dining room table, where we sit across from each other, stirring our espressos with tiny silver spoons.

Rossi drinks his in one gulp. When I take a sip and my stomach makes the kind of sound that implies either extreme hunger or an urgent need to use the restroom, he is kind enough to pretend he doesn't hear it.

"I have made some progress with the clue," he says, playing with the small handle on his espresso cup.

"Oh?"

He looks at me and nods. A long silence follows, during which I watch his jaw clench at least four times. I refuse to drink any more coffee for fear of filling the quiet space between us with that noise again.

He tilts his head back and runs his hands through his still-damp hair. "Ms. Campbell—"

"Remy," I correct.

"Remy," he says in his accented baritone, and my stomach flips. "I believe you are innocent, and I am working to obtain proof so the Chief will be assured as well. I also think you have a right to know what was written on that paper. There must be some reason Fabio chose you, but I don't want to put you in an uncomfortable situation. If I talk to you about what was in that envelope, you can't share the information with your family. Or boyfriend." His eyes raise to mine, and I snort. Clearly, his intel is outdated.

"I want to know what the clue says. I don't expect I'll be able to help at all, though."

He looks at me the way Lil sometimes does when she wants me to stop being self-deprecating, and I can't decide if it's annoying or delightful.

Rossi stands up and gestures for me to follow. He leads me into a bright room, the walls covered in ceiling-high arched windows and bookcases, where another heavy, wooden desk like the one in his office at the police station buttresses the wall. Maybe he collects them.

Rossi leans over the desk and jiggles the mouse to wake up his computer. I watch the muscle in his forearm tighten. Something deep in my body flutters.

It's just a forearm, I tell myself.

When he looks up at me, I offer a wobbly smile. The corner of his mouth ticks up, but he clears his throat and turns to the monitor when it lights up. A window on the screen shows an enlarged photo of the clue.

"*Ecco*," Rossi says.

I lean in. The clue doesn't make any more sense to me zoomed in at 500% than it did in Rossi's office. The characters are familiar, recalling various tagged hoodies and house signs in college. "It's all Greek to me," I joke.

"Etruscan, actually." He bends to point out something on the screen, and our shoulders press together. He seems very focused on the clue, and since I don't want to interrupt, I make sure my shoulder stays nice and tight against his. The problem with this is that our faces are also very close, and when he speaks, his deep voice sinks right into my belly. "Look, the writing goes from right to left."

I follow his finger across the text. "Can you read it?" I ask.

Rossi shakes his head. "No, but I had it sent to an Etruscologist in Umbria who can. It was a straightforward translation. Etruscan hasn't been fully deciphered yet, but she knows a lot more than the Zalśar."

"Isn't the professor worried about being tracked down by the Zalśar? They want to know what it says, too. They could make her tell them."

"She is an Indiana Jones type. Professor by day only," Rossi says. "I think if she could, she'd take the Zalśar out herself."

"I wish she would," I mumble. Rossi nods, and we both stare at the Etruscan letters again. At the bottom, there are five characters much smaller than the rest—a fourth line that I hadn't even noticed on the tiny sheet of paper. "What's that?"

"The professor wasn't sure. A jumble of letters. S, B, L, D, M. No vowels. Nothing translatable. It might be a code within the Zalśar organization. We are working on it."

I mouth the letters, trying to match them to the symbols on the computer. "Maybe they are initials for members of the Zalśar," I say hesitantly, not wanting to make a stupid suggestion to a professional investigator. "L for Lewin. When we parked, he called the man in the courtyard Stefano. And you told me that woman's name is Maelle. That's S, L, and M. I mean, it's only five letters, so probably not, but…." I trail off when Rossi straightens beside me, disengaging shoulder contact.

"Yes," he says, and I exhale. "Yes, it is possible. I will call the office and let them know to check the letters against our records of the active members." I'm grinning as I watch him walk out of the room on his cell phone.

When he's been gone for a while, I pull out his desk chair. Another heavy piece of wooden furniture, slightly resembling a throne, that requires the strength of both my arms to budge. When I sit, my toes don't reach the ground.

I settle one leg beneath me and look at the clue again, following the letters right to left this time. Their shapes start to make more sense. In fact, many of the letters now seem obvious; more angular and ancient versions of the ones that compose the English alphabet.

The symbols on the screen belonged to a people so legendary that the Medicis allegedly sought to preserve their heritage and knowledge through the art of the Renaissance—one of humankind's most extraordinary cultural movements. A people so incredible that a vainglorious group of European criminals commits thefts at the Vatican to uncover their secrets.

I start in the seat when a text notification pops up on the screen. I open it without thinking.

The message is from Valeria. The same Valeria, I assume, that the mail was addressed to. A Valeria who perhaps used to live here. Likely with Rossi. There's a small photo in the corner, but all I can make out is what I deduce must be a perfect face. Because look at Rossi.

The words are Italian, but the *baci* and the *amore mio* at the end don't require advanced translation. Maybe Valeria still *does* live here.

"*Cazzo*," I say, trying out one of Alberto's favorite swears.

"What's wrong?" Rossi's concerned voice arrives just before he does. The message is still open on the screen. He bends over my shoulder to read it. I turn the same berry red as my shoes.

He closes the text box without replying to her, then regards me for a moment in the giant chair. Oh God. Rossi is going to kick me out. He's never going to free me. Innocent people don't creep on other people's messages, probably.

Rossi leans back on the desk, and his shirt stretches across his chest. A vision I will carry with me to jail. I close my eyes to lock it in place.

"So," he says. "Do you want to know what the clue says?"

Chapter SEVEN

ROSSI READS ME THE TRANSLATION from Etruscan, first in Italian and then in English.

"The professor sent it to you in English?" I ask.

"I did the English," he says, scribbling something on a piece of paper. He hands it to me. It's his translation alongside the Italian.

"Wow," I respond. "It sounds terrific in English." In the way of compliments, it's a little clunky. But I think I see his mouth threaten a smile, which would be horrible; even the memory of his smile from the other day makes me dizzy. That is not where my mind needs to be and not where this Valeria person would want it.

I give myself a shake and look back at the paper in my hands.

The lion that fell the steed/Il leone che abbatté il destriero

In the ring/Nel cerchio

Of the first true king/Del primo vero re

"What happens now?" I ask.

"Now, we try to figure out what the clue means and get to the next one before Fabio can. The problem is, not many of the officers are art history types."

I shift in my seat. I mean, I don't expect to crack the case, but if I could help, at least it would give me something to do. I hold my breath.

Rossi points to the door.

Dammit.

I use both hands to push away from the desk, and the chair makes an awful scraping noise on the ceramic tiles.

"You can take them with you if you prefer to read in your apartment," he says as I rise.

I pause. "What?"

"The books." He points to the door again. Beside it, there is a table stacked with dense old volumes with leather spines. "Most are in Italian, though, so it might be helpful to have a computer and an internet connection. You can stay here to do your research." He gestures to the desk.

"My research?"

"Only if you want to, of course," he hurries to add, standing up. "I don't mean you have to do anything. I just thought it might be more interesting than listening to Alberto shout bad words at his phone all day." His hair falls into his face, and my fingers flex with the urge to run my hand through it. "And I could use someone who knows a little about this stuff."

The proof at last that a degree in the humanities isn't completely worthless. Though, I'm not sure my mother would agree that getting to work on my own criminal case in order to prove my innocence justifies a background in art history. Knowing she'd disapprove makes Rossi's offer all the more appealing.

I grab the biggest book in the pile and pass the rest of the morning hunched over tomes about Rome's history, flipping through the indexes and checking all the pages that are listed under *leone* (there are many) and *cerchio* (there are none). Rossi lets me use the search engine on his phone—mine is still in evidence at the station—to look up words I don't know while he fires off emails from his computer.

My back starts to ache, and I try to scooch the low table I'm working at closer to the brocaded armchair I'm sitting in. The table barely moves.

"How the hell did you get this furniture into the apartment?" I ask, pulling my chair closer to the table instead.

"It came with it," he responds without looking away from the computer.

"Did they build it in here?"

"Some of the pieces."

"Really? How do you know?"

"The apartment has been in the family for a long time. My father grew up here."

My pulse jumps. "Did you, too?"

Rossi looks at me over his shoulder, chewing his lip. He shakes his head. "I was raised in Sicily."

One more Italian to check off my possible first kiss list.

We work until it's time for him to go to the station, and I return to 3A with Mnemosine—Rossi offers me the cat before I even have to ask.

I spend the second half of the day listening to Alberto yell at his phone, and I get down a few new swears in the front of my guidebook. I'll take it with me tomorrow and have the internet or Rossi tell me what they mean.

Later that night, Rossi comes by with some pizza and a can of paté for the cat. On his way out, he puts his hands in his pockets and leans against my door frame. He tells me Mnemosine can stay if I want her to. I do, I tell him. He asks me if I'll come back up in the morning. I say I will, biting my smile between my teeth.

He straightens, and his expression turns serious, like he's

just remembered something horrible he has to tell me. Or like he's just been struck by reason and realized it is entirely inappropriate to have me hanging out with him in his apartment.

My heart drops. "What is it?" I panic.

"I forgot to pick up coffee for you. I promise I will make you all the espresso you can drink tomorrow."

"What the hell, Rossi," I choke out. I reach out a hand to shove him for scaring the shit out of me. My palm lands flat against his chest.

He covers my hand with his own before I can pull away, pressing my fingers into the space just above his heart. He bends ever so slightly forward when he speaks. "Sorry," he says in a soft voice.

My lips part, and I'm not sure what I intend to do with them, but before I can make up my mind, Rossi drops my hand and steps back out into the hallway. "Coffee in the morning, then? I picked up some art history books in English from the American University for you today. They might be helpful."

"It's a date," I say and immediately want to slam my face into the wall. But Rossi just nods.

"*Buona notte*, Remy."

Two days later, I am googling the Etruscan kings of Rome on Rossi's computer with the Rome guidebook open on my lap when Rossi's phone rings. It's sitting on the desk beside me, and the number comes up as unavailable.

"Incoming call," I shout to Rossi, who is busy in the kitchen. He kept his promise about the coffee and has since included a few meals and the occasional modest glass of wine. Today, for dinner, he is preparing something "light": eggplant parmigiana.

"Who is it," he shouts back?

"It doesn't say," I answer over the sound of popping oil. "But it's not your work tone."

"Answer it."

"Really?"

"It's probably just a telemarketer."

I swipe my finger across the screen and try out a hesitant, "*Pronto*?"

A woman's voice responds. "*Pronto*? *E tu chi saresti*?" I don't need to know Italian to know she is not happy I answered the phone.

"Um, *un attimo*," I manage in a strangled Italian accent as I hop out of the chair. I slide into the kitchen in my socks. "It is *not* Alberto," I mouth to Rossi, my hand over the phone. Something flashes in his eyes, and then he sighs, reaching for the phone.

"*Salve*, Valeria," he says, turning his back to me.

I slink back to the study. Rossi's voice is low and severe as he speaks with her. I can hear her arguing through the receiver, even from the other room. Then silence.

"Everything okay?" I ask when he comes in.

Rossi avoids my eyes. "Fine."

He looks sad, and I don't like it. "Are you sure?"

Rossi nods, rubbing the back of his neck. "Dinner will be ready in half an hour."

"Perfect," I say, pushing the chair beside me out for him. "That gives me plenty of time to show you what I found out about Tarquin the Elder."

He sits, and we spend the next thirty minutes talking about Rome's first Etruscan king, *the first true king*, whose name I caught in the Circus Maximus chapter of my guidebook the night Mnemosine found me.

The next day, when Rossi's phone rings, I stiffen.

The call with Valeria yesterday was…not great. Rossi never fully recovered after their conversation, and I still feel guilty for setting her off. If it is Valeria on the phone again, I should ready myself to hightail it out of the apartment.

"*Pronto*," I hear him answer. There is a short silence, and then he laughs. An adorable, deep chuckle. My feelings around the phone call shift to something less akin to contrition and scarily similar to jealousy. I have to stop myself from going into the room. If I were to see him smiling at the phone, I might growl.

I'm stewing at the thought of Rossi being so happy to hear from Valeria when he laughs again, closer. Apparently, they made up last night. It's not my place to care, but oh God, do I.

"Yes, the pasta, so much pasta. And chocolate?" Rossi asks into the phone as he comes around the corner.

He's speaking English? I don't know if this makes me feel better or worse, especially when I see his face split into a grin. That damn mouth. "Thank you. You too. Here she is."

He stretches the phone toward me. I push back into the chair. "Who is it?" I mouth.

"Lilliana."

"Lilian?" I repeat. My jaw falls open. My sister is a reprehensible flirt. I snatch the phone and am about to tell her as much, but she speaks first.

"Is he as delicious as he sounds?"

"Oh my god," I hiss, standing. I lean to see Rossi at the dining room table and tell him I'm stepping into the hallway. He nods. "What did you say to him?" I ask Lil as soon as I'm outside the door.

"Tell me what he looks like," she insists, ignoring my question. "Javier has been out of town for work, and my phone calls with your detective are the only thing keeping me going while I'm alone with the kids. It's spring break, you know. I'm fucking drowning in snacks and weird-ass YouTube videos."

"What do you mean *phone calls*?" I ask. I know Rossi said he'd been in touch with my family, but I thought he meant that he'd, like, called to update my dad. Not that he'd been placating my sister with his sensuous voice during her stint as a stay-at-home-mom.

"I'm not as bad as Mom. I've only called a couple of times."

"You've all been calling Rossi?"

"Your voice got all breathy when you said his name."

"Shut up."

"But he's hot, right?"

"He's..." I swallow. He's gorgeous, kind, a great cook, and I spend an inordinate number of minutes in the day thinking about his smile.

And, *he's taken*.

"I knew it," Lil cuts in with a sigh. "Anyway, after you called Dad, he told Mom what was going on, and she lost her goddamn mind. And of course, Dad didn't know anything—not where you were, what had happened. But he had Rossi's number, so she called it. They've pretty much been on the phone together ever since."

I groan. "How did I not know this?" He'd offered to let me call my family at least once a day, one time even tried to make me, but I'd never heard him on the phone with them.

"I think she times her calls for when you aren't around."

Figures. "Do you think she's driving him crazy?" The last thing Rossi needs is another asshole to deal with on the phone.

"If she is, he hasn't let on. Rossi is the picture of patience," Lil continues. "I think Mom might be falling."

That puts two Campbell women in the slog. Three if you

count Lil's horny housewife fantasy. "Yeah. He's nice," I say noncommittally.

Lil snorts. "Don't tell Eric. He's taking this all pretty hard."

My eyes widen. "Has he been calling Rossi, too?" I ask in a high voice.

"Not that I know of. He's too busy posting 'BRING REMY HOME' all over his social media. Eric is kind of a celebrity over here these days. The media loves the handsome fiancé campaigning for his innocent betrothed schtick. He's really good at it."

My stomach turns. I'm not sure if it's the thought of my story being splashed all over the news that is so awful or the fact that Eric is reveling in it. And, *betrothed*?

"We aren't even together!" I protest, my voice so loud it bounces off the walls.

"Interesting. You should let Eric know."

"Is he seriously calling me his fiancée on the news?"

"Does it matter what he calls you?" She doesn't give me a chance to answer before she fires off her next question. "Is Rossi a big guy?"

"He's above the local average, I guess."

I can practically hear her roll her eyes. "I know what kind of pants Italian men wear, okay? Don't play me."

"Jesus, Lil," I mutter, but my mind goes to Rossi in his sweatpants, and I bite my lip.

"I'm waiting."

I shake my head. "You have a problem," I tell her.

"Seems to me like you might be the one with the problem," she counters. I can hear the kids screaming in the background. The familiar call of "D-O-N-E" resounds in the distance—little Carlito is ready to have his butt wiped.

"I love you," I say. "Take it easy on Javier when he gets home."

"If I end up with a fourth child, you can blame it on Rossi's voice."

"That's weird."

"God, it's so sexy."

"You already got to marry your tall, dark, and handsome foreigner; this one's mine."

"I knew it," she all but screams into the phone. "You want to bang the—"

"Bye," I shout over her before hanging up the phone.

I take a couple of minutes to compose myself before walking back into Rossi's apartment, Lil's words echoing in my head. Stupid big sister is always right—I do have a problem. I have a few of them, in fact. And most of them involve my feelings for Rossi.

The way he is so familiar already, how it's so easy to be with him. That tingle I get when he smiles at me.

Rossi opens the door right as I reach for the handle and takes the phone from my hands, looking behind me, up and down the stairs. I push past him into the apartment, and he follows, locking the door behind us.

"It was quiet out there for a while; I was worried something had happened," he says. My shoulders drop. Rossi thought I'd tried to make a run for it, and I'm reminded that for him, the problem is keeping me from escaping. It's his job to be stuck here with me.

Rossi and I are here because we have to be, he has to be, and when it's all said and done, none of it means anything.

"Are you okay?" he asks when I don't respond.

I scoff. "Yeah, sure, about as okay as you were yesterday after your call with Valeria." Rossi's brow creases, and I keep going. "You should be nicer to your girlfriend, Rossi."

I'm not sure why I'm defending Valeria. Maybe because I

would have been furious too if I were dating Rossi and some mystery woman had answered his phone. Maybe because he's been nothing but amazing to me, and it is the only thing I have to hold against him.

Rossi looks at me, confused. I cross my arms, walk to my chair, and slump down in front of a book about Greek sculpture.

He comes up right beside me. "Remy?"

"What?" I snap. It's not Rossi's fault that I like him so much–well, maybe it is a little bit—but I am angry. Angry that the one beautiful thing in this crummy situation exists in my head. Angry that Eric, the man who I am supposed to go back home and be with once this is all over, is thriving not just in spite of my situation but because of it.

Rossi sits down on the edge of the low table in front of me. "Valeria is not my girlfriend."

Excuse me? My heart races in my chest. "It's none of my business," I respond. Even though I very much want it to be my business.

"Maybe not, but since you are here, you should know some things."

I look up at him. "What should I know?"

"Valeria and I were a couple until a few months ago. She lived here, too. You noticed some stuff around, I'm sure. And the mail." I cringe when he brings up the pile of letters I peeked through, but he doesn't say it accusingly. "We are still figuring some things out. We were together a long time, and it is difficult to untangle our lives."

I think of Eric. How easy it was for him to untangle himself from our life together. "Of course."

"I just," Rossi pauses, his hands in his hair. "I just didn't want you to think I'd be cruel to someone I care about. It has been hard on both of us. But you're not wrong. I should be nicer."

Not too nice, I want to add, but I'm too busy trying to hide my smile.

Chapter EIGHT

ROSSI DOESN'T SAY ANY more ABOUT VALERIA, but he does invite me to stay in his apartment while he's at the station that afternoon. We've fallen into an easy rhythm. I show up in the mornings with Mnemosine and get a little thrill every time I knock on the door. For better or worse, Rossi expects me now and always welcomes me into the apartment fully dressed and mostly dry.

He prepares the espresso while I feed the cat, and then we both hunker down in the study—me in a pile of books and Rossi scanning (likely classified) documents on the computer—until I start to get grouchy and need to eat something.

Sometimes, I hear Alberto's muffled swearing. His voice comes from the floor below, echoing up the stairwell. I imagine him sitting outside my apartment, verbally abusing his phone. I wonder if he knows where I am. I wonder what he thinks I do all day if he doesn't.

Rossi and I make a good team, bouncing ideas off each other, translating back and forth. Rossi is the kindest, most physically impressive colleague ever, who is also great at cooking and smelling delicious, which is a particular issue when we are bent over a book reading together.

We are careful not to let our shoulders touch, nor our fingers or knees or any other body parts. Not since, in a fit of excitement after discovering details about the original construction of the Circus Maximus buried in one of the textbooks he brought me from the university, I reached up and grabbed him by his biceps.

It took me way too long to let go, and we were both red by the time I did. Five more minutes passed before I got my breathing back under control.

I also finally talk to Eric.

Our call is brief and includes a lot of sighing and swearing on my part and explaining and begging on Eric's.

He's angry I didn't find a way to reach out to him sooner, which is pretty rich, considering he is well aware of my situation. I can only push the point so far, though, because he's not wrong. Rossi has offered me plenty of chances to make contact.

I yell at Eric for all the fun he's been having garnering the world's sympathy through interviews and Facebook posts, for reveling in his newfound fame, and not doing anything to help me.

But once we get that out of the way, our conversation isn't all bad.

He's requested time from work so he can come to Rome, be here for me if I need him. The thought of Eric anywhere near Rossi makes my skin crawl, but I just thank him and tell him I should be home before that becomes necessary. I tell him that I am very well taken care of here. He doesn't ask, so I don't tell him just how well.

Before we hang up, he says he misses me, that he can't wait to have me home. I say it back. Because Eric is my real life, and I am lucky to have someone who cares and is worried and is waiting for me. I tell myself I even mean it.

After the call, Rossi and I instate more prudent boundaries.

Detective Rossi and his sidekick Remy Campbell. No more grazing elbows, no more talk of exes. He is the consummate professional. I try, but whenever I zone out, all I see in my head is his mouth, his naked chest, the way his fingertips pressed into the tomato he was dicing the other night.

Every time it happens, he gives a little fake cough and turns away. One time, I think his eyes sparkle, and his lip twitches up like he knows what I'm thinking about and doesn't hate it, but that could just be my vagina playing tricks on me.

Sometimes when Rossi is gone in the afternoons and evenings, I roam around the apartment trying to remember the Italian words for all the things inside and outside. Unlike my apartment, which has two windows that both look into a narrow, walled-in alley, his opens up to the street. There is a busy cafe with metal tables across the way where old men gather to drink tiny coffees over newspapers and smoke cigarettes and argue. If a game is on, the voices are directed at the television.

The cigarettes and soccer make me nostalgic for the outside Roman world, but I'm glad to at least get a small taste of it here.

From the corner window, I can see to the end of the street, where a crumbling aqueduct intersects the neighborhood. I check each view for a conspicuous landmark, but there is nothing specific—just a lot of well-maintained white and yellow buildings and pretty little gardens.

Every few days, we have a rainy morning, and the tables outside the bar are wet and empty, the umbrella stand by the door filled to bursting. Inside, I can see the men in their sports coats, jammed shoulder to shoulder in front of the bar. I recognize the regulars now. My favorite I call Geppetto. He is old and little and always smiling. If I ever make it down there, it will be hard not to give him a hug.

This, I suppose, is what it feels like to live in Rome, outside of the tourist hustle and bustle in a little neighborhood with cafes and restaurants filled with locals, somewhere off the so-called beaten path.

It's a feeling I like. A feeling I could get used to and maybe already have.

There is not much of Rossi in the apartment, no old photos or trophies, but I discover a bit about his father. Pietro Rossi loved Rome and the law. With the exception of a small collection of old Italian poetry that Lorenzo said belonged to his mother—Petrarch, Aretino, Leopardi, Alighieri, and surprisingly, Michelangelo di Ludovico Buonarroti Simone, aka Michelangelo—every book in the apartment has to do with one or both of Pietro Rossi's favorite subjects: Roman history, Roman legal history, History of Italian Law, the Italian constitution, the influence of the Roman Empire on modern politics, and any work by Greek historians and philosophers that impacted things along the way.

"It must have been hard for your dad to leave Rome," I say to Rossi one night over dinner.

His jaw pulses, and he puts down the *arancino* he's been eating, picking up his wine instead—a red from a small vineyard outside of Catania. I do the same, staring at the piece of fried dough he just set on his plate, the stringy scamorza his teeth tore through. The wine tastes like cherries and plums and volcano, and I let it sit on my tongue as I wonder how a half-eaten ball of flour, cheese, and rice can be such a turn-on.

"He never really did," Rossi says.

I swallow. "I thought you grew up in Sicily?"

"Yes, with my mother and two siblings and our grandparents."

I give him my best "oh, shit, sorry" face. I had assumed that Rossi's whole family was off on the island.

"Your dad?" I ask.

"He passed away a few years ago."

"I'm so sorry."

Rossi shakes his head a little and takes another sip of wine.

"We were never very close," he says. We are both quiet for a moment before he goes on. "He was good friends with Chief Marchetti. They went to law school together." His shoulders sag. "I think that's how I got the position. How I made detective so young."

"I'm sure that's not true."

He huffs a laugh, but it's not a sweet sound. "After what happened on my last case, it is a miracle I'm still with the Polizia di Stato. If things don't go well this round, I'll probably be sent back to Sicily to write parking tickets for people I went to elementary school with."

I swirl my glass and watch the ruby wine spin. "What happened on your last case?"

"I let someone get away. The Commissioner wanted an arrest, and I just...."

I reach out to take his hand but pause before my outstretched fingers reach his. "You'll get the bad guys this time."

He curls his fingers into a fist, leaving my hand splayed between us. "I hope so."

I already hate Fabio, and the thought of him getting Rossi fired makes my ears pound. "You will," I insist. When he doesn't look at me, I give him a gentle kick under the table, letting my foot drop next to his. "Hey," I say when he glances up.

He smiles, and goosebumps cover my skin. "*We* will get them, Remy."

Something deep inside me twists. In these moments, even

having just my toe this close to his is electrifying, almost alarming. Like the spark between us might build into something dangerous if we aren't careful. Or maybe it's just me who feels like I'm about to burst into flames every time Rossi's nearby.

As desperate as I am to solve the clue, to have Rossi find something or someone who can exonerate me, I'm not as eager as I should be for this all to end. I'm not looking forward to going back to the way things were—the life where I'm just a beauty line marketer from Phoenix and not up to my neck in art books all day puzzling through vague Etruscan prose to outplay a group of haughty European criminals.

I'm not ready for a normal without Rossi.

I'm flipping through a thick and musty Italian book that indexes the contents of the Capitoline Museums when I see it: a marble statue of a lion with its claws and teeth pressed into the stone back of a horse.

I let out an embarrassing, high-pitched scream, and Rossi is in the room before it's over.

"Are you hurt?" he says. His voice is shaky and even deeper than usual as he looks me over. His eyes sweep over my body, every little piece of it. My skin goes hot.

I lift the book in front of my face to hide my surely massive pupils and show him the picture. "The lion that fell the steed," I breathe.

"*O mio dio*. You found it." His hand ranges through his hair, and he looks like I just told him he won the lottery.

"I don't know for sure," I hurry to clarify. I should have taken the time to do a little more research before the screeching. "But maybe."

I set the book down and run my finger over the description,

looking for a date. Luckily, those don't require much translation. "325-300 BCE," I say, frowning. "That's like 300 years after Tarquin the Elder ruled."

He leans down to look, leaving a safe six inches between us. "That's true, but look at the archaeological notes. They found it in the Circus Maximus."

Holy shit, holy shit. "Holy shit," I exclaim out loud. "This could totally be it, right?"

He nods and gives a tight smile. "It totally could be, Remy."

The first thing we find online says that the statue is on loan to the Getty Villa—which would mean the clue likely isn't hidden on or near the *Lion Attacking a Horse*. But since that exhibit ended at the end of February, the statue could be anywhere now. He sends an email to the Director of the Capitoline Museums to ask about its whereabouts before he has to leave.

Rossi is going into the station early. He has tracked down some witnesses from my lunch with Fabio and thinks he might be close to locating the kid who served us. Rossi believes he'll have enough evidence to absolve me of any wrongdoing if he finds him. I'd be off the hook. Free.

I try to act excited when he tells me about it. And I am, but only because I wonder what things might look like between us if I wasn't stuck in here with him because of legal reasons and he wasn't my policeman babysitter.

"Alberto is already downstairs, but I told him you were napping and not to bother you."

"Alberto must think I spend a lot of time sleeping."

Rossi chews his lip a little and makes a sound of agreement. I feel a zing low in my belly at the thought of Rossi lying about us to the other agents. I like that I'm his deep, dark secret, that I abscond to his apartment every morning and stay until the sky is dark, that we pass all these hours together, just the two of us, alone.

Although the truth is not that sexy and primarily includes reading and food, a girl can dream.

"Good luck," I say.

Then I remember something from my new shiny Italian phrase book that Rossi bought me. "*In bocca al lupo*," I call to him. *Into the mouth of the wolf.*

"*Crepi il lupo*," he responds. *May the wolf die.*

And with that very graphic exchange, he leaves.

While he's gone, I find more references to the *Lion Attacking a Horse*. The statue was found in a stream bed below the Palatine Hill, beside the Circus Maximus—which was constructed under Tarquin the Elder, the first Etruscan king of Rome—where it had stood in ancient times.

As the clue stated, *In the ring of the first true king.*

At some point, as early as the 1300s, it was brought up and displayed in the central courtyard of the Campidoglio, the home of Rome's capitol. The lion was the predominant symbol of Rome until the she-wolf replaced it.

Later, both ancient artworks were booted in favor of a bronze equestrian statue assumed to be of Emperor Constantine when Michelangelo revamped Piazza del Campidoglio at the behest of a Farnese pope.

That bronze still stands in the center of the Capitoline Hill. Only, it turned out to be Marcus Aurelius.

And Michelangelo did not want it there. He already had a different piece in mind for the spot.

There is a note in one book about a Hellenistic sculpture in Rome that Michelangelo referred to as "The Marvelous" and that one of his students restored in the 16th century.

Michelangelo wanted the *Lion Attacking a Horse* at the center of the piazza.

Suddenly, all the lions make sense. The creepy painting by DaVinci in the Pinacoteca that Fabio laughed at, the amulet the Zalśar stole with the lion-headed pendants, the statue.

The lion guards the secrets of the Etruscans. It represents a Rome that belongs to and owes its glory to them.

"Remy, you should see this," Rossi says when he comes into his apartment that night. I drop my pencil and disengage my legs from where they are twisted beneath me.

"What is it?" I ask, hobbling over to where Rossi is staring at his phone by the door.

"The Director of the Musei Capitolini just emailed. She said that the *Lion Attacking a Horse* was on loan at the Getty Villa but arrived back in Rome just about two weeks ago. The same day you got here."

I wince. The Commissioner is going to eat that up. "Is it back on display?" I ask.

He looks at me and smiles. My heart races. "It is," he answers.

"Did you already send someone?"

"The email just came in. I'm going to call the Chief Inspector, but we have to act slowly, carefully. We don't want to draw the attention of the Zalśar. It could endanger the case and the art. We should be able to get someone over there tomorrow, but since we don't know what we'll find, we need to be thoughtful with our approach."

"Right, of course. But you think the statue is what we've been looking for?"

"I do. You did an amazing job, Remy Campbell." He puts

out a hand for me to shake, but fuck it, I go in for a hug. I am, potentially, an investigative genius. I deserve a cuddle.

As soon as my arms are around his waist, I feel the tears prickle. I haven't had a hug since Lil threateningly embraced me at Sky Harbor International in Phoenix and whispered in my ear that if I didn't at least add one kiss to my list, she would disown me as a sister.

Rossi stiffens at first, holds his breath, but when he exhales, his body softens, and his arms settle around my neck—which has me bawling in mere seconds. He makes shushing sounds and presses one hand to the back of my head, pulling my face closer to his chest. The fabric of his shirt is already soaked through with my tears, and when my nose starts to run, I try to pull away, so I don't end up wiping my snot on his top, too. But he leans his cheek on the top of my head and keeps me there.

"It's going to be okay," he whispers into my hair. "Soon, this will all be over, and you can go home."

At that, I cry so hard I start to laugh.

"What is it?" he asks.

I lean back to look at him.

His fingers drift down my sides to my waist, and I shiver as he holds me there.

"I just…" I just want him. I want to taste his mouth and feel the weight of his body above me. I want to test the durability of every piece of heavy wooden furniture in this apartment in the most amoral way possible.

My palms spread over the damp fabric of his t-shirt. I'm staring at his lips.

Rossi drops his hands from my hips and steps back. He looks away when he clears his throat. "Tomorrow is going to be a big day."

I wipe the leftover moisture from my cheeks and nose in an attempt to hide my face.

"Do you have anything to eat in the apartment? I can make something if you're hungry," he offers.

I shake my head. "All good." My voice comes out hoarse.

In truth, all I have to eat downstairs is a bag of Mulino Bianco Abbracci cookies, but it will have to do for dinner because there is no way I'm dragging this discomfort out any longer than necessary.

Rossi walks Mnemosine and me down to 3A. "She'll miss you when you leave," he says as he hands me the cat. I take her and shut the door without responding. I head straight for the cookies.

Chapter NINE

ROSSI IS AT THE APARTMENT to let Mnemosine and me in the following morning, but he leaves after. *Likely to avoid me*, I think, my chest compressing. He does ask me to stay until he gets back, at least.

Almost sixteen hours later, the apartment door slams, and I jump in the chair, ramming my head into the heavy brass lamp on the desk in Rossi's office.

"Remy?" he calls from the foyer.

"In here," I shout back. I shove the stack of papers I've been conjugating Italian verbs on to pass the time under a volume about Medici architecture in Rome.

Rossi walks in, untucking his shirt, and I look back at the book, crossing my legs and willing the vision of him topless to dissipate from my mind. Praying that when I speak again, I'm semi-coherent, that I don't embarrass myself like I did last night.

Of course, the reason I do my reading in his apartment and not my polizia-funded suite downstairs—other than the faster internet—is to enjoy this moment every evening: watch him come home and undo himself, pour a glass of wine, and stretch his legs out before him on the couch. I stay so I have a reason to steal glances of his face when he asks me if I found anything good, so I can revel in the way the air shifts when he leans forward to listen to whatever it is I've dug up.

And he cooks me pasta.

Tonight it's late, though, and he seems agitated. He doesn't sit down on the couch, and I shift in the seat to see him better.

"Alberto wasn't downstairs," he says, a hint of irritation in his voice. "Why would he leave?"

"*Che cazzo ne so*?" I try on for size. *How the hell should I know?* Rossi's eyebrows pop up, and he shakes his head, but he's smiling. My heart flutters.

"I have good news, Remy." He comes and stands in front of me, reaches out like he might squeeze my shoulder, but doesn't. "You've been cleared."

My stomach flips.

As much as I hoped, in the beginning, that this situation would just hurry up and be over, I don't want it to be. I've been stuck in this apartment building for two weeks, and I've gotten more joy out of researching the first clue than I experienced in five whole years at my job in marketing.

"You found the server?" I ask, bending to pick up Mnemosine, who's been twining between Lorenzo's legs. I rest her on my lap, and he pets her as he talks. She starts to purr. I've never understood an animal so thoroughly.

"Yes, I found him. Got a huge lead out of him, too. The poor kid was terrified. He told me all about your lunch with Fabio." Rossi's eyes flash dark, and I am happy he hates Fabio as much as I do, even if it's for different reasons. "Chief Marchetti did some background work, and there is now nothing to incriminate you in the case. You've been labeled an unwilling accessory."

I shrug. I've been called worse.

He pulls a phone out of his back pocket, my phone, and

hands it to me. It powers right up, fully charged, and starts buzzing with messages and voicemail alerts.

"Thank you," I say, placing the ringer on silent.

Rossi bites his lip, right on the dark spot he's been abusing since this all started.

"What?" I ask.

He rubs the back of his neck, looking like whatever comes next is not good news at all. I cling to the cat, steeling myself. "The Commissioner would like you to remain in Rome in case they need help identifying any of Zalśar's agents. I'm so sorry, Remy, I could talk to him and maybe..."

My breath rushes out in a laugh—the sound of manic, inappropriate relief. He cocks his head and looks at me, uncertain.

"I've been in Rome for over two weeks and have barely seen anything. I'm not ready to leave yet." I don't add that the thought of never seeing him again makes me want to puke a little.

He nods, and his eyes light up. I forget to breathe. "I thought we could celebrate," he says, walking to his bag. He pulls out a 2012 Solaia. The same bottle of red wine my dad special ordered for my graduation. My throat tightens. "A *brindisi* to your breakthrough yesterday. And your innocence."

The way he emphasizes my innocence makes my face go hot. "I'll grab the glasses," I offer, dropping Mnemosine to the ground.

He grips my wrist with gentle fingers and turns me. "Not here."

"My apartment?" It seems like a weird choice, but I'm not against it.

He lets go of my arm and slides his hand into his pocket. "Now that you don't have to be stuck inside, I thought I could show you around the city." His voice is different, less sure.

"In the middle of the night?" It's more of a statement than a question, more giddy than incredulous. There is something crumbling between us, and it is making every nerve in my body snap to attention. The invisible barrier that has kept us in check these weeks is in heaps at our feet. I was a suspect. He is a detective. It wasn't flirting; it was professional courtesy. They weren't semi-indecent early morning coffee dates; they were discussions about the Italian legal system.

But now, it's just us. And none of the pretense.

He looks at his watch and seems surprised when he sees how late it is. But I've already strapped on my sandals and am heading for the door.

We walk from the apartment past the Basilica di San Giovanni in Laterano up to Via Labicana, around the Colosseum (just the sight of it gives my heart a kick), and down Via Dei Fiori Imperiali, where statues of emperors salute us from the side of the street. We take swigs out of the bottle as we go, and every time my lips close around the glass, I get a heady rush thinking about how Rossi's have just been there.

He takes a left up a quiet side street, and we arrive at a locked gate that they use to funnel tourists out of the Roman Forum during the day. Rossi lifts himself up onto the wall beside it and reaches down for my hand.

"Detective, are we breaking into the Roman Forum?" His lips turn up as he pulls me up close beside him, onto the base of a marble column that's stacked on top of a detailed relief. It feels sacrilegious to put my feet anywhere near the millennia-old carvings, but the marble below my shoes has survived a lot more than a tipsy, mid-twenties tourist.

Rossi jumps off the Arch of Septimus Severus, and I shimmy myself down into his waiting arms, thinking about how much more fun this crime is to commit than the one I was being accused of. His broad hands press against my ribs, and my breasts tingle at the closeness of his fingertips.

We pick our way along the uneven, moonlit stones of the Via Sacra. I trip on the carved edge of a fallen capital—and consider doing it again after the high of having the muscles in Rossi's chest flex against my back as he saved me from eating ancient pavement.

When we reach the House of the Vestals, he turns on his phone light and guides me up a rickety, rusty metal staircase inside the ruins. At the top, we emerge into an opening that looks out over a quiet, dream version of the Eternal City.

His silhouette stands out against the glow of Rome, like the outline of a strong-shouldered Roman god. "Come here often?" I ask, trying to ignore the building heat low into my belly.

"I do," he answers.

"Hm." I grab the wine. It's empty, but there is a backup bottle in his bag. "For the view, I'm sure."

"When I'm on a case, I like to come up here to think. It does help that you can see the whole city. Hard for Rome to hide her secrets when she's laid out before you." Oh, my.

He hesitates, then adds, "This is the first time I've ever brought anyone."

I turn away to hide my smile. "I'm glad the Commissioner is holding me hostage in Rome," I say, taking in the sprawling city, golden lights glowing up and down the streets, the gray shapes of ancient buildings jutting out against a dusky sky spattered with stars.

Rossi sits down in the grass, and I sit beside him. He has the second bottle open, and we both take a long drink.

"You'll have to leave the apartment," he says, leaning back on his hands as I rest the bottle between us.

"Oh."

"But you'll still need protection, of course. I was thinking, if it feels safe for you, you could stay in my apartment, and I will sleep in Signor Moretti's extra room across the hall. That way, you won't have to worry about Fabio, and I can still..." he pauses. "I'm also happy to find another arrangement. Whatever you want to do, Remy, I'll make it happen."

"I'll stay with you," I say, lifting the bottle again. The lights that flood the Colosseum's exterior seem to sparkle.

Rossi lets out a long breath and rakes a hand through his hair. It sticks out sideways. Our silence stretches a second too long. "You should make a list of the things you want to see and do while you're here." He's speaking hurriedly, gesturing to the night. "There are the obvious places you must visit. But I also know a bunch of smaller museums and sites I think—" I shift, and our arms graze, sending goosebumps over my skin. He swallows mid-sentence. "I think you'd enjoy. There's one place where you can go underground, and..." He trails off and looks at me.

His chest rises and falls, and when I dare to look up into his face, his eyes are nearly black, but they are blazing. They are molten. And their heat moves into my body, spreading, pooling.

The wine is strong, and we are alone with Rome spread out below our hill. Still, I whisper. "There *is* something I've been dying to do." I reach out a hand before I can reconsider and run it through his thick hair. Then I shift myself in front of him and do the same with the other. His eyes are wide with surprise, but as I drag my fingers back, they close. I trace the lines of his face with my gaze, taking in the perfection that I never let myself enjoy in earnest: the strong cheekbones, the full lips, his dark lashes. I feel a shock of anger as I think about Valeria hurting him, and my right hand closes in a tight fist in his hair.

A growl escapes from deep in his lungs, and my body shudders. His eyes shoot open. He looks mortified.

"Remy," he says in a hoarse whisper. My insides are liquid.

I weave the fingers of my left hand through the hair at the base of his neck and clench my fingers. I want to hear that noise again. "Yes, Lorenzo?" I breathe.

As soon as his name is off my lips, his are pressed hard against my mouth. Our bodies collide, and his powerful hands crush into my back, my waist, holding me impossibly close.

Lorenzo leaves me at my door with a brush of his lips against mine, and even that small, sweet gesture is enough to make me nearly lose my mind. Mnemosine follows me in.

I somehow manage to get my head on straight enough to brush my teeth and change into pajamas. Knowing he is just a floor above me, sleep does not come easily. I lay in bed cuddling the cat and thinking about Lorenzo, about our kiss.

It was like taking the thrill of my first kiss at the Colosseum and multiplying it by a thousand. Maybe a million. There was the advantage of being an adult kissing another adult, and having a bit more direction and knowledge about the dynamics and anatomy, of course. But it was so much more than that.

In that kiss was a lifetime of anticipation set ablaze in the grass of the Palatine Hill. I'd been waiting since I was fourteen for my knees to go weak again, but all of me fell apart in Lorenzo's arms. And he held me together.

I feel like I could set the world on fire. I will find the amulet. I will help Lorenzo catch Fabio and the others. I am smart. I am strong. And I will *not* go tearing up the stairs to bang on

Lorenzo's door and beg him to kiss me like that again. Not until sunrise, at least.

This last bit requires a certain amount of conviction I'm not sure I possess, so I take a melatonin and content myself with the lingering smell of Lorenzo's apartment in Mnemosine's fur.

The sun is blazing when I wake up, and the clock Lorenzo picked up for me says it's just past nine. I look around for Mnemosine to make sure I didn't smother her in our sleep. I'm surprised she hasn't gotten me up yet; she's never let me sleep past six without putting up a fight. Like me, she is not one who misses a meal without complaint.

The cat is sitting upright in the corner of the room like a very voluptuous lion at guard. Maybe she knows I spent the night dreaming about ravaging her owner. Judgy little feline.

When I pick her up, she remains tense in my arms, and I start to get a nervous tingle in my stomach, a feeling that something is wrong.

What if the Zalśar saw us last night? They could have followed us back to the apartment. They could have done something to Lorenzo.

I don't give myself a chance to elaborate on that thought. I fling Mnemosine over my shoulder and run out of the apartment, taking the steps two at a time. I'm panting when I reach 4B. My ponytail is half undone and three inches right of center. My pajamas are—I look down—covered in oil stains?

I slam my fist into Lorenzo's door anyway.

"Rossi?" I call. Then, because that doesn't feel quite right anymore, I say, "Lorenzo?"

I know, reasonably, that he is probably fine. But my gut doesn't seem convinced, and neither does Mnemosine, who is bristling in my arms. It feels like forever before the door opens, and I am on the verge of hyperventilating when it does.

Which makes it hard not to vomit when I see a beautiful, elegantly dressed, fully coiffed woman standing on the threshold. "*Lei sta bene*?" she asks me. *Are you all right?*

I nod as I take her in. She is put together in all the ways I never am and never will be. She radiates confidence, certainty. This woman burns on the outside.

Valeria.

I swallow the ugly noise building in my throat and shove Mnemosine toward her. They both recoil, so I hug the cat back to my chest. "I was just bringing her home."

She regards me, my sloppy clothes and hair and unwashed face. "You must be the American."

I nod again.

"Do you speak Italian?" she asks.

"Not much."

She smiles like she already suspected the answer. "You can keep the cat. I don't need her fur all over my clothing."

My thoughts reel out. Had Lorenzo been lying to me about his breakup? Have they been together this whole time?

At this point, I am not above stealing his cat. I clear my throat. "I'll just need her food, then," I say to Valeria.

"Lorenzo keeps it somewhere in the kitchen," she tells me, and I want to yell at her that I already know. I want to cry at the way his name sounds on her lips. But I flip-flop my way past her and make a show of looking for Mnemosine's favorite cans of paté. I'm shoving them into one of Lorenzo's reusable shopping bags when I hear Valeria say, "Ah, the *pigrone* decided to drag himself out of bed."

I stand up, and Lorenzo is glancing between Valeria and me with a look of absolute horror on his face. He is wearing a pair of boxer briefs, and my throat constricts. I try not to imagine them sleeping together after our kiss on the Palatine.

"What are you doing here?" he asks in English, and my heart threatens to burst from my ribs. What *am* I doing here? I misread everything. I am the forever idiot throwing myself at the wrong men. A giant fire hose is putting out all the flames that ignited inside of me last night, and it takes all my strength not to puddle on the floor with them in a weepy mess.

But Valeria answers. "I told you I was coming back for the conference."

Lorenzo shakes his head. "Next week, you told me next week you'd be here for the law thing." He looks at me with wide eyes. I look at my feet.

"No, Lorenzo," she says with a sigh. "*La societá della giurisprudenza romana* meets tomorrow."

His voice is raised when he responds, and their conversation becomes a volley of Italian words at a consistently attenuating volume. Mnemosine has stuffed herself between a chair and the wall, and I coax her out while Lorenzo and Valeria have at it behind me. I make it out the door with the cat, but I hear Lorenzo call my name before the lock clicks.

"Wait, Remy. Please," he says as he steps into the hall in his underwear. He's running his hands through his hair, and it is as wild as ever. Looking at him hurts.

"I won't say anything," I tell him, focusing on the cat.

"What do you mean?"

"I mean, I won't tell Valeria. Yesterday you and I were both excited and got caught up in the moment. All the wine and the news." I raise my face. He looks confused, so I continue. "The kiss last night," I state, trying to keep my voice light. "It was no big deal."

"No big deal?" he repeats, and the way he says it makes my breath hitch. His eyes are the darkest brown. His mouth is... God, it's perfect. I make myself look away. That damn kiss was the biggest deal, the best deal. The kiss I've been waiting for since I was fourteen. And nothing more, apparently.

"I've got Mnemosine's food. She can stay with me."

Lorenzo buries his face in his hands and swears, saying all the bad Italian words I learned from Alberto in quick succession. Then he looks back at his door. Probably thinking of the gorgeous woman he left behind it.

"Thank you," he says, turning back to me, and I wonder if he is thanking me for taking care of his cat or for my silence. He scratches Mnemosine under her chin. "*Fai la brava per la zia* Remy," he tells her. *Be good for Aunt Remy.* I am the cat's aunt now.

"No problem," I reply with a forced smile, turning for the stairs before he can see the well of tears in my eyes.

"*Ci vedremo presto, Remy,*" he calls from behind me. *We will see each other soon.*

Chapter TEN

AFTER FLEEING THE SITE of what was, without a doubt, the most scandalous moment of my life, I flop onto my bed beside Mnemosine.

A mere seven hours ago—after the wine but before licking the sweat off Lorenzo's neck while he cupped my ass with his simultaneously capable and tender hands on the Palatine—I'm pretty sure I agreed to move into his apartment.

He can't believe that is still going to happen.

I know I can't.

I find my phone and dial Cassie's number, ignoring the 271 unread text messages. She doesn't answer.

"Hey, friend," I say after the beep, trying not to sound frantic. "Remember me? Call me when you get this, kay? Love you."

I stare at the phone for a while, hoping she'll see she missed a call from her best friend, who has been MIA for weeks, and run away from work to talk, but she doesn't. So I go with my next best option and beg and pray to whatever higher power holds precedence in Rome to get me out of this mess, or better yet, to get me out of this country. "Please, please, please," I plead out loud, my voice as desperate as the humiliation worming in my belly.

At one point, I suspect Mnemosine rolls her eyes at my theatrics, but the Commissioner *has to* send me back to Phoenix. What's the alternative? I live with Valeria and Lorenzo until the case is over? Watch them walk out of the bedroom with their tousled hair and missing clothing every morning. Suffer in silence as they kiss and cuddle and whisper sweet Italian nothings in each other's ears.

I would die.

I'm sighing into the pillow when there is a knock on the door.

Alberto! The gods have answered.

Leaping from the bed, I tug on my ballet flats (not the red sneakers with the laces Lorenzo bought me) and grab my purse, which has been hanging by the door of 3A since I arrived here.

The plan is to make Alberto take me to the station, where I can talk to someone about getting out of Italy. I will stay with Cassie until my flight and never have to see Lorenzo again.

I just wish that thought didn't feel like a knife twisting in my chest.

What a surprise it will be for Alberto to see me—and awake—after being told I've been napping for the past two weeks. I hope he doesn't think I've just been lying in bed crying this whole time. I was solving crimes, dammit.

But if he doesn't know I was at Lorenzo's, I doubt he knows I'm the one who cracked the clue. I square my shoulders, but my cheeks are warm when I open the door.

They burst into flames when I realize it is Valeria, not Alberto, in the hall.

"Um," I say with all the eloquence of a girl who unexpectedly comes face to face with the woman whose boyfriend she just made out with for hours.

Valeria reaches out, sweeps a piece of hair off my forehead, and looks me up and down. I suck in my belly. I can't help it.

Her hand falls from my face to my shoulder, and she gives it a gentle squeeze. "Get some clean clothes," she says, "and come with me."

Not what I was expecting.

My brows wrinkle. "Why?" I ask.

"You need to relax, Remy. All this *dramma* is not good for your face." She waves her long, manicured nails in the air between us. I scratch at the side of my chin.

I may have a stress zit or two, but I don't think it's that bad until I survey Valeria's perfect skin. She might have a point.

I choose my cutest clean dress to bring with me, overcome with a need to impress this woman, and when I grab my fancy undies, Mnemosine gives me a look that screams, *Traitor*!

"She seems perfectly nice to me," I hiss at the cat before following Valeria out of my apartment and up to Lorenzo's. Or hers, I guess.

I hesitate at the door, but she takes my hand and pulls me over the threshold. "*Dai*," she says. *Come on*. "Lorenzo ran out of here just after you did."

She leads me to the bathroom. I sit on the toilet seat, and she perches on the edge of the bath after grabbing a familiar bottle from the cabinet. The newest PetaLuna logo—approved by yours truly—peeks out from between Valeria's fingers.

"Is that the PetaLuna Marigold and Amethyst Bubbling Bath Soak?" I ask. Wow. I guess the European marketing campaign I started in the fall took off.

"Yes." Valeria turns on the water and holds her hand underneath until she is satisfied with the temperature. She pours the bath soak into the steamy stream. "Sorry, I know it smells like… What's the word when fruit goes bad?"

"Rotten?"

"*Esatto*. I know it smells like rotten fruit, but it's the only one he kept when I moved out."

I laugh, relieved. At least now I know Valeria had moved out. Which means maybe they'd also broken up? That this is all some sort of misunderstanding, and I'm not a homewrecker, and Lorenzo isn't a horrible human being, and my histrionics were all for naught.

A tiny flicker of hope reignites in my chest.

Also, the bath soak does smell like spoiled fruit, and I had told the product development team as much before it launched.

Thank you, Valeria, for the vindication—on both counts.

She drags a hand back and forth through the water. "It's ready," she tells me. I stand and wait for her to leave before I shrug out of my t-shirt. When she doesn't, I make a noise that I believe is international for, "A little privacy, please?"

She stands. "Americans," she sighs as she turns to the wall. I slip out of my clothes and into the water, maneuvering small mountains of sickly sweet bubbles over my more intimate parts since it seems Valeria is going to be staying with me.

The water feels amazing. I let my eyes close.

"The temperature is good?"

"Perfect," I answer, sinking lower into the bubbles.

"He likes you, you know."

My shoulders stiffen, sending a small wave toward my toes. "What?"

"Lorenzo. You're his type."

I can't tell if my entire being is blushing or if the water is too warm.

I'm his type? *Did he tell her he likes me*? The memory of his hand on my thigh comes flooding back, his mouth on my collar bone. All sorts of things start happening to my body, and I fidget under the bubbles.

Valeria is watching me, waiting for me to say something. My brain stumbles over all the possibilities.

"So, you're a lawyer?" It's the first thing that comes to mind, other than begging her to tell me why she thinks her (hopefully ex) boyfriend is into me.

"I am."

"Like his dad," I say.

"Pietro Rossi was my professor. That's how Lorenzo and I met."

"That's cute," I manage.

She smirks. "I guess Lorenzo hasn't told you much about his father."

"No, not much."

Valeria crosses her arms. "*Ascolta*, Remy." *Listen*. "Lorenzo needs someone to love his way. I wanted him to fight. Fight for his father's attention, for his promotion. For me. Lorenzo is not a fighter."

"Okay," I say, blinking.

She goes on. "What Lorenzo needs is someone who will be there for him. The way his father wasn't. The way I couldn't be. Someone who won't leave every time things get difficult. Someone who will stay. Someone who will be *here*." Our eyes meet, and her brows rise almost imperceptibly. Oh.

Oh.

All of this just to tell me to stay away from Lorenzo. Because one day, in the probably not-too-distant future, I'll leave Rome. And she doesn't want him getting hurt. I must say, the bath as a conversation opener is a bit excessive, but points for style.

And, of course, I don't blame her for wanting to protect him, but my heart cracks a little anyway. Because she's right. I'm going home, and it would be selfish to start something that can't go anywhere.

Lorenzo isn't off-limits because of Valeria. He's off-limits because of me.

Valeria and I break our gaze when the sound of pounding footsteps crushes through the apartment, followed by the sound of sirens on the street.

"Valeria," Lorenzo's voice shouts.

"*Nel bagno*," she calls back, squatting down and reaching for my hand.

He bursts through the bathroom door and looks very, understandably, confused.

"*Che* é *successo*?" she asks Lorenzo, squeezing my hand tighter. *What happened?*

"Thank God you're here, Remy," Lorenzo says, crouching beside the tub next to Valeria.

PetaLuna Body Soak might smell like month-old bananas, but the bubbles are indefatigable, and my modesty is maintained under the water. Though *I* am very aware I am naked, and for a brief moment, as I glance between their faces, I think, *Ah, this is how threesomes happen.*

But then I notice Lorenzo's left eye is swelling, and Valeria is speaking again.

"I brought her up to the apartment as soon as you called me," she says. And now I'm lost.

"Lorenzo?" I ask.

"It's Alberto," he says. "The agents were at the museum last night, and you were right, Remy, the *Lion Attacking a Horse* was the answer to the clue—"

"They found the amulet?" I squeal.

"No, they found another clue, but it's a huge step forward. Everyone is impressed with your work. Your research was pivotal to the case. We couldn't have done it without you, Remy."

I grin so hard my face hurts. Valeria very loudly clears her throat.

"Right," he looks at her, then back to me. "The Zalśar found out we knew where it was, but since they couldn't get it first, they sent someone to get something they could use as collateral. You."

"Me?"

"I've been having Alberto tailed; I didn't trust him. Not since you told me about his phone calls. I didn't have anything concrete on him, and I didn't want to tell the whole team because it could have ruined our hit if he heard something. Only the Chief Inspector, his tail, and I knew. That's why I tried to have you spend so much time in my apartment."

"To keep me away from Alberto?" I ask. I guess that's as good a reason as any, but not what I had been hoping for.

He looks out of the side of his eye at Valeria, then back at me. "That's not the only reason."

Valeria purses her lips.

"The tail called me because they saw Alberto heading toward the apartment. Chief Marchetti had already pulled him off the assignment, so I called Valeria and had her bring you here. Alberto broke into the apartment and started tearing through your things, turned the mattress, the tables. I called the Chief for reinforcements and then approached him." His hand drifts to his purpling brow, and I feel guilty for wanting to kiss it. "I tried not to get physical, but he went for the cat."

"Mnemosine!" I stand in the tub, sending foamy water sloshing over the side into Valeria's lap.

Lorenzo turns away and knocks his face into the cabinet, setting himself up for a second black eye. "I have her," he says as he rubs his cheek, still facing the wall. Valeria mutters a *porca miseria*—for God's sake—under her breath and has a towel around me in seconds.

"Let me get her dressed," she says to Lorenzo, "and we can talk about the damn cat at the table." He peeks over his shoulder before leaving, and she glares at him. I smile. Then she glares at me.

"Thank you," I say to Valeria as I step out of the tub. She warned me off of her ex, but she also might have saved my life by bringing me up here. "For the bath and the rescue."

"Don't thank me, Remy," she interrupts. "Just tell me you won't drag Lorenzo along on whatever romantic foreign fantasy you think you are living out here. He deserves better than that."

"Latin," I say, studying the photocopy of the clue the agents discovered under the base of the *Lion Attacking a Horse* at the Capitoline Museums. Valeria had to leave for a meeting, and Lorenzo and I are sitting across from each other at his dining room table, exactly where she left us: acceptably separated.

She doesn't know that even with three feet of Italian chestnut tabletop between us, I can still feel the heat of his hands on my skin from last night, which makes it hard to pretend that nothing happened.

"You studied Latin?" he asks, looking up at me from his own copy.

Our eyes hold for a moment before I look away. "Just for a couple of years in middle school."

I tell him a little bit about my teachers, our Mythology Fridays, the time they had a bunch of adolescents very questionably celebrate the fertility festival of Lupercalia instead of Valentine's Day—without the blood rights and animal sacrifice, of course.

I don't mention that those teachers introduced me not just to Rome's history but to Rome itself the summer after eighth grade. I don't bring up the trip at all. After the scolding from Valeria, now is not the opportune time to confess my decade-long infatuation with this city and the men who live in it.

"As for the actual Latin, I just remember the basics," I tell him after five minutes of unnecessary expounding. "You know, first declension endings, *semper ubi sub ubi*, that kind of thing."

"*Semper ubi sub ubi*?"

"Oh, um," I blush. Because apparently, deep down, I am still a fourteen-year-old girl. "Always where under where."

He looks at me and chuckles. My heart drums a happy little song in my chest.

"It's a start." He points at the clue and then reads it out loud. "*Sub cavea leonum, osculum regni est.*"

"Under…something….maybe cave lion…something something is." I frown. "Should we try online?"

He shakes his head. "Too many variables."

"We are going to need a professional," I say, glancing at him.

"A few experts at the American University and La Sapienza who have worked with us before already have copies and are coming up with some best options. Translation is so subjective with Latin; we can't know for certain what the words mean."

Kind of like when Valeria told me I was Lorenzo's type.

She also said he wasn't a fighter, and he disproved that when he walked in with a black eye after taking on Alberto in my old apartment. Maybe she was wrong about both things.

"Remy?"

I release my lip from where I've been grinding it between my teeth. "Sorry, I was just thinking."

"If you are afraid about the Zalśar coming after you, don't

be. They wouldn't try something like that again; it's not their M.O. In fact, I'm not even sure Alberto's break-in was sanctioned. I think he just got desperate."

I nod, trying to look as if yes, this thing about which I should be concerned was the thing I was worrying about. And not some comment Valeria made about Lorenzo liking me.

He goes on, "But we are taking precautions anyway. No one knows about this apartment, and I'll be with you always. Actually," Lorenzo says, focusing on a knot in the wood, "I thought it might be best if I stayed here with you instead of sleeping at Signor Moretti's. But I don't want you to feel uncomfortable, especially after what happened on the Palatine."

He said it; he's acknowledged our tryst. But it is no relief. My body aches in inappropriate places, and across the table, Lorenzo shifts in his seat.

"I have an extra bedroom," he adds as if I didn't already know.

"Yeah, sure. That makes sense." I try to sound casual. No biggie, just two—one for sure—sexually charged adults sharing an apartment and being stuck with each other all day and all night without any chance of recourse for their burning desire.

Valeria is going to be pissed.

I peek over at Lorenzo, the suggestion of a smile on his lips, and Valeria's words clang in my mind.

He deserves better than that.

I need to be fair to Lorenzo and stop feeding this thing between us, stop trying to drag out my teenage daydream. We hooked up, and it was amazing, but I am mature enough to treat him like a friend without secretly trying to make him want to kiss me again. He pushes his hair back from his face, and my fingers twitch.

"Great, then it's decided," I say, standing from the table. I slap my hand on the wooden surface to drive out the urge to reach out and touch him. "I am going to call Eric and let him know what's going on." I'm not sure why I say this, maybe because it feels like a way to build the wall back up between Lorenzo and me—for my own sake, as a way to remind myself that this isn't my whole world.

If it bothers Lorenzo, he doesn't let it show on his face. "Your phone is on the charger," he says. His eyes scan mine. "Please let me know if you need anything while you're here, Remy. If there is anything I can do for you."

My conviction buckles. Lorenzo will have to start being far less considerate if I have any chance of making it through this with my heart in one piece.

Chapter ELEVEN

I SIT DOWN ON THE EDGE OF LORENZO'S GUEST BED, prepared to tell Eric everything. Well, most things.

Or just that I am going to be staying in Rome a while longer.

The hope is that hearing his voice will remind me why I loved him and why I want to go back to Phoenix. Eric is my cold shower, of which I will need many now that I will be sleeping in bed sheets that smell like Lorenzo. Not that I sniffed them as soon as I shut the door.

I take a deep breath and look at my phone.

There are three missed call notifications from the last hour and all the pressure in my chest releases. I am so giddy my finger is shaking when I hit the button and the call goes through.

Eric can wait.

"Is it really you?" Cassie rasps out when she answers.

"It's me, you ass. Why didn't you answer earlier?"

"I was in a meeting. At my job."

"Well, I was on the verge of being kidnapped."

Cassie does not laugh at this. "What the actual fuck is going on, Remy?"

"Nothing. I'm fine," I hurry to reassure her. "I'm super safe, like all the protection. Lorenzo has got me totally covered."

"Lorenzo sounds like a condom."

I choke a little at the thought of Lorenzo and a condom. "Lorenzo is a detective, Detective Rossi. He's my person here."

"He's your person?"

"No. What? I mean he's the guy who has been overseeing my safety since all this shit started."

"You don't have to be so snappy. I was only asking."

"I know. I'm sorry," I say, my shoulders slumping. "Please forgive me, sweet bestie, who I miss so much. It's been a weird couple of weeks."

"I miss you too. Even though it's your fault I've been a panicky mess since I started work."

"Would we say it was my fault, though?"

"Shay told me I can't blame you."

"Shay from the bar? I knew I liked her."

"Can I see you?"

"I think so. The police cleared me, so I'm free now. Did you know they thought I had something to do with the theft of that amulet from the Vatican Museums?"

"Rem, I think the whole world knows."

I groan.

"Don't worry, that's old news now. But I still expect you to tell me about your date with Fabio."

"I guess we never did get to have that *aperitivo* or that conversation."

"Can you meet me this afternoon? I have a break at two for lunch."

"Send me an address. I'll run it by Lorenzo and let you know."

"So, he's not a condom. He's your father."

Ew.

I would like very much to refute this assertion, but if I

argue, I'm worried it will be obvious. She will see right through me, and rehashing last night with Cassie will not make it easier for me to sleep down the hall from Lorenzo tonight.

"He's…well, you'll see," is all I say.

Cassie texts me an address for a bar in Piazza di Pietra. When I ask Lorenzo if we can go and meet her that afternoon, he has the audacity to grin.

Clearly, he harbors none of the anxieties about meeting my best friend for a drink together that I do. In fact, he almost looks excited. He tells me he can drive, or we can take the metro, which will require some walking.

"Walking," I answer.

"Good," he says.

Since it is already almost noon, we get ready to head out. I ask Lorenzo if I need a disguise, something to keep me hidden from the Zalśar. He tells me he doesn't think it's necessary, but with the texted permission of Valeria, we concoct an outfit for me from her suitcase—which, I notice with satisfaction, happens to be beside mine in the spare room and not in his.

I am offended that they think a few sophisticated wardrobe pieces and a different hairstyle are a functional guise, but when I look in the mirror, I have to agree. Gone is the ponytailed, flowy-dressed co-ed. In her place is one badass bitch in excellently tailored pants. I try on a pair of Valeria's shoes, but Lorenzo shakes his head and hands me my berry ballet flats.

In true Italian style, I leave the shirt unbuttoned one button below where I usually would. My mother would cry. For a brief moment, Lorenzo looks like he might too. It is not the reaction I was hoping to elicit, and I'm disappointed that Cassie's father comment wasn't so far off base.

When we walk out of the apartment, it's my turn to want to cry, but for very different reasons. I squeal in delight, and it takes all of my willpower not to throw myself into Lorenzo's arms, overcome by the pure joy of the Roman sunshine on my face.

"It's Rome!" I beam at him. I inhale a huge breath and hold it in my lungs, wanting to feel the city in every part of my being, wanting to have it live in my cells.

"Same Rome as last night," he offers, looking amused.

I smile. It might be the same Rome, but last night was not about Rome. It was about Lorenzo and me and the little part of the city we carved out for ourselves above the Forum. Last night was about finally giving in to that undeniable pull between us, the one that feels like fires lighting in my blood. The one I promised Valeria I'd ignore.

"There's our *fermata*," he says, drawing back to the present. He leads me underground into the Manzoni metro stop and a waiting subway train. In four stations and four short minutes, we get off at Piazza Barberini.

We come up the stairs, and in front of us is Bernini's sexy Triton Fountain.

I glance at Lorenzo in his tight gray t-shirt and think he'd also look pretty good soaked in water, legs straddling.

"Do you know what they say about the Fontana del Tritone?" he asks, looking down at me. His eyes do that thing where they get intensely dark.

"I don't," I squeak, trying not to get lost in them.

"The legend is that if you toss a coin in, you'll come back to Rome."

"Isn't that the Trevi?"

"It's both."

"Are you sure?"

"I promise."

"In that case," I open my purse and sift through the debris on the bottom. "Damn."

"Here," Lorenzo says, digging into his pockets, but he comes up short too. He shrugs an apology.

I sigh.

The Fates have spoken.

Valeria has spoken.

I need to get myself together and stop thinking about Lorenzo half-naked on a throne of dolphins. I'm leaving when this is over, and who knows if I'll ever be back.

For me, for Lorenzo, I have to cut it out. But it's hard when just looking at him makes my knees ache.

He smiles. "Next time."

"Next time," I say, still hoping there will be a next time, even if I shouldn't.

I'm not at all embarrassed when I come around the corner of the cobblestone alleyway and into the piazza, screaming Cassie's name at the top of my lungs. She is screaming too, and we both run, falling into each other's arms.

"God, it's good to see you," I sob into her neck.

"I think it's the longest we've been apart since freshman year of college."

"I'm amazed I survived."

When we let go of each other, Cassie snorts. "What are you wearing?" she asks, taking in Valeria's fitted, ivory button-down and virgin wool trousers.

"Duh. It's a disguise," I explain.

"Are you supposed to be a middle-aged lesbian elementary school teacher?"

"Mean." I run my hands down my front, my legs, giving

myself another once over. "I thought I looked pretty hot," I say, pouting.

"You do. Forty-something schoolmarm is my kink."

I wrap my arms around her again and tell her I love her.

Cassie tenses. "Don't look now," she whispers in my ear, arms tightening around my back, "but I think you're being followed."

I feel my face pale and swing my head around.

"Way to be discreet," she mumbles beside me.

It's Lorenzo, one hand in a pocket and the other in his hair. I bark out a relieved laugh, turning back to Cassie.

"That is the detective I was telling you about."

"*That* is Detective Rossi?" She looks at him, then at me. Then, quietly, so only I can hear, she says, "He makes me want to get myself arrested, and I'm not even into dudes."

Then he's beside us, and he's reaching out to shake her hand. She winks at me when she goes in for the cheek kisses.

"Are you joining us for a drink, Lorenzo?" she asks him.

"No, no. I'll leave you two alone to catch up." He turns to me and places a hand on my shoulder. A shiver runs up my spine. "Remy, if you need me"—I gulp— "I will be inside at the bar."

"Great, okay. Thanks, Lorenzo." *I've got this*, I think. *Cool as a cucumber.*

"It was a pleasure to meet you, Cassie," he says with a slight bow to my best friend.

"Likewise," she answers, grinning.

I wave at his back while he walks away.

Cassie looks at me, her brows so high they threaten to disappear under her dark chocolate curls. "What was *that*?"

"What was what?" I ask without meeting her eyes. I sit down at a metal table and pick up the menu.

"Remy Elizabeth Campbell, I demand the truth."

"The truth is," I look at the closed door that Lorenzo walked through, "he's great. But like you said, in a fatherly way." I cringe on the inside but keep going. "Besides that, there's this woman that he's sort of involved with, and she's smart and gorgeous, and she let me play dress-up in her clothes today. So…" I trail off. It's not exactly a lie. Still, I feel bad not being honest with Cassie. But it's better not to fuel the fire that is Lorenzo.

"Shame," she says with a shake of her head. "But it's probably for the best." She sets her huge purse onto her lap and reaches inside, pulling out a jar of peanut butter and a bottle of Cholula hot sauce. "These are for you."

"Thank you?" The peanut butter has been opened and partially consumed.

"Eric sent them for you. A taste of home, or whatever."

I'm speechless.

"I know," she says, acknowledging the surprise on my face. Eric was always good at roses and fancy dinners but rarely hit the gift nail on the head. Sending me comfort food essentials from the States is his best success to date. "He even broke international import laws to do it."

Eric committing the crime of shipping illegal foodstuffs into Europe doesn't sound like a big deal, but knowing his political prospects, I'm sure he felt like a certified Clyde to my Bonnie. I'm touched.

"You can keep the PB," I tell her, pushing it across the table. When she reaches for the hot sauce, I slap her hand away. "Have you been in touch with him?"

"With Eric? Yes. It turns out he's grossly obnoxious when he's worried. Calls every day."

"He does?"

"Remy, he has been beyond freaked out since everything

started. Completely distraught. Especially because he felt like he could never get a hold of you."

"I called him once," I argue.

She leans toward me over the table. "Have you not gotten in touch with him yet to tell him you're out of custody?"

I bite my lip. Guilty.

"What he did this winter was awful, Rem. But I think he's back—the same friendly, thoughtful, dorky, hunky Eric you fell for that first week at university."

I draw circles on the table with my finger. "How do you know?"

She points to the hot sauce. "It is your favorite."

I shrug.

"Look," she says, taking my hand, "Eric knows he fucked up, but he loves you, and he wants to fix things."

"Since when are you such a fan of Eric?"

"Since he showed me how much he cares about my best friend and told me, again and again, ad nauseam, all of the things he would do to win her back and how he'd treat her like a goddess when he did."

I narrow my eyes at her.

"I swear," she says, putting a hand over her heart. "His words, not mine. But you know what? You deserve to be treated like a goddess, dammit, and Eric is desperate—like, pathetically so—to give you that."

Cassie's words do warm some part of my heart that has been looming in the shadows, but it's hard not to draw comparisons. It took Eric losing me to realize he could be treating me better. Lorenzo has been doing that from the first moment we met.

"Just promise you'll call him," Cassie says.

"I will," I smile. I wouldn't mind hearing Eric beg for my forgiveness. If he does a good enough job, I might even accept, and then we can move on from his misguided megalomania and carry on with our lives—together. I could love him again if I tried.

Cassie orders a bottle of organic Orvieto Classico when the server arrives. He returns with the bottle, two glasses, and a collection of small dishes filled with olives, potato chips, and breadsticks.

We clink our glasses, and Cassie tells me about Shay, who stayed in Rome instead of moving on to Greece. She found a job at a hostel near Cassie's new apartment, and they spend all her free nights together. Shay is teaching Cassie how to knit.

"Knit?" I repeat.

Cassie crosses her arms. "It's a much more creative art form than people realize."

I smile. My best friend may not know it yet, but I can see the twinkle in her eyes clear as day. Cassie is falling in love.

"Don't look at me like that," Cassie says, flinging a potato chip in my direction. "Tell me about you."

I recount my date with Fabio since that's where we left off. Cassie laughs so hard she almost shoots an olive out her nose. Then when I tell her about the end of the date, she says, "If I ever see him again, I'll kick his ass so hard."

"Same," I say, throwing back the rest of my glass.

The sun is shining, but a gentle breeze works its way through the small streets that feed into the piazza and finds us at the table. The wall above the bar is covered in a cloud of bougainvillea, erupting in unseasonable clumps of magenta blossoms on account of the hot spring Rome is having.

Across from us, the Temple of Hadrian's colonnade borders the piazza. The surrounding buildings are built up against it, into it—worn and softened irregular marble abutting the formal, ordered facades of pale yellow, nineteenth-century government offices. A vision so quintessentially Roman, my heart beats louder just to bear witness.

It is a glorious day, and I'm leaning my face up to the sky when Cassie yells, "Shit!"

"Gotta go?" I blink at her, then reach for the bottle. I tip it into my glass, but nothing comes out. I giggle, way tipsier than I have any right to be after a half bottle of white.

"Can I see you again soon?" she asks, collecting her things and her peanut butter off the table.

"Yes, but bring Shay next time."

She smiles and kisses my head. "Call Eric, ok?"

"I'm gonna call 'im," I say, with barely the hint of a slur.

"Not now," she clarifies. She waits for me to confirm I will call later, preferably after a decent meal.

"Tell your hot Italian dad he better keep you safe," Cassie shouts as she walks off.

I press my palms to my warm cheeks, but Cassie is too far away to see my face turn red.

As soon as Cassie reaches the far side of the piazza, Lorenzo is at the table. He has a carryout box in either hand.

"You were watching me," I say, reaching up to poke him in the chest.

"Sorry," he says with a small smile. "But it *is* my job."

I'd groan, but my stomach does it for me.

"Here," he says, taking the seat that Cassie left. "I ordered you the polenta fries and a side of meatballs." He lays the food out on the table and opens the packages.

"I also have something else to share," he says with a sparkle in his eye. He scoots his chair closer to mine. I bite my lip.

Lorenzo leans toward me, his mouth so close to my ear his breath tickles. I clear my throat.

"I received the translations for the second clue," he murmurs.

"Awesome," I say, my voice high. But I *am* excited. With the translations in, I will have something else to focus on and think about all day. There is a crime to solve and an amulet to find. I still want nothing more than to stick it to Fabio and the rest of his pretentious gang.

Lorenzo straightens in his chair. "Tomorrow," he says, "I thought we could go to the university to do some research?"

"I'd love that," I answer. "Detective Rossi and his sidekick Remy, back in the game."

He laughs at this and rubs the back of his neck.

"Should we go over the translations?" I ask.

"We will review them at the apartment. It'll be safer. Right now, we need to take care of you." He pushes the fries toward me, fills up my water glass.

I look at the food, Lorenzo's profile, the ruins, and the Renaissance palaces, the rectangle of perfectly blue sky above us. I am enamored with all of it. And that makes me feel better. The crazy thing my pulse is doing is not only about the handsome man in front of me, slicing a meatball into fourths for me to eat. It's about Rome, and Rome will always be here for me—always has been.

I'm not giving Rome any other choice but to promise me this won't be the end of us.

"I want to go back to that naked merman fountain," I declare before forking a chunk of meatball into my mouth.

Chapter TWELVE

WE DO NOT GO BACK TO THE FOUNTAIN. The little bit of sleep I got the night before and the excitement of the morning hit me like a block of travertine as soon as I finish chewing the last polenta fry. There is a bus stop nearby, and we catch the 51, which dumps us out right around the corner from Lorenzo's apartment.

He helps me up the stairs, and I shuffle into the spare room where I very carefully remove and hang Valeria's fancy clothes—which I am proud to have not spilled on even a little bit—and then crawl into the sheets beside Mnemosine.

I wake up with the imprint of the pillowcase on my cheek. The room smells amazing, so I know Lorenzo has been cooking. I put on some clothes and peek my head out of the door, refreshed and ready to get going on the next clue.

Voices float down the hall from the kitchen—the deep rumble of Lorenzo's words as he speaks, Valeria's gentle laugh.

They sound close, playful—like old friends or lovers.

I take a deep breath and push through the nagging tangle of disappointment in my chest. Maybe it is a day for making up.

I shut the door again before curling up in the covers and calling Eric.

"Babe," he answers. "How are you?"

Eric doesn't act mad at me for not calling sooner or more often; he just keeps saying he's happy I'm okay, that I can put it all behind me now. When I announce I'm staying a while longer to help with the case, he stumbles a moment but then says that he's proud of me.

At some point, I'm just saying things I know will set him off, but he resists all of my provocations and tells me, at last, that he has never regretted anything as much as letting me go.

"To Rome?" I ask.

"That too, I guess, but I mean the break-up."

I think of all the mornings I woke up panicked and depressed in Camila's bottom bunk after I had moved in with my sister. I remember wondering how I'd ever put my life back together and trying to figure out what my future looked like on this new trajectory. He swept the world out from under my feet, and I had no idea how I would land back on them. My vision blurs. "Yeah, that was pretty shitty," I say. My voice comes out high and tight.

Eric tells me how awful he feels about everything. I make small noises to emphasize the enormity of his fuck-up. He says sorry for all the things he should say sorry for while I pet the cat.

"Do you think you could ever forgive me?" he asks.

I bite my lip. "I'm not sure."

Eric sighs. "I understand. I don't know if I can forgive myself either."

His voice is so sad, so desperate, that I ache a little for him. "Eric," I say. "I want to try." It will be hard to forget what happened, but forgiving isn't about forgetting. It's about leaving the bad stuff in the past and moving forward.

I had my oats to sow too, and now that we are back on even footing, I don't have anything to hold over his head.

Even if I did, I wouldn't want to. Eric's apology was pretty perfect.

"Fuck, Rems, I've missed you so much. If you were here right now, I'd show you just how much."

"Really? And how would you do that?" I ask.

"You know how," he whispers.

I know he's blushing when he says it, and I smile. That's the Eric I wanted to spend my life with—humble, caring, gentle. Cassie was right; he is back.

"I've missed you, too," I say.

"When you come home, Remy, I want you to move back in."

I hesitate. "Are you sure we should do that already?"

"I've never been more certain about anything in my life."

I hesitate. "We can talk about it later."

"Okay. Just know, the house has felt empty without you in it."

"When did you become such a cornball?"

"When I realized I royally fucked up and let the love of my life get away."

I laugh.

"Seriously, Rem. I mean it."

My throat tightens. "I should go," I tell him.

"I'll call you tomorrow," he says, then pauses. "I love you."

"I…" My mouth closes, opens. "Bye, Eric."

I put the phone down beside me and press my fingers to my lips.

This is good, great even.

I'm like a little toy train that has been popped back on the rails after a bump in the track. I can now move onward, chug merrily along toward the life I had been building with Eric. Things between us already feel almost normal. And when I see him, and he holds me again, it will be just like none of this ever happened.

The conversation went so well that I am barely aware of the ice-cold ache in my belly.

Opening the bedroom door, I step into the hall, and this time the house is quiet. It is past eleven, and I know we all had a hell of a day, so I assume Lorenzo and Valeria have gone to bed. Since Valeria is here for another two days, I am sleeping in the guest room, she's sleeping in Lorenzo's room, and Lorenzo is taking the couch, so we can all live together like some dystopian Three's Company.

I plan to grab some food, and if Lorenzo isn't up to tell me about the translations, I'll see if I can find a Latin dictionary somewhere and work on them myself. When I pass the living room and don't see Lorenzo on the couch, I shake off the icky feeling I get. Even with my relationship with Eric on the mend, Lorenzo kissed me less than twenty-four hours ago, and my pride is a little hurt.

I'm not paying much attention when I come into the kitchen, but I notice the considerable step Lorenzo takes away from Valeria.

So, they weren't in bed, but they were huddled by the oven, where I could just walk in and see them.

I freeze. "Sorry," I mumble. "I just got off the phone with Eric and thought everyone was asleep."

"Eric is the boy in America?" Valeria asks.

"Sure is," I say, standing up a little taller and looking at Lorenzo. His mouth twists, and I don't miss the sharp look Valeria gives him.

"*Brava*," Valeria says, clapping her hands once. "I'm sure you can't wait to get back to him."

I open my mouth to respond. *Yes*, I should say, *I can't wait*, but the words don't come. I look down at my feet; then, I risk a glance at Lorenzo.

He's watching me, but as soon as our eyes meet, he turns and gestures toward the stove. "Valeria and I were just trying to get the fire to—" he is saying, but Valeria interrupts him.

"I doubt Remy is very interested in what we were just doing, Lorenzo."

He looks at her for a moment—his jaw clenched—then drags a hand over his mouth. "Right."

I tuck my hands into my elbows and don't get any closer. "I just came out to ask Lorenzo about the translations."

I don't mention the food. Suddenly, I don't have much appetite.

"I have a file for you on the desk in the office."

"I'll grab it," I say. My voice doesn't waver at all, and I hurry out of the kitchen.

As promised, I find a file on the desk marked with the initials R.C. It's resting against a stack of books which I assume are for me to go through, so I gather them all in my arms and take one last peek around the room in case there is anything else I might want to stash away with me in the guest room.

I'm about to shout thanks as I walk back past the kitchen, but I snap my mouth shut when I see them. Lorenzo is facing away from me, and Valeria's pretty fingers wrap around his back. His hands are on the counter as he leans into her, over her. His head is bent close to her face.

Oh my god, are they kissing?

No. Lorenzo would never do something like that with me here after last night.

Would he?

My stomach twists.

I tiptoe like hell out of there, though I'm not sure my quiet steps manage to compensate for the violent thundering behind my ribs.

When I'm shut back in the guest room, I tell myself it doesn't matter. And it doesn't; it shouldn't.

Lorenzo and Valeria. Remy and Eric.

Everything is just how it is supposed to be—happy new beginnings all around.

I wipe the wetness from my eyes and crack open the file.

Lorenzo and I are like two negatively charged magnets for the next few days, invisible forces holding us always at a distance.

For my part, I'd call that force self-preservation. Despite the very positive direction things are moving with Eric and the possible necking I witnessed between Lorenzo and Valeria in the kitchen, I can't quite get my body to concede that the Lorenzo thing is over. The physical memory of his kiss is sometimes overwhelming, even when I'm safely on the other side of the room. Just the sound of his voice can make my nerves go haywire.

Given a chance to do it all again, it would be hard, if not impossible, to resist.

More troublesome, my heart has melded the Colosseum kiss and the Palatine kiss into a single, imposing, pulse-wrecking memory. They overlap in my dreams, creating an alarming collage of desire, joy, and a word I shouldn't name—a word that has no right taking up space in this situation.

Seeing Lorenzo and Valeria in the kitchen together should be enough for me to turn off the very drippy feeling faucet in my chest. But sometimes, I think I catch him looking at me or smiling at something I say, and all the feels come flooding back out.

God damn it. I'm staring again.

I bend my head to the page in front of me. The second clue—*Sub cavea leonum, osculum regni est*—is printed at the top of the paper. The translations are bolded and listed below as bullet points. There are over fifty, but we've narrowed down our general focus.

Under the den of the lions is the mouth of the kingdom.

I have this one translation highlighted and keep going back to it. It is, admittedly, not necessarily accurate. Osculum can mean several things other than mouth, including kiss and lips, both words I don't feel inclined to be using on repeat with Lorenzo. It also can translate as orifice—and just, no.

Yesterday, Lorenzo and I visited the American University. He spoke with the professors who provided the translations, and I spent some time in the library, where I compiled a short list of sites around Rome that fit the description of the clue in some way or another. We will check some of them out today, which means lots of uncomfortable time stuck together in his itsy-bitsy Italian car as we drive around Rome.

While at the university, I met the Dean of Humanities, Dr. Hill, a total Robert Langdon type (sexy professor book version, not movie, though Tom Hanks has his own thing going on). He gave me a tour of the campus after I'd found what I needed in the library and told me to come by his office the next time I'm in the area. I've already told Lorenzo I have more research to do there, which is true, but also, I just want to play pretend university student. Being back on a college campus with interesting, intelligent people like Dr. Hill—who just happens to look like Idris Elba in a well-worn tweed suit—was thrilling enough to keep my mind off other things.

Not just Lorenzo but also the emptiness that swells inside me every time I think about returning to my job at PetaLuna in Phoenix. I could look around for something else when I get there, but it would be nice to know I'll have some financial stability while I settle back in, since my settling in will likely occur in Eric's condo—our old condo.

He's asked me again the last two days if I'd move back in and, at this point, I have no legitimate reason not to. Maybe the whole forced proximity thing that has done such wonders for my lusting here will work with Eric, too.

"So, we'll do the Circus Maximus first, right?" Lorenzo asks from the desk, interrupting my thoughts. I turn to him, but he keeps his eyes on the computer.

I shuffle the papers I'm holding. "Yes, yeah. Circus Maximus first. Sounds good." The Circus Maximus isn't my most promising prospect, but *cavea* also translates as theater and auditorium, and we need to cover all our bases. Not to mention, it was part of the answer to the first clue and the original location of the *Lion Attacking a Horse* statue, so it seems like a decent place to start.

"I'll get the car keys," he says before disappearing from the room without even once glancing my way.

I sigh.

We are quiet and incredibly awkward in the front seat of his Fiat Panda. Just like yesterday, he asks if I'd like to pick the music, but I tell him whatever Italian station he likes is fine. After that, he doesn't speak again, and I stare out the window as we wind through neighborhoods of ancient walls, past the south side of the Colosseum, and down the rows of umbrella pines that edge the Palatine.

I haven't been to the Circus Maximus in eleven years, and the park is still just as big and open and visually unremarkable as it was when I was fourteen. Except for a few standing ruins, there isn't much to investigate, but we decide to do a lap or two anyway.

The arches of the imperial palace run along the side of the Palatine Hill on the northern border of the park, and I point to them. "For theater, I suppose the clue could have also meant that. In which case, the Circus itself could be the mouth of the kingdom. But I can't think of any connections between the palace and the Etruscans."

Lorenzo makes a sound that could really mean anything. He's looking at his feet as we walk, and I'm not even sure he's listening to me.

"Also, referring to the *ring of the first true king* as an orifice doesn't really seem like something a bunch of stuck-up criminals like the Zalśar would be down with."

He hums in what might be agreement, shoving his hands in his pockets.

I stop walking. We can be weird together in the apartment and in the car, but right now, we are trying to solve a crime, and he seems a million miles away. Finding the amulet is the only reason I'm staying in Rome, and I need this win to carry with me wherever I land in life. I need to beat Fabio, show him he was wrong to use me, that he picked the wrong woman. I need to silence the doubt, the little voice inside of me that says it's better to do the easy thing, disappear into the background. The voice that always told me to keep my fire hidden because it was best for everyone else.

If this is my chance to burn, I damn well plan to.

And if Lorenzo thought the Circus Maximus was a stupid idea, he should have just told me. If, on the other hand, he is daydreaming about Valeria, he should cut it the fuck out.

"Lorenzo," I say, crossing my arms and turning to him.

He looks up, his full lips a perfect little "o" of surprise, his thick lashes casting shadows on his cheeks. "Yes?"

"Did you hear anything I was saying?"

"Of course, you talked about the palace and the, that word, orifice."

"Lorenzo, I need your head in the game." It feels good to take charge but also to have an excuse to shout at him that doesn't directly involve my muddled, inappropriate feelings.

He apologizes, and we keep walking, scanning the ground and the few stones around the arena for signs. We find nothing.

"I talked to your mom last night," he says.

I roll my eyes. I called my parents a couple of days ago and, not surprising at all, got two very different takes on my decision to remain in Rome. My dad is all for it; my mother is horrified that I would continue to endanger myself for what she deems absolutely no reason and that, heaven forbid, I should dare impose myself on Lorenzo. "Thank God that good man is willing to put up with you and keep you safe," she told me as she very audibly opened a bottle of wine and poured at least half of it into a glass. "You better not get in his way, Remy; he has work to do. I don't see why they'd need you around." I could hear my dad laughing in the background, causing her to mumble, "It's not funny, Joseph."

It made me want to stay in Rome forever out of spite.

"Did she tell you to send me home if you were sick of me?" I ask.

"No, she just wanted to make sure you were safe."

Or that he was, from me. But I know my life will be easier for the next few weeks, or until this is all over, if I don't have to deal with her constant concern on top of everything else.

"Did you manage to convince her?" Since the Alberto thing

went down, there have been a few instances of worry that my safety might be in jeopardy, but nothing serious.

"I told her my number one priority was to take care of you and keep you safe. I told her that I was happy you decided to stay, happy that you trust me enough to be here still. And I thanked her and your father," he says, looking at me, "for trusting me with their daughter, because I need you, Remy."

My entire nervous system forgets how to function. Fuck me. How does breathing work?

"For the case, I mean," he amends. "We need your help. Without you, we never would have gotten through the first clue, but because of what you figured out, we are beating the Zalśar at their own game."

I kick a pebble down the sloping bank of the Circus Maximus and watch it roll down to the track. "I don't think this is the place," I say. "What's next?"

Chapter THIRTEEN

THE BASILICA OF SAN CLEMENTE is located about two blocks behind the Colosseum. A few tourists have trickled this way, but for the most part, the sidewalk acts as a stage for Italians coming in and out of the Poste Italiane across the street or the pizza by the slice place next door.

We've checked out a handful of other sights over the past three days, including the tomb of Pope Leo X in the Basilica of Santa Maria Sopra Minerva and the fountain of the four lions in Piazza del Popolo. We also stopped at a place called Caffe Leone near the Etruscan Museum at Villa Giulia, but that was primarily an excuse to caffeinate after an excessive lunch.

We've found nothing. I was wrong every time.

And to make matters worse, the Chief told Lorenzo this morning that someone leaked the second clue to the Zalśar. Now we are again in a race against those ridiculous assholes to solve it. Even Europol is getting involved.

The entrance to San Clemente is not well designated—just a large green door on the side of the building, partially hidden behind a pair of linden trees. On either side of the marble work that borders the door is a stone carving that I can only describe as hilariously phallic.

"What is that symbol?" I ask Lorenzo.

He bites his lip a little like he's trying not to laugh. Maybe deep down, we are both fourteen-year-olds. "I have no idea," he says.

I tilt my head to look at it. "We should google it," I tell him. "'Pope Clement Marble Penis.' What could go wrong."

"I, in no way, want to be involved," he says. But now he's smiling.

The tension of the past few days falls away from me in a cloud of exhaust from a passing tour bus. It's so loud and stinky that neither of us is required to speak for a moment, and I let myself enjoy this sense of ease between us, the laughing crinkle in the corners of Lorenzo's eyes.

I can keep this up. I can make it easy.

"Shall we?" I step forward to open the door, but he gets there first, and his hand grazes my chest. He flinches, and when I walk past him, I press myself against the other side of the door frame.

All right, I take it back. I can't make this easy.

I look around the interior of the church when we've passed through the atrium. The apse practically glows, the goldwork in the Byzantine mosaic catching the light from the clerestory windows. The same brilliance bounces off the gilded ceiling.

The current building dates back to the 1100s and is a mix of styles from medieval to Baroque, with recycled elements dating back to the Classical period.

It's an ecclesiastical time capsule, but not what we came to see.

San Clemente, as it stands today, was built upon a fourth-century basilica converted from the home of a Roman nobleman, which was built upon a villa from the Roman Republican era—with various other incarnations along the way and in between.

It is a long shot as far as solving the clue goes. Much longer even than the Circus Maximus.

All we have to go on are a few vague facts. Pope Clement I, to whom the church was dedicated, was imprisoned by Emperor Trajan. Trajan's father hailed from the area of Todi and, according to some historians, traced his lineage back to the Etruscans. Trajan was also, at least once, referred to as the Lion of Rome.

As we make our way across the temple's nave, I realize that Trajan's Forum is a much more likely location for the amulet, or the third clue, or whatever else might be waiting for us. I mentally add it to my list of sites to visit.

But Trajan isn't the only reason we are here. Two floors below us is a Mithraeum, a sanctuary for the Cult of Mithras built in the 200s CE. The main area of worship was known as a cave. Mithra was often conflated with the Etruscan god Usil, and one of the most prominent symbols of the Mithraic Mysteries was a lion-headed figure.

I know it's a stretch. But Lorenzo has assured me numerous times that the Zalśar aren't known for sticking to the facts. Like the reality that none of them are even Etruscan.

And the answer to the first clue was just obscure enough to make me think it might be possible.

Lorenzo buys two tickets for the self-guided tour of the underground excavations and shoves a ten-euro bill in the "Donations for Restorations" jar beside the window. The woman behind the counter thanks him, and when his eyes focus on her, she blushes and stammers out a string of Italian nonsense.

I give her a sympathetic smile before turning to follow Lorenzo into the dimly lit staircase. I wonder if now is a good time to tell him that I suffer from a very particular form of claustrophobia specific to underground spaces—especially dark ones.

I hold my breath as I walk behind Lorenzo. The light fixtures are every three feet or so, but they only light a portion of the walkway. To my right, there is nothing but a haze of shadowy stone—and 2000-year-old Italian ghosts, probably—that I try not to think about.

I take a deep breath and clamp my eyes closed, knuckles white against the handrail.

Something touches my arm, and I throw my hand out in front of me in a heel palm strike. My eyes react a second slower, and I see Lorenzo's stunned face just before I make contact.

"Fuck," I gasp at the exact time he grabs his nose and grumbles, "*Che cazzo*?"

"Oh my god," I say, fumbling toward him. "I'm so sorry." I'm worried about his face—the bruises from Alberto are just starting to fade, and I know the hit to the brow has been giving him headaches—but I refuse to turn my back on the eeriness behind me.

I wheedle my way between Lorenzo and the nearest light fixture, reaching for his hand and pulling it away from his face so I can see the damage.

He doesn't yank his hand away, but he does maneuver it out of mine. "It's fine," he says. "I turned just in time to get the least of it. Good hit."

A fine line of dark red seeps from his left nostril, and I get a swooping feeling in my stomach. It's not a lot, and I'm not blood-phobic, but seeing blood on Lorenzo's face—because of me—makes me dizzy.

"Here." I reach down and pull the hem of my dress up toward his nose. It's not my best emergency reaction, but I'm desperate to make the blood go away.

He steps back, pinching the bridge of his nose. "Tissues?" he asks.

"Tissues. Right." I open my purse and pull out the same pack of tissues he gave me at the police station three weeks ago. I hand it to him, but I'm sad to see it go, the only souvenir from my first, and hopefully, last, arrest. He takes out two and hands the package back. Sweet relief.

When I grab them, my hand is trembling.

Lorenzo looks at me, his brow drawing together.

"Are you all right?" he asks. His voice is funny, the tissues still pressed to his nose.

"I should be asking you. You're the one who just got sucker-punched in the face."

"You're breathing strangely," he says.

"Am I?"

He removes the tissues, sniffs his nose, then leans toward me. Now I'm not breathing at all.

"And you're pale," he tells me.

I reach up and touch my cheek. My skin is warm and sticky, not in a sick way, but in an anxiety-attack way. My shoulders slump. "I sort of forgot to mention that I am not a huge fan of creepy subterranean spaces. Not even cool archaeological ones."

"You're scared?" he asks, his voice and eyes filled with concern.

"No. I mean, sort of," I mumble. "But I'll be fine." I think I see something move behind him, and I shiver.

He notices my gaze, looks over his shoulder. There is nothing there. "I'll take you back upstairs."

"Absolutely not." I straighten my back and step away from the wall I've been pressed into. "I can do this."

He hesitates, looks back up the stairs. "You don't have to," he says.

"I *do*, actually."

Without another word, he comes up next to me, filling all the scary darkness between me and the wall, and puts a stiff arm around my back, resting his fingers so lightly on my shoulder I barely feel them. But I know he has my back and my side, and the gloom beyond the light isn't so threatening anymore.

Lorenzo takes a deep breath, and we venture further into the buried basilica.

Once we are out of the stairwell, the space opens up, and despite the buttresses and low ceiling, the darkness and the walls don't feel quite as oppressive. I reluctantly shrug out of the circle of Lorenzo's protective, if not very affectionate, arm. His shoulders fall back, and his jaw relaxes. I see the tension go out of him as I step away.

I cross my arms and try not to scowl as I turn into the right aisle of the fourth-century church, praying that ancient feats of engineering that have stood this long won't decide to collapse now that I'm here. The crypts in San Clemente are for clergy only, and I'm very okay with making sure that sort of favoritism is maintained.

Ahead of us, a small group of visitors follows a tour guide who holds a German flag above her head while speaking, waving it as if to draw back anyone's wandering attention. German is a difficult language to tune out. If my inability to focus on anything besides her voice is any indication, I don't think the brandishing of the flag is necessary. Lorenzo seems to feel similarly, and we dawdle near the stairs until the group passes through into the central nave.

The lower basilica contains more early medieval wall paintings than nearly any other site in Rome, and portions of fresco cling to the block wall of the right aisle, giving it the appearance of a large-scale island nation map. I study the plaster fragments, hoping there might be some hidden hint in the artistry. But alas, the map does not lead us to our treasure.

After a clean sweep of the right aisle, I snap a photo of *The Descent of Christ into Limbo*, a fresco at the end of the hall—Jesus has the same wonky pirate eye Lil gets when she's had too much to drink—and then we cross over into the nave.

The space is mostly empty. The German sightseers disappeared to the lower level and then exited out to the main church before we even finished checking the aisle. Otherwise, there are just a few solo tourists who do a quick lap and depart—probably because it's damn scary down here. When I see the entrance to the lower level looming in the corner, I sympathize with their unwillingness to wander down those stairs alone.

I'm in here with a police officer and still can't get my heart rate to settle.

By the time we've checked the altar and the left aisle, leaving not one stone unturned in the most literal sense, a crushing, horrible weight presses down on me, and it has nothing to do with the tons and tons of marble just feet above my head.

"There's nothing here," I growl, plopping myself down on a chunk of broken column.

"We still have to check the lower level," Lorenzo remarks, missing the edge in my voice. He points to the other end of the aisle. "The stairs are back near the tomb of St. Cyril. And if we don't find what we need down there, we try again tomorrow somewhere else."

I've dragged Lorenzo all over Rome for nothing. It will be a miracle of saintly proportions if the Zalśar don't solve the second clue before we do. I drop my head into my hands. "My mom was right."

I hate to say that, even under the best of circumstances. But it's true. San Clemente is the tenth place we've checked out. Lorenzo is a damn detective. He must have noticed I have no idea what I'm doing. I lift my face. Lorenzo is watching me from a few feet away. He has his hands in his pockets and frowns when our eyes meet.

"Why do you keep indulging all of my bad ideas?" I ask, wiping my nose on my sleeve. "I'm just wasting your time."

Lorenzo crouches before me but doesn't come closer. "You solved the first clue with a few books while stuck inside an apartment."

I look away, bite my lip. "That was luck, Lorenzo, and you know it. I'm some random tourist who happened to know just enough to land myself in this mess in the first place." My cheeks are hot, and so are the tears behind my eyes.

Lorenzo shakes his head and whispers, "Remy." I'm so surprised by the gentleness in his voice when he says my name that I shudder. "Your ideas are good. They are far better than what anyone at the station has come up with. These things take time and work. I wasn't lying when I said we need you."

I look at my feet and shrug.

He ducks his head to catch my eyes. "We haven't solved the second clue yet. But we will. I promise."

His words bring back our conversation over a dinner of arancini and red wine from the slopes of Mt. Etna. It must have been at least a million years ago, as time relevant to our kiss seems to exist in my mind. I'd told him he'd get the bad guys. I want that to be true, but the longer we search and find nothing, the less I believe it's possible.

Then I remember what he said about losing his position in Rome if he can't close this case. "Why would you trust me with your entire livelihood?" I mumble under my breath. It makes me want to hit him again, knock some sense into him this time.

I glance at his nose before my eyes drift to his mouth. I wince when I notice the puffy peek of lip I caused, and my fingers go to my own mouth in sympathy. I feel so bad about the accidental blow that I let myself imagine other ways I could make him see reason.

Lorenzo clears his throat and stands. "Now, let's get downstairs and see what we find." He reaches a hand toward me, and when I reach up to take it, and our palms slide against each other, tightening, he doesn't flinch or cringe or pull away.

I look down the aisle, past the altar of St. Cyril, to the Stygian darkness beyond the small archway that leads below the basilica. "The Gates of the Underworld," I murmur.

The corner of his mouth turns up, the side I didn't slam my hand into. "No, those are in Naples."

I smile back. "Fair enough. It still looks spooky as hell, though."

Lorenzo squeezes my hand, tugs me a step closer to him. "I've got you, Remy."

I'm too distracted by the way he laces our fingers together to care where he's leading me as we follow the shadowy stairs another few hundred years into the past.

Chapter FOURTEEN

I HUDDLE CLOSER TO LORENZO, and not just because he smells like warm bread and fresh-cut soccer field and something I can't pinpoint that is spicy and soft all at once.

There must be some sort of short in the first-century electrical. The lights down here are flickering, and unlike the open floor plan of the excavated basilica above us, this level feels like something Daedalus designed to hold monsters. Heavy iron grates and bars block off pitch-black corridors that line the halls. The stairs fall deeper into the earth and then rise again, letting us out into dead-end rooms, many of which have seating carved into the stone and amphorae leaning against the bricks, seemingly in readiness for subterrestrial visitors.

The echo of running water filters through the maze of walls and ancient Roman alleyways, and we find a spot where the ground opens up to a gushing spring. People have thrown in copper-colored euro one-cent coins like a wish fountain. The bright, shiny metal contrasts against the pale green moss that covers the side of the structure where the water pours out.

"Where does the water go from here?" I ask Lorenzo. The stream is so loud, I have to raise my voice.

"I'm not sure, but a lot of these springs were channeled

towards the Forum and into a great sewer that drained into the Tiber. The Cloaca Maxima."

I snort, remembering the year my mother decided to play hobby farmer but gave it all up when she learned that chickens lay eggs out of the same hole from which they defecate: the cloaca.

From the spring, we move on to the imperial Roman mint and explore rooms built from tufo-blocks. The only overhead light comes in streams through occasional tunnels in the ceiling that open to the floor above.

In addition to the light, the grates also conduct the sound of the tourists exploring the ancient basilica, so we don't miss the blood-curdling scream and chants of "*Un voleur, un voleur. Arrêtez le voleur*!"

I grip Lorenzo's arm in a way that will leave nail marks and turn to him wide-eyed with my stomach in my throat. For all I know, *voleur* means the spirits are rebelling, and I'm about to be buried alive. Much to my mother's chagrin, I was never confirmed in the Episcopal church, and I'm not sure if that will count for or against me when these Catholic ghosts send me to my judgment.

The fact that I don't wet myself right there is a testament to the cool confidence I see in Lorenzo's features. He rests a hand on my shoulder. "It's French," he says. "Thief. There was a thief."

I press my hands to my eyes. "Thank God," I mutter.

"I should go up there, Remy."

"Right, of course, let's go." I won't lie; I'm not disappointed to cut our tour in nether-Rome short.

He pulls me back. "I'd feel better if you stayed here. Just in case. These kinds of things are common at tourist sites, and usually, it's no big deal, but if the thief is armed or troubled, I don't want to risk you getting hurt."

I open my mouth to argue, but he cuts me off. "Please." His eyes leave no room for argument.

I nod. Police officer has got to police, and I've got to put on my big girl panties and chill out. I take a deep breath and smile. "Go get the bad guy, Detective Rossi." I barely have a chance to squeeze his arm before he's off, leaving me alone in a dusky and dank version of my nightmares.

All we have left to check out down here is the Mithraeum and the Mithraic school, and I might as well put myself to use and search it while I'm waiting for Lorenzo—even if curling up in a ball and hyperventilating until I pass out and am no longer aware of my surroundings sort of sounds like the more appealing option.

I go back the way we came and take the other hall at the fork at the base of the stairs. It seems darker than it did when Lorenzo was here, like some of the lights that had been flickering before have now faded out, replacing the glow of the bulbs with a heavy, ominous silence filled with unknowable dangers and unseeable scary things.

My imagination is an asshole.

Fortunately, the light at the entrance of the Mithraeum and those inside are still shining. The little plaque posted by the entrance pretty much states everything Lorenzo and I went over about the site when we were researching in the apartment. Mithraeums represent the cave to which the god Mithras carried and slayed a sacred bull. The stone benches along the sides of the cave weren't just used for seating during initiations to the Mysteries and cult rights but also for the ritual meal, which strikes me as a good selling point for any religious service.

Some Mithraeums, we read yesterday, also have an opening

that faces the sky. The sun and stars were a reminder of the universe beyond, the changing of the light a manifestation of the passage of time. Thank the bull-wrestling god Mithras, this is one of them. When the lights go out moments later, there is still just enough brightness coming from the channel in the ceiling above the altar for me to make out most of the space.

I wipe a hand over my clammy forehead. Being stuck two stories below street level in near-total darkness is a sick sort of torture. I couldn't even get through *Mockingjay*— reading about District 13 gave me indigestion. To make matters worse, my phone is sitting on the armrest of Lorenzo's car, plugged into a charger that is doing nothing, and there is no chance of me finding my way out of the labyrinth that is the underground without another source of light.

I tiptoe my way to the altar on wobbly legs, moving as quietly as possible so as not to draw the attention of the monsters that slither out in the night and fill the shadows. Sitting down, I press myself into the back of the stone sculpture, trying to hide from the dark.

With my hands squeezed between my legs to keep them from shaking, I close my eyes and try to pull up a thought, an image, anything that might help settle me down. I land on Lorenzo's face before he ran upstairs, the easy calm of his expression.

He's so confusing. Most of the time, since the kiss, he acts like if he gets too close to me, he might contract leprosy. But there are other moments where he's so sweet and gentle and close that I feel like we've known each other forever—like, despite the ocean and thousands of miles, some version of us has always existed.

I tell myself he was probably my dad in a past life. That is the equal parts sad and disturbing vibe that Cassie got when she saw us together.

Still, I wish I understood what is going on in his head, what it is I am doing to make him so standoffish. Does he take his marching orders from Valeria too? They have been talking a lot on the phone, and their conversations don't leave him grumpy like they used to. I imagine with their romance possibly rekindled, at least based on what I saw happening in the kitchen, she'd expect him to keep his distance from me. There is no reason she should trust me to make sure that happens, regardless of what I promised in the bathroom.

I suck in a tight breath and swing my head to the left. Despite the raging rush of blood in my ears—Valeria and my panic-induced tachycardia are both to blame—I hear footsteps outside the entrance to the Mithraeum. Hopefully, Lorenzo has come to save me, but I'd throw myself into pretty much anyone's arms at this point.

I hesitate, however, when I hear whoever is out there speaking French. There are two people, a man and a woman, and they are getting closer.

I tuck my knees into my chest and hold them there, praying whoever is out there will walk past, but I already know I won't be that lucky. They stop at the temple's entrance, and I peek around the edge of the altar.

My blood turns to ice.

When I was in the station with Lorenzo detailing my misadventure with Fabio, we talked a little about the gorgeous woman Fabio met that night in the bar. Maelle. Lorenzo mentioned she'd recently done time at a prison in France. As I take in Maelle's familiar long legs and Bella Hadid–grade cheekbones from my spot on the dusty floor, I wish I'd thought to ask what she'd been in for.

When I pull my head back, my shadow shifts on the ground, and I know Maelle and her mustachioed accomplice see it because they both go silent.

"Fuck," I groan into my hands.

"Who's there?" she asks in English.

Maelle doesn't know this, but confronting an infamous criminal—who happens to be a living, breathing human being and not a terror-fueled hallucination—doesn't feel as daunting as it should right now when I'm all jacked up on adrenaline. I've spent the past two hours facing one of my deepest fears. She may have gone to prison, but I've managed to not vomit on myself once since I've been down here.

I stand up and turn to them, keeping the altar between us. "Hey," I say. I even wave.

The young man beside Maelle scratches his chin in the most caveman way possible, which is very incongruous with his fancy facial hair. He gives a tiny shrug as if he's decided it is a bit strange to find me hiding in a Mithraeum, but nothing to be too worried about. Maelle, on the other hand, steps closer. It appears her brows are trying to bunch but can't, and a petty part of me is glad to know at least some element of her physical perfection is by way of injectables. Not even botulinum toxin can keep her mouth from twisting when she recognizes me, though.

"*C'est une farce*?" she asks the man, who blinks back at her, looking bewildered, like a mime pantomiming shock. She turns to me. "Did Dekker do this?"

"Dekker?" I ask.

She glares at me. I guess those muscles still work. "Yes, Dekker. We know he has a contact in the police force. I didn't realize he was working with Lewin's little toy."

I clench my fists. "Lewin's little toy?" I rumble at her.

She folds her arms, raises her chin. Since she's at least six inches taller than I am, the whole looking down at me thing works upsettingly well. "Don't act sillier than you already are. If you had half a brain, you'd have left Rome as soon as they cleared you."

One benefit of having a big sister is that I spent a decade and a half of my life fighting someone taller and better-spoken than me. "If *you* had half a brain, I wouldn't have had to be the one to solve the first clue," I shoot back. It might be immature, but I see the blow land.

Maelle rebounds with sarcasm. "Oh, you *are* smart," she says. "Lewin always knew how to pick his women." I don't miss the hint of jealousy in her voice, but I'm not desperate enough to go there.

"I am not Lewin's woman."

"Oops, I forgot. You've been tagging along at the heels of that handsome detective like a lovesick little puppy." Holy shit, is Valeria reporting to the Zalśar? Embarrassing. Maelle's information is questionable, but her use of it is effective.

As my blush spreads, Maelle adds, "Where's your big, strong officer now?"

I grimace.

"That's right. He had to run away to catch the 'thief,' and left you all alone, didn't he? We sent him on quite the chase. He won't be here to protect you like he was with Alberto. You are all by yourself down here, Ms. Campbell, where no one can hear you scream."

I clench my jaw and give her a tight smile.

I'm no longer a puppy. I'm a cornered wolf, and someone is about to get bitten.

My list of physical talents isn't outstanding, but it's not nothing. I can run fast, maybe not for long, but long enough to hide in another part of the excavations. First, however, I need to get past Maelle and her goon. My dad taught Lil and me how to hit, and what I did to Lorenzo's face is nothing compared to what I could do if I tried.

But there are two of them, and there is no way I can fight them both.

I look at my purse on the ground by my foot. I've always kicked with my left. If I could get the man with the bag, I might be able to take Maelle and escape.

She also has grossly underestimated the volume of my scream.

Prepare to have your eardrums shattered, bitch.

I open my mouth and am about to go full psychotic banshee when Lorenzo's deep voice reverberates through the Mithraeum. He's calling my name from above.

"Remy! Remy, where are you?" Lorenzo's footsteps pound above us.

"*Merde*," Maelle snarls. Then she looks at her guy and points to me, speaking rapid French. I don't have to understand what she's saying to know she wants him to shut me up, fast.

I bend my face up to the circle of light above me, the grate that opens to the basilica. "Mithraeum, Mithraeum," I shout at the top of my lungs until the man is within five feet of me, and I've got to move. The benches take up most of the side aisles, and there isn't much room to maneuver, but I hook my shoe under my purse strap and launch it at his face. It misses by a lot, but he does turn to see what just flew through the air.

I take the opportunity to slide out around the other side of the altar. When I pass Maelle, I shove my shoulder into her ribs, knocking her onto the bench.

Then I'm running through the darkness, but not to escape. As I go, I keep shouting for Lorenzo, and he calls back: Remy.

Rossi. Remy. Rossi, we go back and forth in the most high-stakes game of Marco Polo I've ever played. His voice is coming from the staircase we came down near the Tomb of St. Cyril. But I know there are two ways out of the bottom level, and I have to get to the other set of stairs.

If Maelle and her accomplice make it there first, they could get into the main church and out the back atrium without being caught. And frankly, fuck that.

I just need to block the exit long enough for Lorenzo to catch them first.

As I get closer to the stairs, I hear the sound of running behind me. Maelle's shoes click against the millennia-old mosaic floors. I thought women only wore heels in these scenarios in the movies—I bet she doesn't even have a hair tie.

Despite her ridiculous choice of footwear, Maelle is pretty fast, and since I am running blind, it doesn't take her long to gain on me.

From somewhere in the ruins behind us, I hear a solid thud, and a man cries out in obvious pain. Then Lorenzo is calling for me again, and I shout that I'm almost to the exit. I race around a dark corner and feel someone smack into me. We both huff out a breath, and then it's on.

Maelle and I are at the base of the stairs, and she's pulling at my shirt to get past me. I'm reaching for her hair. We scramble up together, her kicking me off her leg, me biting her hand like a pair of feral cats. At the top, I stumble back a couple of steps when Maelle punches me in the boob.

She smirks at me before turning to run. I go full little sister and leap on her back.

My arms and legs tighten like vices as she tries to pry me off, slamming my back action style into the brick buttresses—or trying to. We'd both fight in the same weight class, and she doesn't have the strength to do much with me wrapped around her body.

"What is wrong with you?" she mutters as we crumple into a heap onto the floor.

I consider her question. My face is scratched up and stinging, and I'll probably have a bruise near my right nipple. But none of that matters. When I see the look on Lorenzo's face as he comes loping up the stairs and finds me restraining Maelle on the ground like an aggressively clingy toddler, I don't feel a thing.

Lorenzo's hand goes to his heart as he takes in the tableau. "Remy, you're incredible," he breathes.

Maelle makes a sound reminiscent of a gag, and I know it's not from me accidentally choking her because my arms turned to rubber as soon as Lorenzo opened his mouth.

"The dude with the Captain Hook stash?" I ask Lorenzo before releasing my hold on Maelle.

"He ran himself into a wall and went down. Backup should be here soon; they'll take care of him."

I pull my arm out from under Maelle's shoulder and scooch back so Lorenzo can zip-tie her hands. "Why did you come back?"

"I got a call out to Chief Marchetti as soon as I was on the street. We have agents all over this area because of the Colosseum. They took over the chase."

"So there really was a thief?"

"There was someone pretending to be." He cocks his head and looks at Maelle. "Now, he's just one more person we have in custody who can testify against Ms. Toussaint."

He pulls her up off the ground. I give a small clap as I stand too, and Maelle turns her face to the wall.

Lorenzo pauses with one hand on her wrist. He runs the

other through his sweat-dampened hair. It's all mussed up, and his cheeks are all flushed, and it's a good thing I was already breathing heavily before he showed up.

He looks at me, bites his lip. "I feel like a jerk for leaving you down there. I shouldn't have done that."

I shake my head. "I was fine. I did fine."

He takes a deep breath and closes his eyes. When he opens them, they lock on mine. "When I got back, and the basilica was cleared, I knew something was wrong. I can't believe I was such an idiot." He hesitates, then swallows hard and adds, "You could have been taken, Remy. Or worse. They could have—"

"But they didn't. You had a bad guy to catch, Lorenzo. You made the right choice."

Lorenzo glances at Maelle, then back at me. His eyes gleam as his swollen lip turns up in a smile.

"You caught the bad guy, Remy."

Chapter FIFTEEN

WE SPEND THE REST OF THE AFTERNOON and much of the evening at the police station. After giving my statement about what happened at San Clemente, I lounge around Lorenzo's office while he finishes up some reports. His desk is still a disaster, and I can't control my impulse to shove everything into more stable-looking piles. A document envelope falls off of one of the stacks. It has my name written across the front—in Lorenzo's handwriting—and underneath that, in bold letters, it says: CONFIDENZIALE.

"What's this?" I ask, checking if the seal is loose.

"What?" Lorenzo is chewing his lip and bent over his laptop. He doesn't look up.

"This big fat envelope with my name on it."

His eyes shoot to me, and he reaches out, taking it from my fingers so quickly that they are left holding air. "Nothing. It's nothing."

I intend to rip it back out of his grasp and tear it open before he has time to protest, but just then, a group of officers and station staff barges into the already cramped space to congratulate Lorenzo on Maelle Toussaint's arrest. He throws his hands in the air and gestures to me with his head.

"*Era tutta lei*," he tells them. *It was all her.*

I beam at him, not just for the credit he bestows upon me, but because he's a really good guy. He returns my smile, and if it weren't for the barrage of handshakes, cheek kisses, and chants of "Capitana America," I would have forgotten anyone else was in the room.

We get back to the apartment just past eight, and I fall asleep on the couch while Lorenzo prepares my favorite pasta—carbonara. He wakes me up to eat, but I only get a few bites in before he's helping me to the bedroom.

"Tomorrow," he says, tucking me in, "we are taking a day off. We can do whatever you want. Drive to Maranello and race Ferraris, swim in every lake between here and Switzerland, visit Mercatale Val di Pesa and drink all the Solaia. I'll take you anywhere you want to go."

Mnemosine jumps up onto the bed and squeezes in beside me. Lorenzo runs a hand along her side, and the cat and I both arch our backs.

"The bar across the street," I say through a forced yawn meant to veil my unintentional writhing.

"What about it?"

"That's where I want to go. To watch Italy play in the World Cup Qualifier. And to meet Geppetto."

Lorenzo laughs. "*Ogni tuo desiderio é un ordine.*" *Your wish is my command.* He pets the cat again but watches me, almost like he's waiting to see if I'll react the way I did before.

"Today was fun," I say, rolling onto my side to disguise the way his hands on the cat make me press my legs together. I remember all too well how his fingers feel on my skin, the warmth of his palms on my body.

"You're very brave, Remy. *Forse anche troppo.*" *Maybe even too brave.*

I laugh. No one has ever called me brave before, except my father, and I didn't believe him either.

"You know that, right?" he adds.

My heart squeezes, and I tell him to turn off the light on the way out.

That night, I have a dream that I'm at the Colosseum, and kitten Mnemosine is talking to me. "It's because of memories like yours," she tells me, "that they had to invent a goddess like me." I ask her what she means, what I'm forgetting that is so important. "Don't act sillier than you already are," she hisses in Maelle's voice. I drop-kick her over the Arch of Constantine.

When I wake up and find Mnemosine still snuggled up beside me, I give her extra scratches behind her ears before carrying her out for breakfast.

Lorenzo has the espresso maker on the stove, and there is a white paper bag on the counter with a red logo stamped on the side—Bar Nona—that he hands to me after I've fed Mnemosine her favorite can of pate. I sit down at the table and peek inside. There is an assortment of all the very best Italian breakfast pastries. I go right for the chocolate croissant.

"This is very nice, but you know I want to actually *go* to the cafe across the street, not just eat their takeout?"

"The game isn't until noon, and for the full Roman bar experience, you have to start with breakfast," he points to the pastry in my hand, and I take a bite. "But since their espresso *non é molto buono*, I thought I'd spare you and make coffee here."

"Lorenzo."

"Yes?" He turns to me as I'm wiping powdered sugar from my bottom lip. His eyes linger there for only a second.

"Your Italian is showing."

His brows bunch, but then he smiles down at the Moka maker. "I know, I'm sorry."

"You don't have to apologize to me for speaking your own language."

"It's just that," he lifts the coffee off the burner as it starts to bubble over and pours it into the waiting cups, "sometimes the words start to mix when my mind is busy with a problem I'm having trouble solving." He looks at me, and his eyes flicker between mine.

"You mean the amulet?" my voice comes out way huskier than I expect it to for such a simple question.

He nods and turns away, grabbing the coffees and bringing them to the table.

"So, who are you rooting for in the match today?" he asks, pulling out the chair across from me.

I look at him like he's crazy, take one more bite of my croissant, and then run into my bedroom. When I come back, I have on an almost twelve-year-old, number 10, Italian National team captain's jersey. I packed it to wear for the game we are going to watch today. When I bought it on my last trip, I didn't have boobs, but I don't dislike how it fits now, tight across the chest and knotted up on the side with just a hint of tummy showing.

Neither does Lorenzo, if the way his cheeks turn red as I pose in his kitchen is any indication.

We get to the bar early and snag a table with a decent view of the big screen television in the corner. I insist on buying our first round, and we settle in with a couple of beers while we watch the pre-game.

I'm wearing a pair of Lululemon running shorts, my red

Nikes, and I have my hair in a high ponytail. I couldn't look less Italian if I tried, but it doesn't stop everyone who enters from shouting, "Forza Azzurri!" when they see me. I'd usually be embarrassed by that kind of attention, but by the time I'm two Peronis in, I'm shouting it back.

Eric is a huge fan of soccer, plays it, follows it. It always drove him nuts that the only games I was ever enthusiastic about watching were Italy matches. In retrospect, he bore a strange hostility against all the things I loved about Italy.

But Eric isn't here, so I let my Italian freak flag fly. Specifically, the one emblazoned on my left breast that jiggles around every time I throw my arms into the air or bounce in my seat—a move that's only intentional a couple of times when I notice Lorenzo is looking in my direction.

By kick-off, we've somehow each got a giant glass of gin and tonic in front of us. About halfway through the drink, Lorenzo is as loud as the rest of the crowd and me. When he yells at the television, I find myself grinning at this version of non-detective Lorenzo. He's so loose, happy, and unburdened, and every time he jumps out of the chair when Italy gets close to scoring a goal, he slaps the shoulders of all the people around him, then leans forward and squeezes mine before sitting back down.

I study the side of his face as he talks to the man next to him during a substitution. I follow the line of his jaw up to his ear, his eyes, and the thick lashes that blink at me once when he turns and smiles before continuing his conversation. There is a hint of a shadow on his cheeks, even though I'm sure he just shaved this morning.

Tipsy soccer Lorenzo is adorable. It's like seeing who Lorenzo was before he became all responsible and serious—a glimpse at a carefree teenager Lorenzo who is terrible at hiding the fact that his eyes keep snagging on my boobs.

I trace his lips with my eyes. They are a touch pinker where my palm hit his mouth and full as ever but not swollen.

The trouble I'm sure a young Lorenzo got into with that mouth.

I squint, looking closer.

Oh my god. His mouth.

I somehow manage to not spit out my mouthful of gin and tonic before gasping.

Lorenzo looks at me, startled. His hand shoots out, and he grabs my arm protectively. Detective Lorenzo mode reactivated. "What's wrong, Remy?"

"Nothing's wrong," I say, but I know my eyes look wild. I can't believe I didn't connect the dots sooner. It feels so obvious. All this time, I've been wondering why he's so damn familiar. "It's just…"

He raises his eyebrows for me to go on.

"I can't believe I didn't realize before now."

"Realize what?"

"Your face, it's almost the same—"

Lorenzo sits bolt upright in his chair and digs both hands into his hair. "Look, Remy, I can explain—" he croaks at the same exact time I exclaim that he looks just like the Italian National team center forward, number 11.

"What?" I ask.

"What?" he responds.

I gesture toward the screen where Lorenzo's doppelgänger is about to take a corner kick. "He's like, your twin, but younger."

Lorenzo exhales a huge breath, and his hands fall to his sides.

"Not that you look old," I correct. "He's just, you know. Less old."

"Thank you?"

"He's really cute," I try.

Lorenzo laughs and looks at me from under those damn lashes. "So are you," he whispers, and the kindling in my belly goes up in flames.

He stands and grabs our glasses. "Another?"

Another could be dangerous. "Yes, please," I answer.

I watch him walk away with my lip between my teeth. I wonder what the hell he thought needed explaining, but by the time he makes it back to the table with two-overfilled cocktails, the game has gone into overtime, and there is no space for conversation. The bar is filled with the sounds of sucked-in breaths and groans and sighs—until Italy scores a goal in the final thirty seconds of the second period, and the tension is shattered in a burst of frenzied cheering.

Lorenzo leaps to his feet, kicks his chair behind him, and takes one long step, so he's right in front of me. Before I know it, I'm in his arms, my feet above the ground, the sides of our faces smashed together—and I think, *This is the happiest I've ever been.*

When he sets me down, his cheeks are flushed.

"We should go celebrate," I say, hooking my pinky in his because I feel unsteady without his taut chest pressed into mine, without his strong arms holding me to him.

He uses that small spot where our skin meets to pull me closer. "Where should we go?" he asks.

The Palatine, I want to scream. But it is the middle of the day, and it would sound more than a little desperate. I'm scanning my brain for a suitable answer that doesn't broadcast the fact that I want to rip his clothes off when he tugs on my hand.

I look up. *Your apartment* probably doesn't work either in that case.

"Your phone is ringing," he says.

"Oh." I pull my hand reluctantly away and fumble in my purse, finding my phone and holding it in front of me just long enough for us both to see who's calling.

ERIC ARMSTRONG is stamped over a photo of us together that I'd never gotten around to changing. I silence the call.

"What about Campo dei Fiori?" I ask, pretending nothing happened, but the corners of Lorenzo's mouth have turned down. The phone rings again before he can respond.

I groan.

"You should answer," Lorenzo says. He takes a step back, away from me.

I want to reach out and stop him. "I...It'll just be a second." I lift the phone, grimacing when I press the little green button.

"Hey, Rems."

"What is it?" I say.

"Whoa, everything okay?"

I glance over my shoulder to where Lorenzo is leaning against the bar, very obviously *not* watching me. "Yeah. Sorry. I was just in the middle of something."

"No worries, babe."

"So," I say, trying to subdue the obvious impatience in my voice, "what's up? Isn't it like five in the morning there?"

"Sure is. I'm on my way to the gym, but I got a notification on my phone that Italy won the qualifier. I wanted to call and say congratulations. I know you were looking forward to being there for the game."

I hesitate, probably because I'm experiencing symptoms of actual shock. "That's...sweet, Eric."

"I thought I could call later when I'm back home, and we can talk about the chairs for the new dining room table."

Right. At some point, I'd agreed to help him with the Remy-andEric 2.0 Condo redesign.

"I'm going to ask Lilian and your mom if I can pick up some of your stuff this afternoon, start putting it away," he adds.

I frown. "I thought we decided to wait on that."

"Remy, you've already told me you'll move back in. As far as I'm concerned, we can wait as long as you want to make things official again, but in my mind, there's only you."

My stomach turns over on itself. I am the worst kind of human: doing everything Valeria told me not to with Lorenzo, flirting with a man when I will soon be moving in with another. I rub my temple with my free hand. "Okay, sure. Call whenever, and we can talk about the chairs."

"Love you, R.C."

"Talk soon."

I take a big breath and put my shoulders back, plastering a big fake smile on my face—Lorenzo's typing on his phone when I approach.

"What about lunch?" I ask. Lunch sounds neutral, friendly. Public.

"Actually," he says, not meeting my eyes, "something big came up at the station. I have to go in."

"I'll come with you."

His jaw pulses once. "I might be there late. You stay home and relax. There is some fresh bread and prosciutto cotto in the fridge. And a kilo of that creamy caciocavallo you said you liked. I can prepare some panini before I go."

Lorenzo hasn't left me alone for more than a trip to the corner market since the whole Alberto thing went down, and now he's going to be gone for hours?

I try to smile. "Don't worry about me. Capitana America can figure out how to put a sandwich together."

"Good. I'll see you later then." He digs into his pocket and pulls out the key to 4B. "You can keep this copy."

Lorenzo hands me the key to his apartment and leaves. I look at it in my palm and have the urge to laugh at the parallel dysfunctions in my life. My relationship with Eric. My relationship with Lorenzo. The idea that I've somehow managed to agree to move in with both of them in the same week. It's only when I feel a hand on my elbow that I notice my giggles have turned into tears.

"*Tutto bene, signorina*?" It's Geppetto, and he's just as precious up close as he is from Lorenzo's living room window, even though he smells a little more like Sambuca than I'd imagined he would.

"*Si, si,*" I respond. "É stata una partita intensa." I nod toward the TV screen. *It was an intense game.*

He calls the bartender and orders two espressos, passing me one when they arrive steaming in front of him.

"*Dove si gioca l'amore,*" he says, eyes sparkling, "é sempre cosi."

Where love is at play, that is always the case.

Chapter SIXTEEN

I'M SCROLLING THROUGH MY TEXT THREAD with Eric as Lorenzo drives me to the university to do research. Screenshot after screenshot of bath towels and dish sets flies by. Eric's insistence on making it "our" home—which I have reminded him, it already was once—is both considerate and exhausting.

The truth is, I could not give less of a shit about what water glasses he orders. It has been four days since Maelle's arrest and three days since the soccer game, and I haven't made any progress with the clue or Lorenzo.

Well, that's not true. I've found a surefire way to keep Lorenzo from getting all freaky uncomfortable with me: I talk about Eric. A lot. Then we are just two people talking about one other person, and there is no talk of us. Not that there is an us.

Eric's text chimes.

> Babe, you've got to tell me which sheets to order ASAP...
>
> Doesn't matter. Whatever you like, I respond.
>
> It's like you don't even care about the house, R.C.

Ding ding ding! I am about to tell him bravo for finally realizing, but that will just land us in one of our endless arguments about how all I ever think about is what's going on in Rome, and he's back in Phoenix putting a life together for us—one built upon sustainable bath towels and non-toxic cookware.

Lorenzo stops at a red light. "Which ones?" I ask, showing him the almost identical sets of eco-friendly sheets. "For my bed at home."

His jaw bunches. "Oh," he mumbles, but he looks at the screen, chewing his lip like he's seriously considering the options.

"Eric needs to know immediately. It is a bedding emergency," I tell him. Lorenzo doesn't even crack a smile.

"The ones with the stripes," he answers right before the light turns green.

I pull the phone back to my face and look closer. One set has a delicate, flax-colored pinstripe running through the fabric. Lorenzo's right. They are nicer than the plain, a little more exciting, and I know Eric already ordered a super boring duvet cover.

"Yeah, definitely the stripes," I concur before texting Eric.

I like the ones with the stripes.

Oh, dang. Sorry, babe, I just ordered the ivory sateen. But I can cancel if you want.

No biggy, I write back. They're just sheets.

Just sheets, and also another glaring example of our incompatibility. I sigh loud and long. Were we always like this? It seems like, after having dated for seven years, I'd have a better sense of who we are as a couple.

Maybe Eric just never asked before; he never checked in to see what it was I wanted.

Neither did I.

I glance at Lorenzo out of the corner of my eye.

All relationships have their challenges, and people aren't supposed to agree about everything. Just because Eric and I have different tastes in sheets doesn't mean we aren't meant to be. If we work at it, we will remember how to exist again in that bubble of contentment we once shared.

That tiny, uncomplicated bubble of PetaLuna and Eric's campaigns and easy affection and endless, mind-numbing complacency.

There's no air for setting fires inside bubbles.

I drop my head into my hands.

"Are you okay?" Lorenzo asks.

"Eric ordered the plain sheets," I mumble. And I know that even this simple phrase is dangerous ground, enough to scare Lorenzo off for hours. Conveniently for both of us, he's just parked at the university and is about to leave me with Dr. Hill for the afternoon.

I hurry out of Lorenzo's car before my words have a chance to settle.

After a quick detour to the language department, I head to Dr. Hill's office.

I've met some of the graduate students on campus, and they've confirmed that the consensus among the entire student body is that Dr. Hill has brought sexy back to art history degrees. He somehow manages to look like a total DILF in a button-down, tie, and plaid vest.

I already have the feels for art history, and he really makes me itch for a Master's.

"I had an idea," he says, pulling a book from the shelves behind his desk. Dr. Hill does not know all the details of the case. He is aware that someone in his language department helped with translations. He has been told I am to be allowed access to whatever materials I request and also that I am to never be let out of his sight (which I hope Dr. Hill has concluded is because Lorenzo is worried about someone doing something to me and not the other way around).

He also knows everything I've told him about the clues—information I probably should not have shared. Not because he's dangerous, but because I'm pretty sure one of the forms I signed when I agreed to stay in Rome was a confidentiality agreement. Oops.

He sets a book between us on the desk: *Etruscan Funerary Rites*.

"I know you are focusing *in* Rome, but what about the Metropolitan City of Rome Capital that extends far beyond just the city itself?" He flips past the title page and the contents to a map. "Here," he says, pointing. "All these sites lay within the boundary of the *Cittá Metropolitana*."

On the map are many of the cities that Lorenzo drew for me that first day in apartment 3A, and my tummy tightens at the memory. I can't believe almost four weeks have passed since then, and after spending nearly every hour of every day of it together, my and Lorenzo's relationship has only become more strained.

"Thanks. I'll take a look." The book is thick, dense with images and descriptions of every crypt cataloged throughout Etruria. Etruscan cemeteries, it turns out, are serious business—entire cities built below the ground or up from it.

I start with the ancient city of Veii, less than ten miles northwest of Rome. An archaeological site in the area is known as The Tomb of the Roaring Lions. It is one of the oldest painted tombs in the entire Mediterranean and proof that the whole Etruscan-lion love affair goes way back, at least 2700 years.

As far as the clue is concerned, the site doesn't give me much to go on. Outside of the whole cave of lions bit, it doesn't fit.

I run into the same issue with the Tomb of the Lotus Flower, the Tomb of the Lionesses, and the Tomb of the Bacchantes at the Monterozzi Necropolis in Tarquinia, north of Rome. Lions detailed in vibrant reds and yellows adorn the gables of the underground rooms, floating above trump l'oeil doorways and altars painted into the plaster thousands of years ago.

Prides of the large felids stalk the walls of the burial chambers. But there is a significant lack of *osculum*—no kisses, no lips, no other orifices. Not even anything that could be interpreted to fit the description "mouth of the kingdom."

The tombs are all frescoed rooms with dirt floors, and if there is anything below that, there would be no way to find out.

When I turn to the section on Cerveteri, my heart speeds up a little.

Cerveteri—known to the Romans as Caere, Caisra to the Etruscans—was one of the city-states that comprised the Etruscan League, the twelve Etruscan settlements that allied in the sixth century BCE to form an economic and religious powerhouse. The same Etruscan League that Fabio and his syndicate of twits strive, but fail, to emulate. The original Zalśar.

It is also where a team of archaeologists discovered a tomb filled with golden treasures in 1836—including one very precious and currently missing amulet.

I slam the book shut and grab my phone to text Lorenzo. I know he was looking forward to a few unafflicted hours away from the torture of my company, but too bad. We have some graves to explore.

"Find something?" Dr. Hill inquires over his wire-framed readers.

I nod. "Can I take this with me?" I ask, but I'm already stuffing the book into my bag next to the copy of Anna Proudfoot's *Modern Italian Grammar* that I snagged earlier from the head of the Italian department.

He gestures around his office. "Take whatever you need, Remy. I can't wait to hear what you've come up with."

As soon as I'm in the car, I thrust the book from Dr. Hill into Lorenzo's hands. For the first time in days, I feel like maybe I might be onto something. Thank you, sexy genius Dr. Hill.

Lorenzo holds the heavy book against the steering wheel, his big hands gripping the sides carefully like I've just passed him a human child and not a thirty-pound reference encyclopedia of death. The sleeve of his faded black t-shirt tightens against his bicep as he bends his arm to keep the book raised before his face. It is annoying how his torso can make something as simple as a crew neck look like it was cut just for him.

"Page one hundred and sixty," I say, a breathy order.

I follow the path of his muscles to where the tendons in his forearm tense as he flips the pages with all the frustrated physical energy of Bernini's *David*—the only inanimate object that's ever made me have inappropriate thoughts. The golden skin of his upper arm tightens when he wets a finger on his tongue to turn the page. I squirm in my seat.

When Lorenzo is weird with me—which is almost always since the soccer game—I don't let myself look at him too closely. For one, I don't want to make things worse, further whatever uncomfortable vibe he's already getting by staring at his frustratingly full lips or the hints of inviting anatomy his clothing can't camouflage.

And two, it causes a very distracting clenching low in my

belly that is hard to reconcile with the fact that somewhere thousands of miles away, Eric is working so hard to piece our life back together, hoping we can be a couple again.

The force of the Lorenzo magnet is strengthened by proximity and ogling. But this is fine—just me admiring a male body much the way Michelangelo might have before contorting himself for endless hours to paint its rock-hard ridges all over the Sistine Chapel.

No one said being a lover of fine art was always easy.

Lorenzo's voice cuts through my thoughts. "The *Sarcophagus of the Spouses*?" he asks.

It takes me a second to register his words. The way his ears turn pink when he looks at my face doesn't help. Dear God, was I drooling? I lean over the armrest to see what page he's on. He shifts his body toward the window, and I roll my eyes, but really I'm grateful he didn't run away.

Half the page is taken up by a single photo of the most romantic coffin I've ever seen. A man and woman, sculpted from terracotta, recline on some sort of fancy ancient sofa, snuggled against each other. His arms reach around her, and they are both smiling, so happy to be close and in love. And maybe even glad to be heading into the hereafter, because they are together.

I haven't had a man's chest pressed against my back since Lorenzo saved me from falling in the Forum, and Eric isn't a cuddler. He *is* the kind of guy who'd want to share a cemetery plot, though, to save a tree or something. The thought of being immortalized in stone with Eric makes my stomach turn. I'd rather face the afterlife alone.

I shake my head. "Page one fifty. Sorry." I apologize, even though my error is his fault for having his bewildering arms exposed.

When he finds the page, I confirm that he's landed in the

right place this time. His lips move as he reads about the Banditaccia Necropolis in Cerveteri and the lion statue, carved from tufo stone, excavated there in the early 2000s. He rubs a hand over the scratchy shadow on his chin. "Yes. It makes sense," he says without looking at me. He's probably afraid of what kind of crazy he'd find on my face. I wish Eric would text me to break the tension.

"Should we go to Cerveteri?" I ask.

"Now?"

"Dr. Hill said from here the drive should be less than an hour. If we get there by five-thirty, we'd have a couple of hours of sunlight to look around."

He clenches his jaw. It pulses. "I can't."

"What do you mean?"

"I can't go right now," he says, looking out the window.

"Why?" I demand. Isn't this his job, to find the amulet?

"I have plans this evening."

I press my lips together, exhaling through my nose. Lorenzo turns to me. He shrugs guiltily like a naughty little kid who just got caught hiding dirty magazines under his pillow.

My insides turn to lead, and all I want to do is crawl inside the Sarcophagus of the Spouses and hide forever. Lorenzo is going on a date.

In my mind, there is a flurry of people I'm mad at, but the most painful one to acknowledge is myself. No one asked me to throw myself into the case, to spend every waking moment (that's not already occupied by thoughts of Lorenzo) thinking about the clues and the amulet or how to say *I want to lick your face* in Italian.

Lorenzo is allowed to have a life outside of work, outside of me. But I am resentful that I don't. Or I do, but it is far away and not very exciting. Maybe Eric was right; my single-minded focus on all things Rome isn't doing me any favors.

"Cool," I manage, yanking the book from his hands and laying it in my lap, willing its weight will ground me in some version of reality that's not so sucky. "I'll stay in and do some more research."

I want to ask him where he is going, who he is meeting. He hasn't mentioned Valeria coming to town, and I'm desperate to know if there is someone else. What a scoundrel. I bet he's out gallivanting when he leaves me during the day too. The police station is a good cover when you are stringing along a lot of lovesick ladies. How many women are there? Why do I have the worst taste ever in men?

"How are things going with Dr. Hill?" he asks when he parks below the apartment. Despite the fifteen minutes of my fuming silence and his uncomfortable throat-clearing that collectively made up our car ride, neither of us rushes to get out.

"Fine," I answer.

"Has he been following your research?" He glances at me, and his face is expectant, maybe even hopeful. I don't know what to make of that.

"I guess."

The corners of Lorenzo's mouth fall. "So yes?"

"Sort of," I offer.

Lorenzo chews his lip. What is he trying to get at? Maybe he wants me to thank him for being so gracious and leaving me alone with the enigmatic Dr. Hill for hours at a time. Fine, here.

"He's remarkably interesting," I say, tracing my finger over the words on the cover of the book. Lorenzo watches.

"Good," he mumbles as my pointer finger drags along the letter A.

“He’s so thoughtful,” I add. “Always keeping an eye on me, anticipating my needs.” My voice grows thicker when I see Lorenzo bite his lip as I shift the book in my lap and the hem of my skirt rides up on my thigh. “Always so close.”

It’s true. Dr. Hill is great. But I am not talking about him anymore. I’m taking one more walk on the Remy and Rossi tight rope before he goes out, and I’m stuck at home imagining the depraved things he’s doing to someone else with his hands.

I play with the hem of my skirt. This is a dangerous act because I am the only one who will get hurt when the tent collapses. I’m the freak show who will be left buried in the detritus. I spread my hand over the skin of my leg.

“So close?” Lorenzo repeats back. His voice is husky, and it is the ovation I was seeking for my performance, the confirmation that I can make him ache a little, even if it isn’t as devastating as the pull he has on me.

I straighten and smile as I unbuckle my seat belt. “I mean, you’ve seen the man. I’m not complaining.” I hop out of the car and don’t look back.

Chapter SEVENTEEN

I PACE AROUND THE APARTMENT. Lorenzo has been gone for twenty minutes, and already I'm jittery. Before he left, I locked myself in my room to avoid the mental self-flagellation of seeing him dressed up and about to get some. He didn't even knock to say goodbye.

Mnemosine is watching me wear tracks on the tile floor, and we both agree, I'm pretty pathetic.

I flop onto the couch and try to concentrate. I'm not as convinced about Cerveteri as I was this afternoon in the car. I've gone over maps of the Regolini-Galassi tomb, where the amulet was discovered. Most of what was found there ended up in the Vatican collections, and almost all the metalwork is ornamented in tiny, golden filigree lions—a chest plate, a brooch, bracelets.

I drew a line between the Regolini-Galassi tomb and the site of the stone lion statue. From there, to the Tomb of the Painted Lions—which no longer contains painted lions because they disintegrated after the tomb was broken into and exposed to the outside world. Much like my pride these past few weeks.

Sighing, I shove a pillow behind my head. *Under the den of the lions is the mouth of the kingdom.* Lions, lions everywhere, but not one single osculum of the kingdom.

One of Mnemosine's toy balls digs into my back, and I pull it out and toss it to her. She swats it once, then bats it back. I conjugate *osculum* in my head to the tune of "Funiculì, Funiculà," trying not to think about the osculum on Lorenzo's face pressing into someone else's.

I roll the ball to Mnemosine again. This time, she holds it under her front paw and looks at me, her fluffy neck scruff a golden-white mane in the sunset light. She is as regal as any feline ever sculpted. She puts the Medici lions to shame.

As I admire her, a giant, flashing *DUH* scrolls across my mind, and goosebumps spread over my arms.

The Medici Lions are best known for flanking the stairs of the Loggia della Signoria in Florence, where they've kept guard over an open gallery of publicly displayed antique and Renaissance statuary for over two centuries.

But before the lions moved to Florence, they spent a couple of hundred years as centurions at the Villa Medici—in Rome.

I throw my legs over the side of the couch, reaching for the cat. "You *are* the goddess of memory," I say, nuzzling my nose into her fur. I cradle her in my arm as I head for the bookcase in Pietro Rossi's office. I've already read through the book I'm looking for, and my hand goes right to its flaking paper spine. *I Tracci dei Medici a Roma*. Traces of the Medici in Rome.

I snap the yellowing pages back and forth until I find what I'm looking for, the chapter on Villa Medici. I breathe the words out as I read them, running my finger along as I reweigh what's written with new eyes.

The book states that construction on the villa was completed in the late 1500s by Cardinal Ferdinando de' Medici, years after Michelangelo's death. Still, certain design inventions were rumored to be credited to the artist. The purpose of the palace was to assert the Medici's presence in Rome.

Or, as some might suggest, to reassert the Etruscan presence.

The Grand Dukes of Tuscany employed the villa as their Roman seat of power until 1737. Their palace on the Pincian Hill was a Renaissance manifestation of those the Etruscans had built mere miles away on the Palatine thousands of years before.

I take a deep, shaky inhale. The next chapter screams itself off of the page.

When the Medici male line went caput, possession of the villa passed to the short-lived Italian Kingdom of Etruria—named for, of course, the very part of Italy ruled by the Etruscans, and then by the Medici.

The freaking villa was entrusted to the freaking kingdom of Etruria—it's so on the nose, I laugh out loud.

The kingdom was dissolved by Napoleon and integrated into France, which is how, five hundred years later, the Villa Medici is known polyonymously as The French Academy in Rome.

I get online and find the Academy's website. Nowadays, you can book tours, visit the gardens, and see discordant modern art displayed in the gallery of Villa Medici. There are also limited and unquestionably haunted guest rooms available in the Medici apartments.

Den of the lions. *Check.*

Now for the osculum.

Before giving myself too big a pat on the back, I need to figure out how the rest of the clue connects to the villa. As I strum my fingers over the keyboard, considering my next move, I notice Lorenzo's messages don't pop up in the corner of the screen like they used to.

No more surprise shoutouts from Valeria.

I'm not sure if I'm disappointed or relieved by this as I scroll through photos.

One of the most repeated panoramas of the villa is a view of the cream-colored facade from the gardens, with St. Peter's erupting in the background. The basilica, in all its subtlety, rises from the chaos of Rome like a saint-crenellated Leviathan.

I open a new window and type VATICAN WORD ORIGIN into the search box.

The results are varied; there is some significant debate about the etymology of the word Vatican. I'm desperate to find an osculum in there somewhere but not desperate enough to concede that the Latin suffix is related in any way to the root word anus—despite Reddit user hobbitusrex82's extensive research. I refuse to believe that the Zalśar are referencing buttholes in their clues.

I think about Lorenzo and holes and shake my hands out before trying again.

I find more than one source that says Vatican is an Etruscan loan word, an ancient name for the area of the Vatican that refers to the site of a mythical oracle.

An oracle could sure as hell be considered the mouth of a kingdom.

I try to force Mnemosine into a high five, but she is not having it. I'm jazzed anyway. This is probably the smartest I've ever been, and I want to commemorate the moment. I peek out the window at the bar across the street and imagine going down by myself for a celebratory cocktail.

The idea is tempting, but despite the brave face I put on, I'm still a little shook about my close call with Maelle. I hate Lorenzo for not being here to enjoy this breakthrough with me. He's the worst.

I head into the kitchen to drink Lorenzo's wine in retribution, pouring a glass of yummy red blend from Ragusa and sipping it as I dial Lil's number. She's at work and can't talk. I call Cassie, but she's on a train to Venice and has lousy reception. I even try my parents and immediately regret it when my mother starts asking me about Lorenzo and how he's tolerating having me around all the time. I hang up as soon as I have a chance to tell my dad I love him and thanks for not being awful.

At this point, I could call Lorenzo and pray he answers, and if he does go full crazy and ruin his date with some self-indulgent praise, or I could call Eric.

I finish my glass of wine and pour another before closing the shutters and curling up in the armchair I use for research in Lorenzo's office.

"Hi, Rems," Eric answers.

"Hey," I drawl. My voice is thick with drink, and all the excitement of my Vatic-non-anus discovery is a jailed tremor in my body, energy in need of escape.

He pauses. "Hey, yourself." His voice is lower now, and I'm surprised when it does things to my insides. Maybe being Eric's girlfriend again when I get back to Phoenix won't be *all* bad.

"I was just thinking about you," I lie.

"I think about you all the time," he says. I want to ask if that's true, but I hear the sound of his car keys clanking onto a table.

"Where are you?" I ask instead.

"Just walked into our house. Where are you?"

"Alone in the apartment."

"Alone?" he barks. "Is that safe?"

"Eric," I say. "I am *all alone* in the apartment."

"Right," he says, and his voice is a husky rasp up my spine. I sigh, grateful this is working, that I'm feeling something. My breathy relief elicits a groan from Eric. "I wish you were here," he says.

"What would you do if I were?" I run my fingers under my top and along the edge of my pink lace bralette, then slip my hand into the waistband of my PJ shorts.

Eric doesn't hesitate. He narrates a super graphic erotic adventure for both of us to enjoy, and I am impressed with his storytelling skills. Eric has picked up some new tricks in our time apart, but it doesn't bother me. His breathing is heavy as he speaks, and I'm replying in little gasps as my body goes full starfish on the armchair; my limbs are everywhere.

The truth is, other than my kiss with Lorenzo, I've been celibate since Eric and I broke up. I've never done anything like this before, but clearly, I'm a rabid horndog and need this release more than I realized.

"And then I've got your nipple in my mou—"

"Fuck," I choke. My brain has done something bad, and this mental porno starring Eric and me has a new leading man. I keep trying, but all I see is Lorenzo, his forearms, his bare feet, his big hands on my naked stomach.

"You like that?" Eric asks, sounding hoarse and smug.

I try to place him back above me, but it doesn't work. It's just a fantasy, though, so I go with it, Lorenzo's hard body planted on top of mine. "Yes," I murmur. I like it a whole lot.

I'm panting, writhing, in the chair, the phone beside me on the table. I have one hand in my underwear and the other in my hair.

"I'm so close, babe," Eric breathes into the phone.

"Me too," I manage. And I can honestly say I've never gotten myself this hot before. It helps that behind my lids, all I see are Lorenzo's hungry eyes.

Eric moans right as the door opens.

"Oh my god," I shout, falling out of the chair. I reach for my phone and knock it below the table. Eric's X-rated noises are blasting through the speakerphone. I fumble, trying to reach it.

"Remy?" Lorenzo's voice falters from behind me as he says my name.

I spare a horrified second to look over my shoulder. Lorenzo's eyes are wide as he takes in the scene. My bra dangles from the armhole of my sleep shirt. My shorts are tucked up into the side of my undies. I can only imagine my hair looks like I was wrestling wolves.

And from under the table, a man's voice grunts, "Rems, that was so fucking good," right before I can hit the little red button of safety.

I take a second to rearrange my clothes and clear my throat before I stand.

"How was your date?" I ask—my traitorous voice shaking —as I turn to Lorenzo with my arms crossed.

"Date?" His face is flushed.

I do a double-take, look him over top to bottom. He's staring back at me in what I can only imagine is abject horror. He just witnessed the leper having phone sex. But I shake my head; something is very wrong. There's a sheen of sweat along his forehead, and his hair is as messy as mine. His clothes stick against his skin. My heart sinks, and I feel a weird heaviness in my limbs that is reminiscent of guilt.

"Are you wearing shin guards?" I stammer.

Lorenzo has dropped what is very obviously an athletic bag at his feet. He also looks like he might vomit, and I don't blame him. I want to puke, too.

"Yes," Lorenzo answers after what feels like a hundred years of excruciating silence. He makes the single word sound like a crack in the very fabric of the universe, dissolving the petty version of reality I'd been consumed by since he told me he had plans.

Yes, I am wearing shin guards. Yes, I was out playing soccer.

What were you doing, Remy Campbell?

My cheeks are as red hot as the scarlet A that is branding itself onto my chest, and I claw at the space above my heart. There, inside me, a sense of soul-gutting regret is being pumped out in time with my pulse, traveling around my body until every tight, itchy part of me knows that I am a complete and total fucking idiot.

I am a fool.

I am racked with guilt. Not because I imagined Lorenzo while I had phone sex with my prospective future fiancé. Not because thinking of Lorenzo and his lips on me while I touched myself propelled me into a state of sexual arousal I've never achieved single-handedly, not because it made me ache for him in more ways than I already do.

No. I feel guilty that Lorenzo caught me with Eric. I feel horrible that he heard Eric's moaning, his gravelly finish.

I feel like I betrayed Lorenzo. Which is insane.

My phone rings, and when I see it's Eric, my instinct is to chuck it as hard as I can at the wall. But I answer as Lorenzo watches, his feet shifting beneath him. I tell Eric I will call him back tomorrow.

Then to Lorenzo, I say the words that I should have said weeks ago, as soon as I got the chance—before my infatuation hit record levels of crazy. I have to push them through my teeth. They fight to stay inside.

"It's time for me to go home."

The words come out a tangle of emotion, a knot that settles on the ground between us. Lorenzo's lips turn down, his brow creases, like he is mentally trying to pick this sentence apart. Like it might mean something different if he manages to get through to the core of it.

"You want to leave?" he asks, his voice so gentle I wince. I might imagine it, but I think his voice trembles. My heart sinks lower in my body, collapsing into a puddle of toxic, impossible feelings.

"I…" I have no idea what to say. The truth is not an option.

Lorenzo takes a step toward me, nearly tripping over his gym bag. He catches himself, steadies his legs and his breathing. From the other side of the room, he reaches out a hand toward me. "You don't have to go, Remy."

I let myself look at his face, and this real version of Lorenzo in front of me is even more amazing than the one I conjured in my mind during the call. The shadow of his lashes on his cheeks, the confused pout of his lower lip. I want to throw my arms around his neck, wrap my legs around his waist and never let go—which is precisely the reason I must leave.

"I'll have Lil book a flight," I say, not meeting his eyes. I know if I were to find even a hint of disappointment there, I would lose my nerve. On the other hand, if they are brimming with relief, I want to spare my heart and pride the trauma.

We both stand there, frozen, for another uncomfortable minute before I grab my glass of wine and hurry past him—flinching at the way the air between us burns—and into my room.

I call Lil and tell her I need to leave ASAP. She doesn't ask why, just tells me she'll take care of it. I know one day I'll be able to tell her the story of what happened tonight without weeping, and I promise myself I will because I know she will shoot whatever she is drinking out her nose when I do.

But right now, what I'm feeling for Lorenzo is not funny at all.

Chapter EIGHTEEN

"TWO WEEKS?" I hiss into the phone at Lil.

Lorenzo and I have barely spoken all day, barely managed to be within shouting distance of each other without one of us turning red and running away. I've been distracting myself by putting together a little presentation about the Villa Medici, which I thought Lorenzo would be visiting alone. I planned to give him my research with a farewell card and a thank you box of chocolates.

But Lil messed everything up. Big sisters are not to be trusted.

Lil's sigh is loud and deep. "It was the best I could do," she says, not even trying to sound convincing.

"I believe you zero percent," I tell her.

"Fine."

"But why?" I whine. My sister is keeping me captive in Rome under very precarious circumstances.

"No one here wants you until you've figured your shit out."

"Excuse me?"

"You really thought you'd come home tomorrow, get back together with Eric, and move on like nothing happened?"

"Yes. Because *nothing* did happen."

"You have an over-ten-year-old map hanging in my daughter's bedroom to remind yourself of a kiss you've been obsessing about since you hit puberty. Do you think this is going to somehow be easier to get over?"

"My arrest? Yes."

"And the hot detective? I'm not saying there is anything there—"

"There isn't," I interrupt.

"Well, I think there should be."

"Why?"

"You know we still talk, right, Lorenzo and me? He asks questions about you, nothing creepy. Last week he asked me what your favorite movie is."

"And you told him *The Twilight Saga: Eclipse*?" I howl.

The other night, Lorenzo had to work late. When I came out of my room before he left, he had set up dinner for one and shifted the table and the TV, so I could see the screen from my chair. He had the movie paused. Twilight seemed like an epically weird choice until I began to wonder if he was trying to tell me something.

Am I Bella, choosing between Jacob and Edward?

Is *he* Bella?

I barely slept that night.

"You are a giant dick," I add when Lil doesn't say anything, which she can't do because she is giggling too hard.

I try a different tact. "Lorenzo has a girlfriend, Lilian."

"Does he, though?"

"Yes. I told you, I saw them. And I—"

"And you are moving back in with the guy who broke your heart before Thanksgiving because he's standard hot and is good at buying houseplants and choosing biodegradable laundry detergent. Great. Yeah, I know. I hope that makes you happy."

"Jesus."

"It's just two weeks. Suck it up."

"Two weeks for me to plot my revenge against you for when I get home."

"Worth it."

"What do I tell Lorenzo?"

"Tell him that your evil big sister won't let you leave until you can give a full report on all of Rome's hottest parts and appendages."

I swallow, cradle my head in my hand. "What if he wants me to leave?"

Her voice softens. "He doesn't."

"How could you possibly know that. Even mom is convinced he's sick of me." Neither of us addresses the fact that my voice is cracking.

"Listen, you ginormous goober," Lil says, sounding very kind for someone so heartless. "I spoke to him this morning before confirming flights. He said two weeks is no problem. The only issue will be the wedding."

My head snaps up. "What wedding?"

I hype myself up in my room once I hang up with Lil.

Two weeks. I've got this. I can maintain control for fourteen days. A whole month has passed, and so far, I've only thrown myself at Lorenzo once that counts. I've resisted the urge to sprawl across the dining room table in my cutest lingerie for him to find me when he comes home from work. I even manage to keep my eyes averted from his lips when he talks. Or, at least I try.

When I am brave enough to emerge from my room, I find Lorenzo in the study. Two weeks. Countdown starts now.

"Hey," I say in a too-loud voice. I have the folder filled with my Villa Medici research pressed into my chest. I hug it closer like a shield.

Lorenzo turns to me, rising in his chair. "Hey," he responds, just the opposite, so quiet I can barely hear him.

I feel like I should apologize for yesterday, for what he walked into. But I chicken out and chew on my lip. "That was Lil on the phone," I say instead.

He nods his head.

"Two more weeks," is all I manage. I know Lorenzo already knows; Lil gave him all my flight information. But what if she was wrong and he doesn't want me here, especially not for his sister's wedding.

He smiles—a huge grin that makes my stomach flip. "Two more weeks," he repeats, not looking at all like he hates the fact that he is stuck with me for another fourteen days.

My lips turn up in response, and my body is a buoyant mess of lightness. After I've stared at him with my teeth exposed for so long I'm worried it might have become threatening, I take a risk and come up to stand beside him at the desk, handing over the folder on Villa Medici.

He doesn't scoot away.

I look at my feet while he reads, very aware of the sounds of our breathing, the humming noise he makes occasionally.

"This is brilliant," he says, closing the folder and turning his chair towards mine. "How did you even–"

"It was all Mnemosine," I interject. "You named her well."

He lets out a slow exhale. "You have no idea."

"Well, you still have a couple of weeks to tell me."

Lorenzo coughs and looks away, his eyes settling on the folder which he opens again. "Yeah, maybe."

"So, when do we hit up the Medici Villa?" I ask, changing the subject. Mnemosine's origin story must comprise some harrowing, unspeakable event that renders even the most stoic of tall, dark detectives super awkward.

Lorenzo stands and grabs another chair, putting it beside his at the desk. We review the information I've already gathered, make some calls to the French Academy in Rome, and plan our trip to the Pincian Hill. Our elbows touch, and no one scowls. I grin at him when he says he's never read such an interesting, detailed history about the site of the Vatican as the one I've put together, and instead of his face paling or twisting like someone has just latched electrified nipple clamps onto his chest, he even smiles back a little.

Lil is a wicked genius. Two weeks. An endpoint.

All Lorenzo and I needed as a buffer was to know that I am really, actually leaving. Two weeks is not long enough to pursue anything between us—not that that's where his head is, but now mine doesn't need to be there either. And it allows us to work out some more details of the case without the whole time being filled with packing and souvenir shopping.

Two weeks is magic.

Lorenzo preorders tickets for a tour of the villa—we will go tomorrow afternoon—and rubs his broad hands on his thighs, the shape of which I can make out perfectly under his tight jeans. I don't look away. I'm leaving in two weeks.

"Next," he says, "we should talk about Sicily."

"Right." Sicily, where, according to Lil, Lorenzo is supposed to be in a handful of days for his sister's spring wedding. I wonder what babysitter he has lined up for me. I wouldn't mind spending a few days with Dr. Hill, for purely educational purposes.

I'll probably get some underling from the police station though. Which is fine, as long as they don't end up being a turncoat working for the Zalśar like old Alberto.

"I need to be in Sicily by Thursday," Lorenzo says, chewing his lip, "so I was thinking a direct flight from Rome to Catania would be best. A train would be good for sightseeing, but you lose a lot of time." I imagine Lorenzo gazing out the window of a blue striped Trenitalia passenger car as the Italian countryside whirs by.

"It's a shame to miss the Strait of Messina, though," he adds, looking at me.

I shake my head. "Odysseus would disagree with you." Two weeks does not include time for Lorenzo to fight his way through Scylla and Charybdis.

"Airport then, and rental car. Or train? To Nunziata."

Nunziata must be where the wedding is, where Lorenzo is from. I wonder what kind of place breeds men like Lorenzo. "Train," I answer. "Someone will lend you a car if you need it."

"Good point." He takes a deep breath then mutters "*facciamalo.*" *Let's do this.*

His leg is bouncing, which it never does, and he seems a little tense as he opens up a new window in the browser and starts searching for airline tickets. Mnemosine picks up on it too and jumps into his lap. I am strong and do not pet her.

He starts to nibble at a fingernail, and now he's making me nervous.

"Everything okay?" I ask.

He looks at me, tries for a smile. Are his ears pink? "I haven't been home in over a year," he says.

"Do you miss it?"

His smile falls away. "I do. Every day."

Ouch, my fragile little heart wants very badly to hug him. Hugs might be reserved for my last seven days here, though. Two weeks is not enough of a cushion for the level of bodily contact hugging would precipitate.

He turns back to the monitor. "Late morning okay?"

"Sure." I shrug. I'm just going to be stuck here anyway, thinking about how warm I felt inside when Lorenzo had me help him plan his trip to see his family, imagining what they look like, who he is with them.

He gets to the checkout screen. "I need your passport," he says, filling in little Italian boxes of information.

I squint at the screen, blink, then glance at Lorenzo, the quiet upward curve of his lips. I press my palms into my eyes and rub, then check the computer again. Apparently, we are *both* going to Sicily.

For all I know, I'm floating when I go to the bedroom to find my passport and fumble through my luggage. My heart is as flustered as I am and skips in irregular beats in my chest, making everything feel swoopy and sideways. Lorenzo wants to take me to Sicily. Or maybe he has to, but either way.

If I go to Sicily, I get to meet his family. I want to meet his family. I shouldn't, but I do. The thought of seeing where Lorenzo comes from, the world he grew up in, is too good. He's spoken little about his father and said even less about Sicily, his mother, siblings, and grandparents. There is a whole person inside him I've never met.

But why the hell would he bring me to his sister's wedding?

I pass the little blue book to him with trembling fingers, sliding my chair closer to his when I sit back down.

His eyes pause on my picture, his pointer finger resting against my signature messy bun. I was nineteen when I got my new passport and was disappointed that my photo looked so much like the one I got for my Italy trip when I was fourteen. I did most of my physical maturing in my early 20s; before that, it was the same baby-faced soft cheeks and big eyes for years.

Lorenzo's breathing does something funny.

"What?" I ask. He's seen the picture before. He had custody of my passport until I was cleared. Maybe now that he has the passport in his hands, he's having second thoughts.

"You look just like..."

I raise my eyebrows, willing him on.

He lets out a tight laugh and then hands me the passport. "Will you read me the expiration date?"

I read it to him.

He thanks me and clicks a button.

Confirmed. Two tickets for passengers Lorenzo Rossi and Remy Elizabeth Campbell. I steady myself, white knuckles gripping the desk.

What will his family think when he shows up with that American girl who accidentally helped some asshole steal an amulet from the Vatican Museums?

I start to sweat as another thought comes railing into my gut, and I feel my face contort.

Ugh. Is Valeria going to be there?

"Remy." The flare of Lorenzo's touch on my arm and the heat where his fingers make contact causes me to almost jump out of my skin. His forehead is creased in concern.

"Yes?" I stammer.

"I'm sorry," he says. "I thought Liliana talked to you about the trip. She told me you'd want to go, but of course, you don't have to come."

"No, I do. I do want to come with you." I temporarily paralyze my speaking parts with these words. Lorenzo's lip twitches. I shake my head and try again. "I want to go to Sicily. I just, I mean, it's your sister's wedding."

"She'll be happy to have you there."

Southern Italian hospitality at its finest. But what about Lorenzo's Italian mother? How will she feel having the woman who has been living with her son in sin—okay, maybe not technically in sin, not outside of my imagination at least, but definitely sleeping in his apartment—crashing her daughter's wedding? I bury my face in my hands.

"The whole family is looking forward to meeting you," he says, and I shiver at the idea of Lorenzo being able to read even a tiny fraction of the thoughts that pass through my mind. Though, in this case, his seemingly clairvoyant response to my inner turmoil makes something tremble against my ribs.

But it doesn't matter that Lorenzo's family is cool with me imposing myself upon them for such an important event if the whole time I'm miserable. I grit my teeth and force myself to ask, peeking at him through my fingers. "Will Valeria be there?"

His brow creases. "No."

"I just thought…"

"Valeria is not coming to the wedding."

I exhale. I laugh, then try to hide it. Valeria probably has some important lawyer-y thing to do. And good riddance. Even Mnemosine gives a satisfied little mew from Lorenzo's lap. Yes, girl, same.

In four days, I'm going to Sicily, where I will meet Lorenzo's entire family and attend his sister's wedding. And it is fine because I am leaving in two weeks.

Lorenzo doesn't need to go into the station, we have nothing to do until tomorrow, and we are speaking and enjoying each other's company without either one of us acting like a nutcase. He announces after an afternoon coffee that he wants to make pasta with cacioricotta in a simple tomato sauce for dinner, but since that's hours away, he has decided he will roll the pasta by hand.

I clap. I should acquire at least one culinary skill during my time in Italy. In the past, I'd been too focused on research, or Lorenzo had seemed too determined to keep us separated for me to pick up any Italian kitchen secrets while he was cooking.

But now, I'm leaving, and that means I can lean over the counter while he creates a little mountain of flour on the marble; I can watch the way his fingers excavate a hole at its center. I can let my mouth hang agape as he works the water and olive oil and salt into the flour with unexpected tenderness.

He runs the back of his hand over his forehead and leaves a streak of semolina behind. I suck my lip between my teeth.

Flour dusted Lorenzo will live in my mental cave of untouchable dreams forever, where I will be able to visit from the safety of my bedroom in a land far, far away.

Lorenzo cuts the dough into pieces. His forearms tighten as he rolls it into strips, his shoulders broad and leaning as his strong hands slice each yellow ribbon of dough into tiny sections.

Then, oh God, he's pressing his fingertips into one of those small, soft pieces of dough, dragging them slowly, firmly back and forth. The piece curls in on itself, a tight, narrow tunnel. It can't take anymore. I'm not sure I can either, but he keeps going. Press, drag, roll, press, drag, roll. No sense of urgency, just a languid, tight sweep of his fingers.

I clasp my hand over my mouth.

He peers down at me, then grabs the next piece. I swear he presses his fingers even harder into the lump of compliant flour, lets them linger there before he pulls it in and over itself. My entire body clenches around the thought of that big hand doing those mean things to that little ball of dough.

I must shudder because he looks at me again. "Want a turn?" he asks in a low voice.

I process his words haltingly. I clear my throat. *A turn to make some pasta*, Remy.

Lorenzo's expression is calm. Just a man, in his kitchen, doing what he loves. I guess it would be nice if I gave him a hand, helped him finish.

Like, in a nonsexual way, of course.

My face goes hot. He's still watching me. Answer the question.

"Yes."

He smiles and places a few pieces of dough in front of me. I pretend to listen to his instructions. I do what he does. I mostly fail. It is hard to roll fresh pasta with shaky hands.

"Next time, we can make anelletti," he says. "It's easier."

I put my hands on my hips and turn to him. "You've got two weeks to make me a pasta rolling expert."

He smirks, and it might be a trick of the light, but his eyes look especially dark. "Two weeks isn't long enough to show you all my tricks." He lifts up his hands in front of his face, wiggles his fingers.

It's official. I'm never going to be able to look at pasta the same way again.

Chapter NINETEEN

The Villa Medici tour Lorenzo booked for us doesn't begin until one forty-five. Since I have a limited number of days left to imprint everything about the city into my bones, I propose we spend the morning being tourists in Rome.

Lorenzo suggests we take the metro to the Barberini stop again to revisit the Triton Fountain. He pulls out a handful of sparkly metal from his pocket, bright, shiny euro coins stamped with miniature versions of Castel del Monte, the Colosseum, and Botticelli's Venus. From the Triton Fountain in Piazza Barberini, we will walk to the Trevi for good measure.

I will toss all the coins into all the fountains.

When we get to the metro stop, there is tape across the entrance and a sign that says "*SCIOPERO*" in bold, red letters. *Strike.*

Lorenzo says he'll grab the car, but I wave the offer off. We have hours ahead of us, it is a gorgeous spring day, and my sandals are worn in enough not to give me blisters.

"Let's just walk," I say, giving my strappy sundress a little twirl. I'm outside. In Rome. My happy place.

Lorenzo looks down the street and then back at me. "Are you sure? Villa Medici is at least three kilometers from here."

"I haven't fully figured out what these kilometer things are yet, but I'm pretty sure you're telling me you are a giant weenie who can't be bothered to walk a single city mile."

"Almost two miles," he corrects.

I open my mouth in feigned horror. "Not. Two. Miles."

"Well, if you're okay with it—"

"Need I remind you that I found my way, all by myself, from Trastevere to the apartment I shared with Cassie—so basically across the entire city—after fleeing a date with a troubled, anti-feminist felon?"

His jaw tightens. "I remember," he grumbles.

"Good," I poke him in the chest. Ow, my poor finger. "Then you know I can handle a couple of miles."

I practically skip as we head northwest, winding through little neighborhoods, across huge streets, past unmarked monuments. I have a general sense of which direction we need to be heading, and Lorenzo lets me wander. He only redirects me once—with a gentle, steady hand between my shoulders—when I get turned around after becoming enraged at the presence of a Burger King across the street from an actual palace.

"You're pretty good at this," Lorenzo tells me as we pop out from a side street on the far side of Quirinal Hill.

"I really am. It is almost like I've been staring at a map of Rome for the past twelve years," I muse out loud.

Lorenzo's steps slow. "What do you mean?"

"Ha, well, funny story." I feel my face flush. "When I was fourteen, I found a map of ancient Rome and hung it on my wall, and it's been there ever since." I gesture at the space around us. "Things are a little different now, but a lot of the big stuff is the same."

"Why Rome?"

"Did I, did I not mention that…" my throat is dry and sticky and resisting—probably because I was a giant weirdo and never told him the truth, and now it's embarrassing. Lorenzo looks like he's worried I might be having a seizure. I force out a laugh and try again.

"I've been to Rome before. I don't know why I didn't tell you. I should have. I'm sorry." I finish with a wince.

"Why are you sorry?"

"You know, bearing false witness, or perjury, or whatever."

"I promise I won't tell the Commissioner." Lorenzo winks.

"Thanks." I smile. "If I get arrested again, my mother might disown me."

"So," Lorenzo says after a quiet minute. His head is tilted toward me. I can feel his gaze on my face, and my cheeks get warm. "How was your first trip to Rome?"

I sigh. "It was magical," I tell him. "I fell head over heels in love."

His eyes widen.

"With the city," I add, pointing at, well, the city. "Thus the map."

"*Oh*," he says.

I stop walking again, an eruption of words I'd kept sealed deep inside rising hot in my throat. "When Eric broke up with me," I hear myself say over the voice in my head, screaming, *Shut up, Remy*. But there are only thirteen days left in Rome, I tell myself. What harm can it do? "I wasn't sure what was next, what I'd do. Lil certainly had some ideas on the matter, and she wasn't wrong. I'd set a lot aside while Eric and I were dating so that we could stay together. Then Cassie was coming to Rome, and I thought…" I swallow. "I thought that if I came back, there was a chance I'd find that again."

"The magic?"

I shrug, fiddle with the strap of my purse. "The love, maybe."

"I understand." Lorenzo's voice is low and close and wraps itself right around my chest.

"You do?" I whisper, tilting my head back to look up at him.

"I came to Rome for the same reason."

He's leaning over me, and somehow our fingertips are touching, just barely, but it feels like little thrums of lightning under my skin.

I wipe something wet off my cheek and look up at the sky—now an ominous, roiling mass of black and silver thunderheads. "When did that happen?" I ask Lorenzo, who has already dropped my fingers and is angling his body into some sort of human umbrella as the ice-cold rain starts to pelt down on our heads.

I reach for his hand again. "Follow me," I shout over a roll of thunder. I start to run, pulling him along with me through a mob of umbrellas. We reach Babington's tearoom just as the sky shakes with a treacherous boom. Lorenzo and I are both dripping wet.

He opens the door for me. "Madam."

I give a soggy curtsy and walk inside. "My English grandmother made me come here on my first trip," I tell Lorenzo as we walk up to the counter. It was the only place she was worried about me seeing in Rome. "I was so afraid of her that I made my teachers add it to our itinerary so I'd be sure to have photos as proof when I got home."

"She sounds lovely," Lorenzo says, smiling.

"Yup, just like my mother."

"I think your mom seems pretty great."

"You are just saying that because you know she adores you."

Lorenzo's cheeks go a little pink. "She adores *you*, Remy. I'm just easier to talk to."

I snort and order us both the Earl Grey and a plate full of shortbread.

When the rain stops, we head back out into the piazza. My dress has dried, but Lorenzo's black V-neck, which he employed in conjunction with his broad shoulders to spare me from the worst of the storm, still sticks to his skin.

He is a walking physiology lesson in muscles.

I am conducting some DaVinci-level artistic observation in anatomy when I skid on a slick patch of black basalt. Lorenzo's hand is around my waist and steadying me before I even realize I'm falling. He sets me down at the base of the Spanish Steps.

"Thanks," I breathe, trying to get my knees to cooperate and keep me upright.

Lorenzo takes a step back and nods his head toward the south end of the piazza. "If we hurry, we can still make it to the Trevi Fountain and back before the tour."

I look down at my sandals. Unless he plans to carry me the whole way—which, gauging by the pull of the cotton across his upper back, he could—there is no way I'm going to hustle my way across a wet Rome in these shoes and survive.

"Maybe later," I say, sticking my rose-colored sandal between us. "I don't think these babies are up for it."

Lorenzo fidgets with his pocket full of coins, then runs a hand through his hair, looking me up and down as if he might just heave me over his shoulder and take off down Via delle Vite with me in his arms after all. "Later," he agrees. I'm just a little disappointed.

Villa Medici is a short walk from Piazza Spagna, just up the stairs and around the corner. The Spanish Steps are still gleaming with moisture, almost iridescent in the sun. Lorenzo offers his arm, and I grip it with both hands for all 138 marble steps—to keep from nearly eating shit again and no other reason.

At the top, we give ourselves a minute to look out over the city. The sun breaks in bursts through the overcast sky and bathes the rooftops of Rome in liquid gold where it breaches the dark clouds. Everything shimmers where the light hits, and the shadows lengthen into dense, tenebrous silhouettes. Our view from the top of the steps is a portrait of the city in chiaroscuro. Lorenzo's eyes glow as he takes it all in.

"There's your magic," he says.

I swallow and look away from him and back toward the gilded domes and sun-drenched palazzi. "Yup."

"I hope," Lorenzo starts to say, then pauses, looking away when I meet his eyes. "I hope that you find what you're looking for. In Rome."

I bite my lip. I shift my purse to my other shoulder. I pick at a broken nail, all before I come out with a shaky, "I better hurry; I've only got thirteen days to find it."

Lorenzo's head bows and he glances at his watch. "We should get going," he says, and I hurry to keep up with him on a much less perilous twenty-first century paved road.

The back of the Villa Medici is visible immediately. The palace is relatively plain on this side, with little embellishment to distinguish it from the other hundreds of palazzi just like it scattered throughout the city. I decide the design is pretty unremarkable and tell Lorenzo as much.

"Just wait, Ms. Campbell," Lorenzo responds with that annoying little sparkle he gets in his eye when he knows he's about to see me eat my words.

There is a military jeep parked on the cobblestone beneath the window nearest the door, where an armed guard waves us by when Lorenzo shows him his badge. We pass through the entrance and make a straight path to the loggia, which opens to the gardens.

As we come out of the gallery, the contrast of light and dark accents the contours of the replica Medici lion statues poised on either side of the central arch—two marble reminders of why we are here. Though it's hard to resist extending our morning game of "regular old tourists" as long as possible. Lorenzo doesn't seem in any rush to let it go, either.

"So?" he asks, leaning his forearms on the marble balustrade beside me.

I shrug. "Not bad."

"Come on." He takes my hand and leads me down the polished, worn stairs and out into the gardens to a red granite obelisk. There are various other statuaries behind it, and past that, a hedge and trees blocking the view of the Borghese gardens on the other side of the wall.

"Ready?" he whispers. He braces me from behind by the shoulders and turns me toward the villa.

The design of the building gives the impression of a fortified castle, with two towers rising from the second story. I've seen it all before when searching online, but the inner facade is a delicate, elaborate collage that the photos I saw did not capture—ancient Roman bas-reliefs interspersed with garlands, medallions, and masks that make it feel more fairy tale than fortress. The Medici coat of arms is displayed above the main arch, claiming ownership of the stories and history that play out on the marble veneer.

From this distance, I can't make out the details in the carved scenes along the wall, but all the same, I feel as if I've been transported two thousand years back in time—like maybe this building with its clay-tiled roof and sculpted white marble exterior somehow drifted from its spot on the Palatine between the Domus Saveriana and the Flavian palace to this much quieter hill on the other side of Rome.

Lorenzo holds a little pamphlet about the villa that he grabbed at the front desk. "It states here that one of the original Medici lions was carved from a capital taken from the Temple of Jupiter Maximus on the Capitoline Hill," he says.

"I wonder how Tarquin the Proud would feel about having one of his columns repurposed into a big cat for the Medici?"

"We do know the Etruscans were fans of lions."

"Fair point," I respond as my gaze sweeps from the villa to the uninterrupted vista beside it. St. Peter's Basilica hovers, golden, in the distance. Behind the row of giant stone Jesus and his apostles that crown the church's roof rises Michelangelo's dome—which from here appears the same color as the clearing sky.

"You're right, not bad," Lorenzo says. He nudges me with his shoulder.

I press my lips together to hold in the contented sigh that fills my throat and nudge him back with my hip, glad we can touch, be close. Happy that we could spend the morning being friends.

I point towards the Vatican. "Remember when you thought I stole an ancient amulet from the museums just past that big church thing?"

"It was all just a ploy for me to get you."

I laugh as my whole body heats.

Lorenzo takes a step away from me. "To get you to work on the case, Remy," he says, looking away from me and waving a hand toward the Villa Medici. "No one at the station would have gotten us here based on the second clue alone."

"I think you said that about San Clemente too, and we know how that turned out."

"I do. We caught Maelle. Or you did. And now that she's talking, we know a lot more about why the Zalśar would have been desperate enough to pull a stunt like sending Alberto to the apartment, why they are willing to take such public risks this year."

"Wait. What did Maelle say? What's going on this year?"

Lorenzo bites his lip, looking a little guilty. And rightfully so, this is stuff he needs to share.

"Maelle told us that this year the Zalśar will add a new member to their council of twelve, something that rarely happens," he says. "Only members of the council can be considered for the position of Zilath. The senior members of the Zalśar have organized this treasure hunt and the clues, and whoever finds the amulet will be granted the position. There are five aspirants, and the Zalśar are divided amongst themselves, each contingent supporting their competitor. Fabio—Lewin—is one of the contenders."

"Do we know who the others are?"

"They were all involved in the theft. Actually, it sounds like their first challenge was to pull it off. There is Stefano Caposanti, who you also met briefly at the villa where Fabio parked. Then a Bastien Dekker we don't know much about."

"The Dekker that Maelle mentioned in the Mithraeum?"

"Same one. Then a Diego Trujillo, who we are pretty sure already left the country. And Maelle. Plus, with what she's told us, I think I can figure out—"

"The first clue—SBLDM. It was their initials!" I interrupt. "And Dekker and Trujillo, they could have been the guards who let us in and out at the Vatican Museum. The one with the crazy eyes and the—objectively speaking—very attractive one."

Lorenzo raises an eyebrow. "Maelle confirmed they were there that day. It's possible."

"Excuse me, did you not think to tell me this extremely important information? I feel like this is the kind of update your sidekick should be privy to."

Lorenzo's cheeks turn a lovely shade of golden pink. "I'd just heard from the station when I was on my way back from the soccer game. I was going to tell you, but then…"

Now I'm blushing too, but whatever color my face has turned, it is not human.

Just then, by the grace of every god ever worshipped in the city, a loud voice announces that the one forty-five tour is about to commence.

Chapter TWENTY

I SPEND THE FIRST TEN MINUTES of the tour waiting for the heat to drain from my face and avoiding any skin-to-skin or eye-to-eye contact with Lorenzo, which is not difficult because he is doing the same.

Luckily, the guide starts with the work of the current French Academy fellows, so I don't miss much—toilet paper sculpture isn't my style, and as I've already established, the whole osculum as orifice thing in *that* sense isn't the Zalśar's, either. The room is beautiful, though, and I try to reconcile the gorgeous Renaissance frescoes and flooring with the incongruous creations of bath tissue shaped like monster-sized internal organs.

I enjoy myself much more when we enter the loggia, the villa's main gallery. The restorations are well done, and to stand there, it feels, I imagine, much as it might have five hundred years ago. Lorenzo and I separate ourselves from the group to look at a detail in the ceiling decoration.

"*Sub cavea leonum, osculum regni est*," Lorenzo repeats the second clue loud enough for only us to hear as we gaze up at the painting.

The fresco is of a woman at the mouth of a small river, a cave opening behind her. The entire loggia is covered in little vignettes like this one. And also portrait after portrait of the

Medicis. My gaze skips from one to the next, my eyes growing wider and wider.

"Lorenzo!" I whisper-shout, pulling my arms back just in time to prevent my hands from taking hold of his biceps. I close my fingers into excited fists instead. "This room could be the den of the lions the clue is talking about." I point to the walls, and he follows my finger to the multiple likenesses of Medici men gracing the hall. "Maybe we don't need the Vatican at all; maybe the clue is right under us." I stomp my foot on the mosaiced marble floor. "Does this place have a basement?"

"Pardon, signori," the guide calls. "We are continuing on to the Stanza degli Uccelli." Lorenzo realizes we are the 'signori' before I do.

"My wife is a bit dizzy," he says, wrapping an arm around my shoulders. "We will catch up in a moment." Lorenzo's words cause an actual sweep of vertigo, and I lean into him. The tour guide nods and leads the others off down another beautiful hallway.

"There was the fountain at the base of the loggia stairs," I say when the voice of the tour guide has receded. Lorenzo drops his arm from my back. "A fountain is a mouthpiece for water, so *osculum* makes sense."

"Yes," Lorenzo says. "People would have originally approached the villa from the gardens and been greeted by the fountain before entering the palace. *Osculum regni*, the mouthpiece of the kingdom."

"There was a statue of Mercury on top, right?" I ask, watching Lorenzo's fingers idle on his mouthpiece as he thinks.

"Mercury also had an Etruscan counterpart called Turms," he says as I drag my eyes back to his. "He was the messenger between gods and men."

I cross my arms and give Lorenzo a once-over. "Someone has been doing his homework."

His mouth twitches up at the corner. "But why Mercury?" Lorenzo asks. We both spend some time chewing the inside of our cheeks.

"This might be a stretch," I say, "but it seems like the Zalśar aren't huge fans of the Papacy outside of the Medici popes. The Pope moved the *Lion Attacking a Horse* statue from an important spot on the Capitoline, remember? They put the bronze she-wolf there instead, and then the Marcus Aurelius bronze. The Vatican did a lot to honor the Roman tradition of the city but gave no recognition to the Etruscan origins or contributions. And the Zalśar are not down with that."

"They are not," Lorenzo confirms, but his face looks as unsure as I am about where I am going with this.

"Have you ever walked through the Raphael Rooms at the Vatican?" I ask him.

"I have."

"Okay, do you remember the Hall of Constantine?"

"Did you go there with Fabio?"

"What? No. We never made it past the Museo Gregoriano Etrusco." I rub a hand over my belly. "But I did visit my first time in Rome. There was one fresco in particular that always bothered me."

"Is that so?"

I nod. "Fourteen-year-old Remy has still not recovered from Laureti's *The Victory of Christianity Over Paganism*." I remember straining my neck to stare up at poor Mercury, all dismembered on the floor. "The ceiling felt so mean."

Lorenzo looks like he might be biting down on a smile. I narrow my eyes at him. "It's not funny."

"Not at all," he says, and now even his eyes seem like they might be grinning.

I flick him on the shoulder. "Pay attention."

"Yes, Ms. Campbell." I shake off my shiver at the note of coy submission in his voice.

"What if," I say, leaning toward him, "Mercury is another symbol the Medici used, like the lion, to celebrate their Etruscan roots? The Mercury on the fountain would let everyone know they weren't a part of the Papacy's Rome, that they belonged to a different tradition."

"It's possible," Lorenzo says, running a hand over his dark stubble, thinking. He looks up at me. "There was a grate under the fountain."

"Well, why aren't we out there seeing if we can get it open?"

Lorenzo scans the tour program. "Let's do it. We can be back inside by the time the guide gets to the Medici Apartments."

We slip out of the loggia and past the fake Medici lions to the fountain. Below the flying Mercury, on the front of the fountain's base, is a large iron grate—that we definitely can't get open.

"Shit," I pout.

"I'll put a call into the station, but it is always complicated getting search warrants for historic and protected sites. We are looking at a few days at least."

My shoulders slump.

"Let's go," Lorenzo says, giving my fingers a little squeeze. "We can catch the end of the tour, see if anything else comes up."

*

My phone rings right as we reconnect with the tour group. The sharp sound ricochets off the plaster walls of the palace's residence wing, making me cringe.

"Sorry," I mumble, scrambling to silence the call. It's Eric.

With an uncomfortable twist in my chest, I realize that it will be incredibly annoying living with someone again who wakes up so early every day—in Phoenix, it's not even six in the morning. Chances are, Eric is already on his way home from the gym.

"Do you need to get that?" Lorenzo whispers close to my ear.

"No."

Lorenzo bites his lip, and we follow the group into one of the historic apartments. The furniture is simple, and there is a baby grand piano in the corner. I'm admiring how the light from the single sunken window illuminates the frescoes running along the top border of the walls when my phone rings again. I turn off the ringer and shove it in my purse.

Then it starts to buzz, and I ignore it, but the droning becomes incessant.

"Your phone is still ringing, Remy," Lorenzo says.

"Yep," I respond and then go back to listening to the tour guide's story of how Galileo—another notable recipient of Medici patronage—once stayed in that very room before being sentenced to house arrest in Florence for undermining the Papacy.

"It might be important," Lorenzo says, eyeing my vibrating purse.

I scowl. Eric probably has a question about my preference for moss green or sea green accents in the guest bathroom, but five calls about a design impasse is pretty excessive, even for him. Maybe Eric *is* calling about more than the color of soap dispensers. I pull my phone back out of my bag and sigh.

"You keep going," I order Lorenzo. "We don't want to miss anything important."

He puts his hands in his pockets, sparing one wary glance at my phone before heading toward the door with the rest of the group. He waves at me from the other side of the room and is the last to leave, shutting the door behind him.

I am all alone in Galileo's old room—possibly one of the few places nicer than apartment 3A, where I spent my first two weeks in Rome, to ever be used as a holding cell. I got Lorenzo's carbonara and Mnemosine cuddles, though, so I might still win.

My phone rings again—call six. I answer.

"What's wrong?" I ask, more irked by Eric's relentless dialing than I am worried.

"Hey, babe. What's up?" he answers.

"I'm busy. Is there a problem, or can this conversation wait?"

"Can't a guy want to talk to his girlfriend?"

I grimace. "We decided no titles until I got home, Eric. I wanted to take it slow, remember?"

"R.C., you're moving in with me in like ten days. I'm pretty sure that makes you my girlfriend," his voice is light and flirty and obnoxious.

"Thirteen days," I correct, and my throat feels scratchy.

"You're so cute," Eric says, misinterpreting the emotion in my voice. "It will fly by. And then I'll get my girlfriend in our bedroom. We can pick up where we left off on the phone."

"Didn't I just ask you not to call me that," I groan.

He laughs. "There is something else I'd like to call you."

I'm sure there is. I have a list of choice words I'd like to call him right now, too. "Let me have it," I say.

"How does 'wife' sound?"

My heart stops beating for a dangerously long time, and when it picks up again, there is nothing but dread cascading through my bloodstream. Probably not the reaction Eric was hoping for.

"Eric, Jesus," I snap. "I told you I'm right in the middle of something. This is a big deal, okay? Not everything is about you, or us, or the bathmats."

"I know," he says, and his voice is flat and cold. "It is all about Rome."

"Right now, yes."

"Always has been."

"What the hell is that supposed to mean?"

"Nevermind, Remy."

"I don't know what you're getting at," I say.

"I think we can both agree that I've been pretty patient while you are over there having your little quarter-life crisis."

"What the fuck, Eric? If you recall, I'm over here because of *your* quarter-life crisis. You're the one who called off our engagement."

He lets out a long, shaky breath. "Sorry," he says. "I just really miss you."

That takes enough of the fight out of me for me to respond at a normal volume. "We will talk soon, okay?"

"Yeah, sure, Rems."

"Bye, Eric."

He hangs up first.

If I didn't think it would echo through the entire villa, I would be screaming.

Eric was the one who broke my heart all those months ago. He left me. Now, he could at least give me the courtesy of allowing me some time to get myself back in the game. Give me some space to find myself in the world of "us" again. Can't he just wait for me to get back before trying to force us into something like freaking marriage? We aren't even officially a couple again.

I want these last thirteen days in Rome for myself.

And then I'll be back in Phoenix, and we can go back to normal just like nothing ever happened.

Thirteen days is barely anything.

Thirteen days will be over before I know it. It will all be over.

A sob lodges in my throat and hot tears spill down my cheeks.

I lie on the bed against the back wall and stare up at the coffered wooden ceiling with blurry eyes. I am going home to live with Eric, but I get nauseous every time he calls me his girlfriend. Not good.

My other options include moving back in with Lil, or if she won't have me, with my parents—which none of us want to see happen. But regardless, I have to go back. I need a job. I need to figure out what I'm doing with my life. I can't just stay here forever. Eventually, my tourist visa will expire, and Lorenzo will have to deport me.

I wipe my eyes on the back of my arm and focus on the patterns in the wood above me as my breathing steadies.

"Huh," I say out loud when I see what appears to be a very tiny M carved into a corner. I prop myself up onto my elbows and keep looking. I find an S, a B, a D, and finally an L. The five aspirants all accounted for.

I stand up and track them around the room in the same order they were listed on that little piece of paper that I stole from Fabio— SBLDM—and end up near the window. I search around the frame but find nothing. Then I do it in reverse and end up back at the bed.

I peek underneath—not even a dust bunny hiding out down there.

I lift the super heavy mattress and let it fall on my back as I crawl onto the bed frame, considering for only a moment how strange I would look if someone walked in. The fingers on my right hand find something hard, and I stretch further to get a hold of whatever it is. I manage to wiggle the object out from under the mattress and into the light—a thin, palm-sized, leather-bound journal. I flip through, and the whole thing is filled with numbers written as Roman numerals. A couple of pages are dog-eared, but I can find no notes in the margins or little stars or highlights that indicate why.

Row after row of Is, and Xs and Ls following no particular order, but there must be hundreds.

I'm about to shove it back under the mattress when I notice a small seal, just as big as a euro 50 cent piece, in the corner of the journal's cover. My skin tingles as I run my finger over the tiny fasces imprinted in the leather.

I recognize the symbol from one of the Etruscan Civilization books in the university's library. There was an entire chapter on Etruscan imagery integrated into other cultures. The motif of the fasces—a bundle of twelve rods wrapped around an ax—originally represented the twelve cities that constituted the Etruscan League.

I hug the journal to my chest. Perhaps it is just a coincidence that I excavated a fasces stamped diary filled with Roman numerals from under a mattress in a Medici bedroom that has every single one of the letters from the first clue etched into the ceiling. But the way my pulse thrums in my ears makes me doubt that.

With the journal stuffed inside my shoulder bag, I remake the bed before running out of the room to look for Lorenzo. It takes all my power not to yell in excitement when I find him on a stone bench near the exit, but I do start bouncing in place.

"You look happy," he says. The corners of his mouth turn down as he takes in my obvious enthusiasm.

"I *am* happy," I confirm, checking the hall to make sure we're alone. "I have to show you something." I dig into my bag.

"The ring?" he asks.

"A ring?" I repeat, my hand freezing around a chapstick.

Lorenzo looks like he swallowed a fly. "Wasn't that Eric?"

"On the phone? Yeah, but that is *not* what I am happy about." I shudder as I think back on my conversation with Eric. "Look," I say, holding the leather journal up just enough inside my bag for him to see the seal of the fasces. He has to lean toward me to see it, and I would be lying if I said I didn't give my chest a little squeeze to make sure my quarter-life cleavage is part of the view.

I know it works because it takes Lorenzo much longer than it usually would to process what I'm showing him—the journal, not the boobs. Those he seems to notice right away.

He clears his throat. "Do I get to see more of what's in there?"

That's a loaded question. "Numbers. Lots of Roman ones," I rasp, not at all articulately. "And the room had the letters carved on the ceiling, Lorenzo. All the letters from the first clue. That's how I found the—"

"Excuse me," an urgent voice interrupts. We both turn to see a stout man in a fancy striped jacket hurrying toward us. He stops in front of me. "Signora Campbell?" he asks.

"Um," I mumble and glance at Lorenzo. My eyes go wide. He has physically transformed into the archetypal warrior on every piece of red-figure pottery from the ancient world, ready to javelin the shit out of the little man in front of me. "Maybe?"

The stranger brushes off my confusion and hands me a letter. "A guest left this here for you. I know nothing else," he sniffs, "so don't bother asking."

I take the letter, and the man bustles back out the way he came.

The envelope is addressed to Miss Remy Campbell, my name written in a flourish, probably by fountain pen. I know who the letter is from before I even open it. The stationary is just as pretentious as the man who left it for me. Lorenzo steps closer.

I groan.

Fabio beat us to the villa.

Chapter TWENTY-ONE

WHEN I OPEN THE ENVELOPE, a pile of photos falls onto the ground. They all appear to be taken from outside the large, arched windows of Lorenzo's apartment. We study them together. Me eating. Me staring adoringly at Lorenzo while he's working. Lorenzo staring adoringly at me? Wait, that can't be right. I lift the photos closer to my face, but Lorenzo is already trying to hustle me out of Villa Medici, one hand gripping my upper arm. His fingers are wrapped around the bare skin above my elbow, and the effect of his touch—verging on the side of aggressively protective—does exciting things to my insides and makes Fabio's irritating epistle almost worth it.

As we come out of the door, I notice a massive red granite fountain across the cobbled street. The basin is at least thirteen feet across and is framed on either side by ancient oak trees. In the distance, behind the fountain, rises the dome of St. Peter's.

"Lorenzo," I gasp, wresting my arm out of his grasp to point. "What if that's the osculum?"

He doesn't even look at the fountain. Instead, his eyes scan the street, behind us, above us, his hands drawing me in close by the waist. "The amulet isn't important," he says, checking his phone and then returning his fingers to my side. "The only thing that matters right now is keeping you safe."

"Fabio isn't here anymore, and if he is, it isn't like he's going to try something." I turn in the circle of Lorenzo's hands and look into his face. "Besides, I've got you looking out for me."

Lorenzo swallows. His hands release from my hips, and he drops them to his sides. Not what I was going for, but I press on. "Finding the amulet is important. It's important to me," my throat feels tight, and I blink down at the sidewalk. I need this victory for so many reasons—one being that I want to see Lorenzo win.

Lorenzo reaches for my chin and lifts my face to his. "We will find the amulet, Remy. But for now, we need to regroup somewhere secure and away from the Zalśar. Somewhere Lewin can't find you." He growls the name.

"Where will we go?" I ask, hoping I don't sound too breathy. All these "we's" he's dropping are triggering irregular heartbeats.

"Home," he answers, and my pulse goes haywire, but not in the sweet, swooping sort of way. Is Lorenzo sending me back to Phoenix? There is no we in Phoenix.

I will hunt down Fabio and make him eat the amulet for this alone.

My mouth is still too dry to demand an explanation when a shiny blue car with red, white, and green stripes running along the sides pulls up in front of us. Lorenzo helps me into the back. I figure he will shut me in like he did when he first took me into custody and take the front seat, but he squeezes in beside me.

I turn and stare at his profile as he speaks to the officer in the driver's seat in rapid-fire Italian that I can't piece together. He pulls his phone out and starts making calls as soon as the car is moving.

I muster my courage and tap him on the shoulder. Maybe I

misunderstood. "Home?" I mouth, and he nods before turning to the front and carrying on with his phone call.

I sink into the chair, watching Rome zip by outside the window before digging Fabio's letter out of my purse.

Dearest Miss Campbell,

To say choosing you to accompany me to the Vatican Museums was a mistake would be an understatement. If only you'd proven to be as dumb and desperate as you were with me at the bar, this would all be so simple.

But alas, your obnoxious persistence is starting to get on my nerves. I recommend you remove yourself from the case before I find a way to make it happen myself.

Or perhaps you're trying to get my attention.

Well, you have it.

If you choose to reconsider your allegiances, we can discover the mouth of the kingdom together. Though I'm not sure a girl like you is up for playing with lions, I have found the combination of ingenuousness and ingenuity you possess to be rather intriguing.

The detective must agree.

He's quite the knight, I admit, but I promise I am a superb example of what seven generations of kings can offer. And remember, signorina, knights provide protection while you sleep, but that doesn't mean there aren't still lions prowling in the garden.

Until we meet again,

Lewin Bumgartner

I scan the words one more time, a flicker of hope coming alive inside my chest once the urge to dry-heave at Fabio's disturbing come-on passes. He manages to be equal parts offensive, unsettling, and, conveniently for me, indiscreet in his invective: as of the writing of this letter, Fabio had not found the third clue. This means Lorenzo and I still have a chance to beat the Zalśar at their own game.

The same Lorenzo who, according to Fabio, must find me intriguing—hopefully enough so that I can convince him not to send me home.

I take a deep breath and steel myself. I'm pretty sure Lorenzo has no grounds on which he can force me out of his country legally. Out of his apartment, sure, but I can figure that out later. I am staying, and before I leave, I will make sure I have one particular lion begging at my feet.

I grab Lorenzo's hand. He looks at me, surprised, but doesn't pull away. He lowers his phone from his ear.

"I am staying here," I tell him. Trying to channel all of my inner fire and supposed intrigue into my eyes, I pin him with my gaze. *You can't make me go*, I tell him. *Don't even try*.

His phone chimes, and he cowers into his shoulders.

My brows tighten. "What was that email?" I ask.

"I—I'm sorry, Remy. It will be safer, quieter. I think it is for the best," he says. "But I can't make you do anything you don't want to do."

"You can't?"

"I mean, I don't want to force you to leave, but we need to consider your safety."

"How long do I have?" I ask, taking his phone from his hand. The email notification subject reads *Flight update notification*. Below that, all I see is a departure date—tomorrow.

"What the heck, Lorenzo?" I cry so loudly that the driver whips his head around to look at us. I ignore him. "I was already going to be leaving in thirteen days; now I don't even get that time."

Lorenzo looks devastated. "I wish you could spend all of that time in Rome, enjoying it, not dealing with this case. I wish I had time to show you everything, Remy." He bites his lip, leans his face toward mine, just close enough for me to feel his breath on my cheek. Good thing I hate him now, or this would be risky. I'm glaring at his mouth when he continues. "And I know that being stuck in Nunziata for an entire week when you have so few days left in Italy will be awful, but right now, I don't know how else to keep you protected."

His home. We are going to Lorenzo's home. Early, before the wedding. I am going to spend an entire week with Lorenzo's family. That's four more days than we'd planned to be there. My hands should not tingle. My body should not feel all warm and gooey. But they do, and it does.

"Nunziata?" I ask, pressing my nails into my palms to make sure I'm not in the middle of a very vivid dream fantasy sequence that involves cop cars and Lorenzo's birthplace.

"Yes," he says, his gaze flicking between my eyes.

I lean my head back on my seat. I laugh. Lucky for Lorenzo, these police car seatbelts are super constricting, and I'd never be able to get my arms around his shoulders or my legs across his lap if I flung myself at him the way I want to right now. But I can imagine.

Lorenzo relaxes somewhat beside me. "You're not mad?"

I smile up at the ceiling of the car. "No, I'm not mad about a week in Sicily." His mouth turns up at the corner. "But next time," I add, "maybe lead with that."

When we get back to Lorenzo's apartment, we are greeted by a very displeased Mnemosine and the smell of expensive perfume. Lorenzo's hand stills on the door handle. Then he sighs. Valeria comes around the corner from the kitchen with her hands on her silk-pantsed hips.

All of my well-dressed Roman ghosts are coming out to haunt me today.

"Hi, Valeria," I say.

"Remy," she answers with a curt nod. I can't blame her. I spend a ludicrous amount of time with her boyfriend and an inappropriate amount of that time thinking about him in unmentionable ways.

Plus, I'm going with him to his sister's wedding. And she is not.

"Excuse us a moment," Lorenzo says, getting all up in Valeria's space and backing her into the kitchen without so much as a glance back in my direction.

I grab the cat and all but run for my bedroom. I've learned my lesson about walking in on those two. I do not need to witness their steamy reunion. I start packing, ignoring the ache behind my ribs.

Sooner than I could have hoped—and in far less time than is required for even a quickie on the kitchen counter—there is a knock on my door. I nearly trip over myself in relief as I rush to open it.

"Valeria is going to head out soon," Lorenzo says.

"She is?" I ask.

"But she needs your help with something first."

I narrow my eyes at him. "She what?"

Lorenzo shrugs and chews his lip. "She told me she had a women's issue and asked if I could send you in."

I straighten my back and grin. I've got this. Homegirl just needs me to loan her a super plus, and then we can go on pretending we don't hate each other. "Where is she?" I ask, smiling at Lorenzo as he fidgets with the hem of his t-shirt.

When he gestures toward his bedroom, the tight cotton slides up along his abdomen, and a strip of hard, golden-brown skin taunts me as I slip past him and to the room with his bed in it, that I've never been on, to talk to his make out partner, who definitely has.

"What's up?" I ask Valeria as I come into the room and get a lungful of Lorenzo. I've walked past his door a thousand times but never breached the threshold. The bed is, of course, heavy, solid wood. But the bedding is light—rumpled, cream-colored linen sheets under an ivory cotton slub duvet. The bedside tables are covered in books, mostly about the Etruscans. One, though, says simply ARIZONA on the spine. My heart leaps into my throat.

"Shut the door," Valeria says from a sleek leather chair in the corner.

I do as she asks and stand in front of her, nervous that I might burst into flames if I chance sitting on the bed.

She looks me over and nods. "Well, it's obvious you've never made it into the bedroom before. Thank you for taking some of what I said to heart, at least."

I shift my feet. "You're welcome."

Valeria looks at her pretty red nails. "How does your boyfriend feel about you going to meet Lorenzo's family?"

The question catches me off guard. I turn away. Admitting I haven't told Eric yet does not seem like it fits well with Valeria's agenda, but neither does arguing that Eric is technically *not* my boyfriend. So I lie, sort of. "He didn't have much to say about it."

"He's going to be okay after you leave him, Remy."

"Eric?"

Valeria's brow wrinkles. "Lorenzo."

"I know."

"He's not yours. He is not your plaything. Please, remember that."

"I know," I say again, but my voice is louder, tighter.

"Good," she murmurs and stands up.

"Do you need a tampon or something?" I ask.

She blinks at me.

"Lorenzo said you had a women's issue," I clarify.

"And you assumed that implied menstruation?"

"Well....yes."

She waves a hand toward me. "You are the issue, Remy."

"I see that now."

She falls back into the chair and exhales, pressing her fingers to her brow. Vulnerable Valeria makes me extra uncomfortable. "Are you all right?" I ask.

"I'm worried about him," she says, looking at the wall like she can see right through it to wherever Lorenzo is twisting his shirt in his fingers.

I crouch in front of her. If Lorenzo were mine, I wouldn't love any of this either. "You have nothing to be worried about. Since you left the last time, Lorenzo and I have barely made eye contact." Today notwithstanding. "We haven't even been within touching distance for the last two weeks." Except for all of the times he swooped in to save me before and after the villa—arms around my shoulders, hands on my waist. Not important. "You guys are good," I tell her.

And I mean it. I don't want to be that asshole. My Lorenzo fantasies will continue to exist in the confines of my mind and whatever hapless nerves and hormones connect to that particular region of my brain.

She bows her head, shakes it. "You don't understand."

"Maybe I do, a little bit?"

She raises her face so our eyes are level. "You don't," she snaps. "He's spent so much of his life reaching for this impossible idea, searching for something that doesn't exist. And if you do anything to make things worse for him, you will regret it. I can promise you that."

She's not wrong. I would never forgive myself if I screwed up Lorenzo's life. "Got it."

Valeria huffs out of the chair and runs her hands over her cashmere tank top. She's beautiful, even when she scowls at me before exiting the room without another word. I scramble up to standing and hurry out the door behind her, not wanting to loiter in Lorenzo's bedroom.

After our talk, Valeria changes her mind about leaving and sequesters Lorenzo in the dining room after dinner. I fail to ignore the deep, thundery edge of Lorenzo's voice as I lay in bed that night. I try harder than I should to make out Valeria's saccharine responses.

Twelve more days in Italy suddenly feels like a dangerously long time.

Chapter TWENTY-TWO

ONCE VALERIA HAS LEFT THE APARTMENT and Lorenzo has gone to bed, I call Eric to tell him about Sicily. Our conversation goes about as well as my chat with Valeria. I was not anticipating the news would make him so crabby—maybe *he's* the one on his period.

"You are going with this detective to his home? For a wedding? Doesn't that seem a little unprofessional to you?" Eric argues for the third time since we started talking.

Yes, very unprofessional. And I'm thrilled. "It is his literal job to protect me, and since he has to be in Sicily for the wedding, and things are getting weird in Rome, I have to go with him."

"There must be someone else who can babysit you while he's away."

I force myself to take a deep breath. It only aids in making me sound like an unfeeling sociopath when I respond. "I thought you'd be happy I was leaving Rome. You've always been so jealous of how much I love it."

"Fuck Rome. I want to know if it's the detective I should be jealous of," he sneers.

"The detective's name is Lorenzo," I say. "And don't forget, Eric, I'm not the one who broke things off between us."

"How many times do I have to tell you I fucked up? I'm sorry."

"So many times."

He sighs, and it echoes between us. "At least you called this a relationship," he murmurs.

A gross error on my part, but I don't need to kick him when we are both down. "I'll be home in twelve days and desperate for Mexican food. Want to take me out for a margarita and an obscene number of tacos when I get in?"

"Sure." His response is dry and sour sounding. Whatever. I tried.

Lorenzo and I leave early the following day, and our twelve euro, last-minute tickets get us from Rome to Catania in under an hour and a half. Next: a train to Mascali and a quick cab ride from there to Nunziata—which will give us some time to flip through the fasces-stamped journal I still have in my purse and pretend that we are cryptologists who know how to read Roman Numerals.

As we come out into baggage claim, a beautiful woman with bounding black waves and a dark pink mouth shouts, "Lollu!" Lorenzo smiles—in the big, cute, teethy way—and lifts his hand to wave at her.

We aren't even in Nunziata yet, and already we are being besieged by the Lorenzo Rossi fan club mere hours after another slap on the wrist from Valeria. Worst of all, he seems thrilled to be running into this particular member.

"She looks nice," I mumble.

"Don't be fooled. She is nothing but trouble," Lorenzo answers, but he's grinning. Then he's stooping and lifting and swinging her around, and I'm looking for the nearest bar.

"*Fratellino*," she laughs, hitting him on the shoulder and at once becoming one of my favorite humans. "*Mettimi giú.*" *Put me down, little brother.*

I smile as she steadies herself in front of Lorenzo and realize I'm shaking in my sandals. She has his same lashes and lips, but where his hair is dark brown, hers is the color of ink—though just as thick and amazing, and her eyes are storm-cloud gray. She catches her breath and looks at me.

"*Benvenuta,* Remy," she says, eyes sparkling. She pulls me into a hug, and I squeak a ciao as her arms tighten around me. *Keep it casual,* I tell myself. It isn't like I am here so he can introduce me to his family, so we can all get to know each other and prod into each other's pasts or make plans for Christmas while his mother laments her lack of grandchildren.

I can imagine what that would feel like, though.

"I'm Mary," she says into my hair, "and I am so happy my brother brought you home to us." And oh no, an embarrassing number of tears manifest behind my eyelids. My only response is a strangled grunt of emotion.

She holds me a little tighter, gives me a chance to blink away the wetness before letting me go. It shouldn't matter. It doesn't, really. But this is not the awesome, super-not-crazy first impression I would have liked to make.

Yesterday, between the Villa Medici and Valeria, my body discharged a Vesuvian apocalypse worth of adrenaline, and it rocked my mental bedrock. Thus my inelegant disintegration into a blubbering, gooey mess inside the reach of Mary's arms. The fact that Lorenzo's sister gives the best hugs and I only have a single week of my life to elicit as many of them as I can, has nothing to do with my questionable emotional reaction.

Or that is what I tell myself.

We collect our bags from the carousel and head for the parking garage. "Thank you so much for picking us up," I manage after a lot of sniffing and swallowing and a couple of concerned looks from Lorenzo.

"Lollu hasn't been back in so long I was worried he wouldn't find his way home," she says, jabbing an elbow into Lorenzo's side. "And I was desperate to meet you after everything he's told us. The pleasure is all mine." She smirks at her brother.

My pulse quickens, and Lorenzo's lip curves over his teeth like he might go feral on her. Mary's smile widens; clearly, she is unfazed.

"We can drop Remy off at the hotel first so she can rest, and you can take me to the house," Lorenzo tells Mary as he puts our bags in the trunk.

"What hotel?" she chuckles. I look at Lorenzo. He won't meet my eye.

"Remy is staying with the other guests, right?"

"Are you kidding? Mamma made up your and Tano's old room extra special as soon as she heard you were bringing her."

Lorenzo's face pales. "*O dio*, Mary," he says, running a hand through his hair. His eyes flick toward me, then back to her. "*Non é cosi.*" *It's not like that.*

"Talk to Mamma about it. There's no hotel room."

Lorenzo takes me by the shoulders, bends his face down, so we are eye to eye, mouths just inches apart. He looks panicked, and inside I'm screaming too, but in an inappropriately excited way. "I'll figure it out, Remy. I'm sure there is still something available in town. If not, then by the beach."

"Lorenzo," I say, resting my hand on his arm. "We've been sharing an apartment for weeks. We can manage a few nights in the same room." I ignore the way my insides flutter at the thought, trying not to notice the warmth of his skin under my fingertips. "Okay?"

All right, so maybe Valeria has a valid reason to hate my

guts. But I know we can make this work—as friends. What's the difference between sleeping twenty feet apart versus three.

He shifts his feet, and I try not to be offended by the way he grimaces when he says, "*Va bene.*"

Mary watches the entire exchange with a grin on her face, then slaps her baby brother on the shoulder. "Ah, Lollu, é troppo bello averti di nuovo a casa." *It's really great to have you home*, she tells him

As Mary drives us north along the coast to Nunziata, I watch the horizon alternate between the deep azure of the Ionian Sea and the green and golden ribbons of vines that have been twining along the Sicilian hillsides for millennia. Life is good. The Zalśar, Fabio, and Valeria are hundreds of miles away. It is the middle of the night in Phoenix, and Eric hasn't bothered me yet.

I'm in Mary Rossi's car, wondering which sphere of Dante's *Paradiso* looks like the interior of a Citroen C3. And Lorenzo is in the back seat laughing at something his sister said.

The sound is so sweet it sets goosebumps on my arms, and I glance back at him. He's sprawled out, arms spread along the backs of the seats. His legs are wide, and I think it would be very nice to crawl between them. Lorenzo's lips turn up, and the corners of his eyes crinkle as he watches me watch him.

Non-detective, Sicilian Lorenzo is relaxed and cool and makes my blood hot in a whole new way.

Frick.

I stash the moment away in my Lorenzo vault of reveries and force myself to keep my eyes forward for the rest of the ride.

When we get to Nunziata, Lorenzo and I hop out of the car under his mother's apartment building—a faded red–plaster, two-story palazzo on a narrow one-way street where Lorenzo spent his childhood. Mary hugs me again and kisses my cheeks before taking off to meet all her female relatives at the hairdresser for the wedding hair trial. She invited me to come, but I declined.

I'm tired from the trip, but I'm also not here to spend time alone with Lorenzo's family. Insinuate myself into their lives. That would be a bad idea. After one car ride, I already want to be Mary's best friend. A whole afternoon together would put me on precarious footing in the "don't get too close" department.

Lorenzo opens up the apartment door. I walk inside and am overwhelmed by the feeling that I've stepped into some secret recess of his heart.

"I'll take the bed by the window," he says as he flips on the lights in the hall. "It can get drafty in that corner. Especially in the spring. I'll make sure you get the best mattress either way."

"Okay," I respond, but I'm too lost in this microcosm that is Lorenzo's other life to pay much attention to what he's saying.

A fan oscillates in the kitchen off the hall, and the smell of a simmering Sunday sauce wafts in waves through the apartment. On the walls are sepia-tone photos of unsmiling men and women; a few modern, colored prints show young children I assume are Lorenzo with his siblings and cousins.

I trace a finger over a small, mischievous face that is recognizable on account of the pouty lips and gorgeous eyelashes. "It's baby you," I say, turning to Lorenzo. But he is not beside me.

Lorenzo is down the hall, standing in front of an open door and looking like he just got wet willied.

"*Porca misera*," he groans as he drags his hand down his face. *Bloody hell.*

I hurry up beside him, and the problem is immediately apparent.

In the room Lorenzo shared with his older brother growing up, there are no longer two beds. There is one—and it might not even qualify as a queen. A framed painting of the *Madonna and Child* hangs above the headboard. Between the two sets of pillows rests a tiny bouquet of citrus blossoms tied together with a white ribbon.

It seems his mother did get the wrong impression. He shuts the door and starts opening others.

"What are you doing?" I ask.

"Trying to remember where she keeps the extra blankets. I'm making up the couch."

"What?"

"You take the bed. I'll sleep in the living room."

"Don't be ridiculous."

He glowers. "I'm not letting you sleep on the couch. Don't even try."

"Lorenzo, I don't see the problem."

He stops walking, turns his head toward me.

"It's a pretty big bed," I go on, though we both know this is not true. "I think we can manage."

"You mean," he cringes, "you want to *share* the bed?"

"Jesus, it wouldn't be that terrible, would it?"

"I don't—"

"We are both adults, aren't we? People do this kind of thing. It isn't a big deal." Lorenzo doesn't look convinced. I'm not either, but I'm not making him sleep on the couch.

"What about Eric?" he asks, rubbing the back of his neck.

Right, Eric. Obviously, I will not be telling Eric. There is nothing to tell.

"Eric will be fine," I say, waving a hand in the air. Have

I always been so full of shit? I briefly wonder if I should feel guilty about this lie I'm telling myself, but the truth is, Eric and I have talked about what things will look like when I get back to Phoenix, but I'm still in Italy, and I am a free woman who can sleep in Lorenzo's bed—with him—if I want to.

As friends, of course.

Lorenzo chews his lip for a very long time. "We can do this," I say, punching him on the shoulder.

He sighs, shrugs in surrender. "*Dio Santo, aiutami*," he murmurs as he carries our luggage through the door. *Dear God, help me.* Damn. Knowing that Lorenzo is so unenthusiastic about sleeping beside me sure puts the brakes on the heat building in my belly at the same thought.

Not for the first time, I wonder if Valeria has got her information all wrong. This is not a man I could break. But he sure as hell might take me down.

Lorenzo shows me where I can put my things and then ducks out of the room like it's on fire, mumbling something about a call to work. I hang up the dress I brought for the wedding in the mostly empty wardrobe that once belonged to Lorenzo's brother, Tano, then unpack a couple of other pieces that threaten to become offensively wrinkled if left in my luggage.

When Lorenzo doesn't reappear, I take the opportunity to do some casual snooping. On the wall to the right of the bed, lined up on two Ferrari-red shelves floating one above the other, are several soccer trophies with Lorenzo's name engraved on the bases. Medals dangle from hooks on either end of the shelves.

I chuckle to myself at the thought of Lorenzo the jock until I remember the way he looked when he came in from his soccer game the other night. My thighs quiver and I have to squeeze my legs together to repress the memory. These are not thoughts one should be having before a platonic sleepover. I move on.

A shiny, black particle board desk beside the door houses a yellowing computer monitor and some deteriorating shoeboxes, which I assume contain decades-old love letters and other middle school memorabilia. Along the back, lined up side-by-side, are small bottles of half-used men's cologne.

I sit down on the end of the bed and run my hands over the gold brocade of the comforter—out of place in the otherwise teenage boy–centric decor—chewing my lip as I contemplate Lorenzo's closet.

He's shared so little about his past. I wonder what skeletons he may be hiding, what secret parts of himself he's left buried in small-town Sicily.

But since I'm not a total weirdo, I leave the closet undisturbed and go for the nightstand instead. I tease the drawer open by the metal knob. And, oh my.

I stare, and a pack of Durex Comfort XL stares back. I reach for the box, a plan forming in my mind. As long as Lorenzo and I fail to address the elephant in the room—not the one in his pants, never the one in his pants, don't look at the trophies, Remy—as long as we keep tip toeing around the fact that we've kissed (and it was fucking amazing), we will never be able to relax, horizontally, beside each other. But maybe if we can joke about it, it will ease the tension. Haha, look, you wear gigantic condoms. Lucky Valeria. I promise I won't do anything untoward to you in your sleep.

Okay, not that. None of that.

Maybe the condoms aren't Lorenzo's. Maybe they are his brother's, and we can relish the awkwardness of that revelation together. I am willing to sacrifice Tano's privacy for the greater good.

I take a deep breath and shake out my arms, stretch my neck. I'm going to fix this, and Lorenzo will love having to sleep with me, dammit.

I have the box of condoms in my hand when I open the bedroom door. I'm shaking it in front of my face, calling Lorenzo's name in a voice that teeters between flirty and facetious, when suddenly I'm gulping just to breathe, and my life flashes before my eyes.

Since my date with Fabio, I have felt fear—being brought into the station, Alberto's attempted abduction, Maelle cornering me behind an ancient altar two stories below street level. Valeria.

But this is the first time I've thought, *This is it. This is how it ends.*

Only, I'm not that lucky.

Chapter TWENTY-THREE

I PULL MY HANDS BEHIND MY BACK, but it's too late.

Saveria Rossi has just witnessed me call her son hither while brandishing a box of condoms in my hand, playing it like a goddamn tambourine. Somehow I remain standing, not dead—engulfed in a burning burst of shame—even when an older woman I assume is Lorenzo's grandmother snickers over Saveria's shoulder.

His mom's face is unreadable and looks so much like Lorenzo's that I have no hope I might be wrong about who she is.

I open my mouth to say something, preferably something coherent and semi-intelligent, though I'd be proud of myself for sputtering out a *ciao* at this point. Before I manage to make words come out of my face, Lorenzo's grandmother reaches behind me for the condoms and hands them to Saveria, who walks past me into the room and places them back in the nightstand.

"*Binvintu, zita miricana*," his grandmother says to me, in a language that might be a distant cousin of Italian and that I don't understand, taking me by my now free hands. "*Tu puoi vieniri cu nui.*" Saveria slips back in front of me, not a single hint on her face to give away what she might be thinking. Lorenzo's grandmother smirks. My eyes dart around the hallway for an escape. What if I've broken some code in the guest-host relationship that the Greeks imported when they first colonized the island 2800 years ago and am now, by some ancient magic, going to be turned into a pig?

Or worse, what if Lorenzo's mom hates me forever?

The two women guide me to the kitchen, and I comply without a fight, accepting the forthcoming consequences of my idiocy. Lorenzo seems to have evaporated from the apartment altogether, which means there is no chance of rescue anyway.

His grandmother pulls out a seat and pushes me into it while continuing to talk. Her words form a unique patchwork of sounds, some familiar and others foreign. The (albeit one-sided) conversation reminds me of the old buildings we saw on our drive to Nunziata. Her vocabulary is a linguistic collage, the dialectical equivalent of the merging of Greek columns and Moorish arches and Arab-Norman cathedrals with Byzantine mosaics. Mementos of invaders whose artistry and prose soaked into Sicily's soil, worked their way past the limestone and lava crust into the island's heart, continuing to exist in Sicily's monuments and the mouths of its grandmothers.

Lorenzo's grandmother sits down beside me, blinks at me when I don't respond. "*Nun parra talianu*?" she asks, looking amused.

"*Mamma, sei tu che non parla Italiano*," Saveria responds, and I think, the way her lip turns at the corner, she may be smiling. *Mamma, it's you who doesn't speak Italian.* "*Ecco*," *here*, she continues, placing a heaping plate of pasta in meat sauce in front of me on the table.

"Grazie," I say, pressing my hand to my heart. Like mother like son.

While I eat, Saveria introduces herself and her mother, Maddalena, who lives in Mary's old room and is known to

Lorenzo and his siblings as Nonna Nena. Saveria apologizes for not being there to greet us when we got in, and I notice for the first time that her hair seems to be halfway through some sort of style renaissance. They left the salon as soon as Mary told them we were at the apartment because we'd be hungry from the trip; naturally, she needed to feed us. She says nothing about the condoms.

At some point in the conversation, it occurs to me that the words coming out of both our mouths are Italian, and it makes me feel like I just shotgunned a dozen espressos. I, Remy Campbell, am speaking Italian with Lorenzo's mother. She seems to understand what I'm saying, so maybe I'm even a little bit good at it.

For four weeks, in between all the pining and sleuthing, I've dedicated every free minute to learning Italian. The guidebook was a good refresher, and the textbook Lorenzo brought was even better. Once I had my phone, I watched all my favorite rom coms dubbed in Italian. Dr. Hill arranged for me to sit in on some lectures. The Italian department provided books and even helped me find a tutor who I worked with during two of my trips to the university.

I didn't toil away in secret over Italian-English dictionaries and newspapers I found in the hall with the intention of one day impressing Lorenzo's mother by being able to communicate with her. Improving my understanding of the language was important to the case. It was vital to the research. But I'd be lying if I said I didn't start trying a little bit harder to get all my verbs conjugated correctly when I found out we'd be coming to Sicily.

This is my first opportunity to give my foreign language abilities a test run, and if it scores me a few bonus points with Saveria, so be it.

I don't stumble once until she asks where Lorenzo is. I shrug, and her eyebrows rise, and I focus on the pasta again.

When I've cleared my plate and received the pleased Italian mother nod of approval, Saveria enlists me to help her and Nonna Nena fill three hundred and eighty white organza pouches with candied almonds to distribute as favors at the wedding.

That is how Lorenzo finds us, huddled together at the kitchen table, Saveria translating incriminating stories Nonna Nena is telling about Lorenzo and Tano from Sicilian into Italian and smiling at me when I laugh.

Lorenzo pauses in the doorway, and we all look up at him. Maybe I should be embarrassed that the naked joy on my face matches his mother's and his grandmother's, even though they haven't seen him in over a year, and I've been without him for an hour tops. But I don't care. I'm not even mad at him for abandoning me after we arrived. I'm sandwiched between two of the women he loves most in the world, and it feels good here.

But whatever face I am making when Lorenzo walks in, he makes the opposite—all pale lips and wide eyes.

Lorenzo shakes his head, and his features clear. He takes an unsteady breath. "What's going on?" he asks, first in Italian, then, looking at me with a raised brow, in English. His tone makes it sound like he just found us cooking meth and not filling frilly little bags with nuts.

Saveria and Nonna Nena don't bother to answer. Instead, Nonna Nena goes to Lorenzo and pulls him down by his ears so she can kiss his cheeks. Saveria serves another dish of pasta, which she lands on the table beside me before pushing Lorenzo into her chair.

"*Grazie, Mamma,*" he mumbles, but he still has me pinned

like I'm a Zalśar clue and he's trying to figure me out. His eyes narrow, and I glare back. The smile I'm biting down negates the dirty look, though. Suspicious Lorenzo is pretty cute.

He takes a bite of the pasta. "*Allora, di che cosa stavate parlando*?" he asks with an adorably forced nonchalance. *So, what were you all talking about?*

I straighten in my seat. I've been looking forward to flaunting my newfound fluency in front of Lorenzo, but now that my moment has arrived, it feels an awful lot like stripping myself naked for his inspection—which, under the circumstances, would require at least a glass or two of wine.

Panicking, I glance at Nonna Nena and then Saveria. She gives me a slight nod.

"Your mom was just telling me about your soccer trophies," I respond, my face flushing as the words tumble out of my mouth in very uninspired, regular old English. "Why didn't you ever tell me you played in the national league?"

Lorenzo sighs and looks at his mother, who makes an indifferent sort of noise before turning her back to him.

"That was a long time ago," he says.

"Nonna Nena told me if you'd stayed in Sicily, you could have gone on to play in Serie A, in Catania. That's a big deal, Lorenzo."

"I wanted to be in Rome, not Catania."

"Couldn't you have played in Rome?"

Rather than answer, Lorenzo raises his eyes to mine. "You've been working on your Italian?" he asks. There is a strain in his voice I don't understand.

"A—a little," I stammer, feeling warm in my cotton ruffle top.

"If you were talking to these two, you were speaking Italian. The only other language either of them knows a word of is Sicilian." He gestures toward his mother and grandmother, who busy themselves with the dishes and pretend they aren't watching us like hawks.

I look away from him, biting my lip while I wait for the stutter of my pulse to settle. Telling Lorenzo such a simple, silly thing—that I've been cramming Italian in my free time—is a more embarrassing confession than I'm prepared to make.

"I've been studying when you're at work," I say, looking up from the lace edge of the tablecloth I'm rubbing between my fingers just in time to see his face nearly collapse. "And Dr. Hill let me audit some classes at the university," I add, not mentioning the fifty times I've watched the new *Emma* in Italian.

"Why didn't you tell me?" he asks after clearing his throat, his knee fidgeting twice between us.

"I wanted to surprise you," I say, holding my breath.

Lorenzo grunts, not meeting my eyes, and takes another bite of pasta, keeping his attention glued to the acanthus-edged plate in front of him.

My chin quivers.

I didn't expect Lorenzo to throw a party when I busted out my Italian skills. But I did kind of hope he might be a little excited—that he'd give me one of his sweet smiles. Maybe even a hug? That we'd drink a bottle of wine together while he quizzed me on the subjunctive tense.

I never imagined I'd render him speechless. And broody. And sullen.

I feel a hand on my shoulder and remember to breathe. "*Vieni*, Remy," Saveria tells me in slow, sweet Italian, "I will show you where the towels are. You can take a shower and relax for a bit in your room before dinner."

I give Saveria a shaky smile that echoes the feeling in my belly as I stand, and she hooks her arm in mine, guiding me out of the kitchen. At the door, she stops, turns her face back to the table. "*Tanto*," she says, her voice turning hard, eyes shooting daggers over my shoulder. "*Io devo parlare con mio figlio.*" *I need to have a talk with my son.*

After a shower, I crawl into bed. Alone. Not that I expected Lorenzo to hop under the sheets for a midday snuggle, but it's out of character for him not to check in. The whole bed ordeal has shot his avoidance into overdrive just when things were starting to feel normal between us.

I pull out my phone to google hotels in the area. There is one, and it is indeed full up. The Airbnb results are equally dire. I find something in a small town about fifteen minutes away and am about to book it out of sheer self-preservation when a text comes in from Eric.

There's a picture of a puppy (cute) he saw on his run and an upcycled bookcase (questionable) he bought for "our" home.

> Sorry I was such an ass about Sicily, he writes.
> Bring the dog home, and I might forgive you, I answer.
> Did you make it to the detective's town?
> Yep.

Getting into the details feels unnecessary since Eric and I are not officially together. Our coupleness is contingent on a few things, and a major one is existing on the same continent again. I don't see how it would do any good to detail my Nunziata sleeping arrangements in a text message. *Oh, you're decorating the bedroom you want to share? How sweet! I'm sleeping a foot away from the sexy detective I can't stop fantasizing about. Don't worry, though; he's suffering through every second.*

I glance at Lorenzo's side of the bed and sigh. My phone buzzes in my hand.

What's his family like? Eric asks.

They're nice.

Fancy?

Normal.

Maybe a little scary?

Are you trying to ask me if Lorenzo is in the mafia?

Yes.

Stop.

I get to kiss you in eleven days, R.C.

I shudder and send back a thumbs-up emoji.

When I recheck the hotel listing, the room is no longer available. I drop my phone onto the bed and groan into my hands.

"Remy?"

I scramble out of the sheets and stand to face Lorenzo, who seems to be suspended within the frame of the door.

"Your sister wasn't lying," I say, pointing to my phone. "There isn't a room available within twenty miles at least."

"I know. I went out to check after my call."

This should not be disappointing. Or offensive. It should not make my heart want to flee from my body in search of a new, more worthy host. "Oh," I say, trying to remember what one usually does with their arms while standing.

Lorenzo takes a few steps into the room, the bed between us. We both glance down at the lightly rumpled blanket. The indent my head left on the pillow.

"We will be fine," he says, running a corner of the pillow-case between his fingers.

"Totally," I affirm. "It is only for a few nights."

"Six," he answers, rolling his shoulders back. "Six nights."

We meet each other's eyes, then both look back down.

I chew my thumbnail. Lorenzo clears his throat.

"I am going to visit my goddaughter, Matilde, at my uncle's house before dinner. Would you like to come?"

"I'd love to," I rush to answer. If the invitation is him extending a hand of peace across the mattress, I am going to white-knuckle it. "I mean, if that's okay with you. I don't want to intrude," I add for the sake of diplomacy.

"I didn't bring you to Nunziata to keep you locked in a house with my mother. Not that she would complain." He looks at me. His eyes twinkle. "She said she was very impressed with your Italian."

"She did?" I murmur, my insides experiencing a level of warm and fuzzy hitherto unknown to me. Lorenzo's mouth threatens a smile.

"Matilde will be harder to win over," he warns.

I grab my purse and shove my hand in. When it reemerges, my fingers are full of Kinder Bueno bars I panic purchased at the airport in Rome in case I got hungry during the flight.

I wink. "Secret weapon."

Lorenzo chuckles, and I have to keep myself from dancing in place. "Using chocolate to win a child's favor is cheating," he says, crossing his arms.

"I, Detective, am many things, but a cheater is not one of them."

The amusement drains from his face, and he takes a step back. "Of course not," he says.

I open my mouth to respond, then stop short. *What*? Weren't we just talking about hazelnut cream-filled candy bars?

"Come on," Lorenzo says with a stiff nod to the door.

Zio Peppe lives in an old, white farmhouse on the outskirts of town. The building backs up to open land, which is the first place Zio Peppe takes me after releasing me from a welcoming bear hug. He doesn't spare as much attention for Lorenzo and instead sends him inside to get Matilde up from her nap.

Zio Peppe runs his hand over his bald head and tells me in Sicilian-sprinkled Italian how the land has been in the family since the Moorish conquest for sure, and possibly longer. He pulls out his wallet and shows me a byzantine coin he tilled up a decade ago. He keeps all the other treasures that have surfaced on a shelf in his garage and some in an old coffee tin, he says. A veritable depository of Sicilian history perched and packed like tchotchkes around his home.

In 1928, when Etna erupted, the lava flow missed the village of Nunziata, but it took out much of the surrounding area, including the family's land. "But this," he says with his heavy island accent, resting his hand against the thickest, gnarliest olive tree trunk I have ever seen, "survived. This tree has stood here since the Norman invasion. After the eruption, my father used its cuttings to grow every other olive tree you see in the orchard."

I make a mental note to google the lifespan of olive trees while Zio Peppe glances at me expectantly. I look around at the dense rows of lush olive trees that are no spring chickens themselves if they were planted essentially a century ago.

"*Incredibile*," I offer, but Zio Peppe's eyebrow crooks up, unsatisfied with my paltry compliment.

Fine, I'll give him the real Remy show and do what I've wanted to do since I saw the tree across the field. I spread my arms out and hug it, taking all its thousand possible years of resilience and abundance in my arms, squeezing the trunk the way I'd like to squeeze Lorenzo every time I get a peek into his heart, his past, his people.

Zio Peppe rests his hands on his hips and grins, his big

round belly rising—my display of appreciation finally on par with his level of pride. "*Ora, ti faccio vedere i pomodori.*" *Now, I will show you the tomatoes.*

When we get back to the house, I'm holding my white t-shirt out in front of me like a basket. The cotton is full of deep red datterino tomatoes. Zio Peppe is one hell of a gardener, and his skill, combined with all the goodies Etna left behind in the soil, means ripe tomatoes year-round. So ripe, in fact, that more than a few have burst against my top.

Zio Peppe holds the door for me and directs me to the kitchen. As I spill the tomatoes from my shirt and into the sink, I hear a small intake of breath behind me and turn in time to see a set of wavy, golden-brown pigtails take off down the hall.

"*Lei é qui*!" a sweet, bright voice announces from the other room. *She is here*. This assertion is followed by a droning hum of anticipation that is cut off sharply but only briefly by Lorenzo's voice issuing anguished orders, like, *Stop!* And, *Please, no*, which makes me curious enough to wander in.

And it is with a seed-stained, semi-see-through shirt that I meet every extended member of Lorenzo's Nunziata family.

The first to introduce herself is Matilde, who willingly accepts my offer of chocolate and tells me all of the English words she is learning at the Scuola Materna. I meet Matilde's parents: Zio Peppe's son, Nicolas, and his wife, Maristella. Nicolas's identical twin sisters, one of whom kindly bleaches her hair, though I can hardly tell them apart regardless. Michela, a beautiful, curly-haired goddess who keeps my wine glass full. All of Saveria's brothers and sisters, all of their spouses, all of the cousins.

Lorenzo's family tree has more branches than the ancient olive grove in the backyard.

I look to Lorenzo for help at some point when a great aunt

starts grilling me, but he seems a bit ruffled himself, eyes wide and manic like I imagine my own must look. His brother Tano sweeps in and saves me, pulling me onto the balcony where his husband Roberto is already hiding.

"Thank you," I say, wiping a hand over a few remaining seeds stuck to the front of my shirt.

Tano chuckles. "I've been rescuing Roberto from similar situations for years. You have to forgive Lorenzo. You're the first person he's brought home to the family. He'll get better."

My cheeks burn to match my tomato-blotched top. I make a series of useless sounds to clarify, once again, that *it's not like that.* My fingers twist nervously in my shirt as I unsuccessfully attempt to explain.

"Don't worry about that, either," Tano says, about my clothing, I realize, and not the fact that his brother's intentions with me are not romantic. "I texted Mary to bring you something to wear for dinner. I figured Lorenzo was too overwhelmed by the aunts' interrogation to think about it."

I look at Roberto, who nods at me. A nod that says, *Yes, all the Rossi children are unbearably thoughtful.* Yes, it is impossible not to fall in love. Yes, Remy, your heart is in trouble.

And it's true. My heart is in such big trouble—and getting bigger.

It expands when Saveria greets me with a hug at dinner, when Nonna Nena winks. It balloons as I laugh with Mary as she tells me how she was named for her grandmothers, Maria and Maddalena, but how she refused to go by anything but Mary after being read the story of Mary Magdalene in bible class during her first year of elementary school. Michela's snarky asides, Roberto and Tano's hand squeezes, Zio Peppe's insistence that I return tomorrow to pick more tomatoes. All of it threatens to make my chest burst open right there at the dinner table.

For the most part, Lorenzo is quiet but attentive beside me. His jaw pulsing occasionally. Once, he sets a hand on my shoulder as he asks the table if he can bring them anything back from the kitchen (yes, wine), and I have to press my lips together to keep from looking overly excited about the fact that he is touching me.

After the meal, a tired Matilde wanders over to us and reaches out her arms. Lorenzo lifts her into his lap, brushing the hair back from her face as she burrows into his shoulder.

"*Non sei molto confortevole Lollu,*" she says squirming. *You aren't very comfortable.* "É tutto troppo," she pokes his chest, "*duro.*" Everything is too...hard.

Oh, the joy of being able to jab freely at that muscular torso.

"Come here," I tell Matilde, pulling her from Lorenzo's lap to mine. From experience with my niece and nephews, I know that I am not too hard to rest on. I have been assured multiple times—much to the chagrin of my ego—that I am the perfect amount of squishy. Matilde curls up with her head under my chin, my arms wrapped around her as we rock in the seat, Lorenzo watching.

Under Lorenzo's gaze, I fight to keep my breath calm as Matilde's slows. He doesn't look away from me until she's asleep. We whisper above her head as he lifts her tenderly from my arms. I wish I knew what he saw, what he was thinking. I guess my face isn't completely transparent if he didn't run away while I was internally shouting at him about how I want to have his babies and rock them to sleep on my squishy body, how I want to rock him to sleep—or something like it. He carries her to bed, smiling at me over his shoulder.

But when we get to his mother's house, Lorenzo is as distant as ever. After brushing my teeth, I come in from the bathroom and find him smooshed into one edge of the bed, a blockade of pillows propped along the side of his body. I'd laugh if I weren't busy swallowing the heat in my throat.

I crawl into my side of the bed, facing Lorenzo's back. His shirt pulls against the muscles in his shoulders, and everything in me aches to put my hand there, feel the heat of his body with my fingertips, search for his pulse and make it mine.

Six nights. I only have to make it six nights.

"*Buona notte*," I say, tucking my hands under my head.

Lorenzo turns off the light. "Good night, Remy," he answers into the darkness.

Chapter TWENTY-FOUR

I SCOOT MY CHAIR CLOSER TO THE KITCHEN TABLE, and Tano fills up my plastic cup with more of the plum-colored wine. We clink our drinks together.

It's the end of our third full day in Sicily, and one of the uncles has busted out a few packs of Sicilian playing cards. The family has divided into three distinct groups. I have fallen into the childless, loud, and tipsy cohort and am relegated to the kitchen with Tano, Roberto, and the cute cousin, Giacomo—who I suspect has just outgrown the teenage table—as well as the twins, Michela, and Lorenzo. He has barely spoken all night, hasn't touched the wine, and has little Matilde perched on his knee.

Since that first night here, Lorenzo has mounted Castel Sant'Angelo–level defenses against my person. I've tried to get him to sit down with me to go through the journal that I found at Villa Medici, but every time he stammers out some excuse and disappears. If he comes into the house and finds me with his mom or sister, his face pales. Once, when Mary was showing me old photo albums, he even had to steady himself against the wall.

I take another sip from my cup and refuse to acknowledge

the way something inside my chest wobbles when Lorenzo chuckles as Matilde tries to tickle him.

Giacomo leans in close to me to explain the rules of *sette e mezzo* while Roberto deals the cards. He pushes a piece of my hair behind my ear when it keeps falling between us, and I don't move away when he inches his seat closer. Giacomo is a harmless, albeit shameless, flirt who smells like coconuts and smiles every time our eyes meet.

And I'm enjoying every second of it.

He makes a vaguely inappropriate comment about the *asso di bastoni* card—the ace of clubs, only in this deck it is a single giant actual club—and I shove him on the shoulder, laughing. Giacomo covers my hand with his and winks.

I hear a strained groan beside me and turn to see Lorenzo folding Matilde up in his arms as he stands. His mouth is set in a distinct frown when he looks at me. "*Prendo qualcosa di dolce per Matilde,*" he tells us all. "*Fammi sapere quando la lezione di carte e finito.*" *I am going to grab something sweet for Matilde. Let me know when the card lesson is over.*

"*Fai veloce, Lollu,*" the blond twin says. *Be quick.* "*Altrimenti Giacomo proverà di insegnare a Remy come giocano i Siciliani a scopa.*" *Otherwise, Giacomo might try to teach Remy how the Sicilians play scopa.*

I snort, and the tops of Giacomo's cheeks turn a faint shade of pink—maybe not so shameless after all.

I don't have a lot to thank Alberto for, but all those hours he spent outside apartment 3A definitely bolstered my familiarity with Italian swear words and obscenities. I still have the list penciled into the back of my Rome guidebook. Next to the entry for *scopare,* I wrote *to fuck* in flowing cursive. Scopa is also a traditional Italian card game.

"It was a clever joke," I say, looking up at Lorenzo.

He scowls before walking away, and the whole group erupts in laughter. I stick my tongue out at his back, and Matilde giggles over his shoulder.

Tano sighs when Lorenzo is out of the room. "*Povero Lollu*," he says. *Poor Lorenzo.* His eyes are sad when he looks at me, his expression expectant like I might somehow know how to help him find the kid he grew up with, the one hiding inside the big, grumpy asshole Lorenzo. Like maybe I can bring him back.

I chew my lip. I've seen glimpses of that person, and I get why Tano misses him. But Lorenzo has made it pretty clear since we got to Nunziata that he's not interested in letting me in. I've already invaded his work, apartment, family, and childhood home. That's as far as he will let the conquest of Remy go. I am not the girl who can draw out his easy smile, his laugh. I can't help him remember the joy of being young and free, the way sunshine and love felt when he was still unburdened by the complexities of an absent father, his job, the challenges of his adult relationships with women.

Still, though. I have to try.

I push back in my chair, put my cards down. "I'm just going to—"

"*Vai, allora.*" *Go then*, Roberto says, smirking as he reaches for my cards and Lorenzo's, reshuffling them into the deck.

I hesitate at the entrance to the dining room. Lorenzo is in the back corner with Matilde. He has her propped up on the top of polished credenza beside a platter of Sicilian biscotti, cannoli, and little fried balls that look like donut holes. He's pretending to try them all, and whatever he's doing with his face is making Matilde roar, her short little chestnut pigtails bouncing up and down with her shoulders.

It is all horribly precious, and when I feel a tightening in my right side, I know for sure the scene has cast a spell on my ovaries and invoked ovulation. Abracadabra, put your babies in me.

I shake my head. I need to ask Tano for the exact percent of alcohol per volume in the neighbor's basement wine so I can pace myself better from now on. Lorenzo is my friend, though, I think. And even if he doesn't see it that way, we've been through a lot together. Detective Rossi and his sidekick Remy. It's normal to want to make sure my main man is doing okay.

Not main man, just main Rome man.

No. Not main. Just man. I'm just looking out for some man. A man whose voice makes my ribs feel too small, who sets my skin on fire when he forgets not to touch me, whose smile will keep me awake at night for years to come. A man who wants nothing at all to do with me or my body or my lips, even though I can't stop thinking about his.

I rub a hand over the space above my heart, jumping when I notice Saveria watching me from behind a fan of black-backed playing cards. Even with her mouth hidden, I can see the corners of her eyes curl into a smile.

Deep breath, Remy.

I step into the room, and halfway to Lorenzo, my phone rings from the butt pocket of my jeans. The volume is low, but that doesn't stop Lorenzo from looking right at me. His brows crease, which I take as a good sign because he seems confused that I'm there, which means he hasn't noticed me ogling him from the threshold.

But now I'm staring again, and he knows because he's still watching me, clearly wondering what the hell I'm doing standing frozen in the middle of his mother's dining room.

The phone rings again, and I slide it out of my pocket, not

breaking eye contact with Lorenzo until the screen is in front of my face.

Lil.

I smile and am still smiling when I look up to see Lorenzo's shoulders sag as he turns back to Matilde.

I give myself two seconds to dream about massaging the tension out of Lorenzo's bunched back before I swallow the ache in my throat and answer the phone.

"Are you in a club?" Lil asks.

"The dining room," I yell into the receiver. "What's up?" I plug the ear that the phone isn't pressed into and manage to make out pieces of Lil's story about Camila and Carlito and an unfortunate episode with a pair of Fiskar's blunt tip scissors and the moral implications of getting hair extensions for your second-grade daughter. As I pass Saveria on the way out of the room, her eyes lower, and she glances back at Lorenzo. I pretend not to notice.

When I've closed myself in the bedroom, I open the balcony doors and step out into the quiet night.

"At the consultation, Camila told the stylist she wants to fill in blond on that side. She envisions a sort of Cruella-chic look, I think. I am all for encouraging autonomy and decision-making, but my hold on the PTA vice chair position is tenuous at best. I'm not sure it could survive me sending my kid to school as Lily Munster for the rest of the quarter."

"If anyone could pull it off, it's Camila."

"I know. I'm going to let it happen. I hope she hates it, though, so I can hold it against her when she's older and wants to make even more ridiculous life choices."

"Fair."

"Speaking of ridiculous life choices, how's Sicily?"

"Rude."

"Go on."

"It's amazing. Lorenzo's family is incredible and warm and loud and would probably make Mom spontaneously combust," I laugh, leaning out over the railing, a salt breeze tickling strands of my hair against my face. "No, that's not true. They'd get her nice and buzzed on homemade wine, and Mom would love every second of it despite herself."

"Homemade wine sounds dangerous."

"Pure trouble. But delicious. You and Javier could add an Italian grapes section in the shop, bottle it, import it, and make a fortune. And God, the olive oil. Don't tell your husband, but it's better than any oil I've ever tasted in my life. I had to refrain from putting it on my gelato last night. I want it on everything."

"Mmmm," she hums. "Tell me more."

"There are tons of kids, all crazy. Your three would fit right in. Carlito and Matilde could wreak all the havoc together."

"And Dad?"

"Zio Angelo has a classic car collection. Doesn't speak a lick of English. But they would get along great, looking at engines and wheel wells or whatever the hell it is that men do with cars."

"Cool," Lil says. "Sounds great. When's the wedding, again?"

"Tomorrow."

"No, not that one. I mean the wedding you've been planning in your head to Detective Rossi."

"What?"

"Why else are you fantasizing about your entire family visiting his hometown?"

Oh no, why am I?

"Stop it," I whine. "You know it's—"

"It's not like that? You are, you know, only sleeping in his mother's house and going with him to his sister's wedding."

"Because I have to."

"What's the deal, anyway? Are you in the guest room? Bunking with his grandmother?"

"Funny story, now that you mention it. Lorenzo and I are sort of sharing a bed."

"Sort of sharing a bed?" she barks back at me.

"Yeah, and he hates it. Every night he constructs a little fortress of pillows between us like he can't trust me not to plunder him in my sleep."

"Oh, little Remy. Have you ever heard of morning wood?"

I sigh into the phone. "If only giving Lorenzo erections was the problem. I think it's more that he hates me."

"I'm sorry," Lil says quietly.

"For what?"

"You've got it so bad for him, Rem."

"Do not," I counter, but my voice is shaking. I look back over my shoulder at the bed.

"He sleeps in his little Italian man-panties, doesn't he?" she asks.

I'm about to argue that Lorenzo wears normal-sized boxer briefs—a fact I know on account of sharing a washer and drying rack and for no other reason—when the call waiting tone drones in my ear.

I pull the phone down to check who's calling, shaking my head when I see it's Eric. "I should take this," I mumble.

"Eric?" she asks.

"How'd you know?"

"That boy has been in a *mood* the last few days."

I groan. It probably hasn't helped that I've been ignoring his calls and responding via emoji to all of his text messages.

"Good luck," Lil chirps and hangs up.

My finger hovers over the green button. Other than a few texts, Eric and I haven't spoken since I got to Sicily, and yesterday I canceled his call when I was out with Tano and Roberto. I've been a jerk.

I squeeze my eyes shut and answer. "Hi, Eric," I say after settling the phone against the side of my face.

There's a muffled sound on the line like he's lifting weights and has me on speakerphone. Or he's crying.

"Eric?"

"I—I have to tell you something, Rems. I messed up, and I am so sorry, but I need to be honest."

My breath hitches in my throat. "Okay."

"Just listen before you say anything, please."

I nod, though he can't see me, and he goes on.

"I've been really fucked up about this whole Sicily thing. It just feels wrong, like I should be the one there with you, looking out for you. Instead, you are with some dude you barely know, and he's doing *my* job."

I make a faint noise of acknowledgment.

"Last night, I went out and had too much to drink. I just kept thinking about you, there, in this guy's house. About how I've spent the last seven years vying for you to like me as much as you like some goddamn city."

All right, that's just silly. "It was never a competition between you and Rome, Eric."

Eric huffs a humorless laugh. "You're right. It was never a competition. Rome always won. Every anniversary was Italian food and *Gladiator* on the couch. When I bought you that bottle of expensive Pinot Noir from Napa on your birthday, you questioned if I even really loved you because I gifted you a California red. The way you get heart eyes whenever you talk about Italy, the time you asked if I'd wear an Italian national team jersey in bed. Your tattoo. But I tried anyway."

I bite my lip. When he puts it like that, it doesn't look great. But I *was* a good girlfriend. I put him first in every other way, in everything, always. "Eric, you know that what we had went beyond all that."

He clears his throat. "Last night, I brought someone home from the bar."

"Oh."

"She's someone I met over the winter when you and I weren't together. It just sort of happened."

"We still aren't together."

"I slept with her, Remy. On our new sheets."

I cringe. Eric means the sheets I didn't pick; the ones Lorenzo didn't like, either. I hope they ruined them.

"You have nothing to say?" he asks, his voice ragged.

"We haven't made anything official, Eric. You're a free man."

"You don't even care, do you?" he scoffs.

"I—" I run a mental inventory of my current feelings, and he's right. The fact that he hooked up with one of the attractive women who flooded his Instagram stories months ago doesn't bother me. No, that cold, sinking sensation inside me has nothing to do with Eric.

I've been pretending all this time we could go back to the way things were. But Eric's got my number. I'm in love with Rome. And that's just half of it. I feel furious with myself for having wasted so much of my time here catering to some farce in Phoenix.

My eyes start to prickle, and I cough to clear my throat. "I'm sorry." I hate that I apologize, but I mainly say it to myself.

Sorry, Remy, for not giving yourself a chance to set fire to that thing inside you, for not living these weeks in an incandescent storm of heat and brilliance.

But that wouldn't change the way Lorenzo feels. As much as I love Rome, it's painful to imagine myself ever being in the city again without him.

"No," Eric says, "I'm sorry. I'm the one who messed up. I shouldn't be putting that shit on you. I hope I can make you see how much I love you one day, R.C. I hope we can still try when you get home."

I murmur, *Maybe*, insist his apologies are unnecessary and don't roll my eyes when he asks if he should install a dog door at the house, my anger turning to numbness.

When we hang up, I crawl into bed with my clothes on, preparing Lorenzo's pillow barricade along the center of the bed before stuffing my face in the pillow and crying.

I don't know how long I've been weeping under the covers when Lorenzo comes in, but it takes me a few big, shaky breaths to stop. I can hear him changing into his pajamas in the corner behind me, the gentle click of buttons, the rustle of his pants as he pulls them off, and the soft brush of cotton on his bare skin as he pulls on others.

I have to press my hand against my mouth to keep from sobbing again.

When he lifts the cover to crawl in beside me, a cool gust of air brushes my neck, and I shiver. I try to steady my breathing. Feign sleep. It doesn't work.

"Remy?" he says, leaning over the pillow fort to look at me. I close my eyes. His breath is minty, and his pajamas smell like the apartment in Rome: warm, musky, delicious. "Are you all right?"

"I'm good." My voice is hoarse and broken.

One of his hands falls near my shoulder, then stumbles in the semi-darkness for mine. I very consciously do not moan at the way his fingers graze my body on the search. Lorenzo squeezes my hand.

"You'll be home soon," he whispers. The words elicit a whimper, and my shoulders begin to shake as the tears barrel from my eyes.

Lorenzo pulls his hand back, pushes himself off the bed. "I'll come back later," he says, and then he's gone, and I am free to fall apart in the childhood bedroom of the man I've fallen in love with.

Chapter TWENTY-FIVE

I PUCKER UP IN THE MIRROR and swipe on some Chanel Ideal red, check my teeth, then step back to give myself a head-to-toe once-over.

My dress is a super hot, dark emerald, flutter slit trumpet gown that I had packed for the gala Cassie's company is hosting at the MAXXI, which she'll be attending with Shay instead before they escape to the south of France for a long weekend. She brought up international elopement procedures the last time we talked. At least one of us is heading toward a happily ever after.

The slit in my dress pulls against my thigh, just high enough to be sexy without scandalizing the old-gen Italians, and my boobs look great but well within the realm of wedding-appropriate. The back laces up, so I'm bra-free, but I made sure to double knot the ties when I yanked them closed.

I brush the big, 1950s glamor curls the hairdresser gave me over my shoulder and smile. I haven't had a chance to dress up for a long time, and it feels good.

I needed this after spending hours last night tumbling down the woe-is-me rabbit hole after Lorenzo left the room.

No one loves me. No one wants me.

Well, Eric claims to, but he also just banged some bar

hookup on our new bedding, which didn't bother me until my pride got involved—a sore spot that Lorenzo kept pressing this morning by avoiding me at all costs.

Settling my hands on my hips, I wink at my reflection in the mirror. There are other Italian fish in the Mediterranean, and I'm going to the wedding looking like fresh bait, ready to reel them in.

I move to the bed and double-check the buckles on my strappy, ruby stilettos.

"Ready," I call as I grab my clutch and stand up.

The photographer came by earlier. She snapped countless photos of the family looking like Gucci models, and then a series of Mary in her childhood bedroom and beside the portrait of the Madonna with her brothers. When the photographer finished, Tano hustled Mary, Saveria, and Nonna Nena into a car so they could do a quick lap of photo-ops with all the aunts and cousins before the wedding. Lorenzo stayed home to clean up, and I finished getting ready. Tano is supposed to come back by the house to take us to the church.

I pull my shoulders back and step into the hall.

Lorenzo comes around the corner from the kitchen with his head down, texting. He is in a midnight-blue suit, fitted to accent his shoulders, his waist. The shirt underneath embraces every muscle that constitutes his torso and is unbuttoned just enough to give an agonizing preview of what that torso looks like naked. His pants hug his hips and curve around the muscles of his ass.

I didn't get a good view during the bustle of the photoshoot, but I should have known he'd look upsettingly attractive all dressed up.

The very chemical composition of his pheromones, the contours of his face and body, are an adrenaline shot to my heart.

I can't control the feeling, but I wish I were better at hiding it, especially when we've been so busy shunning each other all day.

I didn't tell him about my call with Eric. Why would I? I don't have any desire to humiliate myself further, announce to the world that all the men in my life are so quick to find themselves with others. Besides, Lorenzo seems content never to speak to me again outside of what he has to say out of necessity.

Like, "Tano is on his way."

Lorenzo shoves his phone into the pocket of his impeccably tailored suit and looks at me.

He blinks once, and even from across the room, I can hear his inhale.

The look of bewilderment on his face is satisfying. The way it makes my face heat up and my belly tighten less so.

"Is it okay?" I ask, a hint of false concern in my voice as I look down to examine my dress. That's right, Lorenzo, this is the woman you separate yourself from with a wall of pillows because it is just so awful to have to share a bed with her.

The woman you kissed and forgot the next day.

Eat your heart out, assface.

"Remy," he says, running his hands through his hair. "You look…" it comes out half stammer, half breath.

"Careful, you don't want to make Valeria worry."

His brow creases, he practically growls. "It is Eric who should be worried."

Goosebumps shoot down my arms. "What does that mean?"

He looks away, his jaw pulses. "Nothing," he says, shaking his head. "We should go down to the street."

I hurry to block his exit. "No, I want to know what you mean."

"It doesn't matter."

But it does matter because he's not allowed to say things like that when he acts the way he does.

The way he kissed me, held me, on the Palatine, like the desire had been eating him up, only to turn around and make out with Valeria in front of me the very next day. The way he always tried to keep at least two feet between us and was horrified by the thought of having to share a bed. The way he always talks about how happy he is for Eric and me.

And now he tells me Eric should be worried. About what? Me breaking my ankle in these dangerously tall heels? Or something else. The something else that I sometimes think I sense in the darkness of Lorenzo's eyes, in the twitch of his lip.

"So, nothing your girlfriend would care about?" I raise my chin, dare him to tell the truth.

Lorenzo's eyes search mine. "Why do you think Valeria is my girlfriend? I thought we'd gone over this."

"But…" I feel a little dizzy. "But you've been talking to her a bunch. She calls all the time."

"That's true. Valeria is moving back to Rome, and we are friends."

Friends? "She was supposed to be here at your sister's wedding."

"That was the plan a few months ago. Things changed. Now you're here instead."

My pulse stutters a little at this like maybe I'm not just here by default, but because he wanted me to be. That can't be right, though. He can't stand to be close to me. I think of the night in the kitchen when I saw them together and try not to shout. "You kissed her!" I say. "I saw you kissing the evening after you fought Alberto." The night after you made my knees go weak the way I'd been waiting for all these years.

Lorenzo recoils when I say this, eyes huge. "What are you talking about?" he asks. His voice is rough.

"Don't pretend it didn't happen. I walked right past. I saw you two together."

"Remy, no."

"Actually, yes. Yes, Lorenzo, I did."

His shoulders slump forward, and he grabs his chest, looking like someone just put a sword through his ribs. "You think I am the kind of man who would do that?"

My mouth falls open. "I—I don't know. I mean, I hardly know you, really, right? And you did do it. Didn't you?"

His phone rings, but he ignores it. Our eyes lock, and I'm desperate for him to prove me wrong. *Tell me you weren't kissing Valeria,* I beg him in my head. *Please.*

He looks away. "It wasn't what you think," he answers.

I swallow hard as my heart shrinks in my chest. "Whatever, Lorenzo." I walk past him to the door. "If that was Tano on the phone, we should hurry up."

Lorenzo clenches his jaw and raises a fist to the wall. He leans his forehead against it and takes two deep breaths before pushing away.

"Let's go," he says, leaning around me to open the door, ever careful not to let our bodies touch.

The yellowing stone church, Chiesa Madre della Madonna dell'Itria, is a three-minute drive from the apartment. And that is only because every street in Nunziata is so narrow you can only go one way, and we have to skirt the entire edge of the town to get there.

Walking would have been faster. Walking would have spared us all these three soul-crushing minutes of discomfort.

Tano and Roberto are all smiles when we get in the back seat, but they spend the entire ride looking at us anxiously over their shoulders. When we arrive, I thank them both and find Michela—her caramel curls a beckoning corona of salvation—among the loud, lavish guests gathering outside the church.

I cling to her gold lamé-covered arm and follow her to a pew about halfway down the aisle that some of Lorenzo's other young cousins have claimed. Giacomo winks at me from the far side of the wooden bench as I slip in beside the blond twin. I throw double finger guns his way, and he looks confused.

During the nuptials, I am a weepy mess. Lorenzo and Tano walk Mary down the aisle. That moment and everything that follows is heartrendingly beautiful, fairytale perfect. While the church choir sings "Ave Maria," I close my eyes and try to imagine my own wedding—the one that always felt inevitable. I hear Eric's voice in my head obsessing about pesticide-free peonies and nopales party favors. Even in my imagination, he gets mad at me when I suggest we serve Italian wine.

I might as well have punched myself in the sternum for the way it makes the breath shrink in my belly—the absolute unequivocal acknowledgment that Eric and I are very much not meant to be. A truth I withheld semi-successfully from myself since I got to Italy. Still, the thought of returning to Phoenix, how hard my heart will ache when I do, almost makes me not care. If I can't have Italy—if I can't have Lorenzo—does it matter if I move in with Eric despite everything? If I don't expect more?

Something bright and hot comes to life in my chest, building until it pounds firm and loud behind my ribs, drumming realization into my blood.

I shake my head, pressing my lips together.

No, I cannot move back in with Eric.

Because we don't belong together. And also because I *do* expect more—for me. I packed too much of myself away for too long to be with him. But now, I've opened those boxes, dusted off the daydreams, and torn the bubble wrap off my old hopes. And instead of being satisfied to see the sunlight, they've grown hungry and powerful.

There are things I love, things I am good at, and I will explore them. I know what I want, and I won't settle. Not in life and not in love.

A tear slides down my cheek.

Oh, Lorenzo.

I replay our conversation in my head, holding on to the delicate image of his face when I suggested he'd kissed Valeria—my small, fragile hope.

From where we sit, I can't see any of the Rossis besides Mary. I know Lorenzo is up front somewhere beside Saveria as he watches his sister, smiling at her. If I had a view of him—all dressed up and emotional beside the altar—I might not survive the vows. As it is, I barely make it.

The bride and groom kiss, and I wipe away the remnants of my tears. Michela pulls some tissue from her purse and dabs my eyes before leading me out into the piazza.

From the far side of the courtyard, I watch Lorenzo come out of the doors and down the steps at the front of the church. His grin is so wide that my lips feel compelled to rise at the corners in response. The midday light floods his face, making him even more impossibly handsome, a Riace bronze in a custom wool suit and Ray-Ban Aviator Classics. He takes off his sunglasses, and our eyes meet across the piazza. Both our smiles falter in unison. Still, he continues toward me and is standing beside me when the crowd—with a sort of frenzied recklessness—launches brown paper cones of rice at Mary and Francesco.

The newlyweds duck their heads, laughing as they try to fend off the assault. Francesco takes off his jacket and shields Mary from the white grains the guests torpedo in their direction. She wiggles out of it to kiss him. The piazza erupts in cheers as Mary and Francesco stare into each other's eyes, cheeks flushed, mouths just tipping open.

They are so in love my stomach turns.

Lorenzo presses against my side as the mob closes in on the newlyweds, showering them with sexual innuendo now instead of rice. I shift my body away from his and lean into Michela to ask if she can give me a ride to the reception.

"*Certo*," she responds. "You and me, Remy, all night long." She gives a little shimmy, glances over my shoulder at Lorenzo, and smirks.

I laugh.

Lorenzo shoves his hands in his pockets and stalks off toward his brother, shouldering his way through the feral mob of geriatric Sicilians fighting for a chance to kiss the bride.

I squeeze myself into the backseat of Michela's Passione Red Fiat 500 convertible, crammed between the twins in a space only wide enough for two child-sized humans. Giacomo hops over the door and slides into the front passenger's seat without the use of his hands, which are clutching two bottles of prosecco. He pops them and passes one to me and the other to Michela, who gives it back.

Giacomo shrugs and reaches his bottle towards mine. We clink the glass together, and I take a sip while trying to crouch below doorframe-level to avoid being seen.

"*Ma che fai?*" Michela laughs at me. *What are you doing?*

"This is a wedding in Italy. I'm the one driving; no one cares if *you* drink in the car."

Not even Saveria? I want to ask because it's her I'm worried about. Heaven forbid I make a bad impression on the mother of a man I'll never see again once my time in Nunziata is up.

Michela raises her eyebrows at me. "*Bevi*," she commands. *Drink*. And I do. And then the music comes on, and I drink some more.

We are parked in a long line of vehicles that wraps around the edge of the piazza. They are all so close that bumpers are whispering against each other. After passing the prosecco to the twin on my left, I pull myself forward enough to turn in the seat. Tano and Roberto's Audi is right behind us. Lorenzo is already sitting in the back seat, arms crossed, staring at me through the windshield.

"Hi," I mouth, raising a hand.

"Hi," his lips say as he raises his hand in return. He leans forward between the two front seats, resting his elbows on his knees. He's close enough that I can see the way his chest heaves with a heavy breath, the lift and fall of his Adam's apple as he swallows. His mouth starts to move again, but I'm distracted by the sound of ignitions starting up. Applause arrives in a wave from the front of the line, where a car covered in ribbons and roses pulls into the street. Mary waves her bouquet out the window like a conductor's baton, and the motorcade responds with a symphony of honks that continues all the way to the reception hall.

I spend the ten-minute drive toward the sea holding my hair back and raising my free arm into the wind, resisting the urge to angle myself sideways in the seat so I can look back at Lorenzo, wishing I knew what more he'd had to say.

*

I finger comb my convertible-wrecked hair as we walk up to the castle. Because that's what it is: a white-washed, eighteenth-century country keep with crenelated towers that look out over the Mediterranean.

Before the main meal, there is an outdoor cocktail hour. The guests amble in, mingle, and find seats at the glass tables under a vine-covered veranda. A hush settles as the first pulls of an accordion echo over the lawn. A six-person marching band plays ahead of the newlyweds, who the guests greet with hurrahs and a standing ovation like we didn't just shout ourselves hoarse four miles ago outside the church.

Lorenzo is sitting with one of Francesco's brothers, his back to me. He doesn't see Saveria come by and kiss me on the forehead, but I see her bend over to whisper in his ear. I watch his shoulders rise as he laughs at something while the band plays Paolo Conte's "Via con Me." I trace his profile against the greenery when he turns his head to the right to take a drink of water. Michela nudges me as the dishes start arriving at the tables: charcuterie, freshly shucked shellfish, pizzette—and more prosecco.

We are already an entire day's worth of food in when the white-gloved staff invites us inside. The interior of the reception hall is *Godfather*-meets-*Jersey Shore* chic. Satin ivory curtains cover the floor-to-ceiling windows, and the room is lit up like the inside of a disco. The head table is at the back of the room, framed by an arch of white flowers, glitter, and twinkling lights, and the rest of the tables fan out on either side like the colonnades of St. Peter's Square in Rome.

I sway a little when I stop at the seating chart, and not on account of the prosecco.

Of course, it makes sense that tables for the formal dinner

would be assigned. I just didn't expect to find my name at this particular one.

With a steadying breath, I gaze at my table. Saveria is there, smiling at Roberto as he pulls out a chair for Nonna Nena. Tano watches the tender moment between his husband and his grandmother with hearts in his eyes, taking his seat and draping his arm over Roberto's when he sits beside him.

Two unoccupied chairs remain.

"Remy."

I jump at the sound of Lorenzo's voice—or the closeness of it, of him, stating my name like a fact. Or maybe an answer, but to what question?

He clears his throat. "Are you enjoying yourself?" he asks.

"How could I not? Just look at them," I say, my shoulders falling as we admire Mary and Francesco. "Have you ever seen two people so in love?"

I can feel his gaze turn to my face, and I have to fight to keep my breath even. When I turn to him, his jaw bunches, and he drops his eyes to his feet, speaking to them when he says, "Mary is easy to love; Tano too. My siblings have never had trouble where love is concerned."

I wonder if the words hurt as much coming out as they do to hear. The heartbreaking implication that he is different from them in this way. Did his father make him think that? Valeria?

But there's me, Lorenzo. There's me. And as hard as he's tried to keep it from happening, I've fallen head over heels. I reach out for his hand, and just as my fingertips graze his knuckles, he straightens and takes a step away. "We should sit. They'll be serving another course before the dancing begins."

I hug my elbows and follow Lorenzo to the family table, reaching for the menu as soon as I sit down to use as cover for my burning cheeks.

Luckily, it looks like there will be enough food and wine tonight for me to drown a lifetime of relationship sorrows in. The hour we just spent eating and drinking outside counted for only one-seventh of the meal plan.

A train of carts, each operated by two members of the wait-staff, travels between tables, delivering plates from silver, lidded trays. The first course: *saccottino di ricotta e miele* and a glass of grillo white wine.

As soon as the plates are cleared, the music begins. Michela pulls me from the table and onto the dance floor, and I don't protest.

The afternoon progresses into evening course by course with half-hour-long dance breaks in between. *Mezzi pacheri* with clams and plum tomatoes, then Chubby Checker and Shakira. *Bistecca alla fiorentina* followed by the Black Eyed Peas and Jovanotti.

I dance like I did with Lil during parties in our living room growing up, unselfconsciously. It might be the six hours of drinking that does it—though, between the food and the sweat, I don't even feel tipsy anymore. I think it's more that everyone else is busy having fun and not worrying about looking sexy or trying not to embarrass themselves. So I don't either.

Lorenzo is no stranger to the dance floor. Francesco's more mature female relatives draw him out into the music, and once a woman about my age in cheetah print who I've seen giving him eyes all evening drags him by a sleeve onto the floor.

His go-to move is some sort of Italian foxtrot that the older women can't get enough of. He smiles down at them as they twirl around the dance floor, and they run their hands up and down his sides way more than is necessary.

Not that I'm staring, but I do maybe throw a fist in the air when I see him fake a fit of coughing the second cheetah girl's hands find their way into his ass pockets. After a sip of water at our table, he comes back out, alone, and joins me and Michela and the cousins.

Lorenzo tries, but his freestyle is nowhere near as on point as his ballroom. When the Eurythmics hit, he's lost. I don't even attempt to stifle my laugh. Lorenzo straightens and leaves with a tight nod to the group. I spend the rest of the song and all of my lobster risotto that's served after feeling like an asshole.

As the empty dishes disappear, I notice Nonna Nena is becoming increasingly animated across the table, clapping her ringed hands together as she eyes me and then Lorenzo. The lights stay bright, no music cues up from the DJ stand, but people are beginning to circle the edge of the dance floor.

I lean into Tano on my right and ask him what they're doing.

"*U'nozzu,*" he answers, his eyes glinting at me, but not as brightly as Nonna Nena's.

"The what?" I ask, but no one hears because Lorenzo pushes back out of his chair, grinding out a firm, "No." Saveria tells him to sit back down, and he does, pouring a double shot worth of Amaro Averna into his glass and down his throat as soon as he's back in his seat.

I look around the table for answers, but none are forthcoming.

I steel myself and turn to Lorenzo. "What's going on?"

He scrubs his hands over his face. "*U'nozzu* is a traditional dance."

"I don't see the big deal."

"It's a courtship dance." His hands fall to his sides, and he looks at me with wide, worried eyes, maybe even frightened. "For unmarried couples."

"Lorenzo, what's about to happen?" I demand just before

a riot of grandmothers tugs us from our seats and into a small group of couples waiting on the dance floor.

The dance starts slow, and the audience claps in time with the music. I am stiff as I try to figure out the steps, but no one else seems too worried about the fact that I alone have no idea what I'm doing. The dance is nowhere near as horrifying as Lorenzo's face implied it would be.

Lorenzo and I aren't required to touch much—except for our palms, which is enough to create problems for my heart—but we must face one another the entire time.

"Sorry I laughed," I say, hoping to at least clear some of the air.

"Don't apologize. I'm not a dancer."

I should argue this point. I've spent a good portion of the night watching him glide around the dance floor like a hot detective Gene Kelly, but I don't because I'm pretty sure I'd tell him that.

We are quiet for a while, taking in each other's faces.

Lorenzo looks away. "I didn't kiss Valeria."

"What?"

He turns back to me, his eyes holding mine as he steps closer. "That evening, I was upset because—" he stops, shaking his head.

"Because?"

Lorenzo takes a deep breath. "It doesn't matter. But we hugged, that's it. There was no kiss. Nothing has happened with Valeria since—" Lorenzo drops his eyes. "Since I started working your case."

"Oh," I breathe, and I believe him, and I'm mad at myself for ever thinking otherwise. Because I trust him entirely.

But if they never kissed, then all this time…

"Why were you crying during the ceremony?" he asks in a low voice, and I realize that my eyes have begun to water again.

"I—" I must lie. "I wasn't crying."

His eyebrows crinkle, and he tilts his head, pressing his hand ever so more solidly into mine. "It must be hard for you," he says.

My throat tightens. "You have no idea," I murmur.

Lorenzo takes a deep breath, his lashes fanning out above his cheekbones when he looks down at me. "I'm sure Eric is suffering, too," he says.

I choke on the violence of my laugh, causing the line of dancers to bump against each other. "Yes, he's miserable," I snort. So miserable he's probably slamming his side piece on his vegan leather couch as we speak. And good for him.

Lorenzo frowns. He blinks at me.

And then the music ends. I step back and curtsy to Lorenzo; he bows in return as the lights start to go down.

The DJ shouts something incoherent into the microphone, and the dance floor floods with young people. I turn away from Lorenzo and begin walking toward the full glass of Etna Rosso that is waiting for me at the table. A familiar, twangy Latin song intro blasts through the speakers.

I make it two steps when a hand slips around my waist from behind.

I spin, expecting to see Giacomo with that tequila boom boom shot he's been threatening to make me try.

Instead, it's Lorenzo. He draws his hand back, raises it palm up in between us, an offering.

"May I have one more dance?" he asks.

Chapter TWENTY-SIX

THERE'S GOT TO BE A CATCH.

I look up from his waiting hand and around the reception hall. Maybe this is "U'nozzu" part two. First, they force you to dance around to some hundred-year-old tambourine music, and if you survive palming each other for five solid minutes while being forced to look into one another's eyes, they make the couple take a run at something else. But "Despacito"? Seems unlikely.

So what is he doing?

Maybe he thinks his Eric line of questioning made me feel bad and wants to make it up to me. Lorenzo is nothing if not thoughtful to a fault.

But, like, has anyone in the history of the world ever foxtrotted to sexy Reggaeton before? Is it even possible?

I blink, my attention returning to the space between us. At some point, my hand found its way into his. I must not have noticed because it feels like it has always existed there, in the gentle squeeze of his fingers. His other hand slips under my arm and settles on the back of my shoulder. I wonder if he feels me shiver.

This is more contact than he usually allows—which is zero —but we are a safe, middle-school dance distance apart in all the places it counts. I smile as I rest my free hand on his side. Beggars can't be choosers.

My eyes flutter closed as his hand drifts to my waist, but they fly open and upward when I realize Lorenzo is singing. His deep voice rumbles low in my belly as he serenades me with Justin Bieber's opening. It should be hilarious, Lorenzo belting out Bieber while we sway in place a ruler-width apart. It should be.

But I can't laugh. I can't even swallow. Lorenzo's eyes are holding my mouth prisoner, and it's just sitting there uselessly on my face, awaiting orders.

His gaze drops to my neck, then lower until he's taken all of me in and left every nerve shaking in his wake. His eyes find mine again, and I see something flash there. Doubt? Worry? It doesn't matter because he shakes it away and spreads his palm against the bare skin of my back. He releases his other hand, and my arm remains raised, statue-still. Lorenzo runs his fingertips along the inside of my arm, from my fingertips to my shoulder. My head falls back. He trails them down my ribs, and I press my lips together. His hand sinks into the dip just above my hip, and he pulls me into him right as the Spanish drops.

If this is some variation of Lorenzo's good cop/bad cop, I'm not sure which one I am getting, but I hope he sticks around. This version of Lorenzo does not foxtrot. But he definitely uses handcuffs in the bedroom.

Lorenzo holds me tight against his hips, and I cling to his jacket, using the rise and fall of his chest to remember when to breathe, though both of us are exhaling in gasps. He dips me, bends into me, and as we come up, I claim his neck for support, one hand sinking into his hair. His mouth opens on a groan.

I squirm in his arms, press my chest against his, rub every

bare piece of my flesh against some part of his body. His arm wraps tighter around me, his fingers splayed just above my ass and resting on the place where the top of my panties would be if I had any on. I know the exact moment he realizes I'm bare underneath my dress because all the places our bodies are touching tense at once, and one, in particular, stays that way.

Lorenzo's eyes go wide, and his touch lightens, almost like he's embarrassed about what his body is communicating. I cannot allow that.

I hitch my hip up on his side, the slit of my dress barely resisting. His hand reaches down to grip my thigh, his fingers sinking into the flesh so close to the places I want them. Lorenzo drags his bottom lip through his teeth, and I press my hips harder into his on the next roll of our bodies because his need is just a tiny reflection of my own, and I'm aching everywhere to feel him on me.

We have gone from two kids at a middle school dance to two adults who may be carted off for lewd acts in public if my body has any say in the matter.

The only way to get closer is for our faces to meet, and they do, cheek-to-cheek. I feel the rough drag of his scruff on the side of my lips. His warm breath tickles my ear.

Any remaining restraint I had melts away with the friction of our clothing, our skin. I can't be this close and not have all of Lorenzo. I run my tongue along his jawline. He rakes his teeth against my neck. I've never wanted to taste another person's mouth as badly as I do right now. And what do I have to lose?

I pull back just enough to look into his face. Our mouths are there, swollen with want and panting against each other. Our lips brush, and everything in me convulses with unresolved desire.

"Lorenzo," I breathe against his mouth as the song ends.

And then he's putting me back together, carefully, gently—like a breakable doll that's been flung through the air and lands with its body parts all out of order. But the only part of me that feels like it might not recover is my heart.

"Remy, I—"

"Why?" I rasp. My insides are on fire. My throat is filled with flames.

He rubs a hand over his brows, the fingers of his other still lingering in mine. "I thought I could do it—be your friend. But having you here has made it so much harder." He steps closer, rests his forehead against mine. "I'm sorry, Remy," he whispers. "I'm so sorry."

Lorenzo can't have me here. But I am here, and now I'm not that happy about it either.

He spends the rest of the reception at a different table with different women while I simmer in his words—the fact that he just dirty-danced me into molten goo because he thought he was trying to be a good friend. I scream myself raw on the dance floor when the DJ plays an aggressive remix of Franz Ferdinand's "Take Me Out," making Giacomo visibly nervous. When I find Lorenzo to tell him Nonna Nena is ready to head back to Nunziata and Tano said we could take his car, he flinches when I touch his arm. I all but snap my teeth at him in return.

He's the one who asked to dance, who managed to forget for the entire space of "Despacito" that he loathes being near me. But he thinks it's all right, I guess, to be an asshole, because he said he was sorry.

I despise him. I have to. It is the only feeling powerful enough to shut the others up.

When we get to the apartment, Lorenzo helps Nonna Nena to her bed. She insists on giving us both a goodnight kiss, and I grab her a glass of water from the kitchen while she has Lorenzo turn down her sheets.

She is talking to him in low tones when I come back, and he seems flustered. I go to the room to give them some privacy and to get out of my shoes. I unbuckle them, wiggle some feeling back into my toes, and try not to think about what happened while Lorenzo and I were dancing as I dig my pajamas out from under the pillows. Go figure: I have the best sexual experience of my life on a dance floor with a man who can't stand to have me around while his entire family looks on. I wonder what the priest at table sixteen would have to say.

If I hurry, I can change before Lorenzo comes in and save him the horror of seeing me undressed.

My dress, however, does not cooperate. The cute bow I made on my lower back when I tied myself into my dress this morning has become a constrictor knot after multiple tipsy re-trussings in the lady's room. I'm still struggling when Lorenzo enters the bedroom, looking a little like maybe his grandma just told him his childhood dog he loved didn't actually retire on the *masseria*.

"Could you help?" I ask, wriggling my hands behind me.

He looks up at me, bewildered—maybe he expected me to be in his mom's room since we now have the luxury of an extra bed—then sits down to take his shoes off, placing them next to mine.

"Can you just get the bottom knot?" I try again. "I can't reach." I turn to show him what I mean. His features tighten.

"I can't," he says.

"Just pull it. It should come undone."

"Remy," his voice is gravel, somewhere between a groan and a growl. "I can't…touch you."

I turn on him, eyes like daggers.

This is ridiculous. He's ridiculous. And, if I'm honest, it hurts that this vacillating repulsion he feels toward me is so insurmountable that it makes him incapable of helping me out of my damn dress.

"You can't untie my dress? We were just dancing together," I remind him. "And somehow, you survived." I don't mention that, if the hard heat against my hip was any indication, he didn't hate it, either.

"We were surrounded by people," he says. His throat is tight.

"So, you need witnesses in order to be close to me." I cross my arms, take a step closer. This is beyond absurd.

He clenches his jaw. "Yes," he grits out. "I do." His eyes flash to mine before he looks back at the ground.

Somewhere inside of me, something wild rears its head. My chest rises, falls. "Why?" I ask. I'm holding my breath. The word feels like a match, flickering through darkness.

Lorenzo stands, looks up at the ceiling, pushes a hand through his hair. It turns into a fist, and the noise he makes reminds me of our first kiss on the Palatine. My heart pounds in response, my body pulses.

He drops his face back to mine, our eyes lock, and heat pumps in waves through my mind. His gaze is hungry, starving, a fire in desperate need of oxygen.

I open my mouth, willing my response to be the bellows. "Untie my dress, Lorenzo."

He shudders, and I take a step closer, turning my back to him. Lorenzo runs the featherlight touch of his fingertips along the laces that crisscross over my back. They fall to the dip of material that grazes low on my hips—a tingle races down my spine. A moan echoes in the space around us, and I'm not sure which of us made the noise, but his hands become more urgent.

I feel the fabric loosen as the knot comes undone, and then the brush of his lips on my shoulder, behind my ear. His hand pushes at the strap of my dress, and it falls down my arm as his breath caresses my neck. "What's this?" he murmurs into my hair, his finger grazing the small tattoo on my upper ribs—a compass rose with the number seven inside. For Rome, a promise to myself when I turned eighteen that I would find my way back to a love that made my knees forsake their function.

Instead of answering, I press against him. One strong hand comes around to hold me, tightening against my belly—the length of my body is suspended against his, and I feel him there, wanting.

His other hand is in my hair. "I know I have no right to do this," he says into my skin, trailing his mouth along the goosebumps blossoming on my shoulder. "Tell me to stop, and I will."

If he lets go of me now, there's no way I'd be able to stand. There's no way I could walk away from this moment and not regret it for the rest of my life. I turn my body within the circle of his arm.

"I want you," I say into his mouth, tugging on his bottom lip with my teeth. "Only you."

"You are all I've ever wanted," he murmurs back, then he takes my mouth with his, in a kiss so deep, I feel it ripple through the most secret corners of my body, in places heat and longing have never reached before.

Lorenzo pushes me out of my dress while my fingers fumble over the buttons of his shirt and fight with the buckle of his belt. When my dress falls to my feet, he inhales, looking at me. Everywhere his eyes settle, bonfires ignite beneath my skin.

He leans forward, kisses me on the forehead. "You make my heart blaze, Remy Campbell."

I launch myself at him, tearing his shirt from his body, helping him kick his pants and his briefs to the ground. I run my hands over his hard stomach, his back, his arms, as he kisses an eager trail from my collarbone to my breasts. I stumble back onto the bed, and he is there with me.

The sensation of his scruff on the most neglected expanses of my skin makes me arch against the mattress, and I'm certain that the firm grip of his hands on my inner thighs is the only thing keeping me from floating away. His tongue finds its way back up my abdomen, to my mouth, and he kisses me so fiercely my thighs quiver.

His fingers help to ease the mounting ache, but I want more.

"I need you," I gasp, rising to pull him over me, tugging at his arms to settle him against the stretch of my body.

We are both panting as I reach into the bedside table and grab one of the condoms stashed there, pushing it into his hands. His fingers tremble as he takes it.

"Are you sure?" he asks, watching my eyes, my face, for any sign of doubt.

"Yes, Lorenzo," I say. I lick a stream of sweat from his chest, tighten my hands on his taut back and dig my nails in. "I am really fucking sure."

His hesitation evaporates, and soon, he's there with me, and we are moving against each other like the future of humanity depends on it, like if I don't touch all of him at once, the world might cease to exist.

Then just when I think nothing has ever felt so good or

right, we come undone together in a crushing burst of sweat and need and pleasure.

We hold each other tight, unwilling to give the moment even an inch of space to fall apart. Lorenzo's breath is cool against my skin and as unsteady as my own.

I kiss his cheek, let my lips linger on his damp skin, and I wonder if Lorenzo is as terrified as I am.

After that, how can I ever pretend to be okay with anything less?

Chapter TWENTY-SEVEN

I WAKE UP WITH THE THICK BROCADED QUILT pulled up under my neck, my shoes set on the ground beside me, and an open bottle of acqua frizzante on the bedside table—right between the box of condoms and a rosary.

The roller shades are closed, and the room is dark. I did not have the mental wherewithal to maneuver myself under the covers after the countless plates of pasta and the liter of red blend that ended up in my glass at lunch, which means Lorenzo must have gotten me to bed and tucked me in.

I don't know if it's still the day after the wedding or the next, but based on the noise coming from beyond the door, I am the only one in bed. I turn on a light and find my phone in my purse—seven p.m.

Lorenzo and I spent all morning locked in the bedroom, sustained by the eight courses plus cake we'd consumed at the wedding. But by midday, our reserves couldn't keep up with the near-rabid need to keep touching, and Saveria came home, so we ventured to Zio Peppe's for lunch.

I bite down on the squeal that battles to broadcast from my body, flinging my arm out beside me, where the pillow wall of resistance has been razed, demolished by endless hours of kissing, and cuddling, and having real-life (and not just in my mind) sex with Lorenzo.

Grinning, I read through my pile of messages from Lil. They are all variations of her emotional response to the single text I sent her after the wine hit at lunch and a series of follow-up questions I'll get to later.

For now, she can take my, "I'm sorry I didn't trust you when you told me simultaneous orgasm is real," and use her imagination to fill in the blanks.

I push myself out of bed and take a look in the mirror on the back of the bedroom door. My hair appears to be levitating above my scalp, and my sundress looks like re-gifted tissue paper.

I figure I can sneak out of the bedroom and into the bathroom, where my toiletries have been stowed, before anyone sees me. I slip on my sandals and open the door. It screeches like a cat in heat.

Mary's head pops out of the kitchen, and I sigh behind my smile.

"Remy," she calls. "I need your help."

I attempt to flatten my dress with one hand and my hair with the other as I pass through the living room. A chorus of voices greets me. "*La bella addormentata!*" "*Pensavo che gli americani sapevano bere.*" "*Mangia la stigghiola che ti metterá apposto.*" Jabs about sleeping beauty and Americans' inability to drink. An order to eat something called *sitgghiola* to get myself fixed up.

Aunts, uncles, fiftieth cousins twice removed shout from the overburdened couches and the crowded table. I shrug and laugh, and they laugh back. In a kind way. A way that makes me feel like part of it all. Saveria gives me a small smile that I return.

"What's *stigghiola*?" I ask Mary as I pull out the chair beside her at the kitchen table.

She fakes a gag.

"So if one of the aunts offers, I say I'm allergic?"

Her face goes still, serious. "Remy, you can't lie to *le zie*."

I open my mouth to tell a different lie about how much I'd love to eat all the mystery things and apologize for my bad joke, but the corner of her mouth twitches up, much the way her brother's does.

"They can sniff it out," she whispers, looking at her family gathered in the other room. "Trust me. I've been trying my whole life."

I exhale on a giggle.

Mary stands and grabs a big bowl out of the sink, setting it on the table between our seats. "Mamma wants to make *macco di fave* for the dinner tomorrow, which means we get to peel all of these tonight," she says, settling in beside me.

Tomorrow is the last day in Nunziata for the newlyweds before they head back to Catania, and our last day before we return to Rome. "When we were at Zio Peppe's earlier, the aunts decided we'd be having the last lunch at Nicolas and Maristella's house. There will be dinner, too?" I ask, not sure I have the internal capacity to withstand two full-size Sicilian meals.

"Indeed." She smiles. "Since we are all leaving Nunziata, they must feed us threatening amounts of food to assure the mothers and grandmothers we will survive until we return. They're probably already planning the menu for your next visit."

My next visit?

My stomach teeters with my pulse between the excitement of that possible future and the realization that Lorenzo and I, in the throes of our pent-up passion, have not spoken at all about *any* future.

Chill out, Remy.

It's only been like fifteen hours since I first saw him naked. Of course we haven't talked about holiday visits with his family yet.

I shake myself and glance into the bowl that Mary propped between us. Inside is what I'd approximate to be at least my body weight's worth of dried, shell-on fava beans soaking in water. Mary gets going, and I follow her lead, discarding the skins onto the red-checked cotton table cover. Her pile grows much more speedily than mine does, maybe because I'm busy scanning the mass of people in the other room for her brother.

"Lorenzo went for a walk with Nonna Nena and Matilde," Mary says, glancing at me and then back at her fava beans. I imagine Lorenzo with his grandmother on one arm and his goddaughter on the other. My heart swells so aggressively, I think Mary can sense it because she adds, as if to see if I might burst like one of Zio Peppe's overripe tomatoes, "He likes to sneak them out and buy them ice cream."

I look up at her, and whatever she sees on my face makes her give my sticky, fava-covered hand a gentle squeeze. We both reach back into the bowl.

We are quiet for a moment before she speaks again. "When Lollu said he was bringing an American girl, we were all so hopeful he'd found the one."

"It's not like that," I say out of habit, but I want that not to be true anymore. It's not true anymore, right? "I mean, things are..." My throat is tight, and I don't manage to finish my thought.

"I know, I know," Mary helps me. "He's just held on to that story for so long."

My head shoots up. "What story?"

She studies me a second and then huffs a laugh, pushing her dark waves out of her face with the back of her arm. "Lorenzo would kill me if I told you."

"But obviously, now you have to."

"He never mentioned why he studied English?"

"No. I just assumed you were all preternaturally good at languages. I mean, what the hell? Your English is better than half my contacts on Facebook."

Her chin rises a little at my compliment.

"You can't tell him I told you," she says, holding my gaze with her sharp, gray eyes.

I put out my pinky, and she seems unsure of what to do, so I give her a cursory lesson in American elementary school omertà. After we've both kissed our knuckles and I've sealed my lips and thrown away the key, she dries her hands. She must need them for the story.

"When Lorenzo was sixteen or so, he met an American girl and fell in love. I don't know what he was thinking, maybe that he'd magically bump into her someday, but he became obsessive about his English. In high school, he even worked at the gelateria every day after soccer practice to pay for private lessons."

"Wow," I say, but deep down, I am starting-to-see-spots-in-my vision jealous. Completely envious of some random American adolescent whose Italian fell so in love with her, he sacrificed his teen years scooping gelato just to be able to communicate in the case they ever found each other again—a girl who stole Lorenzo's heart before I could.

"Honestly, it was a little *pazzesco*," Mary adds, tapping the side of her head.

I grab another bean to give my hands something to do other

than clench in baseless outrage in my lap. "I didn't realize you get a lot of tourists here."

Mary chuckles. "I think you're the first American to set foot in Nunziata since World War II. He didn't meet her here. He was spending the summer with our father. If I'd been around, I would have smacked some sense into him then, spared him the decade-plus of drama."

I think back to what Valeria told me about how Lorenzo had always been searching for something impossible to find. Maybe this is what she meant.

"I just can't help but think it's the reason he is so stuck on staying in Rome," Mary says, almost to herself. "Not because of Papá, but because he's still hoping this girl will show up."

My heart stutters. "Rome?" I breathe.

She squints at me, but we both turn away when the door flies open. A giggling, chocolate ice cream–covered Matilde is settled on Lorenzo's hip, his arm around her, and just as I imagined, Nonna Nena's hand is laced in his other arm.

Matilde leaps off and skids into the living room. Lorenzo leans his ear down to his grandmother, whose gesturing implies a very intense conversation. He locks eyes with me over the top of her head, and it might be the lighting, but his face looks red. He nods when she reaches up to pat his cheek, and we both watch Nonna Nena shuffle down the hall.

Or I pretend to. Really, I'm clenching every part of my body below my neck to keep it in place—my heart, my uterus, the spot between my legs that leads to both.

Mary clears her throat beside me and gives me a look that I can't read before standing and gesturing her brother toward her chair.

"*Tocca a te, fratello,*" she says to Lorenzo as she leaves the room. *Your turn, brother.*

Lorenzo slips into Mary's vacated seat and kisses my temple. "Did you sleep well?" he asks.

"Very," I answer, looking up at him, trying to erase the space of twelve years in his face, his features.

Lorenzo reaches into the pot of unshucked fava. I watch his mouth move, hear most of what he says as he tells me a story about Nonna Nena punishing him with a year of peeling beans after he used a neighbor's open window for shooting practice, but all I can think is, *Rome*.

Rome?

It's impossible. It should be impossible.

But what if it's not?

I shake my head. There is no way Lorenzo was that boy at the Colosseum, that he carried that kiss with him as long as I have.

That would be insane.

I reach out and run the back of my fingers along his scruffy jaw, up into his hair. He looks at me, his lip caught between his teeth in a smile, his eyes as hungry, and dark, and hot as ever.

I apologize to Mary in my head and to the institute of secret-keeping in general because there is no way I am holding up my end of that pinky promise.

We park down a dirt road and hike through shrub-clad rocks interspersed with prickly pear and tall amber grass toward the sea. The beach is a stretch of white sand and water so clear and blue it makes the cloudless sky look almost dull by comparison.

And it is all ours.

Lorenzo shakes out a blanket for us to lay on but ends up draping it around my shoulders when he sees me shiver. The breeze is brisk, but the sunshine offsets the cold. The temperature has nothing to do with why goosebumps bloom along my skin, but I keep the blanket on anyway, to arm myself, my heart, for what I've been waiting since last night to ask.

Lorenzo sits down, and I sit between his legs facing the water. He wraps his arms around me, kisses my hair.

If Lorenzo was not the boy at the Colosseum, I'll be fine. Whatever we have right now is all I've ever wanted. My knees might never work properly again on account of all the kiss-induced weakness they've suffered the past two days, but that is a consequence I am more than willing to accept.

I might still be a little jealous of that teenager who stole his heart all those years ago, but I could get over it with enough direct access to his lips and naked time together.

But what if it *was* Lorenzo at the Colosseum? What would that mean? Is destiny a real thing? Am I crazy for thinking this is even possible?

I take a deep breath and tell myself to stop being a baby and clear my throat and...

"Did I ever tell you how I found Mnemosine?" he asks.

I look back at him over my shoulder, and he nuzzles into the side of my face. Okay, he can go first. "I recall that you were reading *The Theogony* at the time. Goddess of memory, right?" I'm pretty impressed with myself for remembering any of what he told me that morning after seeing him shirtless, fresh out of the shower, and in those sweatpants.

Then again, I doubt I'll ever forget any of our time together. I hope so hard I don't have to.

He brushes his lips against my ear. "Yes. It was three years ago, and my father had just passed. After law school, I got the detective position with the Polizia di Stato because he knew the Chief. Valeria and I were fighting all the time. I missed my family, and I was thinking about leaving Rome. I couldn't remember why I wanted to be there."

His legs squeeze against mine, and I lean back into him.

"I grabbed *The Theogony* by chance out of my dad's bookcase and started walking. I ended up at the Colosseum. There's an old, worn down stone—"

"On the southwest side." My heart pounds.

Lorenzo hesitates. "Yeah, that one. I sat there and opened the book to a random page. I wasn't paying much attention to the words. I just needed to be doing something. Then I heard her."

"Mnemosine?"

I feel his nod against my back. "She just appeared—this tiny, fluffy kitten with runny eyes—while I sat on that stone and read about the goddess of memory."

"Lorenzo," I say, turning around to face him, my knees tucked beneath me. "Mary told me why you studied English."

He sighs, but he's smiling. "Did she really?"

I drop my gaze. My fingers play with a button on his shirt. "She said there was a girl. An American girl and…."

"And?"

I look up into his eyes. "Do you still talk to her?"

He sweeps my hair behind my ear, and his eyes are so earnest and dark I want to look into them forever. "I do," he answers. My heart beats everywhere inside me at once. He reaches up to hold my face between his hands.

"It was you, wasn't it?" I whisper.

Lorenzo smiles.

"When did you know?" I ask.

He runs his thumbs under my eyes, sweeping away a few stray tears I didn't realize were falling.

"I suspected early. As soon as I saw your red running shoes when we came to take you into custody."

"My shoes?"

"The night at the Colosseum, you had on red sneakers."

"From my dad."

"Of course that wasn't a lot of evidence to go on, so I might have taken a little advantage of my position at the station to do additional research during the investigation."

"The REMY CAMPBELL file!" I smack him on the shoulder. He catches my hand and kisses my knuckles, slowly, one by one. "Super creepy," I add in a husky voice that undermines my indignation.

"I know." His words whisper against my skin.

"Why didn't you say anything?" I ask, scooting closer in the sand so I can press my mouth against his neck.

He laughs. "Remy, if you kissed someone and they'd forgotten, would you be in a rush to bring it up?"

I lean my forehead into his. "It was my first kiss. I never forgot." I leave out the part about being in love with him ever since and kiss him again instead. Our mouths go from soft and sweet to hungry and insistent as I fall on top of him in the sand. "Living in your apartment and not being able to touch you was torture," I tell him.

"You have no idea."

"I thought about you all the time."

"Not all the time," he says, raising his eyebrows. "I remember finding you thinking very hard with Eric after my soccer game."

"Trust me, whatever you saw had nothing to do with Eric."

He rolls me over, pushes my legs wide with his knee, and presses himself in between them. He rubs against the seam of my jeans. I moan.

"Were you thinking about this?" he murmurs into my ear.

"Pretty close," I breathe, arching into him. He runs his teeth along my collarbone. "Less clothing, though."

After we've committed at least two separate crimes on the private beach, Lorenzo feeds me a panino, and I ask him, "What now?" between bites. I mean *us*, what now with us, what happens when two people—who've been looking and waiting—find each other again?

"Now we go home and get packed before dinner, so we are ready to fly back to Rome tomorrow morning and find the third clue before Fabio does."

He's right, of course. We've neglected the case for way too long. But my mouth feels dry and sticky when I say, "Yeah, fuck that guy."

Lorenzo's face falls, and he runs a hand along the outside of my thigh. "I'm going to miss that mouth when you leave."

Leave? My stomach twists when I remember my flight to Phoenix is only five days away. Waking up in his arms has made it easy to forget this is all about to come to an end.

Lorenzo is the kind of love you come home to. The kind of love you package up and keep inside your heart for strength when you need it most. And I am supposed to just walk away from that?

But maybe this is it, twelve years of angsty yearning appeased by seven days of "That's Amore" playing on a loop inside my heart and then farewell. Maybe we were never meant to be forever, just two falling stars blazing past each other, intersecting for one magical moment in time.

That doesn't happen twice, though, does it?

He found me, and I don't want him to let me go. I want him to keep me, always. I want our together to be its own eternity.

Chapter TWENTY-EIGHT

The thought of never seeing Lorenzo's family again makes my heart feel like it is being stomped to death by every last one of Hannibal's war elephants. There is a lot of hugging and kissing and *arrivederci*, but Lorenzo still hasn't mentioned anything about me extending my stay (preferably forever), so I suffer through our goodbyes as the black hole within me gapes wider and wider.

As soon as we are on the plane, I pull out the leather, fasces-stamped journal from Villa Medici in a desperate attempt to channel my feelings into something that doesn't look like despair, which I'm worried is plastered all over my face.

"Do you think they meant for one of the aspirants to find the journal?" I ask Lorenzo. Their initials were carved across the coffered ceiling, after all. Fabio must have come pretty close to uncovering it before we did since he'd been staying at the Villa Medici.

"Maybe. Whatever those numbers are written inside, it seems pretty certain they are connected to the five people vying for the council spot."

"Yeah," I murmur. Still, I can't help but think there's more to it. "I just feel like I'm missing something."

"That's why you're so good at figuring things out. You keep looking past the obvious."

"We've done a lot of looking for the third clue, and three weeks later, we've still got nothing."

"False," Lorenzo says, shifting his gaze to the journal in my lap. He rests his hand on top of it and angles his mouth closer to my face. "I'm pretty happy with what we've managed so far."

I swallow and cross my leg away from him as he leans back into his own seat. A private beach is one thing, but just because the plane is packed doesn't mean I have the willpower to make respectable bodily decisions where Lorenzo is involved.

Luckily, it is a short flight, and once we get in his car, he puts in a call through to the station and has us back to the apartment in record time with zero police interference.

By dinner, I can confirm with absolute certainty that every piece of furniture my bare backside has met in the apartment is rock solid. Except for the bookcase, which is how I ended up staring at Saveria's old poetry books while trying to brace the shelves with Lorenzo behind me.

For dinner, Lorenzo feeds me *pasta al forno* and opens a bottle of Solaia.

"Are we celebrating something?" I ask. It is the same bottle that he brought home the night I was freed, the wine we drank on the Palatine.

"Us?" he offers.

I'd answer, but my throat is choking on the fact that I only have three full days left in Rome. Valeria said Lorenzo wasn't a fighter, but I want him to fight for this thing the universe has tossed in our laps twice now. I need to know that he wants a future in which we are together as desperately as I do.

But he's been left by his father and Valeria. Maybe he is too afraid to try, just to lose again.

Unless.

Unless he doesn't want that future. My track record with men this year isn't great, and I've learned enough not to trust my footing, even with Lorenzo.

"Let's go back to the Palatine tonight," I say.

His eyes darken, and I feel my cheeks flush like we didn't just spend the better part of the day traumatizing Mnemosine.

"We can show those vestals what they're missing," he answers, swirling his wine.

This time we break into the Forum from a small access road off of Via dei Fori Imperiali. Through a gate. That Lorenzo has a key to.

"Really?" I ask as he swings the metal bars open and gestures for me to enter. "A key?"

"I thought I'd be more likely to make an impression if I snuck you in on the Arch of Septimus Severus. It was also a good excuse to get to catch you at the bottom."

"Then I'm disappointed we didn't do it again."

Lorenzo smiles at me and locks the gate behind us. "Next time," he says, and I squash the bleak tremor of heartache that surges in my belly.

The moon is hidden, but the clouds hold the glow of the city. Rome lights itself from within and from above, and it is easy to see the path. Lorenzo takes my hand anyway as we pass the Temple of Antoninus and Faustina. I squeeze his fingers back extra tight.

Instead of walking straight to the House of the Vestals, we loop past the ruins of the Temple of the Deified Julius Caesar. Inside, visitors have tossed offerings onto the crumbling altar in honor of the man who turned Rome from a republic into an empire. The sight of impromptu bouquets piled on the 2000-year-old mound and coins pooling at its base makes me grin. Lorenzo pulls me into a kiss.

"I love the way Rome excites you," he breathes into my hair.

I don't respond because this comment is not the proper lead-in to what I want to tell Lorenzo. But it is close to what I hope he'll one day tell me.

We stroll on, along the southeast edge of the Basilica Julia. When the tall steps up to the basilica end, Lorenzo puts an arm around my shoulders as we drift left to avoid a portion of railing that juts out into the path. As we pass, I stop walking. There is a metal door worked into a recess under the base of the building.

I look up at Lorenzo. "What do you think that goes to?"

"It was one of the original openings to the Cloaca Maxima. It still convenes with the main line as far as I know."

I straighten in his arms and look up, past the broken columns of the basilica, past the edge of the Forum, and to the Capitoline Hill. "The Temple of Jupiter Optimus Maximus would have been there, right?" I point to the western corner of the Forum.

"Parts of it still are, built into the Palazzo dei Conservatori."

"The same palazzo where the *Lion Attacking a Horse* is displayed."

"Same one."

"Designed by Michelangelo."

"*Si, si.*"

I chew my lip. "When we were at the Villa Medici, you told me that one of the original Medici lions was carved from a capital taken from the Temple of Jupiter."

Lorenzo nods.

I grab for my phone but then remember I left everything in

the apartment. Lorenzo hands me his, and I open a Latin-English dictionary. "It could work," I tell him. "Under the den of the lions," I say, gesturing with my head to the Capitoline Hill, "the cloaca of the kingdom."

He's leaning over my shoulder to see the page I've pulled up. "Without the drainage the Cloaca Maxima provided, the Forum never would have existed here. This was all marshland until the Etruscan kings came in."

I smile as a shiver runs down my spine. Lorenzo's encyclopedic knowledge of Etruscan history is definitely my kink. "You don't happen to have a key to the Cloaca Maxima on your person, do you?"

"I don't," he smiles back. "But I know someone who can find us one."

We both glance at the Palatine Hill behind us. I am torn between wanting to spend every last hour of the next few days in Lorenzo's arms and solving this case. When I leave, it would be good to know that I at least exacted my sweet revenge on Fabio. It would be good to know what I am capable of moving forward.

Luckily, most of kicking Fabio's ass will involve having Lorenzo at my side regardless.

"Do you mind if we head home?" I press my cheek against his chest. It has been a long day, and it's already past midnight. Before I drag Lorenzo into the trenches, I should do some more research. And some sleep would be nice, too.

"I'd follow you anywhere, Remy," he answers, running light fingertips across my shoulders.

"Even through an ancient sewer?"

"Especially through an ancient sewer."

If that's true, maybe at the very least, I could convince him to visit me in Phoenix.

*

We return to the Forum the following day, thirty minutes before the gates open to the public. A colleague of Lorenzo's comes along to guard the door while we are inside the Cloaca. He needs to keep out tourists and, more importantly, keep us from getting locked inside.

That I'm going back underground at all says a lot about my determination to see this through. I just hope I'm not putting my faith about making my way into the light again in another Alberto. Lorenzo reassures me we could always follow the drainage channels to the Tiber River and escape there if necessary. Still, I'd prefer not to see that happen, so I am extra friendly with Officer DeSantis.

In the daylight, the Forum is just as magical as it was last night. Spring wildflowers bloom in any spot not claimed by marble or Roman concrete—and even then, in some places, they've managed to take hold in tiny cracks or crevices on the sides of buildings and columns. Bright red poppies carpet the floors of basilicas, and snapdragons and purple larkspur line the Via Sacra.

Lorenzo bends and picks a small bunch of delicate white flowers. "Were you flirting with DeSantis?" he asks, smirking at me as he hands me the tiny collection of blossoms.

"Yes. Do you think it will keep him from locking us in the sewer?"

"I think we'll be okay."

"You should flirt too, just in case."

Lorenzo nods. "DeSantis," he calls to the officer who is already at the door to the Cloaca Maxima. "*Stai frequentando la palestra*?" *Have you been going to the gym?*

DeSantis turns to us and flexes an arm in the air to examine his bicep. He grins. "*Solo un paio di volte*." *Just a couple of times.*

Lorenzo looks down at me and raises his eyebrows. "Was that good?"

"We should definitely be safe now."

As soon as we are through the door, I reconsider my decision. But I fought Maelle surrounded by crypts, and two stories below street level. I can handle some puddles and dark corners.

Lorenzo has equipped us both with headlamps and rubber boots, and we pause inside the entrance to look around. The tunnel spans at least the width of a car, and extensive, water-stained travertine blocks arch over our heads. We follow the flow of the water toward the river and away from the city. Since Rome's modern sewers don't run into the Cloaca Maxima, we only have to wade through rain runoff, so there is no added threat of contracting disease via human waste.

There are a lot of rats, though.

"Hello, little rodents," I say, deciding to make the best of it. "Have you happened to notice a clue floating around down here that leads to the location of a missing amulet?" They go on doing ratty things and ignore me.

"I don't think they understand," Lorenzo offers.

"How do you propose I get their attention?"

"Something more Italian."

"Right. How would a local say, 'Friends, Romans, countrymen, lend me your ears?'"

"*Aó, ascoltate ragazzi,*" Lorenzo shouts into the tunnel. The rats skitter off.

"That works for me."

We walk forward, following the path of the rodents. "I know I may be wrong—again—about this being the answer to the clue, but is it weird that they only sent one other officer with us? I mean, what if the clue is down here? Shouldn't we have some backup or something?"

I feel Lorenzo tense beside me, and I reach for his arm.

"What is it?" I demand.

"Well, the Commissioner has switched the focus of the case. There are a couple of higher-ups in the Zalśar organization that he's working with Interpol to locate. He thinks they are more important than the amulet for now."

"When did this happen?"

"Around the time you caught Maelle," he answers as he runs his hand through his hair.

I cross my arms. "So, you have just been indulging me this whole time like my mother assumed."

"No, Remy," he says, reaching out to squeeze my hand. "The Commissioner thought it would be good for us to keep looking. If the Zalśar think our attention is still on the amulet, they might be less careful with other things."

"So you got stuck playing pretend with me?"

"I asked to be stuck with you. And there's more. After I talked to the server from your lunch with Fabio and had a chance to question Maelle, I noticed a pattern that connects the theft of the amulet to a few other crimes—including one that I worked on recently."

"The one where you let the bad guy get away?"

"Exactly. Thanks to you, I've had time to look into it further without drawing attention from the wrong people."

"The Zalśar?"

"The Zilath."

"What the fuck is that?" I scream, scrambling up Lorenzo and making sure no part of my body is touching the ground. Just ahead of us, the head of a huge, hungry-looking creature is jutting out from the wall.

Lorenzo cradles his hands under my bottom, propping me

on his hip. "I believe that is where one of the sewer branches empties into the Cloaca Maxima, *cara*."

I look closer and concede that he is probably right.

He sets me down, our feet touching. "Where do you think we are right now?" I ask.

"If I were to guess, I'd say we are near the southwest edge of the Palatine. Close to the Lupercal."

"The cave where Romulus and Remus were raised by the she-wolf. Any chance the Zalśar think the twins were Etruscan?"

"If you look at the foundation myths, they'd have evidence to go on that the Etruscans at least influenced some of the story. Before choosing which hill to build on, the brothers took auspices. It is possible that augury came down to the Latins from the Etruscans. And the tradition of the pomerium, the sacred wall."

I frown. "The sacred wall Remus jumped over before Romulus offed him." I never liked that story.

"Don't mess with your brother's pomerium."

"Does this mean we have to go up that channel I mistook for a rabid animal in search of the clue?"

"I think it does," he answers. My heart, which has been relatively calm considering our circumstances, loses all of its cool.

"You first," I grumble.

I follow behind Lorenzo and watch as he hefts himself up into the stone shaft.

"Huh," he says.

"What is 'huh'?" I ask, fidgeting and feeling very exposed all alone in the main channel.

"I found something."

"Is it fuzzy?"

"Not a rat, Remy. Here, grab it." He works his arm out

along his side and shifts so he's partway out of the narrow space. I take a bronze cylinder from his hand, and he jumps down, landing next to me in the shallow water. "You can open it," he tells me, smiling.

I twist the top and pull out a piece of paper.

My whole body tingles. "Lorenzo, it's the clue. And," I say, holding it up for him to see in the glow of his headlamp, "it's in Italian!"

Chapter TWENTY-NINE

THE NEXT DAY IS ROME'S HOTTEST SPRING DAY on record—Phoenix-in-June temperatures but without the luxury of central air conditioning.

Lorenzo has a mini-split in the dining/living room, and we transfer the office to the dinner table. I turn down the temperature on the unit as low as it will go and sit right in the blast zone, which is very upsetting to Lorenzo.

"Careful, Remy," he says, doing a little desperate dance with his hands. "If you sit there, *ti prenderai un colpo d'aria.*"

I laugh. "I'll get what?"

"You'll get a…hit of air. I don't know how you say it in English."

"Well, that's a first. And what will happen if I get this hit of air?"

"You'll get sick," he answers, his brows creasing.

"Trust me, as someone who was raised on ceiling fans and air conditioning, a hit of air is not a real thing. Or at least it's not a bad thing."

He shakes his head, looking unconvinced. "And your hair is still wet from the shower," he mumbles. "*Non va bene.*"

I stretch my leg under the table and run my big toe up along the inside seam of Lorenzo's jeans. "And what a shower it was."

He smiles and relents, and we each look back down at our copies of the third clue.

Il cuore del maestro riposa per l'eternitá
dove i leoni furono trasformati in re.

The heart of the master rests for eternity
where lions were turned into kings.

I groan because I've got nothing in my brain except for the hint of a headache developing behind my left eye.

Lorenzo takes a sip of his third espresso. "The answers to the clues so far have centered around the Capitoline Hill in some way."

I perk up a little. "Then the master is easy—Michelangelo designed the entire piazza."

"Yes, Michelangelo, good," Lorenzo says, jotting something down on a piece of paper.

"But," I add, frowning, "he was buried in the Basilica of Santa Croce in Florence." I slump back into my chair and wipe a drop of sweat off my forehead. Lorenzo looks at me and tilts his head to the side, concerned. I shush him when the look on his face asks if I'm okay. It's not my fault the mini-split is not doing its job.

"I mean, we are talking about someone dead, right?" I ask. "Or does the phrase resting for eternity give out different vibes in Italian?"

"Same vibes," he concurs.

"I need books—anything your dad has on the Capitoline. Everything in the bookcase about Michelangelo."

"At once, *cara*," he says, standing.

I get up too, a little slower and a little dizzy, and grab a bottle of water out of the fridge, chugging half of it. Lorenzo cringes. The only thing scarier to an Italian than a hit of cold on the outside is a hit of cold on the inside.

"I promise, the water is not dangerous," I tell Lorenzo as I pad onto the couch. "Feel free to deliver my materials here. And can you point that thing this way?" I ask, gesturing toward the AC unit mounted on the wall. Ideally, he would pop it off and put it on the ground next to me.

"I'll see what I can do," Lorenzo says as he kneels beside me and wipes a damp piece of hair behind my ear. When he rests his hand on my forehead, I swat it off.

"I'm just not used to the humidity," I explain, ripping off my shirt. "Where I come from, 110 feels more like a dry hell."

Lorenzo studies me a little longer, chewing his lip, and then disappears into the office. He comes back with armfuls of old books and sets them on the low table in front of the couch, organized by subject matter.

"Wait," I say when he starts to go. "I need the pretty word things."

"The pretty word things?"

My head feels as muggy as the air. I force my thoughts and then my mouth to articulate the word *poems*. Lorenzo's expression grows increasingly worried as he watches me struggle on. "The ones the guy wrote. The Michelangelo."

"Remy, I think you should rest."

"I saw your mom's thing the day we got back, when you and me," I mime some form of depressing lovemaking, "on the shelves."

"My mom's book?" His eyes brighten. "You mean her anthology of poetry by Michelangelo."

"Bravo," I manage.

I fall back on the cushions and fan myself. My flight is in two days; I cannot be getting sick. When Lorenzo returns with the book, I only have time to tell him that this is all a weird mistake before passing out.

I open my eyes to darkness.

Lorenzo's hand rests over my heart, like he's been making sure it's still beating, that I'm still breathing, in his sleep. He moved me to his bed at some point. I feel a faint breeze and hear the hum of a floor fan, which means he must have bought one just for me and even dared to sleep with it aimed in our direction.

My throat issues an audible whimper as the impossible happens—I fall even harder for Lorenzo.

I grab my phone off the bedside table where he set it to charge and use the light to find my way into the living room, where stacks of books cover the coffee table. It's almost two in the morning. I've been asleep for three-quarters of a day, and though I still feel like I've contracted whatever disease it was that led to the fall of the Roman Empire, I'm not tired.

Plus, my plane takes off in twenty-seven hours from Fiumicino Airport, so it's now or never if I want to solve this clue while I'm in Rome.

I read about the Capitoline Hill with Mnemosine curled up on my lap until dawn when I tuck myself back in bed beside Lorenzo.

My dreams are a mess, and I can't tell half the time if I'm asleep or awake as my mind fights through all the things I've just read, fact after fact, over and over, trying to fit them like tiles in a vast mosaic that will reveal the secret of the third clue if I can just figure out where the pieces go.

I sleep another day away.

*

The unrelentingly warm weather isn't doing my lingering fever any favors. The fan is on in Lorenzo's room—even though he still insists the forced air from the AC is the reason I'm sick—and I'm sprawled out sweating into his bedsheets.

But none of that matters because I am still in Rome.

My phone rings, and I swipe at it without looking, answering with a gravelly voice.

"You sound terrible," Eric interrupts before I even finish saying hello.

Eric? I shift myself higher on the pillows. I've been ignoring his calls since we last spoke in Sicily. I didn't think we had much more to say to each other.

"It's just a cold," I say. *Or the plague*, I think, remembering those Roman sewer rats. To be determined.

"You were supposed to come home today." He sounds angry that I didn't.

"Well, it seemed unfair to the other passengers to risk contagion or an emergency landing," I reply. In reality, I had nothing to do with the canceled flight. Lorenzo called Lil yesterday and told her what was going on. I get another six days in Rome.

I never thought I'd be so happy to feel like ass.

Eric clears his throat. "I was looking forward to seeing you."

My brows crease. "Why?" I scoff. In his head, are we still happening? Didn't he tell me he was sleeping with someone in our bed? When we ended that call in Nunziata, he'd asked if I'd still be willing to try and work things out in Phoenix. I'm pretty sure I did not commit to that plan. I had hoped that my continued radio silence might drive the point home that I am no longer interested in pretending we belong together.

"I don't like that you're there all alone," he says.

In the kitchen, Lorenzo chops vegetables. I can hear the hum of the Telegiornale on the TV, turned to the lowest volume, so the noise won't bother me. I snuggle my face into his comforter. "I'm not alone."

"Your mom told me Cassie is in Milan for another week," Eric says with an edge in his voice.

A cork pops in the other room, and I smile as I imagine Lorenzo pouring a glass, the way his brows furrow when he takes his first sip. The way he runs his tongue over his bottom lip.

"I'm coming to stay with you until this is all over," Eric says. "And then we'll fly back to Phoenix. Together."

I sit up too fast, and my head spins. "No, Eric."

"No?" he barks. "Remy, I should be there with you." I can almost feel his face redden on the other side of the world as he thinks about the few details he knows about the case, the distance between us, and my stuffy nose.

And as he's probably thinking about Lorenzo, too, who appears in that moment with a steaming hot bowl and a small glass of amber liquid. His t-shirt is coming untucked and clings to the side of his abdomen, so a hint of skin is showing above his pants. I let myself stare at that spot, the memory of his hard stomach tingling in my fingertips.

Lorenzo notices the phone and mouths sorry, backing up out of the room.

"Wait," I say. Lorenzo pauses, watching me, his eyes and mouth smiling. He nods.

"Wait for what, exactly? How much longer do you expect me to sit here doing nothing," Eric argues into my ear, and I wonder how he's managing to ruin this moment from so far away.

I guess Eric and I do need to have the conversation at some point. I haven't been honest, and in some ways, he was right—Rome won. But Eric and I were never meant to be. "Eric, I'll be there in six days," I say, each letter a tiny stab wound in my back. "But I need to make it clear, I won't be moving back in, and you and I won't be getting back together. Ever."

"What do you—"

"I need to rest." I cough on purpose, but my little farce devolves into a convulsive bark.

Lorenzo rushes to put down the bowl and the glass and rubs my back. I hang up without further ado.

When Lorenzo has assured himself that I'm not at imminent risk of hacking myself to death, he heads for the kitchen and returns with a plastic Christmas-themed tray that he rests on my lap. He sets the bowl—filled with a thick soup—on the tray. The heat spreads to all the most dangerous places, but I force myself to focus on the food. I swallow a spoonful. I was expecting chicken and stars, but this is…

"Awful," Lorenzo offers.

I shake my head so hard I make myself dizzy. "It's not awful at all," I insist. And it's not. It's one of the most amazing things I've ever eaten, and I try not to think about how he made this just for me because his sweetness might undo me. I look away from his dark eyes and swallow hard.

"It's delicious," I say, taking two more big bites to prove my point. Lorenzo laughs. The sound makes my heart skip.

"No, Remy. Offal. It's all the bits from the animal. To give your body vitamins and strength."

To my surprise, I don't even gag on my mouthful of mystery meat. "Let me guess, your great-great grandmother's recipe?"

"I found the recipe online, but my mother did make us eat *zuppa di frattaglie* whenever we were sick as children."

"Well, you're still here," and strapping, and perfect. I finish the bowl, and I think maybe I do already feel stronger. Then I throw back the small glass of amaro Lorenzo brought in with the soup and feel something else that takes my breath away.

Lorenzo is propped beside me on the bed, his weight resting on one well-defined arm as he fusses with my pillows. His hand brushes the small of my back, and I turn to look at him. His face is so close to mine. And I am certain he is my person. That this love I feel is meant for him, made for him, and if I lose it, I will never find anything like it again.

"Hi," he says when he notices me watching him. "*Stai bene*?"

I press my fingers to his cheek. I want to cuddle myself into this man's chest and have him keep me. I want to hike to the base of the Palatine Hill together and desecrate the House of the Vestals every weekend for the rest of my life. I want to sneak kisses in Sicily while his mom shows me how to roll all of his favorite kinds of pasta by hand. I want him to touch me like he has since the wedding, with no hesitation, forever.

I try to smile, and my lip trembles. I glance up at the ceiling. Lorenzo's gentle fingers sweep my hair from my temple, my forehead. My breathing falters as he leans closer, my pulse pounding so wildly I can't believe the whole bed isn't shaking as my heart screams.

You love him, it shouts over everything else, all the worries and the fears and the sadness. *Tell him you love him.*

"I want to kiss you," I whisper instead. "But I don't want to get you sick."

"Thanks to all the *frattaglie* I ate as a child, I am constitutionally incapable of becoming ill," he says, pressing his cool lips against my fiery hot ones.

I thought the lowest thing Fabio did was use me to pull off his ridiculous crime, but having Lorenzo come knock at my door that day might prove to be much worse.

"I'll get you better soon," Lorenzo whispers as his lips brush my ear. He rests a hand on my thigh, and I fight the urge to reach out and grab it because if I do, I will never let go. And that's not fair to him. If he wanted me to stay, he'd ask.

Lorenzo's phone rings in the other room, and he pulls back. I drop my eyes to the sheets. Lorenzo resettles the bedding where he's messed it up and then straightens his shirt. "I should get that," he says. "I'll bring you some water, then you should try to sleep." He bends over to kiss me on the head and then grabs the empty soup bowl and the glass before walking out of the room.

If I open my mouth to thank him for being amazing, the sob I'm holding back will take us both out.

I hear Lorenzo answer his phone and the sound of dishes being dropped into the sink. He's using his secret phone conversation voice, the one that I'd always assumed was for Valeria. The apartment door creaks open. He shuts it quietly.

I guess he forgot about the water.

My hand digs under the pillow for the Zalśar journal, and I drag myself off the bed and to the couch, where Lorenzo has outfitted my new office space with a laptop, a cute little cactus that Cassie knit for me, and a small bell to ring in case of emergencies.

"The heart of the master rests for eternity," I murmur to myself as I shuffle through the papers that cover the table, "where lions were turned into kings." My research from the other night is a chaotic mess of barely legible notes, but I flip through them and reread anything I wrote in caps or underlined multiple times.

The Capitoline, composed initially of the Temple of Jupiter Optimus Maximus, was the epicenter of Rome, a symbol of eternity, as far back as the Etruscan kings.

In the Middle Ages, the hill was the site of rebellion and revolt against Papal control.

Then, in 1536, Michelangelo was commissioned to redesign the Piazza del Campidoglio—essentially, Pope Paul III, who was not a Medici, wanted the artist to make over the entire hill. The intention was to shift the focus of Rome from the ancient to the new.

The pope wanted the redesign to turn its back on the ruins of the Forum. He wanted the piazza to face St. Peter's Basilica and the grandeur of the Papacy.

Instead, Michelangelo drew Rome back into the place where the Etruscan kings laid the foundations for one of the most powerful empires the world would ever see.

I have bullet points and timelines written for all significant monuments and buildings. I pull up a map of Ancient Rome on my phone and a Google satellite view of the Capitoline as it stands now on the laptop as I go back through my notes, looking for anything that might lead me to Michelangelo's heart.

The cordonata, a wide, sloping stairway that ascends from Piazza d'Ara Coeli to Piazza del Campidoglio, is the main ingress to the plaza. At its base, the railings are topped by two basalt lions.

At the center of the piazza is the bronze statue of Marcus Aurelius, which I have written NO next to in big, bold letters in my notebook. I don't think his heart would rest for eternity under a statue he wished wasn't there. Unless the Zalśar meant to imply that it was crushed when Michelangelo had to stage Marcus Aurelius at the center of his masterpiece instead of the *Lion Attacking a Horse*, but that seems a little dramatic.

Palazzo Caffarelli Clementino and Palazzo Nuovo are crossed out with a small scribble beside Palazzo Nuovo that says: CAVALIERI.

Next is Palazzo dei Conservatori, built in the Middle Ages on top of the Temple of Jupiter Optimus Maximus. The building now houses the Capitoline Museums and the *Lion Attacking a Horse* statue. Renovation completed by Tommaso Cavalieri after Michelangelo's death.

Palazzo Senatorio, built atop the 78 BCE Tabularium, or records office of ancient Rome, in the 13th and 14th centuries. Renovation completed by Tommaso Cavalieri.

I set a reminder on my phone to look up this Mr. Cavalieri and turn to the next page of my notes.

At the top, it says Santa Maria in Aracoeli, and under that *auguraculum*, circled five hundred times with a massive question mark underneath.

I guess I'll start there.

Chapter THIRTY

I DISCOVER THAT THE BASILICA OF SANTA MARIA in Ara Coeli al Campidoglio sits upon the highest summit of the Capitoline Hill.

The basilica is the designated church of the city council of Rome, which still employs the ancient title *Senatus Populusque Romanus*. The Senate and the People of Rome.

But the site was essential to the city far before Rome became a republic.

At the tallest peak of the Capitoline Hill stood the auguraculum, an open-topped temple that was oriented to the four cardinal directions. The priests sat inside and watched the flight of birds over the roofless temple in a bid to tell the future.

During the period of the Roman Kingdom, newly elected monarchs were brought to the auguraculum, where they would be seated facing south, toward the site of the Temple of Jupiter Optimus Maximus for their inauguration.

The place where lions were turned into kings.

Now, I just have to figure out what it has to do with Michelangelo and his heart.

Lorenzo still isn't back, and when I try his phone, it goes straight to voicemail. I don't want to think the worst—that he's in the middle of some torrid, horny reunion with Valeria and has forgotten about me—but the lack of sleep and the Italian Dayquil I've been popping make me wonder. It isn't like Lorenzo to disappear.

But I've got other things I need to focus on, like making my way to the university so I can question everyone in the art history department about Santa Maria in Ara Coeli.

I tug on a pair of jeans, one of Lorenzo's lightly wrinkled t-shirts, and my red Nikes while I download the ATAC app on my phone. I grab my notes, give Mnemosine a big kiss on her fluffy head after scribbling a note for Lorenzo so he knows where I am, and walk to the Manzoni stop with a body that would rather be laid out in a tub of ice.

The 51 pulls up just as I do, and I hop on. The ride takes about four times longer than in Lorenzo's car, but I also get a sweet, slow tour of the city for my one-euro-and-fifty-cent bus fare. As far as commutes go, it wouldn't be a bad one.

When I get to the university, it doesn't take me long to realize my plan is faulty. Excepting a few students, the campus is empty. A chorus of bells rings in the distance. I sigh.

It's Sunday.

But the library will still be open.

I find everything I can about the church and what was there before and shove the books into my shoulder bag. I'm starting to break out in a clammy sweat and hurry to check the app for bus times. There is a stop I want to make before I go back to the apartment, but nothing leaves in that direction for forty-five minutes. I consider waiting outside, but it is still so hot. I sit down at a table and rest my cheek against the cool wood.

"Remy?"

My head jerks up, and I wipe the back of my hand across my bottom lip—so much drool.

"Hi, Dr. Hill," I say through a wide yawn.

He draws his glasses lower down on his nose and studies me over the rim. "Are you well?"

"Well enough. Sorry, I'm just waiting for the bus." I tap my phone screen and see that an hour has passed. "I take that back. I just missed the bus."

"Why don't you come to my office while you wait for the next one."

I gather myself and my things and follow him out of the library.

"Looks like you found some material," he says, eyeing my bulging purse with a perfectly raised, pedagogical eyebrow. "I hope you got what you needed."

I smile. "I believe I did."

"You seem to be in the habit of finding what you're looking for."

"I hope that's true," I say, tugging the strap of my bag up higher on my shoulder.

Dr. Hill pulls out a chair for me and then sits across from me at his desk. He leans back and folds his hands over his well-fitted Oxford button-down. "I have a confession to make, Remy. My reasons for helping you here haven't been entirely selfless."

In another reality, this admission might have made my imagination burst into a forbidden schoolgirl fantasy sequence. But today, with Lorenzo's baggy shirt tucked into my dirty jeans, a chafed nose, and the knots in my red shoelaces as messy as the ones in my hair, all I can think is, *Fuck, now what*?

He must be working for the Zalśar. I glance at the metal stapler on his desk and wonder if I could beat him to it.

"Perhaps Detective Rossi already spoke to you?"

I swing my eyes to Dr. Hill, who runs a hand over his striped silk tie. Lorenzo is in on it too? I add nausea to my list of current symptoms.

"He has not," I answer, balling my fists under the table.

Dr. Hill chuckles to himself. "It was his idea. He came to talk to me early on in the case to tell me about you. You see, Remy, I have a position to fill."

He leans over his desk, onto his forearms. I scoot my chair back. "Okay."

"It's a research internship—paid, of course—at the Borghese Gallery and Museum. Detective Rossi asked me to consider you, but as you aren't enrolled as a student here, and having never seen your academic records, I didn't have a lot to go on."

"What?" I whisper, worried I am still passed out in a puddle of drool on the library table and not wanting to wake up.

"The problem," he goes on, "is that the position is only open to graduate students."

"Oh." I slump back in my chair. That boat sailed a while ago, and besides, applications were due for the university by the end of November. I know because I already checked with the admissions office. "That's too bad," I mumble. Dr. Hill is about to see me ugly cry, and he must know it because he stands up.

"Remy, I've seen what you are capable of."

My head sags. "I haven't even found the amulet."

"You will," he says with so much certainty that I nod in agreement.

"But still, the deadline for applications was months ago," I say.

"Indeed, it was."

I shake my head. "I'm too late."

Dr. Hill pulls some papers from the top drawer of his desk. He smiles. "And I'm the new chancellor of the university. I think we may be able to figure something out."

*

When I leave the university, I am physically and emotionally exhausted.

And I still don't have any calls or messages from Lorenzo.

I catch the next bus home and skip my detour. The Trevi will have to wait a little longer, even though I'm more desperate than ever after meeting with Dr. Hill to make it there. I need to get a coin in the fountain—some guarantee that Rome and I aren't over. If I tried to go now, I might black out and drown myself in the marble basin, and that would be both inconducive to my big-picture goals and incredibly embarrassing.

I let the weight of my shoulder bag propel me out of the bus and lug it up the stairs of Lorenzo's building and to apartment 4B like a very pathetic San Nicola—the original Santa Claus. I hope there are a few treasures inside and that I didn't just haul thirty pounds of coal home on my achy shoulder. I'd check now, but when I see Mnemosine curled up on the couch, I have an overwhelming urge to do the same. I flop myself onto the cushions and drape an arm over the cat. I'll just relax for a second and then get to work again.

"Remy?"

I struggle to open my eyes. Lorenzo is crouching in front of me, his palm pressed against my forehead. He smiles. I must be doing something right in life if I wake up to a handsome man calling my name every time I pass out.

Lorenzo brushes my hair off my face, his fingers lingering behind my ear. "I'm sorry I left without saying anything. There was a huge breakthrough on the lead we got through Europol."

Correction: I get to wake up to a handsome man with good news.

I sit up and pick Mnemosine's fur off my cheek, using my foot to push my bag full of books further under the coffee table. I'm not ready to tell him about my talk with Dr. Hill.

"That's great, Lorenzo." I grin and feel the extra creases on my cheek from the cushion crinkle further. He stays on the ground in front of me, rests his hands on my legs. "You found the people the Commissioner was after? He's going to love you."

Lorenzo chews his pouty bottom lip, and I must be feeling better because I can't wait to do the same. "Not exactly. This is a lead I've been working with Chief Marchetti. Or that he permitted me to work, really. It's an agent from Europol and me investigating. Remember I told you about Bastien Dekker when we were at the Villa Medici?"

"Yes, my letter B."

Lorenzo lifts a file I didn't realize he was holding and opens it. Inside is a black and white photo of the hot Vatican guard. "You were right," he says. "Bastien Dekker was the man that let you and Fabio into the museum. The fifth aspirant. But also, an undercover officer working with Europol as an infiltrant of the Zalśar for the past two years—who is, how did you put it? Objectively very attractive."

I snort through my no-longer-stuffy nose. "So, you are working with Dekker?"

"He contacted me when we were at Bar Nona, right after Italy won the qualifier."

"*That's* why you left? I thought…."

Lorenzo shakes his head. "You thought I left because of your call with Eric?"

"Yes?"

"After watching how adorably you scream at the TV during Italy matches, I was ready to propose."

As soon as he says the words, we both turn pink.

Lorenzo clears his throat. "But Dekker wanted to meet, and I had to be there."

"Of course." *Fuck you, Dekker.*

"If we play this right, Remy, we will take down the boss."

"The Zilath?" I ask, leaning towards him.

Lorenzo closes the small space between us. "Yes," he whispers against my lips. He cradles my head in his hand, and I lean into it as his thumb brushes back and forth across my cheekbone.

"How are you feeling?

"I'm suddenly much, much better," I breathe into his ear.

"Did you have a good day?" he murmurs into my neck.

"I did," I answer as I pull back, resting my hands on his shoulders. "I think I know where Michelangelo's heart is."

Lorenzo looks so proud. His eyes gleam, and it's not just a normal amount; it's like they are reflecting the sun. My entire body tingles in their brilliance. There's no question where my heart is; it's trying to burst out of my chest and into Lorenzo's. His hand slips up the back of my—his—cotton tee. His fingers splay against my bare back. "If anyone can dig up an old, lost heart, it will be you, Remy."

Three days later, I feel normal again, but I still haven't been able to pinpoint the precise location of Michelangelo's heart in the Basilica of Santa Maria in Ara Coeli. And I've had a hard time getting my finger on Lorenzo's, too.

I leave in seventy hours, and so far, it looks like my soon-to-be-damaged heart is the only one I'm going to have turned up.

And I still haven't mentioned my agreement with Dr. Hill.

Not like I've had many opportunities—Lorenzo spent all day out yesterday with his new bestie, Bastien Dekker—but still, before I say anything, I need to know what he wants. Lorenzo has not once mentioned me staying in Rome. The message should be loud and clear, but all the things his eyes tell me, his lips, his hands, the way he looks at me before I fall asleep and when I wake up…I think those things have something else to say, even if he won't.

But this time, I'm not going to stay with someone because it's easy or convenient. I've done that before, and I've learned my lesson. If Lorenzo wants me here, he needs to let me know.

Besides, I might not get the position at the Borghese anyway. Dr. Hill and I made a deal, and I have a lot of work to do if I plan on holding up my end.

I slam a textbook closed, and Mnemosine glowers at me when the small burst of air from the pages hits her face. I scratch her chin, and we both freeze at the sound of a key in the lock. Mnemosine jumps off the couch and ducks below the coffee table.

Lorenzo told me Valeria would be by. I hoped he meant when he was here, to protect me from her wrath. I suspect I'm in for more than a bubble bath this visit.

I try to disappear below the table with the cat.

"*C'é nessuno*?" she asks. *Is anyone here?* "Remy?"

Mnemosine bolts for the kitchen, drawing Valeria into the living room, where I am squatting in front of the couch. I pop up to full height and wish I'd put pants on that morning.

Valeria smirks. "Quite a hot week we are having."

I tug Lorenzo's t-shirt down over the top of my thighs.

"Hi, Valeria."

She turns back for the door, and I follow. She's brought two large suitcases with her. My legs go so numb I have to reach for the wall.

Valeria shakes her head, and all I see is a blurry mass of shiny hair and red lips. I blink, and a tear thunks against the tile floor.

"Do you need a tampon or something?" she asks, but she's squeezing my arm—and not like she wants to rip it off.

I look down at my feet. "No," I manage.

"Good, then bring this and come help me pack." Valeria lifts one of the large pieces of fancy luggage off the floor, and it looks light as air. I take the handle.

I am, it seems, a bit of an idiot.

I put the empty bag down and wheel it along behind Valeria as she heads for Lorenzo's room.

She opens the closet, the drawers, claiming occasional pieces of clothing and ignoring the pieces of mine that have taken over. I wince when she pulls a pair of my undies out of Lorenzo's sock drawer and examines them. "Yours?" she asks, and I am sure this is the moment she'll attack.

"Weird," I say, watching her dangle them between us. "I have no idea how those got there." This is true and makes me hope really hard that they're clean. When my panties end up in surprising parts of the house, it's because I'm not the one who took them off.

Valeria rests them on the top of the dresser. "He's the happiest I've ever seen him," she says, folding a shirt. My inhale is so loud that she turns, probably to ensure I haven't fainted.

"He is?" I say when our eyes lock.

She stands and takes a blanket from the closet, hands me two corners to help her refold it. "I won't say I'm pleased that you didn't listen to me, but I can't argue that it doesn't seem to be for the best."

"Too bad it's almost over."

She narrows her eyes at me across the quartered quilt. "What do you mean, over?"

"I leave in four days."

"You can't leave, Remy." Valeria clutches her chest. "A man can't live without his heart."

"He hasn't asked me to stay," I say, sounding whiny even to my own ears. "I can't just—"

"I told you how Lorenzo is. He won't fight. He'll assume if you go, it was because you didn't want him."

My lip quivers. "But what if he doesn't want me to stay?"

"Is that what this is telling you?" The quilt is just a small square between us. She reaches over and rests a hand above my left boob. I press my lips closed against a sob.

"Figure it out, Remy," she says. "You promised you wouldn't hurt him."

When Valeria is finished claiming the last of herself from the apartment, I trudge back to the couch, even more confused about everything than I was a couple of hours ago.

Despite what Valeria said, I want to know that Lorenzo would fight for me, that he wouldn't just let me go. I sniffle and swallow past the block in my throat because I already know Lorenzo isn't going to stop me from leaving. His ex-girlfriend just told me so.

I spread out one of the few piles of books that still consume the surface of the coffee table. The others have been scrutinized and put away. *Rime e Lettere* is easy to find because it's the only book on the table that looks as old as what's inside.

I keep thinking about what Fabio told me that first night at the bar. "I am here investigating an ancient piece that we believe inspired a certain project by Michelangelo," he'd said. I know there must be some sort of direct connection between the artist and the amulet, something that links them across time. Fabio was a piece of shit, but none of what he told me turned out to be entirely a lie.

I pick up the book and open it in my lap. I am going to crack the Michelangelo Code.

A hushed gasp falls from my lips as I run my trembling finger over the contents page. The poems are listed by number, each written as a Roman numeral. I close the book again and look at the spine.

Rime e Lettere di Michelangelo di Lodovico Buonarotti Simoni.

M-D-L-B-S. I'd slam my head into the thick wood of the table if I didn't think it might kill me.

The first clue was written in Etruscan; all the text was read from right to left.

The last line of the clue *was* a list of initials. But not of the Zalśar aspirants.

I want to call Lorenzo and tell him, but he's out doing something important. And not begging me to move in with him forever.

I work through the book poem by poem, searching for the English versions on my phone. Reading love sonnets with an actively breaking heart is like the sixteenth-century equivalent of listening to sad music after a breakup, and I try not to snot-cry all over the tanned and crumbling pages.

I blow my nose and flop my head back on the couch. I'm almost a third of the way through the poems and haven't found anything. Then again, I don't know what I'm looking for.

The Commissioner isn't even worried about the amulet anymore. And Lorenzo's work on the case has been good—he's going to catch the big bad guy, and no one will transfer him to Nunziata to write parking tickets for his friends if he doesn't find the missing jewelry. I'd hate to see Fabio take the prize, but maybe everyone is right—there are bigger fish to fry.

But I also don't want to disappoint Dr. Hill. Or myself.

I could be wrong about the poems. It wouldn't be the first time I'd made a misstep in the case. I should be focusing on the basilica or spending some time mentally preparing myself for the giant hit my heart is going to take when I watch out of the plane window as Rome, and Lorenzo Rossi, disappear.

But those things are just logs on the fire, and it's burning too hot to turn my back on now.

I flip the page to poem XC and then type 90. I' MI SON CARO ASSAI PIÚ ENGLISH into the search bar. My hand flies to my mouth when the results pop up.

No. Fucking. Way.

Chapter THIRTY-ONE

I EMAIL DR. HILL IMMEDIATELY.

Thanks to a comment Valeria made and Michelangelo's poem "The Amulet of Love," I have a better idea of what I'm looking for in the basilica. I'm just not sure where I will find it.

Dr. Hill emails me back the next morning with a number for someone in the records department at the *Comune di Roma*. He let them know I'll be calling—on university business.

Lorenzo slams a second espresso and kisses me on the head as I'm leaning over the laptop, making a list of all the documents I need to request.

"Going out with Dekker?" I ask, still typing.

"Yes," he answers, running a hand through his hair. "Will you be okay here again today?"

I gesture to the evidence of my research sprawled all over the table. "I will be great. When do I get to meet this Mr. Dekker?"

"As soon as I've done everything I can to make sure he can't steal you away from me." Lorenzo winks.

I purse my lips. *You better hurry up and do it, then.*

"Hey," I call as he's heading for the door. "Can you send me Valeria's phone number?"

Lorenzo comes and stands in front of me with his hands in

his pockets. He waits for me to look up at him. "Should I be nervous?"

Now that I'm taking the time to examine his face, he already looks a little on edge. I told him those double espressos aren't good for him. "No," I say. "I need her help with something later—a clothing issue."

He tilts his head and looks at me bemused, then pulls his phone out and sends me her contact.

"Thanks," I tell him. "Be safe today." I sure don't plan to be.

As soon as he's out the door, I call the number Dr. Hill sent me and explain what I'm looking for in my most careful Italian. An hour later, an email comes through with a bunch of attachments. I scan through blueprints and city grants for the upkeep of the church and land on the architectural notes for the Baroque renovations of Santa Maria in Ara Coeli.

And there it is, the spot where the master's heart rests for eternity in the place where lions were turned into kings.

Fabio's letter is tucked under my notes, and I pull it out, unfolding the paper. I bet he'd be super pissed if he knew the little trail he left for me to find him led to the answer of the third clue—which makes the discovery even sweeter and is why I have to bring him with me when I go to Santa Maria in Ara Coeli to get the amulet.

I take a shower, make myself an espresso, and text Valeria before I can chicken out.

She shows up two hours later with one arm draped in layers of dark clothing and the other wrapped around three pairs of shoes.

"Does Lorenzo know what you're up to?" she asks before stepping into the apartment. I had to open the door for her. She left her key on the last visit.

"No," I answer. "And you can't say anything."

"Whatever this is for, it better mean you're staying."

"It does." Dr. Hill promised.

When I texted Valeria earlier, I told her I needed to look fierce, and her clothing selection does not disappoint. We spend more time than I intended playing kick-ass Barbie dress-up, but when we settle on an outfit, we are both pleased.

I look like a bad guy, in a good way.

She turns me in the mirror so we can both admire my outfit. I'm wearing a low cut, black silk cami, leather leggings, and black pumps—which I agreed to because they are red-bottomed Louboutins. I'm going to need all the fire I can muster today.

Valeria examines me, running her manicured fingers over her chin, and decides something is missing. She digs in her purse and pulls out a pair of gold earrings, each shaped like the head of a lion.

"How did you—"

"I had a hunch. Give the bastard hell, Remy."

I hug her so hard we both can't breathe. When I pull back, I look out the window. It's starting to sprinkle, and there is no way I will make it across Rome in these shoes if it's raining. "Valeria, you didn't happen to bring a car, did you?"

She narrows her eyes at me. "If Lorenzo has me arrested for helping you, I hope you know I'm holding you accountable."

"Of course, one hundred percent."

We laugh. Seeing her like this makes me understand how Lorenzo loved her, and it makes me love her a little bit too, but maybe that's just the nerves. Regardless, when we walk to her car, and I realize she drives the same Passione Red Fiat 500 as Michela, I hope Valeria will agree one day to be my best Roman girlfriend.

"Where are we going?" she asks when we are both buckled.

Her eyes are a little sparkly. I think she's enjoying the thrill of our adventure almost as much as I am. I wonder if that will change when I tell her she's delivering me to Fabio's hotel.

After spending some time going through Fabio's letter last night, it wasn't hard to track him down. I don't think he meant for it to be.

"Rome Cavalieri," I tell her.

And remember, signorina, he'd written. *Knights provide protection while you sleep, but that doesn't mean there aren't still lions prowling in the garden.*

A quick google search for cavalieri—knights in Italian—in Rome turned up the Rome Cavalieri Waldorf Astoria. The only hotel in Rome that happens to have a pride of bronze lions mounted on the lawn.

Valeria grins at me and shifts the car into first.

"If something horrible happens," I say as Valeria zips in and out of lines of traffic, "will you tell Lorenzo I love him?"

Valeria looks at me and at my lap and somehow not at the road for a really long time. "Tell him yourself."

My phone is ringing.

"Hey," I answer.

"Hi," Lorenzo says, a little breathless. "I was hoping to catch you at the apartment. I have some news."

"I'm out with—" Valeria glares at me. I start over. "I'm out."

"Is everything okay, Remy?"

I see the sign for the hotel in front of us. "Listen, Lorenzo. I need you to have Chief Marchetti and Officer DeSantis in Santa Maria di Ara Coeli in an hour. Plain clothes. Make sure to tell them to stay between the transept and the exits."

"What's the signal?" he asks, and my whole body sets on fire because Lorenzo believes in me so much he doesn't even stop to wonder if I've lost my mind.

"When we move from the tomb of Cecchino Bracchi and to the Chapel of San Gregorio, tell them to be ready to close in."

"We?" he asks.

"I've got to run," I say. Valeria raises her eyebrows at me. "Lorenzo, I—I'll be home for dinner." I hang up the phone. *What?*

Valeria sighs as she drives through the hotel gate and pulls right up to the gold-framed glass entrance. A porter reaches to open my door, but I hold up a finger for him to wait.

"How do I look?" I ask, turning to Valeria in the seat.

"You are a Fury come to life," she tells me, and I choose to take it as a compliment that she's compared me to an infernal goddess of vengeance. That is, after all, a good part of the reason we are here now. "You just need a little more *fiamma*," she adds.

A little more flame. Also the name of Valeria's favorite shade of red lipstick.

She passes it to me, and I swipe it on in the visor mirror.

Valeria gives a chef's kiss when I'm done. I think she loves me back.

I start to thank her, but she rolls down the window and tells the porter to stop standing there staring and open my door. I step out onto the cobbled walk and the porter offers his arm, but I wave him off.

If I'm going to pull this off, I have to play the part. And I'm ready to leave Fabio's dream of being Zilath one day in ashes.

At the front desk, I hesitate before resting my elbow on the counter and leaning forward toward the concierge, who luckily for me, seems to really like my outfit. Or at least the way I look in it.

"I need you to connect me to Tarquin," I tell him, hoping to God I'm not wrong.

"Which Tarquin," he asks in a shaky voice as he stares at my mouth. I didn't realize there was more than one staying at the hotel. That's an interesting piece of information for Lorenzo, but right now, there is only one fake Etruscan I'm worried about.

"The Proud," I answer, giving him a wide smile. *A superb example of what seven generations of kings can offer.* Lucius Tarquinius Superbus—superbus from the Latin for proud or arrogant—the last monarch of Rome. And Fabio's very fitting alias.

Fabio smirks when he opens the door to his suite.

I have my hands on my hips, and my lips turn up in a half-smile. "Hello, Mr. Bumgartner," I manage to say without even a hint of a giggle in my voice.

"Hello, Miss Campbell," he says, eyeing my sexy superhero ensemble. His gaze pauses on Valeria's lion earrings. Excellent. "What brings you to see me today?"

"If you'll let me in, I have a proposal to discuss with you."

His curated brows rise, but he doesn't hesitate to hold out his hand for me to enter. I walk in straight and tall and even wink as I slip past him into the room. He closes the door and follows me, holding a crystal snifter filled with amber liquid as I snoop around the suite. I go to the French doors that lead out to the balcony, pushing back the heavy satin curtain.

"Nice view," I say, and it comes out breathy. Not because I'm nervous, but because I can see all of Rome through the glass, and I love every damn brick and cobblestone that makes it up.

Fabio turns to me and runs his fingers over the clean-shaven skin of his jaw like he's in a men's perfume ad.

I take a step closer and give him a thorough once over. "This one isn't too bad either," I say. And to be fair, it isn't. Fabio is still the most well-groomed, well-dressed, generically handsome human I've ever seen in person.

And he does nothing for me.

However, his apparent need to present himself so perfectly does tell me something important. Fabio wants to be wanted. He's an arrogant asshole who gets off on other people's admiration. I can give him that. In fact, I'm banking on the fact that that is all he's looking for in a woman, hoping the only person he's actually interested in is himself.

I fake a little pout of longing, and he grins.

Poor Fabio. Who hurt you?

"You've done some growing up since our last visit, Miss Campbell."

I laugh but pass it off like I'm in on the joke. Silly, naive, desperate Remy, who played into the Zalśar's plans, is no longer.

Except she's right here. The same girl who had to have another woman dress her this morning. Who wants her teacher to like her. Who has a humongous, forever crush on a boy and no idea what to do about it.

And that's okay. I can be badass Remy *and* still be figuring the rest out.

"I'm glad you noticed," I say.

"Your detective couldn't keep up?"

"I'm here, aren't I?"

Fabio takes a sip from his glass. "So, what is this proposal of yours?" he asks, lounging on the edge of the marble table.

I walk around in front of him and sit down in a massive

armchair, steepling my fingers and crossing my legs as I lean back. "I know where the amulet is."

His eyes brighten, the snifter wobbles once in his fingers. "Impressive, Miss Campbell. What do you want for it?"

"I am aware of the prize. You will get the twelfth spot on the Zalśar council if you recover the amulet."

"Yes," he says blandly, but his cheeks flush, and his knuckles pale around the glass. He wants this bad.

I smile. "As one of the twelve, you can initiate new members to the Zalśar."

Fabio's lips purse, releasing a noncommittal hum.

I lean forward. "I want in."

"And why would I make you a member?"

"Other than the fact that I'll take you to the amulet?" *And other than the fact that I'm the one who was clever enough to find it and you weren't?* I don't add because it will hurt his feelings and ruin my plan.

"But why would you want to join the Zalśar?" he asks, his eyes narrowing as he stares into mine.

Before I have time to worry that Fabio is becoming suspicious, he waves a hand and pushes off the counter. "I mean," he says, coming to stand in front of me. "Why join the Zalśar when we could do so much more together, alone, just you and me?"

Side proposition was not on the list of things I had spent time worrying about before coming here. I slide out of the chair and around Fabio. There is a vanity mirror against the wall, and I rest my palms on the stone shelf beneath it, pretending to examine my lipstick. "You and me?"

Fabio walks up behind me and meets my eyes in the mirror before talking to his own reflection. He turns his head as he speaks—to appreciate his different angles, I imagine. "The

Zalśar have too many rules," he says. "Even if I join the twelve, we could plan our own jobs, sell in the big markets. I already have interested buyers."

"Convince me," I say, bending forward toward the mirror. Fabio starts talking, oblivious to my cleavage. I exhale.

There are two things at this moment that I am grateful for:

1. Fabio is a veritable autosexual.
2. Valeria, the crafty, legal mastermind, who sent me into the hotel rigged up to record his every word.

I check the back of my right earring and keep that side of my face turned to Fabio while he continues to gaze at himself in the mirror and divulge all of his contacts in the underworld of illegal art deals like a big, dumb, self-incriminating Narcissus.

I pay enough attention to ask questions that might lead to information the police can use to identify or track people down, but nothing too explicit as to be obvious. I am here to take down Fabio, but if I can help Lorenzo smoke out other criminals, I'm happy to do it.

Fabio seems pleased that I'm curious, probably because it is a continuing excuse for him to talk about himself and his connections. Then he says something that piques my interest.

"All the members obviously know he's part of the Polizia di Stato, which is how—"

"Who?" I turn, and he gazes down at me. He looks at my lips with a scowl, mad at them for interrupting him.

"The Zilath, Miss Campbell."

I nod and let him continue, but inside I am buzzing. I left my phone with Valeria on purpose. Lorenzo texting me while

I try to seduce Fabio with the promise of the amulet wouldn't help my cause. Plus, these leather pants have zero pockets.

But oh my god, the Zilath is part of the Polizia di Stato? Does Lorenzo know?

Fabio fits a single piece of hair back into place. "Anyway, that is how that unfortunate Turkish gentleman ended up accused. Your detective worked that case as well. He's the reason the man isn't still behind bars."

My heart races to keep up with all the places my mind is going. Lorenzo had said he let the bad guy get away, but it sounds like he did the opposite. Unless…

"We should go," I say, tapping the face of Fabio's Ulysse Nardin watch. "There's a mass at five, and we want to be out by then."

Fabio tears himself away from the mirror and walks into the bedroom. He comes back with a camel-colored jacket and shinier shoes. "Let's be on our way to church, then," he murmurs. "I hope you're right about the amulet."

"I am," I say, picking up the car keys on the gold table by the door and tossing them in the air to catch them again. "And I'm driving."

His jaw clenches and then loosens. "You want to drive my Maserati? Through Rome?"

"That is my intention," I assure him.

"Are you capable of doing this?"

"Baptism by fire." I smile.

Chapter THIRTY-TWO

THE DRIVE, WHICH I PLANNED ON GOOGLE MAPS, is reminiscent of the ride Fabio took me on in the Ferrari 488 Pista when he used me as cover to steal the amulet, only in reverse—which seems appropriate because today, I am using the amulet to make him realize that was a big mistake.

When we pull up beside Castel Sant'Angelo, I give his knee a little squeeze for old time's sake. Neither of us enjoys it.

At the base of the Capitoline Hill, I drive onto Via delle tre Pile, a small street where it is rumored Michelangelo lived while working on the piazza. When the car is in park, Fabio straightens his shirt and jacket and then holds his hand between us. I drop the keys into his palm.

If all goes well, he won't be needing them again any time soon. I'm happy he hasn't seemed to put that together yet.

"Not even a scratch," I say, stepping out of the car.

Fabio shudders. "I'm as shocked as you are."

I laugh because I hate him a little but also because I'm not shocked at all.

But he's about to be.

We walk past the bottom of the cordonata and Michelangelo's two black lions set on the bases at either side. We smirk at each other. We are the bad guys. We know the truth. And I am not at all distracted by the hot cop patrolling the staircase.

Tight dark blue polo, fitted pants with a red stripe up the side, leather boots, and a navy cap. I have to ask Lorenzo if he still has his uniform hanging in the back of his closet. I want him to put it on so I can take it off again.

I tell myself that will be my reward if I pull this off.

Well, one of them.

"Here," I say to Fabio when we reach the base of the adjacent staircase, the one that leads up to Santa Maria in Ara Coeli but looks like it might deposit you right to Heaven's doorstep. We glance up at the basilica. The church was constructed of ancient bricks scavenged from the ruins of various Roman buildings, and the facade is a mosaic of fired clay.

As we take our first of one hundred and twenty-four steps, I'm tempted to grab Fabio's hand. I need something to grip to squelch my bubbling excitement. Acting like a giddy kid right now wouldn't fit the part. But that is how I feel. Walking up the steps, my body is overwhelmed by the same thrill I got at the beginning of a new school year, the day I got my driver's license, stepping onto the plane to leave for Italy the first time.

The excitement of possibility tumbling inside me is so overwhelming, I don't even struggle to make it to the top in Louboutins.

A part of me is disappointed that Lorenzo can't be here to savor the moment with me, but this is my win, something I need. A fuck-you to all the time I wasted banking my fire because it was the convenient or easy thing to do or because it was better for somebody else that I didn't burn too hot.

I look at Fabio, and when he turns to me, I see flames reflected in his eyes. Instead of taking his hand, I squeeze my lips together to hide my wicked grin.

When we enter the church, I take a deep breath. Hopefully, Chief Marchetti and Officer DeSantis are ready and waiting somewhere inside. But if they're not, I am not opposed to taking things into my own hands again like I had to with Maelle, even if Fabio is the kind of guy who wouldn't hesitate to hit me in the face.

Fabio watches me, and I roll my shoulders back and start to talk as we amble from the entrance and through the nave. The basilica is gorgeous, the floors a checkerboard of medieval Cosmatesque stonework and the ceiling coffered, gilded wood. But now is not the time to appreciate the architecture.

"Would you like me to tell you what the third clue said?" I ask to piss him off. To prove once more, I beat him.

Fabio looks as disgruntled as I hoped he would. "I suppose you should."

I pause near one of the twenty-two columns that line the nave, all repurposed from buildings that had stood thousands of years before. My voice is quiet in the huge space, but it is confident. "The heart of the master rests for eternity in the place where lions were turned into kings," I recite to him.

He nods. "The auguraculum, of course."

I hide my scowl. Okay, it's annoying that he knew that, but I suppose he *is* part of a criminal group that likes to pretend they are Etruscan. And I am not but figured it out anyway.

"And the master's heart?" he asks. "We are speaking of Maestro Michelangelo, I assume."

I start walking again, drifting into the south aisle, running my fingers over the bars that block the Chapel of St. Jerome. "Indeed. That part of the clue was a bit harder to unravel. I happened upon a little journal when the detective and I were at Villa Medici. There was a fasces stamped on the front, and I suspected it might belong to one of your friends."

"And what was inside?" he asks, arching an eyebrow.

"Numbers. So many numbers, about three hundred, in fact. Exactly as many numbers as poems by Michelangelo have been printed."

"Ah," he says.

I stop and read a plaque and enjoy how Fabio starts to squirm beside me. I wink at him and wander further down the aisle. "I found the work you were looking for, the one inspired by our favorite ancient piece of jewelry."

Fabio clears his throat. "A poem." He says the word like it is something offensive.

"Yes, 'The Amulet of Love,'" I answer, smiling.

As soon as I read the poem, I knew what I was searching for in the basilica, what I would find. Fabio and I arrive at the basilica's side entrance. There, beside the open door, is the tomb of Cecchino Bracci, illuminated by the sunlight filtering in from outside.

Fabio chuckles, and the sound is as pretentious as the way he swings his jacket over his shoulder. "Cecchino Bracci," he says, studying the elaborate marble work of the tomb. "Michelangelo's pupil. And muse, apparently."

I don't correct him. There is at least one poem of Michelangelo's that references Cecchino Bracci, but it's not the one that led us here.

"I'm not an admirer of poetry, not even Michelangelo's," Fabio says as he moves closer to the tomb, holding his chin in his fingers like he is trying to put on airs. "This, on the other hand," he gestures to the wall, "is true art. The tomb was designed by Michelangelo, you know?"

And I do know that, but it doesn't stop Fabio from giving me a complete education about the details in the marble work.

While he talks, I forgive myself for ever wanting to lick

Fabio's ear and other body parts. As obnoxious as he is, he does know a lot about art. And when we first met, he wasn't entirely awful. He saved that for lunch and every day after.

Fabio turns to me with bright eyes when he is done with his lecture. "Now. Where, precisely, is the amulet?" he asks.

Time for the big reveal.

"Not here," I shrug.

Fabio's lip curls up in the approximation of a snarl. He'd never make an ugly face. "Miss Campbell?"

I step back from the tomb, walking backward into the nave. He follows.

"As soon as I put Cecchino and the poem together, I knew I should find you. I knew that you'd be willing to bring me on if I could offer you the amulet. It wasn't until I reread your letter that I wondered if I was wrong about the tomb."

I stop and look up into his face. He's with me. He nods for me to go on.

"Tommaso Cavalieri," I say. "Do you know of him?" The question is rhetorical.

Fabio huffs. "I'm familiar with his work," he says. "But other than Cavalieri's contributions to the piazza, I don't see how he is relevant."

I nod toward a chapel beside the altar, the Capella di San Gregorio, and we walk there together in silence. How do you explain to a man like Fabio that Michelangelo's heart wasn't contained in his work but in his love for another person?

His heart existed outside himself. It belonged to someone else, and now it rests with that person for eternity in a church built upon the temple where Etruscans were turned into Roman kings.

I think of Lorenzo, our first kiss and second, and the Sarcophagus of the Spouses and eternity, and how I hope he won't break my heart because it's his now.

I blink, clear my throat, and pull Fabio into the chapel beside me.

"I got the plans from the Comune," I explain. "All of the documentation from the renovations the church underwent in the 1700 and 1800s. Most of the tombs in the Capella dei Cavalieri were torn down or built over."

"The Cavalieri Chapel?" he asks.

"Surprise, right?" I walk around the edge of the room. "The tomb of Emilio was here," I say, pointing to the stone bust of someone else who claimed the space much later. I take three more steps and touch a spot on the wall, pressing my palm flat against the cool marble.

Fabio bends down beside me.

"And here," I say. "The tomb of Tommaso dei Cavalieri. The love of Michelangelo's life."

Fabio scoffs, but his eyes are drawn to the tiny corner missing from the tile I am touching. "Open it," he commands.

I hesitate to pry the tile off the church wall, but I am as anxious as he is to see what's underneath. I manage to work my pinky finger in behind the edge and tug. Fabio catches the tile as it falls.

We both gasp and lean in closer. Hidden behind the tile is a stone niche containing one ancient, golden amulet adorned with delicate leonine protomes in a glass case. Before I have time to process the amazing treasure, Fabio shoves me into the wall with his shoulder. An oof bursts out of me as my back hits the hard marble.

Fabio grabs the amulet and gives me the most pompous look imaginable. I keep my eyes focused on his. He doesn't need to know what's going on behind him.

"You said we had a deal," I cry.

Fabio tilts his head and looks at me, the same overly willing, naive little girl he duped into a fake date at the bar on my first night in Rome. He makes a tsking sound. Like I'm just so pathetic, he almost feels bad about it.

In the brief moment it takes for me to bend down and tear off Valeria's Louboutins, I wonder if he's right, if I've made another terrible life choice, but as I watch the first shoe soar toward his smug face, I decide I don't care.

Fabio raises a hand to knock the second heel off course, and I dive for his leg. He falls hard, both hands wrapped around the glass box protecting the amulet. He mutters something not very elegant and kicks his cap-toe leather oxford hard into my shoulder, but he's aiming for my face.

"Fuck me," I mutter when his heel grazes my cheek.

"Only in your woeful little dreams, Miss Campbell." He scoots back on his elbows and stands, running a hand over his clothing, still unaware of the crowd gathering outside the chapel behind his back.

I scramble onto my feet and take a step forward, reaching for the amulet. Fabio laughs at me as he raises it high between us. I can see Chief Marchetti and Officer DeSantis moving towards us through the tourists who have stopped to watch. The hot officer from the cordonata is with them, his hat pulled low over his eyes.

"Time to give up, Miss Campbell. You are in far over your head." He nods toward the case he is holding above me. "The only reason you were ever involved was that I needed someone attractive enough to pass as my companion, and Maelle couldn't walk into the Vatican Museums on my arm after just getting out of prison."

I tilt my head. "You think I'm pretty?"

"I think if we bred, our offspring would rank above avera—"

He doesn't finish because the hot officer steps between us and decks Fabio straight in the nose. The sound of the bones breaking echoes through the church. I hope it never sets right; it will drive Fabio crazy.

Chief Marchetti and Officer DeSantis are on him in seconds, the amulet placed into the hands of the officer who punched Fabio in the face. He brings it to me, and I'm shaking as I take the ancient jewel in my hands.

"You," I manage, and my insides are trembling with unfettered amounts of adrenaline. And with something else that's rumbling deep and loud inside of me.

"Detective Campbell and her sidekick Lorenzo Rossi," he says, running his finger over my mouth. "I couldn't miss the grand finale."

"You broke his nose," I say.

Lorenzo grimaces. "He was talking about breeding with you."

"I would never. Just so we are clear—"

Lorenzo bends, his warm lips finding mine. His kiss is possessive and tender as he cups my bruising cheek and is the kind of kiss that makes me want to have *his* babies. Immediately. Too bad we will be spending my second to last night in Rome giving statements at the police station.

Shit, the police station.

Fabio's words from the hotel room come pounding back into my mind. I pull back, goosebumps on my arms. "Lorenzo," I whisper, glancing over at Chief Marchetti and DeSantis to make sure they aren't listening. "The Zilath is in the police force. Fabio said something about your last case, and I think that it might be—"

"The Commissioner," he finishes for me, nodding.

"You knew?"

"I knew something was off after he pushed so hard for that arrest in our last case. Dekker shared my suspicions, and we put together enough evidence for an arrest. Dekker and I and a small team from Europol brought him in earlier today on a substantial number of charges. The Commissioner is being transferred to The Hague as we speak."

"Is that why you are all dressed up?"

"Official police business. I had to look the part." His lip turns up at the corner. "But I kept it on because I thought you might like it."

"I do. Very much," I answer with my voice all husky. If we didn't have an audience, I'd be happy to show him just how much. Instead, I sigh.

"And you, *cara mia*," he says, looking me over, "look like the world's sexiest fake art thief."

I bite my lip. "Maybe we can play cops and robbers later?" I tug at the handcuffs dangling from Lorenzo's belt to pull him closer.

He makes a sound that tells me he likes that plan a lot and braces my face in his hands. "I'm so proud of you, Remy."

"We got the bad guys," I say, wrapping my arms around his body.

Lorenzo holds me tightly against him, the 2000-thousand-year-old Etruscan amulet of love pressed between us.

Lorenzo comes into his office balancing two espressos in one hand and a pair of thick socks in the other. He sits in front of me, perching on the edge of the desk, and removes the heels that I've been wearing for the past twelve hours—with only a small break when I weaponized them in the Basilica of Santa Maria in Ara Coeli.

Lorenzo pulls the cozy socks over my toes and massages my aching feet. I spent the last two hours going over the recording I got of Fabio at Rome Cavalieri, filling in all the spots that didn't come through well with whatever details I can remember while they are still fresh in my mind.

Fabio's testimony is going to be the nail in the Commissioner's coffin. The date with Fabio was worth it just to know Lorenzo will walk away with such a big win.

My win was big, too. Dr. Hill texted me as soon as he heard I'd found the amulet. I have all of the official papers from the university sitting in my inbox, ready to go with me to the Italian consulate when I'm back in Phoenix. I can get a visa interview in as little as four weeks and, hopefully, get everything processed within a couple of months.

That will give me time to get things settled in Phoenix. Time to find a place to live when I return to Rome.

I still haven't told Lorenzo. I have him to thank for getting me the position at the Borghese in the first place, and I am so excited about going back to school and pursuing something I love in a city I could never get enough of, but it's not the way I'd prefer for him to keep me here, on an eventuality.

Lorenzo's phone rings and he answers. He smiles and laughs, makes a comment about golf.

"Golf?" I mouth.

Lorenzo shrugs and keeps talking.

"Of course, Mr. Campbell. Here she is," he says before handing me the phone. And to me, he murmurs, "I really like your dad."

My throat tightens.

"Remy, you there, kiddo?"

I cough. "Hey, Dad."

"Your mother and I just sat down for the evening news, and guess who popped up on the screen?"

"Oh no. Did Lil get arrested for giving Camilla that awful dye job?"

My father chuckles. "Poor kid," he says. "But no, no one is pressing charges against your sister for her mismanagement of my granddaughter's hair."

I laugh.

"Anyway," he goes on. "I think congratulations are in order. According to CBS, you and Lorenzo are quite the team."

Hearing my dad say Lorenzo's name makes me smile. It comes out easy, like he's been saying it a lot.

"They've got this great shot of you and your detective," he goes on. "Looks like the cover of a *People* magazine."

"I'll have to find a copy when I get back."

My dad hesitates. "He is *your* detective, isn't that right?"

My heart stutters. "It's complicated," I mumble into the phone.

"You want to hear about complicated, ask your mother about how she and I met." I hear my mother protest in the background.

I laugh. "What's she yelling?" I ask.

"She's just loudly declaring how happy I make her."

"I don't doubt it."

My dad clears his throat. "We think you should stay in Rome, Remy. We'll come visit." There is more shouting. "Your mom is nodding. She agrees," he adds.

"I am not nodding, Joseph," I hear my mother say.

"Now she's winking," my dad tells me. My mother laughs, and the sound is sweet.

"I'll see you guys soon," I say, hoping my voice doesn't sound as teary as my eyes are.

"No rush, Peanut. We love you."

"Love you too."

"And one more thing. Tell Lorenzo to stop calling me Mr. Campbell. It's just Joe."

"I'll let him know," I say, swallowing.

"But he should keep calling your mother Mrs. Campbell. Gets her all frisky, works out for me." My mother huffs in mock outrage beside him, but I can hear the sound her lips make against his cheek.

"Ew. Okay. I'm hanging up now."

"Just so you know, kiddo," he says before I can close the call. "You've got more fire in you than anyone I know."

Chapter THIRTY-THREE

We wake up tangled in each other's limbs. My last morning in Lorenzo's bed, and neither of us seems willing to let go.

Lorenzo brushes my hair back from my face.

"Can we just stay in bed all day?" I ask him, nuzzling deeper into his neck. I'd like to spend the day enjoying him, but I am also so tired. It was past three in the morning when we got home.

He pulls me closer, his hand tightening against my back, pressing my chest against his "We can't," he answers.

"Please?" I bite gently on his jaw.

He obliges me with another half hour in the sheets before tugging me out into the kitchen. Mnemosine is clingy, rubbing between my legs and jumping on my lap when I sit down. She mews into my face. At least she doesn't hesitate to ask me to stay.

Lorenzo watches the cat knead my thighs but doesn't second her appeal.

When I'm dressed, we walk down the stairs hand in hand and to the bar across the street, Bar Nona, where we watched Italy win the World Cup qualifier. Lorenzo kisses me at the counter, and I find a table near the back while he orders our coffee and croissants. I'm watching Lorenzo smile and laugh with the bartender and wondering if it will hurt when my heart is ripped out of my chest tomorrow morning, or if maybe, I'll be too dead inside to feel anything at all—when a kind, old voice interrupts my thoughts.

"*Sono contento di vedere che alla fine, l'amore ha vinto*," the man I call Geppetto says. He's stooping behind me, looking over my shoulder toward the bar. *I am happy to see that in the end, love won.*

I shake my head. "*La partita non é ancora finita.*" *The game isn't over yet*, I tell him.

We look at each other, and he raises his fuzzy, white eyebrows at me like he suspects me of lying to him. If only that were true.

"*Lo sa, signora, questo bar si chiama Nona per una delle dee Romane del destino. Abbi un po' di fede.*" He smiles at me with a mouthful of espresso-stained teeth. His eyes twinkle.

"*Aó, Geppetto*," the bartender calls in our direction from the front of the cafe, raising a martini glass full of coffee-colored liquid in the air. "*Il tuo caffé corretto.*"

My mouth is hanging open when Geppetto, whose name is actually Geppetto, winks at me. He shuffles to the counter and takes the glass from the bartender, chugs whatever is inside, and tips an invisible hat at me before leaving.

You know, miss, he'd said to me before gulping down his ten a.m. cocktail. *This bar was called Nona after one of the Roman goddesses of destiny. Have a little faith.*

I discover, after our coffee, that the reason Lorenzo wouldn't let us snuggle in the apartment all day is that he has put together a "Remy's Last Day in Rome" itinerary.

I have mixed feelings.

The thought is appreciated, but unless our day ends with Lorenzo getting the Polizia di Stato to shut down the airport so I'm stuck here with him, the whole experience seems a bit sadistic on his part.

Our first stop is the Trevi Fountain, so at least I know he isn't opposed to me coming back. In fact, he has an entire collection of coins stashed in the console of his car for this exact moment. He takes a photo of me offloading at least fifty euros worth of metal into the marble basin.

Between the hefty offering to the Trevi and the visa application paperwork from Dr. Hill, I feel pretty confident that whatever happens in Phoenix, I'll be back in Rome sooner rather than later.

Lorenzo isn't as certain and, just to be safe, drives us to the Triton Fountain in Piazza Barberini to do the same thing with whatever change we can scrounge up from my purse and his pockets.

We leave the car somewhere near the Galleria di Alberto Sordi shopping mall and walk down Via del Corso, his arm wrapped around my shoulder, my hand pressed into the space above his heart. I don't care where he's taking me; I'm already exactly where I want to be.

"You know," I say as we lean over the railing at Largo di Torre Argentina. "We have the Commissioner to thank for keeping me in Rome after I was cleared. What a horrible decision on his part."

Lorenzo gives a low chuckle. "I think his intention was to use you to distract me."

"Should I be offended that his plan didn't work?"

"Oh, it worked." He bites his bottom lip, drags it between his teeth. "But the Commissioner failed to account for a couple of things, including your investigative genius and my desperate need to impress you."

I lean my head on Lorenzo's shoulder. "I'll always be grateful to him for making such a gross miscalculation."

Below us, countless cats lounge about like reincarnated Roman dignitaries on fallen columns and stone ruins. They chase one another in the Theater of Pompey, turning the site of Julius Caesar's assassination into the scene of an adorable, furry reenactment.

"I've been thinking," Lorenzo says. "Maybe Mnemosine needs a little sister."

He runs his hand down my arm, and I press my lips and my legs together.

Lorenzo blushes, his smile shy like he just suggested we give it a shot right here. "We will be lonely when you go," he says, grazing a kiss against my temple.

You don't have to be, I want to yell at him. All he has to do is ask me not to leave, and I'll stay with him forever. Instead, he leads me into the Torre Argentina Cat Sanctuary at the southwest corner of the archaeological area and smothers me in kittens.

All of the volunteers there know Lorenzo and love him, and seeing him on the ground while a bunch of semi-feral cats climb over his lap in search of his fingers makes my pulse pool in my chest until the beat of it is as loud as the purrs he's eliciting.

I fall in love with every cat we hold, but none leave with us. If Lorenzo needs a consolation kitten because I'm leaving, he will need to choose one on his own.

We eat pizza al taglio at the Pantheon and feed each other gianduia gelato from Giolitti's while sitting on the base of the obelisk outside Montecitorio. We watch a street show in

Piazza Navona, his arms wrapped around me from behind and our faces resting side by side. We visit the terrace of the Altare della Patria and get an incredible view of our time together in Rome—all of our adventures laid out before us.

We eat dinner outside in Via del Boschetto, under string lights and vine-covered palazzi. We kiss like the world is coming apart.

Mine is.

"I love you, Remy Campbell," Lorenzo says long after we've turned the lights off to sleep. And at least I'll have that to hold on to when I go.

When I wake up, Lorenzo is no longer in bed. Mnemosine sits on his pillow with her paws tucked under her, facing me.

"Good morning," I tell her as I stretch my arms over my head and against the tightening feeling in my chest.

She scowls.

"You're right," I agree. "Not a good morning at all."

I reach for my phone, and a wave of nausea rolls through me when I see the time. I'm supposed to be at the airport in two hours for check-in, and I still need to finish packing. Plus, I'll need to find room for all the extra emotional baggage I'm hauling back to Phoenix with me.

I call Lorenzo's name as I pad into the kitchen, but he isn't there. And he's not in the bathroom or the study or the guest room. He doesn't answer his phone.

I take the deepest breath of my life and tell myself he probably went to pick up the car.

But by the time I'm ready to go, he hasn't shown up.

If I don't leave for Fiumicino in the next ten minutes, I will have to sprint through the airport to make it to the plane on time, and I don't have those kinds of mental or physical reserves right now. There's a good chance I'd die if forced to run to the terminal and away from everything I love. Walking will be hard enough.

I wipe my eyes but still have trouble seeing the phone screen when I try to open the Uber app. I'm typing in Lorenzo's address when a knock at the door makes me jump.

I look through Lorenzo's peephole and see two men, neither of them the one I was hoping for. I open the door anyway.

"Ciao, DeSantis," I say, dragging my sleeve across my nose. "Lorenzo isn't here."

"Si, I know. We take you to the airport," he answers, reaching past me for my luggage.

My eyes widen as I realize what he's telling me. Lorenzo isn't coming. There will be no goodbye.

The other man reaches his hand out. "Bastien Dekker," he says. "A pleasure to finally meet you, Remy. Great work on the Zalśar case." His body consumes the entire door frame, but his green eyes and touch are kind and gentle.

"You too," I mumble. I might even try to smile, but my body has forgotten how. "Where's Lorenzo?" I ask, looking back and forth between DeSantis and Dekker. I'm almost too embarrassed to ask. He's not here, and really, that's all that matters.

DeSantis lets out a long, uncertain sound and shrugs. Dekker shuffles his feet as a faint pink tinges his deep, golden-brown cheeks. "Rossi had something important he had to take care of this morning," he says. "He asked us to help out."

I raise my chin and choke back another wave of tears as a new emotion sparks to life inside me.

Good. Hating Lorenzo a little bit makes it a lot easier to leave. He couldn't be bothered to accompany me to the airport after telling me he loved me. He couldn't even let me go in person.

This is the very opposite of fighting for me.

I whisper my farewells to the cat, make one last sweep of the apartment, and follow the two men down the stairs and into a blue police car. How fitting.

Dekker turns around in his seat to talk to me, pressing his shoulder into DeSantis, who is grinning while he works his way through the traffic. The joy on his face feels like a personal affront.

"So, you like Rome?" Dekker asks.

I nod. "Yeah."

"Like, you *like* like it or just sort of like it?"

I laugh because I've never had a super-hero-sized man who hunts international criminals ask me if I "like like" something before. "I love it," I confirm.

"Good," he says with a loud clap before turning around. Now he and DeSantis are both smiling like idiots.

I'm about to ask them what the hell is going on when a call comes in on the radio. All I can make out is something about the Colosseo. DeSantis looks at me in the rearview mirror. "Mi scusi, Ms. Campbell, I have to see to this."

"Um, okay," I mutter as he switches on the siren and the flashing lights—he better be willing to use them to get me to the airport if this takes a long time. We tear down Via Labicana, and the whole time, Dekker looks like he's trying to be serious, but the corners of his eyes keep crinkling.

DeSantis drives right up inside Piazza del Colosseo.

Crowds of people fill the space between the Forum, the Arch of Constantine, and the Colosseum. Only, they aren't tourists. Women dressed in sheer white togas carry olive branches in their arms. Young girls in red wear garlands on their heads and run from boys in tiny gladiator costumes. Men in crimson hold Roman standards above their heads, and others have on crowns of laurel and look like they've just been discussing the invasion of the Gauls with the other patricians.

It's possible I've lost my mind.

"*Siamo arrivati.*" *We are here*, DeSantis says into the radio before turning to me over his shoulder. "Today is Roma's birthday. Today, Roma celebrates."

DeSantis and Dekker get out of the car, and I expect I'll be waiting in the back seat for them to settle whatever hilarious issue arises between a bunch of Italian men bearing wooden javelins, but Dekker opens my door like he's one of Cinderella's footmen and gestures out toward the piazza.

I narrow my eyes at him, but he dodges my silent question, which is a very fervent, *What the fuck*?

The cosplay ancient Romans in the piazza are starting to notice us, and as they do, they fold apart, clearing a path. Dekker gives me a gentle push forward. "Go on, Remy," he says.

"I'm not getting sacrificed, am I?"

"No," he smiles, squeezing my shoulder.

I nod, the back of my neck overcome by tingles. My whole body shakes in time with the pounding behind my ribs, but I put one foot in front of the other and make my way into the tunnel of Vestal Virgins and Roman statesmen. A child in a loincloth tosses flower petals in my face, and behind me, Dekker shouts, "Go time!"

The crowd opens, and Dekker bounds past me. I see Valeria in the mass of people and wave. She waves back, smiling as she aims her phone at me. Someone to my right shouts, "Yes, Daddy!" and I turn to find Cassie, cheering as Shay watches her like the entire universe is wrapped up in five-and-a-half feet of curves and curly dark hair. I start to drift toward them, but

Cassie looks at me like if I get any closer she might bite me, and points further down the cobblestone.

I follow her finger with my gaze, and there, standing atop the age-worn stone on the southwest side of the Colosseum where we shared our very first kiss, is Lorenzo. He has on a metallic jacket just like he did that evening almost twelve years ago. He looks so out of place in the throng of centurions and priestesses I'd laugh, but I can barely breathe.

Lorenzo smiles at me and runs a nervous hand through his hair. The speaker at his feet begins to play—three chords burned into my brain and heart the first time our lips met.

Backstreet Boys' "I Want It That Way" echoes off the exterior wall of the Colosseum. Lorenzo is singing, and then, with Dekker, DeSantis, and three other officers, he begins to dance.

And holy shit, it's embarrassing, and my chest is so overfull with love, and my cheeks ache so bad with smiling that it takes a full five seconds for me to register when the music stops. To realize I'm not dreaming when Lorenzo drops to his knee.

"Remy Campbell," he says. "I have loved you since I first laid eyes on you. I spent over a decade praying I'd find you again, and now that I have, I don't want to let you go." He reaches into his pocket and pulls out a ring—lovely, antique, perfect. As he looks at it, he says, "Nonna Nena gave this to me the night of Mary's wedding. She told me if I didn't get it on your finger, I wouldn't be welcome back in Nunziata. I think that means it's yours whether you say yes or not. But Remy," he looks up at me with flushed cheeks and sparkling eyes. "I'd be so happy if you chose to spend your life with me."

Lorenzo stands and takes my hand. He rests the ring in my palm. I close my fingers around the gold band, squeezing my eyes shut and then opening them again. "Remember after Villa

Medici, when you told me I was going home, but you didn't clarify that you meant *your* home?" I ask, my voice shaking.

"Yes," he answers. His lips turn down in a guilty frown. I run my trembling thumb over the corner of his mouth.

"Waiting to do this until this morning is like that, but a million times worse."

Lorenzo bites his lip, bowing his head. "I'm sorry."

I rest my fingers on the side of his face, tilt his chin back up. "I got the position at the Borghese," I say. "Thank you. Dr. Hill told me you'd asked him to consider me. I have a visa interview scheduled in Phoenix. I planned to be back in Rome as soon as the paperwork came through."

Lorenzo's face fills with pride, but there is a hint of disappointment in his eyes, a flash of sadness. "Dr. Hill and the Borghese will be lucky to have you. Your work on the case was some of the best I've ever seen. You deserve the spot at the museum, Remy. You deserve everything."

I step closer. "You know," I say, the ring clutched in the hand I have pressed against my heart. "I'll need a place to stay."

Lorenzo's eyes brighten. "Yes, absolutely. My home is yours," he finishes softly.

"Thanks." I bite my lip. "And not that I've spent a ton of time googling it or anything, but I'm pretty sure a permit-of-stay lasts a lot longer than a student visa, right?"

"Right," Lorenzo responds on an inhale. He holds his breath, studying my face.

I hold up my left hand between us, the ring settled at the base of my fourth finger.

"I want forever, too, Lorenzo," I say, breathless and smiling. "Of course, I want forever."

He grins and his eyes are bright as he scoops his hand around the back of my neck and his arm around the small of my back.

I cling to him as our mouths find each other, and he holds me when my knees go weak beneath me.

"I love you," I murmur into the heat of his breath.

"I asked Mr. Campbell for permission," he says against my neck.

"It's just Joe," I tell him.

Lorenzo stands me up straight again once our kisses have communicated how much we both want this. How much we need it, like air or water. *A man cannot live without his heart.*

He holds me tight against his chest, leaning his forehead against mine. "So, you'll stay," he says, a reassurance to himself and the universe.

"Always," I answer, pressing myself as close as possible to let him know I'm his. He's keeping me. And he is mine. The look on Lorenzo's face as his bottom lip slides through his teeth makes heat flood into the lowest corners of my belly. His eyes darken. I clear my throat. "But maybe we wait until I've finished my degree to think about that little sister for Mnemosine."

Lorenzo hums into my ear. I wrap my arms around his waist and look up into his face. "Thank you for fighting for me."

"All I did was dance."

"No, though that was very brave too. Thank you for risking it all to keep me here."

"The only risk would have been letting you get on that airplane."

I tuck my head under Lorenzo's chin and curl into his body, looking out at the piazza. Cassie blows a kiss, and I pretend to catch it. Valeria winks at me before walking over to Dekker. But the rest of the crowd has already moved on, distracted by a pair of chariots racing down the cobblestone.

Today, Lorenzo and I will picnic on the Palatine. Tomorrow, we'll tour the Vatican after dark.

And then?

We have our own eternity to uncover the rest of Rome's secrets—together.

THANK YOU

I love to read the acknowledgments section in books—the sweet, thoughtful insights into all of the people and things that made the story so wonderful, who made it possible.

And it turns out, it takes a lot of people and things.

I never would have been able to do this without the love and inexhaustible support of my husband, who kept me well-fed and well-wined and was endlessly encouraging, and my children, who were way more patient with me than I was with them. V.P., Polpettina, and Mr. Mozzarella, you are my everything.

A huge thanks to my dad, who beta read *Remy vs. Rome* from the ground up (well, most of it…), and, when offered the chance to write a line, gave me "you have more fire in you than anyone I know," except he might have said Italian instead of fire. And my mom, who probably still hasn't read it yet (update: she has), but whose creative mind is always in the gutter, and thus, an inspiration.

Kate, thanks for launching this whole thing and being there every step of the way. You are the best friend and best (and only sometimes scariest) sister ever, and I am entirely dependent on you. And Brad, the kids are so lucky to have a fun uncle who helps them remember not all grown-ups are grumpy, over-caffeinated jerks.

Natalie (Bump!), you've been my rock and life-mate for decades now. Your faces are the best and getting excited about

Rome things with you has been a highlight of my life. *Nihil est,* favorite little empress.

Amanda, the AB I didn't know I needed but never could have done this without. I am so glad we got to go on this ride together, and I'll be roaring in your corner until the end of days.

To Gia, Nicole, and Iram, the very talented blue fairies who turned this story into a *real* book, I am honored to have had the chance to collaborate with a group of such brilliant, creative women.

To my early readers, thank you for helping me find my way. And Court, thank you for bringing more awareness to the words and for being such a thoughtful guide.

A huge shout out to my sweet family, especially my grandma, for being excited about the book every time she learned about it, my grandpa for those TEFL lessons in Rome and the green card sponsorship, my fairy godmother, and *le zie*. To the Italians, un abbraccio forte forte e grazie per aver condiviso con me il vostro figlio e le vostre ricette.

To my friends, old and new, who were such awesome cheerleaders, I love you all dearly. For such a shy kid, I am incredibly grateful to have managed such an inspiring group of people to share this life with and who all forgive me a week tucked away with a book to recover my social battery when necessary.

My love for Rome was born in the classroom. I'd like to thank all of the amazing educators in the world and, in particular, a few of those who made such an impact on my life and its trajectory: To the Mr. C's who were super brave and took a bunch of middle schoolers to Italy, thank you. I fell head over heels for the first time on that trip—with Rome, and maybe a little bit with that cute boy on the boat in Sorrento. To Alba and Claudio and the entire study abroad team, I learned so much in Orvieto about Etruscans, Greek lit, art history, and myself. Thank you for sharing your kindness and your knowledge. And Dr. Soren, of course, for being a beacon of classic nerdom and making it extra cool to let my own shine. To the professors in the Italian department at UArizona, you taught so much more than just language—you introduced me to quiet corners of Italian culture and gave me a chance to embrace my curiosity and experiment with the language, all while instilling an irremediable obsession with the subjunctive.

Finally, to the reader: Your mere existence is a dream come true, and I cannot thank you enough for being here. I hope we can go on many more adventures together, but in the meantime, know that I appreciate you taking a chance on this book and sharing your time. It means the world to me.

ABOUT THE AUTHOR

Bonnie Callahan was born and raised in Tucson, Arizona, where she went on to study Classics and Italian at the University of Arizona. After seven years in Italy, she is now back in the Sonoran Desert, where she lives with her Italian study abroad sweetheart, their two kids, and a few bilingual pets. Between raising her two young children and dreaming of Italy, Bonnie found time to pursue her love of writing and penned her first romance. Her idea of a happily ever after includes a solid serving of food, wine, and adorable animals.

Bonniecallahanbooks.com

authorbonniecallahan

Made in the USA
Coppell, TX
24 February 2026

72321106R10215